Advance Praise for
In the Event of Death

"In this poignant story, Kimberly Young explores one woman's struggle to come to terms with a childhood trauma that threatens to cripple her just when her family needs her the most. *In the Event of Death* will challenge the way you think about death and make you laugh and cry while you rejoice in a family's resilience."

—**Tracey Lange**, *New York Times* bestselling author of *We Are the Brennans*

"*In the Event of Death* is that rare novel that is both hilarious and heartbreaking. Young perfectly captures the angst of middle age in this beautifully written story where one woman—sandwiched between her unpredictable teenagers and ailing parents—realizes she can't hold everything together and might as well embrace the messiness of life."

—**Malena Watrous**, author of *If You Follow Me*

In The Event of Death

A Novel By
Kimberly Young

Post Hill
PRESS

A POST HILL PRESS BOOK
ISBN: 978-1-63758-666-2
ISBN (eBook): 978-1-63758-667-9

In the Event of Death:
A Novel
© 2023 by Kimberly Young
All Rights Reserved

Cover Design by Tiffani Shea and Cathy Danzeisen

Interior Design by Yoni Limor

Post Hill Press
New York • Nashville
posthillpress.com

Published in the United States of America
1 2 3 4 5 6 7 8 9 10

*In loving memory of my mother, Gail W. Young,
and for John, my partner every step of the way.*

Chapter 1

*A*fter splurging on a latte, Liz dropped her half-full cup into the trash, feeling overcaffeinated for the meager amount of work on her desk. Her eyes traveled out the window where she spotted yet another vacant storefront with a *For Lease* sign taped to the glass. She reached for the plastic wand on her blinds, twisting off the view.

Somehow, she hadn't seen this downturn coming. But, really, who could blame her? Pink slips, budget cuts, and staycations had been inflicted elsewhere, but not in their neck of the woods. Just last summer, she and Gabbi had been scrambling at full tilt, masterminding weddings in wine country. Bar mitzvahs. Fiftieth birthday extravaganzas. And when Dina Gomez, a local newscaster, hired them to plan her daughter's quinceañera, Liz had been certain that Touchstone Events was poised to explode into new markets.

But here in April of 2008, the phones were eerily quiet. For the umpteenth time that morning, Liz checked her email, but there was no correspondence from prospective clients. When she heard the click of Gabbi's heels on the metal stairs leading from the garage to their office on the second floor, her spirits brightened. Her business partner and old friend was always good company, even when business was slow, even when the shit was hitting the proverbial fan—which it reliably did in the event planning world. Caterers were always running late. AV systems were constantly on the blink. Musicians were forever getting stoned.

Liz looked up to see Gabbi embracing an enormous bouquet of periwinkle and white hydrangeas with assorted greens. The flowers weren't for a client but for their own viewing pleasure. It was an expense they could no longer afford, and Liz raised her eyebrows in silent protest.

"Give me the luxuries, and I can dispense with the necessities," Gabbi quoted Oscar Wilde. Liz groaned, thinking of all the necessities requiring her attention. For starters, their office rent was already a week late. Worse—by far—were the two mortgage payments hanging over her and Dusty at home. But Gabbi, a single mom, had real worries too, and Liz was alternately envious of, and frustrated by, her ability to live blissfully in denial.

As her partner arranged the flowers in a smoke-glass vase, Liz marveled at how put together Gabbi was, even with no meetings to attend. Gabriela Rossi had that gift for plucking out the one chic item in a second-hand store that everyone else had overlooked. Today she was draped in a pink cashmere poncho that softened her curves—curves that still drew the eyes of passing men in the street. In marked contrast, Liz—whom her mother once described with a whiff of disdain as "congenitally skinny"—had arrived at work in her standard slim-fit jeans and pressed button-down. As Gabbi noted years ago, "You're Sporty Spice, Liz. I'm more *Posh*."

Gabbi was humming a little tune, and Liz sensed she had good news of some sort. Finally.

"Remember Karl and Marnie Perkins?" Gabbi asked as she positioned the hydrangeas on the coffee table. "The older couple who hired us to plan their family reunion in Tahoe, like, three years ago?"

Liz nodded, visualizing the affectionate pair who must be eighty-something now.

"Well, Marnie had a stroke in January. Poor thing. It was straight downhill from there. Yesterday she passed away."

"Oh, no—Karl must be devastated," Liz said, getting up from her desk. "Should we send over a note? A gift?"

"He just called me." She paused while adding two cubes of sugar to the water in the vase and met Liz's gaze. "He wants us to plan Marnie's funeral and reception."

"Funeral?" Liz felt a pinch in her gut and stepped back. "We don't do funerals."

"Look, I know you have certain, what, aversions? But hear me out. Karl told me he wants this to be a beautiful celebration of Marnie's life. With her favorite music, gourmet food, a video—the whole shebang."

"But—"

"If you really think about it, Liz, arranging a memorial service is just like planning a wedding, only..."

"Only what?"

"Only the bride is dead."

Gabbi pressed her lips together, forming a thin line. Was she fighting an urge to laugh? Unbelievable.

"Lizzie, you know better than I do how much we need the income," she said, suddenly serious.

Liz dropped her gaze to the floor. In fact, she had reviewed their online bank accounts before breakfast. They didn't have the luxury of turning away business—any business.

But Gabbi knew next to nothing about Liz's condition, a weirdness she had struggled to keep under wraps since childhood. A crippling fear of death had taken root in her the day she watched the men lower Maggie into a small plot of indifferent earth. Years later, when she'd fainted at her Uncle Chet's memorial—the organ music and sickly-sweet smell of Narcissus had ambushed her with memories of that first, unspeakable loss—Liz vowed never to step foot at another funeral.

She lifted her chin toward Gabbi. "Let me sleep on it," she said, intent on buying some time. "I'll let you know tomorrow."

Gabbi fiddled with her hoop earring. "That might be a problem. No *body* can wait."

"You're horrible," Liz said, wagging her finger and fighting her own twisted impulse to smile. She noted the chipped polish on her fingernails. She and Gabbi hadn't paid themselves a full salary since the first of the year. And last night, she and Dusty had quarreled about their property taxes, due later this month on top of everything else. At dinner, the twins had said little as they worked their forks through mounds of lasagna, clearly sensing the tension. Something had to give.

"Listen," she began. "If I agree to this, don't expect me to attend the funeral or reception. I'll work behind the scenes, but this will be your show."

"Deal," Gabbi said. "We could produce this memorial as a one-off, and then return to business as usual when things pick up."

Liz liked the sound of that, and they agreed that Gabbi should meet with Karl Perkins to explore the scope of the service. If they decided to move forward, Liz would develop the proposal and estimate. After six years together, it still surprised her to be the so-called Numbers Person. A history major at UC Davis, she'd come to the world of spreadsheets, Quicken online banking, and tax forms by happenstance. Gabbi had started the business shortly before Liz came on board, and though clients adored Gabbi, she couldn't so much as balance a checkbook. Liz offered to pitch in for a few weeks and soon found herself at the office long after Gabbi had gone home. It turned out she loved nothing better than imposing order on chaos. When Gabbi floated the idea of forming a partnership, Liz jumped. With her boys in school all day, she'd been looking for a way back into the workforce.

Building a small business with an old friend had the pull of destiny.

Before long, the two of them had an understanding. Gabbi was in charge of *The Pretty*: invitations, flowers, linens, music, and food. Liz was in charge of *The Gritty*: contracts, vendor management, logistics, payables, and receivables. Together they were Touchstone Events. They launched just as Silicon Valley began to recover from the 2000 dotcom implosion, never dreaming another recession would dim their prospects so soon.

Despite her best efforts to find things to do, Liz was merely re-shuffling manila folders by 3:00 p.m. She resigned herself to getting a jump on the after-work crowd at Safeway, and an hour later she nosed her metallic-blue minivan into the driveway loaded with groceries. When she spotted Dusty's truck parked out front of their ranch-style home, she felt a tightening in her chest. The event planning industry wasn't the only one vulnerable these days. Dusty's small, residential construction company was getting hammered by the slowing economy. Families were postponing their dreams to build new homes or to improve old ones.

But that was just the half of it. Eighteen months ago, Dusty had taken out a loan to buy a fixer-upper across town, certain they could remodel and flip it for a sizable profit. She'd been reluctant to take the risk, but he'd been so sure. "The Bay Area housing market is bulletproof, right?" he'd said. When he added, "We'll finally be able to set aside money for the boys' college accounts," she'd acquiesced. Now the house was finished, with sleek new kitchen appliances, updated bathrooms, and fresh landscaping—including sunny daffodils that welcomed every passerby. It had been on the market for nearly four months, but the Sunday Open Houses were poorly attended, and the single offer was well below asking. They wouldn't even recoup their investment— they'd be in the hole.

As she navigated through the garage to the backdoor clutching paper bags filled with ground beef and boxes of cereal, Dusty intercepted her. "Hey, babe," he said, taking the sacks into his weathered, muscular arms. She sensed no lingering tension from last night's argument and smiled up at him, noticing the puffiness around his hazel eyes and the glints of gray in his dirty-blond hair. Dusty had always appeared young for his age, but lately he looked every bit his forty-six years. She suspected the same could be said of her.

After putting away the groceries, Liz joined her husband on the checkered couch in the family room and he switched on ESPN. The boys wouldn't be home until after 5:00 p.m., and it was rare to find themselves alone on a workday afternoon. Slipping off her flats, she relaxed into pillows that once upon a time were decorative but now were well-worn and comfy. Dusty reached down to scoop up her feet and deposited her legs across his lap. As he massaged her tired calf muscles, she wondered if he was setting his sights on a romp in bed down the hall. Frankly, she wasn't in the mood. Money problems and talk of memorial services didn't exactly spark her libido. To her relief, he appeared perfectly satisfied watching highlights of baseball players making superman catches while flying over walls into the popcorn bags of fans.

During a commercial break, she reached for the remote and clicked off the TV. Then she told Dusty about the unexpected request to help plan a funeral and reception.

"Do you think we should do it? Or would it hurt our reputation as *fun* planners if people think we're in the frigging death business?"

Dusty searched her face, looking for the right answer to what Liz understood was a tricky question. Yes, they needed the income. But he, more than anyone—more than Gabbi or even her own mother—knew about her anxiety related to her sister's death, her obsessive thoughts and disturbing nightmares. In recent years, she had managed to get things under control and had largely weaned herself off meds. But this new gig could blow open Pandora's box.

"For now, it's just one job," he said, rubbing the stubble on his chin. "Besides, you don't have to officially offer these services. You could provide them as a special favor to existing clients. Folks might actually think better of your business. That you help them out in times of great stress." He paused to take a sip of beer before adding, "Just make sure Gabbi runs these events. So you don't get..."

Nutso?

"...uncomfortable."

Liz nodded. Keeping the funeral thing unofficial and putting Gabbi in charge made sense. She glanced at her watch. Ben and Jamie would be home soon, but there was still time to check her email before getting dinner underway. As her husband returned to ESPN, she padded down the hall to the small guest room that doubled as her home office. Settling in front of her computer, she spotted a message from Gabbi. Subject Line: *Headcount is 150–175.*

An event that size meant they could cover the office rent and pay themselves partial salaries. Liz took a fortifying breath and squared her shoulders. She typed back, *Okay. It's a go.* Then, she started to work up the numbers, feeling both a sense of foreboding and a wave of relief.

Touchstone Events had four days to pull together a huge party (if one could call it that), and given the sluggish economy, every caterer, florist, and musician was not only available but prepared to negotiate. Although she wouldn't allow herself to feel lucky at a time like this, Liz felt comfortable knowing there would be room for healthy mark-ups while still delivering a good value to the grieving widower.

The office hummed at a pace of controlled frenzy that exhilarated her after so many quiet weeks. Jin, the UPS guy, handed her a box of bereavement thank-you cards that Karl would send to dear friends who'd left hearty meals and thoughtful gifts at his front door. Across the room, a rep from Gold Cup Rentals huddled with Gabbi, flipping through binders of place settings and fabric samples.

"We want this beaded flatware," Gabbi said, pointing her finger and rattling the bangles around her wrist. "Those celadon linens."

Manny Lepore, owner of The Flower Hour, sat in the reception area applying yellow sticky notes to select pages of his portfolio. When he caught Liz's eye, he winked and waved. As teenagers, Manny and Gabbi had helped to support their families by tending seasonal plants in vast nurseries along the verdant San Mateo coast. Poinsettias at Christmas time. Long-stem roses for Valentine's Day. And white calla lilies bound for the bridal bouquets of summer. Gabbi had confided in Liz that she'd hated toiling under the fluorescent grow lights and feeling dirt shoved under her fingernails, but Manny had never left the business. They'd remained friends, and now he delivered his freshest flowers at the best prices for Touchstone Events.

While memorial receptions for affluent residents were often held in local country clubs, Karl Perkins wanted a more personal gathering in his wife's beloved garden. Gabbi and Liz knew the venue from previous meetings about the family reunion, and the backyard was blessedly flat. Setting up tables, a buffet and a spot for a live music performance would be no problem. The weather prediction for Friday afternoon set the high at sixty-six degrees, no rain. This forecast would save the Perkins family the mind-boggling expense of a tent, but portable heaters were a must. Liz felt remarkably calm as she jotted down her to-do list. The memorial was shaping up to be just another event.

Thanks to her impeccable filing system, Liz was able to retrieve copies of Marnie Perkins' preferred food and wine items. The spritely woman with soft brown eyes and a stylish white bob had adored ravioli with meat sauce complemented by a full-bodied Cabernet Sauvignon. Liz had already phoned the caterer and reserved six cases of wine from Beltramo's.

Once Gabbi had specified all the rentals and the rep had left, she beckoned Liz and Manny to her desk. She'd learned that the Episcopal church where Mrs. Perkins would be eulogized permitted flowers. While Spangler Mortuary offered to provide them, Gabbi wanted artistic control, and Manny offered a few suggestions.

"When you arrange flowers in a circular wreath, it's a symbol for eternal life," he said.

"Really—who knew?" Gabbi said. She ordered one wreath and several arrangements for the church. Then she and Manny agreed that pink peonies would be lovely for the reception. Karl had given them carte blanche on the floral selections, and Gabbi was sparing no expense.

It occurred to Liz that her partner had been right about the commonalities between weddings and funerals. And it struck her as ineffably sweet that the heartbroken groom wanted to shower his bride with flowers one last time.

Chapter 2

*A*s promised by the local weathercaster, Friday arrived clear and mild. In recent years, Liz had developed a farmer's preoccupation with weather. But while growers in California tilted their faces skyward to search for signs of rain, Liz was always praying for the opposite. So much depended on a dry, sunny day.

Though she was running late to the office, she was the first to arrive, as usual. In two hours, the funeral service would be underway. It was scheduled to run from 11 a.m. to noon followed by the graveside gathering and burial. The garden reception would begin at 1:30 p.m. and end an hour or two later, assuming guests wouldn't linger. Gabbi would be onsite, and Liz would be here, safely stationed behind her sturdy oak desk, reviewing estimates and bills from the myriad vendors working the event. She was well acquainted with them all: the husband-and-wife team famous for their pasta dishes, the chamber music performers who resembled refugees from a Renaissance Faire, and the fleet-footed boys in white jackets who seemed to genuinely love parking cars.

Liz sipped her coffee, relishing the perfect buzz to tackle the paperwork. She logged into her email and found a note from her parents. They were driving home early from

Carmel to attend a funeral. Did they know the Perkinses? She called her father, the Keeper of the Cell, knowing he'd never pick up because he couldn't be persuaded to leave the damn thing on. *"Won't the battery die?"* She left a message and settled into her work. When her phone began to vibrate on her desk, she figured her dad was calling back. Flipping it open, she found an incoming call from Gabbi.

"Morning, what's up?" she asked.

"I've got a little problem. With Zoey—at school. Somehow she managed to break her leg in an intramural soccer game."

"Gabriela," Liz said.

"Obviously, she can't walk and the fracture hurts like hell. It's only thirty minutes to Santa Clara. If I go now, I should be back in time for the reception."

"Which means you don't need me..."

"You need to go to the funeral—to take photos of the family. It sounds weird, but Karl said today will be the biggest family gathering since the Tahoe reunion. And he wants pictures. Yesterday, I told him we'd be happy to help, no charge. The photos don't have to be professional."

"Listen, I feel terrible about Zoey," Liz said. "But we talked about this. Can't you get David to take her to the hospital?"

Gabbi ignored the reference to her ex-husband. They both knew the likelihood of him lifting a finger for the girl hovered around zero.

"Liz, it will be a *closed* casket. Just don't look at it. Meet Karl in the back of the church at ten-thirty before the service starts. You'll be out of there by eleven."

"Jesus-fucking-Christ, Gabbi."

"I'm sorry, I'll make it up to you. Scout's honor," she said. "And Liz?"

"What?"

"The camera's in the bottom drawer of my desk. Left side."

Liz ended the call without a goodbye. She wanted to scream, but she couldn't be angry with Gabbi. They had a longstanding policy of "kids before clients," which Liz had invoked on more than one occasion. She stood up and paced around the office, trying to dispel her mounting anxiety. Feeling no relief, she phoned Dusty—maybe he could snap a few pictures. But the call went straight to voicemail.

She fell back into her chair and closed her eyes, cursing the moment she agreed to this funeral. After reminding herself that she was a grown woman with a family and business partner who depended on her, she fumbled through her pockets and found an elastic band. She wrapped it around her hair and yanked the ponytail tight—a signal to her brain to knock off the nonsense. With all the willpower she could muster, she went to Gabbi's desk, dug out the Nikon camera, and headed to her car. There was still time to go home and change. Though Liz hadn't attended a funeral since college—she'd become extremely adept at making plausible excuses—she assumed that a dark skirt or dress was still the appropriate attire.

Although it was warmer than predicted, a sudden gust of wind chilled the back of Liz's neck as she hurried toward Trinity Church in a black pencil skirt and pumps to match. She noticed a side door in the stone building and gave it a tug but found it locked. So much for slipping in and making her way incognito to the back of the church. Circling around to the front, she stepped through the heavy doors and paused, waiting for her vision to adjust to the dim light. A faint smell of burning wax filled the antechamber, and she could hear low voices in the distance.

Gazing up the narrow aisle that divided the pews, her eyes came to rest on a gleaming cherry-wood coffin flanked by enormous candles. A spray of ivory lilies and woodland ferns softened the edges of the rectangular box. And next to the podium, two towering mixed bouquets offered splashes of color in the otherwise somber church. Where flowers were concerned, her partner had thought of everything.

Holding tight to her purse and camera bag, Liz started up the aisle with the heavy feet of a reluctant bride. Although the casket was mercifully closed, her mind's eye viewed the corpse of Mrs. Perkins with terrible clarity, dressed and rigid in her dark, silent chamber. Halfway to the altar, Liz experienced a peculiar lightheadedness and shortness of breath. *You're okay, you're okay*, she repeated to herself and pushed on. But four steps later, her knees began to wobble. As she grasped the back of a pew to steady herself, someone called her name, but the wump-wump-wump of her hammering heart was deafening in her ears. Collapsing onto the wooden bench, she looked up to find eighty-one-year-old Karl Perkins trotting toward her, his face alive with tenderness and concern.

"Oh, Liz," he uttered. "I had no idea you cared for Marnie so deeply."

She managed a feeble smile in reply. Beside him was the minister, a ruddy-faced man dressed in a thin dark suit and a clerical collar. He peered into her rapid-blinking eyes with a knowing look and took her hand into his warm palms before guiding her to the rear of the church.

"You'll find a ladies' room right there," he said. "Get yourself some water." He lifted the camera bag from her shoulder. "Let's take the photos outside. I'll get the family assembled in the courtyard, okay?" Liz gave him a lame thumbs-up before shuffling toward the bathroom. On the question of God, she was agnostic. But this man instantly convinced her of the existence of angels.

Alone in the dimly lit bathroom that reeked of mold mingled with rose potpourri, Liz splashed cool water on her face, careful not to smear her mascara. She stepped into a stall and lowered the lid of the toilet seat. There, she rested, slumping forward and staring at the cracked tile floor.

In July, it would be thirty-five years since they lost Maggie. Images of her younger sister with tangled red hair and bold green eyes floated across Liz's mind like colored balloons released against a gray, uneasy sky. In 1973, her funeral had taken place on a strangely mild day like this one.

Gripping the wheel of their station wagon, Liz's father tailed the polished black hearse to the cemetery, speeding through yellow lights to keep eyes on the vehicle transporting the youngest member of their family. Next to Liz in the back seat, her mother swiped at tears with a wad of tissues while Liz's older brother, Ned, fiddled with the radio tuner up front. Everyone at the funeral, including Ned and herself, had worn dark mourning clothes to the little church near her school. But just before the service, her mother had emerged from the motel room in a lavender dress; purple was Maggie's favorite color.

At the cemetery, Liz watched as her father, brother, and two uncles carried Maggie, tucked into a tiny pink coffin, across a stretch of clipped grass. Liz groped for her mother's hand, disoriented by the bright sunshine and chirping birds in the neighboring trees. At the very least, she'd expected jagged streaks of lightning and growling thunder to mark the outrageous nature of her six-year-old sister's death.

A small group of relatives and friends huddled near the casket while the minister recited a prayer. The sun began to grow warm, then hot, and Liz pushed up the sleeves of her navy dress. Though she was ten years old and knew better, she worried that Maggie was sweating in that narrow, sealed box. She squirmed, aching to crack the lid and offer her a bit of fresh air. Better yet, a grape popsicle, the kind Mags adored though they always stained her lips.

Instead of offering her sister relief, four unfamiliar men ran straps under the coffin and lifted it toward a newly cut opening in the earth. Liz searched frantically for her father's face, and when their eyes met, he strode toward her, eclipsing the view of the burial. But it was too late. After catching sight of Maggie being lowered into that gaping pit, her knees gave way and her vision telescoped to blackness.

In the musty church restroom, Liz's heart rate began to tick up again. Three times, she inhaled deeply and exhaled slowly, trying to calm herself. It was imperative to arrest these memories and get back out there to take pictures of the Perkins family. Reaching into her purse, her fingers quickly found a small bottle of Xanax pills—"Lizzie's Little Helpers," as Dusty had once called them. That was eons ago, when the twins were toddlers, and every unsliced hotdog threatened to choke her babies. Every backyard pool promised to drown them. And every ember in the fireplace longed to burn them. Liz had relied heavily on the pills back then, so afraid her boys might meet her sister's fate. But she was better now. Infinitely better. She renewed her prescription only for the rare-case need. And today, under these very triggering circumstances, she would allow herself a little reinforcement.

She returned to the bathroom sink and bit one pill down the middle, dropping half into the bottle and swallowing the other with cool water from a Dixie cup. Then she dusted her cheekbones with blush and reapplied lipstick before hurrying outside.

As promised, the minister had gathered the family in the courtyard under a plum tree heavy with the blossoms of spring. He removed Gabbi's Nikon from its case and walked toward her as one might approach a wounded animal. She smiled broadly, determined to appear fully recovered, and met his gaze as he passed her the camera. Yet her hands failed her, and it fell through her fluttering fingertips, smacking the concrete pathway.

"Shit!" she cried, instantly mortified by how the curse word hung in the still air surrounding the church. She reached for the camera and unscrewed the lens cap, barely breathing. Peering down through the viewfinder, the minister's tassel loafers came into focus with perfect clarity—no crack. At last, something was going her way.

It took only minutes to snap a few dozen photos of Karl and his flock of middle-aged children, teenaged grand-kids, and assorted cousins. No prompts to "say cheese" were necessary. The pale, well-dressed Perkins clan stood erect and smiled politely, eager as she was to be done with the shoot. Karl, who wore dark glasses to conceal his weepy eyes, embraced her warmly and thanked her for coming.

As she started back to her car, Liz passed throngs of silver-haired men and women filing into the church for the funeral. Good Lord, had they ordered enough food to feed them all? Climbing into the van, she assured herself that folks didn't eat too much at day events. She slipped the camera bag safely under the passenger seat and prepared to pull away from the curb when her phone rang. It was Gabbi again.

"How'd it go?" she asked.

"Exactly as I expected."

"That bad?"

"Let's just say that the next time I attend a funeral, it will be over my dead body."

Gabbi laughed in a way that lifted Liz up. Rarely was she the funny one.

"We're still at the hospital," Gabbi said. "It's a fairly routine fracture, but they have to put Zoey into a walking cast."

"What's your ETA at the reception?"

"Hard to tell."

For Liz, the harrowing part was over and, with Xanax on board, she was starting to feel back on her game. She told Gabbi not to worry, that she'd get to the Perkinses' home before the party started and make sure everything was going as planned. Famished and still a bit fuzzy-headed, she was anxious to taste what the caterers had cooked up.

It was a godsend that Liz arrived when she did at the impeccably maintained English Tudor home of Karl Perkins. Scurrying to the backyard in what were now decidedly uncomfortable heels, she could see that the sixty-inch round tables were positioned on the lawn, but only a few were draped with celadon linens. And on the brick terrace, glassware and china were still stacked in plastic crates covered in shrink wrap. Men and women in black aprons hustled about, but the catering staff was predictably behind schedule. Over the years, Liz had learned to dress a table and artfully fold cloth napkins with the best of them. She got to work.

Guests began to appear promptly at 1:30 p.m., meandering through a garden graced by blooming white azaleas and ancient stone birdbaths. Two waiters made the rounds with trays of pre-poured Chardonnay, Pinot Noir, and Perrier. Though it was still early in the afternoon, many reached for wine rather than water. It dawned on Liz that these funeral receptions provided welcome social outings for folks who had aged out of the cocktail party circuit.

Feeling restored by a hearty serving of pasta and a fudge brownie, Liz scanned the event landscape looking for something requiring her attention. In the bobbing sea of dark suits and tailored dresses, a woman with auburn hair in a floral print jacket stood apart. She was enthusiastically holding court with a distinguished-looking couple, waving one hand in the air while the other clutched a full glass of white wine. Liz blinked twice and smiled. *My gosh,* she thought, *there's Mom.*

The unexpected pleasure of spotting Joanie dissipated quickly, replaced by a reflexive concern. Was that her mother's first pour of wine? Second? Would she ever stop counting? Liz reminded herself of how healthy and disciplined her mother had become. It had been decades since her mom steeled herself with breakfast Bloody Marys to face the Maggie-sized hole in her life. As she had a thousand times before, Liz vowed to lighten up. Despite the circumstances of this reception, her mother looked lovely. Even a bit thinner than usual. Maybe one of her perennial diets was paying off.

When the handsome older couple nodded goodbye and ambled toward the musicians, Liz drew close, undetected. She embraced her mother from behind, careful not to bump her glass, and enjoyed watching her spin around in surprise.

"Hi, Mom. I had no idea you knew the Perkinses."

"Sweetie, how good to see you!" Her eyes swept down Liz's silk blouse and skirt to her black patent heels and up again. She smiled approvingly. "Marnie took a number of my art history classes at the community college. Such a darling woman. What are *you* doing here?"

"I'm working. This is a Touchstone production." She gestured toward the buffet table and caught sight of her father loading up his plate.

Her mother looked alarmed. "Oh, Lizzie, you don't want to plan memorials. Events for *old* people. Where's the fun in that?"

Joanie was a decade younger than Karl and Marnie Perkins but, at seventy-two, she was still an old person by nearly anyone's measure. Except hers. By her measure, she was still "youngish," as she put it.

"We only do this sort of thing for existing clients," Liz said, feeling defensive. How did Dusty phrase it? "As a favor," she added.

"I think it's smart," her father said, nudging into the conversation and accidentally dropping a sourdough roll to the ground. "I'm all for product line extensions. Anything that pays the bills."

"Exactly," Liz said.

Her mother appeared unconvinced. Underneath it all, was she concerned that Liz was wading into a psychological danger zone with this funeral business? Or did she assume that Liz had tamed her demons by now, as she had? It was impossible to know; they didn't talk about such things.

"The problem is," her father continued, "you're still working by the hour, by the project. You and Dusty need to find a way to make money while you sleep. That's the only way to get ahead these days."

It was her father's new obsession: the notion of making money even after you'd left the building, punched out. While Silicon Valley CEOs crawled under their plush duvets and switched off the lights in their estates, factories in Asia were churning out the computer and telephone components that would add to their personal bank accounts and those of their investors by breakfast time. She and Dusty lived outside that tech world—so close as the crow flies, but so far from their reach. Her father's advice wasn't wrong, merely pointless. She and Dusty didn't have the educational background to move into tech, nor did they have the savings to invest in it.

She gazed into his heavily lined face, noticing the sunburn on his expansive bald spot.

"I'd just hate to see you kids end up selling your business at a fraction of its value. Like I did." Liz squeezed his arm and nodded.

When she was a girl, her father and uncle had owned a small chain of stores that sold auto parts. Items that didn't interest her in the slightest—brake kits, spark plugs, batteries—had put food on their table and allowed her to graduate from college without a single student loan. But when auto supplies moved into Big Box retailers and online, her father had been forced to sell his family business at a discount. As far as she knew, her parents were fairly secure, but not so flush that she and Dusty felt comfortable asking for help.

Liz couldn't see a path to making money while she slept, but she sensed that death-related services would never move online. Families needed help in these sad circumstances. A personal touch. A warm plate of ravioli with meat sauce.

Though she was reluctant to admit it, death might be the only thing to breathe new life into Touchstone Events.

Chapter 3

Standing in front of her kitchen sink, Liz peeled carrots and potatoes for a beef stew and stared out the window where evening began to settle over the sycamore trees. The funeral and reception—minus her embarrassing mishaps at the church—had gone smoothly, and the Perkins family had been grateful for their services. She should have been relieved the day was over, a job well done. But the twins were running late. She could feel that creeping worry that gnawed at her ever since they'd turned sixteen last summer and Dusty surprised them with keys to their own car.

Though their pals teased them that the silver Prius was a "granny car" (in fact, Dusty had purchased it from the widow two doors down), the boys managed to exceed the speed limit on every road in town. Just last week, Ben received a costly moving violation to prove it. As she pulled out her phone to call Jamie, she spotted them rolling ever-so-slowly into the driveway. Ben was in the driver's seat, as usual, but something was wrong.

"Mom, we've got a flat tire," Jamie complained as he shuffled into the kitchen and unharnessed himself from his backpack.

"Second one this month," Ben added on the heels of his brother.

Liz set down the peeler and pushed the vegetable skins into the disposal, too tired to ferry them to the composter out back. "You must've run over something sharp. A nail maybe?"

Ben shook his head and pursed his lips in concern. "No. I'm afraid the Prius has such low self-esteem, it's been cutting itself."

Jamie snickered, and Ben glanced at her, checking to see if he'd scored a smile. Liz turned away to hide her grin, fooling no one, and Ben pumped his arm in victory.

But what school officials were calling a *self-harm epidemic* was no laughing matter. According to Jamie, a girl in his chemistry class had crisscrossed her forearms with a razor blade, leaving a disturbing pattern of red welts. More tragic was poor Mikey Matsen, a former soccer teammate of Ben's who fatally overdosed a few weeks ago. When Liz checked her PTA newsletter every Monday, there was a column called *Teen Health Matters* that encouraged parents to talk with their kids about anxiety and depression. Liz had tried to broach the subject, but Ben turned everything into a joke, and Jamie seemed disinclined to discuss such things. Dusty told her to leave it be. But he didn't fully appreciate the pressure their kids—all kids—were under these days. Ben and Jamie faced ACT tests next weekend, and SAT and AP exams in May. As if all that were a stroll in the park, their school counselor advised the boys to "ramp up" their community service hours. How many canned food drives, charity car washes, and school auctions would be enough?

She peeked over her shoulder at Ben, the blond, husky shortstop who was the spitting image of his dad. As he stood staring slack-jawed into the fridge eyeing the chocolate milk and leftovers, Ben didn't appear stressed in the least. As a rule, he didn't take anything too seriously, with the possible exception of baseball and Maddy Chan, the pretty soccer player who'd kissed him after his game in full view from the bleachers. Here was a boy content with B and C grades and the prospect of a state school. As he chugged the chocolate milk straight from the carton, she groaned.

"Please," she said, "use a glass."

"Like you do?" He closed the refrigerator door and carried the carton to within inches of her nose. She peered into his amber eyes and then looked down to see a trace of plum lipstick on the rim of the container. *Busted.*

At the counter, Jamie slathered peanut butter on a piece of toast and headed to his room where, Liz knew, he would start cramming for a test. Unlike his brother, Jamie was serious about school. About music. Dead serious about video games. As her mother—known as Jo-Jo to the boys—often quipped, "My grand-twins are day and night, sun and moon." Ben, who'd been pulled from Liz via Cesarean section nine minutes before Jamie, was bigger and had crawled and walked first. But Jamie, who'd inherited Liz's dark hair and slate-blue eyes, had talked before his brother and learned to read a year earlier.

Liz finished chopping the vegetables and added them to the broth on the stovetop while Ben settled at the kitchen table, scarfing down quesadillas and humming a popular tune between bites. Like everyone else, she was drawn to his sunny disposition. Yet, as she visualized Jamie hunched over his books, she felt an unspoken kinship with him. They shared an intensity about doing things right, leaving nothing to chance. Not that they didn't have notable differences. Whereas she grew anxious after spending too much time alone, Jamie coveted his privacy. Two years ago, when the twins made the case that they needed separate bedrooms, Jamie volunteered to take the smaller room with one caveat:

that he get a lock on his door. Liz had been against it; Dusty was for.

"Jamie is getting straight A's, and he never asks for a thing," Dusty said. "Wanting a little privacy at fourteen is perfectly normal." He made a fast, up-and-down movement with his right fist, miming masturbation. Liz ignored him.

"What if there's an earthquake—a fire?" she said, her voice escalating. "We won't be able to reach him."

"He can easily climb out the windows. Please," he added, dropping his palms on her shoulders, "don't put your fears on him."

Liz had bristled under his pointed comment. If there was one thing—one thing!—she wanted as a mother, it was to keep a safe roof over her precious boys. To protect them from the toxic swirl of grief, guilt, and loneliness that had smothered her happiness in the years following her sister's death.

In time, however, she reluctantly agreed to let Dusty install chain locks on the twins' doors, allowing her to partially open them to peer inside. Which she rarely did anymore. On any given night, both boys were locked away in their separate rooms, only a ribbon of light escaping from where their doors hung above the wood floors. If either of them was feeling blue or overwhelmed in any way, it was impossible for her to know.

As Liz seasoned the stew, Ben rinsed his plate and drifted out of the kitchen. She heard him knock on Jamie's door and amble inside. Moments later, they were both laughing uproariously, no doubt watching some ridiculous YouTube video or an episode of South Park. She lifted a spoon of broth to her lips, thinking Dusty was probably right. The boys were fine.

Chapter 4

*W*hether it was a lavish corporate gala or an intimate silver anniversary party, Liz and Gabbi always conducted a postmortem to determine what went well and what needed improvement. The term seemed grimly fitting to Liz as she sat across from her partner at Café Borrone on Monday morning to discuss the Perkins memorial. Though Gabbi hadn't arrived at the reception until the caterer had begun to clear the buffet and cork the half-empty bottles of wine, she remarked that everything appeared to have gone precisely as planned.

"Yep," Liz said between bites of a bran muffin. "No snafus, no drama."

"It's nice, isn't it? To manage an event with no Bridezillas? No inebriated tech bros hitting on the wait staff?" Gabbi helped herself to a side of breakfast potatoes glistening in olive oil and looked at her expectantly.

Liz had to agree. The guests had been remarkably easy to please and pleasant to serve. "We didn't have so much as a single vegan complain about the meat sauce."

"So, if we had another client in this 'new sector,' you'd be okay with it?"

"Please don't tell me someone else has died."

"Not yet."

The familiar feeling of being one step behind Gabbi, the bold brunette who was always charging ahead, settled over Liz. Years earlier, they'd attended the same public high school, though Gabbi was always the first to say she came from "the east side, the rough side of the tracks." A year apart in age, they bonded on the girls' basketball team where Liz was a point guard and Gabbi a shooting guard. Gabbi, whose mother was from Mexico City and whose father was of Italian descent, played with a fearless street style—throwing elbows and cursing in Spanish under her breath. Liz quickly learned to favor the younger girl, feeding her balls so that she could take the shot. Which she always did. Even after a string of failed attempts, where the ball clanked off the rim or missed the net entirely, Gabbi would go for it. More times than not, her gutsy play paid off. Now, Gabbi was gearing up to take a shot at the death business. Liz had to ask herself, was she willing to play along?

Gabbi stirred her latte and leaned in closer to Liz. "When guests started to leave the reception, Karl introduced me to an old friend, Anthony Marino, and asked me to see him out. We got to talking, and Mr. Marino made me—*us*—an interesting proposition."

As Gabbi explained it, she'd helped the elderly gentleman with a silver-handled cane make his way through the gardens to the front of the Perkins home. By the time they arrived at a spotless Jaguar where a large man with Polynesian features sat behind the wheel, Anthony Marino had proposed that Touchstone help him "wrap up a few estate issues." Apparently, Karl had told him that Gabbi Rossi and Liz Becker were very resourceful and might be of assistance.

Gabbi acknowledged that what Mr. Marino wanted wasn't strictly event planning. He was a single man with serious heart disease who needed to downsize and get his affairs in order.

"He wants us to plan his memorial service—in advance, of course—so that's a no-brainer," Gabbi said. "But he also wants us to go through his house and help him figure out what to keep for his heirs and what to give away. I suspect we may be clearing out some closets."

"And why would we do that?" Liz was worried about stepping outside the lane of event planning. On the other hand, she was intrigued by the opportunity to put things in order. It seemed to fall squarely into her category of *The Gritty*.

"Because he'll pay seventy-five dollars an hour, a hundred fifty for the two of us."

It was a step down, this hourly wage. But if the work was steady? Maybe she and Dusty could pay some of the bills they'd quarreled about.

As she poked impatiently at her eggs, Gabbi looked ready to start the new job ASAP. Her ex-husband, David, was no longer obliged to pay child support because Zoey had turned eighteen; his checks stopped arriving the month after her birthday. While never an attentive father, he'd virtually disappeared a year ago when Zoey told her parents she was gay. Although the bright, spirited girl had a merit scholarship to cover most of her college tuition, Gabbi was on the hook for her room and board.

"So, what do you think?" Gabbi asked.

Liz reached for her purse and nodded. "I'm in. When does Mr. Marino want us to start?"

"Tomorrow. He's ready when we are."

Though it was a school night, Dusty had scored three seats behind the dugout at AT&T Park in San Francisco, courtesy of a buddy whose house he'd remodeled a few years back. Last season, as Barry Bonds surpassed Babe Ruth and Hank Aaron to clinch the homerun record of all time,

Giants tickets had been hard to find, impossible to afford. This would be the guys' first game in 2008, and Ben had raced home from practice virtually foaming at the mouth. Even Jamie had opted for a live game over a digital one, sliding off his headset and pulling on a Giants cap.

With her boys heading to the city, Liz was free to join her parents for dinner. Only a few miles separated their home from hers, and yet weeks, even months, passed between visits. Since her father had sold his business and her mother had retired from teaching, the two of them traveled more. And, until the recent economic slump, Liz's hectic night-and-weekend schedule of events left no time for drop-ins. But there was something else. Particularly when they were alone, a shifting tension existed between her mother and herself that was unpredictable. As Liz hurried to her car with a tin of oatmeal cookies warm from the oven, she vowed not to linger on that. Yes, they had their past sorrows and resentments, but wasn't every mother-daughter relationship complicated, a wee bit fraught?

Her parents still lived three blocks from the old train station in Menlo Park. "Everybody loves the sound of a train in the distance," Paul Simon sang, but not everyone liked the clatter and vibration of Caltrains nearby. Her family had grown accustomed to the din of the railway, and Liz scarcely registered it as she pulled up to the single-story home dwarfed by towering redwoods. Though the sun was low in the sky, the air temperature was inviting, and her mother's pink and white impatiens brightened the entrance. The light was on in the bathroom that she and her older brother, Ned, had once shared, and Liz made a mental note to call him. They hadn't spoken since Christmas.

She grabbed the cookies and circled round to the back patio where she knew her father would be grilling chicken. He was wearing the royal blue Adidas tracksuit that she'd given him on Father's Day a decade ago. In his right hand was a spatula. In his left, a scotch and soda in the same rocks glass her grandfather had clutched at muggy family reunions in Wisconsin. He raised the glass in greeting. "Want a drink before supper?"

"I'd love one, but I'll get it myself." She jiggled her car keys at him and smiled. "Can't risk one of your double shots tonight."

She stepped through the sliding-glass door and glanced around at the floral upholstered furniture and traditional bronze lamps, feeling a deep connection to the old house. It had been their refuge, a place to start over as a family of four rather than five. And though the early years had been difficult—harrowing, really—they had endured within these sturdy walls, under this shingled roof.

She whistled softly, and Cheddar, their arthritic golden retriever, limped over to bury his head in her knees and wash her palms with his eager tongue. In the kitchen, Liz spotted her mother tossing a salad and tending a pot of what smelled like polenta. She was dressed in a green silk tunic over leggings, and a gold pendant shimmered on her chest. Liz wished she'd worn something other than jeans.

"Come in, come in," her mother said. "Can I put you to work?"

On the table where, a lifetime ago, Liz had served Ned and herself gummy cheese pizza from the freezer—they had quickly learned to fend for themselves after Maggie died—she now laid out silverware and lit the tall, tapered candles. Moments later, the porch door clacked shut and her father shuffled in carrying a carving board heaped with chicken. The sweet, smoky smell of barbeque sauce made her mouth water, and she savored the luxury of having her parents prepare her a home-cooked meal. On evenings like this, she could almost believe the dark years had never existed. In fact, there were no photos from that time, no portraits of Maggie hanging on the walls or beaming from silver frames on the mantle. Only pictures of Ben and Jamie, the generation untouched by tragedy.

Over dinner, they chatted about the surge of troops in Iraq and the contenders for President Bush's seat in the Oval Office.

"I can't imagine why either McCain or Obama would want the job," her father said. "The economy is such a mess." He turned to Liz. "How are things at work? Anything in the pipeline?"

"Gabbi just brought on a new client," she said, relieved to deliver a positive report. "Someone named Anthony Marino."

Her mother stopped chewing and set down her fork. "Tony? I saw him from a distance at Marnie's memorial. You didn't meet him?"

Liz shook her head.

"Well, I've met him. And I'm sorry to tell you he's a Grade-A jerk."

Liz said nothing, preferring not to encourage the sharp turn in the conversation. She reached for her wine glass and took a long, deliberate sip.

"Years ago, Tony's wife, Carol, was the volunteer coordinator at the Boys and Girls Club. She heard I was an artist and brought me onboard to do crafts with the kids. Though she was older, we became good friends." Her mother paused to take a small bite of the yellow polenta. "When Tony left Carol for his receptionist—a girl half his age from the Philippines—she stopped coming to the Club and cried for months." Her mother shot her a severe look. "Like I said, a real jerk."

Liz focused on her salad, trying to enjoy the crunchy cucumber and soft feta cheese. But she could feel the pleasantness of the evening begin to slip away.

"Well, as I remember, the guy's a World War II vet," her father said. "Can't be all bad. He served in the Pacific Theater."

"Maybe that's where he acquired his taste for little floozies."

"Joan, honey, that's enough." His voice was both firm and pleading.

It was Liz's turn to set down her fork. "Gabbi told me that Mr. Marino lives all alone," she said. "During the day, he has only a caretaker with him." The old man did, in fact, sound like a bona fide asshole, but she felt compelled to defend him. Before the downturn, when her business was a happy, chaotic dash from one lavish event to another, such gossip might have seemed harmless. But now, she was in no position to judge clients. Why couldn't her mother see that and simply be supportive? She had a penchant for bursting Liz's bubble, fragile as it was.

"After Tony had a heart attack, he required a lot of help," her mother said. "It wasn't long before his child bride left him for a younger millionaire." She crisscrossed her arms in front of her, looking satisfied. "You know what you call that?"

Liz shrugged.

"Karma."

Liz pushed her chair back from the table, the legs making a disagreeable sound against the wood floors, and stood to serve the cookies she no longer wanted.

Chapter 5

*L*iz and Gabbi met outside the home of Anthony Marino in the hills of Portola Valley. As she locked her car, Liz looked up, taking in the views of the undulating terrain. The Bay Area had endured another year of withering drought. The native grasses appeared parched, the color of dirty straw, in sharp contrast to the lush, irrigated landscapes of the pricey homes nestled into terraced yards and shaded by ancient oaks.

Uncharacteristically dressed in jeans and a zip-up fleece, Gabbi pulled several flat cardboard boxes from her trunk. For her part, Liz shouldered a tote bag weighted with packing supplies and a measuring tape.

"Ready to launch Touchstone Senior Services?" Gabbi joked.

Liz paused to consider the question. Eighteen months ago, she and Gabbi had been hired to produce the fiftieth birthday party for a software zillionaire originally from Texas. The venue had been the entrepreneur's own sprawling estate a mile from where they now stood. Touchstone had orchestrated the extravaganza, erecting a stage and setting up tables for three hundred guests who arrived in boots and bandanas, Western style. After the catering staff had served lobster and short ribs and poured the finest wines on earth, Liz cued the secret performer through her headset. "Send out the cowboy!" Seconds later, flood lights hit the stage and Garth Brooks, electrifying with his black Stetson hat and bucking guitar, strolled out singing "Ain't Goin' Down 'Til the Sun Comes Up." The Crowd. Went. Bonkers.

Afterwards, the elated and visibly drunk birthday boy presented Gabbi and her with a generous tip, a case of fabulous French champagne—and mounds of birthday cake. Gabbi had followed Liz home, and they'd roused Dusty for a spontaneous party, gulping Dom Perignon and eating chocolate molten cake with their bare hands. Before calling it a night, Gabbi slung her arm around Liz's shoulders and they'd clinked glasses, knowing they were at the top of their game. What they hadn't known is that it would be all downhill from there.

"Well?" prompted Gabbi.

Liz glanced up and met her partner's undaunted brown eyes.

"Ready as I'll ever be."

Gabbi wagged her head and laughed. "Okay, Eeyore, let's go."

They climbed the steep steps to the front door of the two-story wood and glass home that must have looked modern in the '70s but today looked inescapably dated. When Gabbi rang the doorbell, Liz found herself holding her breath. What did a "Grade-A Jerk" look like?

The white-haired man who answered the door looked too frail to have ever romanced a young receptionist. And he was living proof that ears and noses continue to grow throughout a human lifetime. Wearing dark trousers and a blazer with a yellowed handkerchief tucked in the breast pocket, Anthony Marino appeared the quintessential Italian gentleman.

He invited them in, and the heavy-set man whom Gabbi had described as Mr. Marino's chauffeur offered them coffee from an exquisite, red-lacquer tray.

"I'm Aasal," the caretaker introduced himself. He had gentle eyes and close-cropped dark hair, and he was wearing an Aloha shirt that revealed his powerful fore-arms. "If there's anything you need, I'm here to help."

Liz and Gabbi followed Mr. Marino into his office where hundreds of books lined shelves on three walls. They settled into chairs that faced an imposing walnut desk. Appearing anxious to get underway, the old man promptly took a seat.

"Thank you for coming on short notice," he began. "Karl Perkins speaks very highly of you." He removed two sheets of paper from a folder and handed one page each to Liz and Gabbi.

"My health is in decline, and since none of my rela-tives live nearby, I must oversee these matters myself." He gestured toward the printouts. "I've made a list of items requiring your assistance."

Liz glanced at his morbid to-do's:

1) Plan memorial service (location: Alta Vista Golf Club)

2) Write obituary (for distribution to SF Chron, SJ Mercury News, local papers)

3) Donate WWII items (Museum? Theater Group?)

4) Give away Italian suits, etc. (St. Vincent de Paul)

5) Photograph furniture and art (send pics to Tony Jr.)

After reviewing the list, Gabbi addressed their new client.

"Mr. Marino, I'm confident we can help you with all of these items. What would you like us to do first?"

"For starters, I'd like you to call me Tony."

"So noted." She laughed, tossing her hair back and flashing a smile that showcased her dimples. "Tony, where do we begin?"

The octogenarian beamed, suddenly enjoying having two women (particularly Gabbi) in his home awaiting their marching orders. Early in their partnership, Liz had been envious of Gabbi's beguiling way with clients. But over the years, she'd learned to appreciate her skill at winning and retaining them.

"Aasal will show you around while I make a few calls. Then we'll put together a plan of action."

The tour started on the second floor in what had once been Tony's master bedroom. His heart condition had forced him to move to a guest suite downstairs, but the palatial room was still largely intact. The inviting four-poster bed with gauzy curtains and gold ties had a woman's touch, and Liz wondered, which one?

She glanced at the framed pictures on an antique dresser, noticing a faded color photo of an attractive family. On the left stood a tall, handsome woman in a pale blue dress. Was this Carol, her mother's friend? Linking arms with her was a young man with a dark moustache wearing a cap and gown, and next to the graduate appeared to be a sister. Liz leaned in closer and recognized the father as a younger incarnation of Mr. Marino. Here was Tony, a trim, middle-aged man in an elegant suit and a King-of-the-World smile. This was the man who would risk it all for the firm flesh and sparkling eyes of his young assistant.

Aasal lifted the photo and gestured for them to come closer.

"Everyone's much older now, but this is Tony's family. At some point, you may need to correspond with them." He identified Carol first. "This is Tony's ex who lives in Seattle near him—Tony Jr.—and his wife and kids." He touched the image of the striking young woman with long black hair and a short skirt. "His daughter, Angela. She's in New York." There were no pictures of the second wife, and he made no mention of her.

Aasal showed them to the walk-in closet. "All these items must go." He reached out to graze the sleeve of a navy cashmere blazer, and it occurred to Liz that it might fit Jamie and bring out the indigo of his eyes. Of course, he'd have no occasion to wear it. Flannel pajama bottoms and T-shirts were fine for playing *Call of Duty* or reading graphic novels in bed. She wondered if he'd even considered attending the junior prom, whereas Ben and his girlfriend had already picked out complementary outfits. Liz had yet to officially meet Maddy Chan, though she'd often seen her leaving the soccer field with her parents. Her mother, Tammy Larkin-Chan, was reportedly a former rodeo queen. Maddy had her father's eyes, her mother's high cheekbones and blue-ribbon smile.

Gabbi entered Tony's closet and stopped in her tracks. She gazed at the suits on gleaming wood hangers, whispering, "Zegna, Armani, Brunello Cucinelli." To Liz, who knew little about fashion, it sounded like a strange incantation.

"Are you sure he doesn't wear any of these?" Gabbi asked.

Aasal nodded. "Tony doesn't get out much anymore. The doctor says his congestive heart failure is getting worse. I drive him to the country club for dinner, and sometimes he goes to the golf course and rides in the cart with buddies who still play. But even the club is casual now."

"I've got a friend who owns a high-end consignment shop," Gabbi said. "He'd flip to get his hands on these suits, and he'd give half the sales revenue to Tony."

"No, the boss wants everything to go to St. Vincent de Paul. That's where Carol took their donations."

Gabbi shrugged, looking mystified that anyone would turn down the chance to make easy money, but Liz suspected the elderly man wouldn't live to spend it.

Aasal guided them downstairs to the living and dining rooms and showed them the furniture, artwork, and Persian rugs that needed to be measured and photographed. Tony wanted a detailed inventory sent to his son, who would determine what to ship to Seattle and what to liquidate.

The last stop on the tour was the garage, where a scuffed-up metal trunk sat on the concrete floor near a vintage Alfa Romeo. Aasal stooped to open the World War II storage box, and this time it was Liz, the former history major, marveling at the treasures within. On top was Tony's U.S. Navy uniform, the color of seaweed, with three black stripes and a star on each sleeve—a high ranking, she figured. The brass buttons with embossed American eagles were still shiny, and the pockets looked freshly pressed. Time may not have been kind to Officer Anthony Marino, but it had done little to dim the regal aspects of his uniform.

Gabbi lifted away the military coat and revealed more of the contents below, including a samurai sword in a tattered leather sheath, and a polished pistol that appeared more recent than 1945. Deeper in the trunk was a gold cigar box full of exotic coins and handwritten letters. For Liz, it was inconceivable that Tony wanted to give everything away. Back in his office, she had to ask.

"Tony, your trunk in the garage—there are so many marvelous keepsakes. Are you sure no one wants them?"

The old man grimaced. "Yes, I'm sure. My son is pleased to be in my will. Happy to accept my cash and assets of value. He simply doesn't want any of my personal items." In his voice Liz heard both bitterness and resignation. "As for Angela, my daughter is a partner at Lehman

Brothers." Pride lit up his face momentarily. "She needs— and desires—nothing I have to give."

While Gabbi assembled cardboard boxes upstairs and filled them with Italian suits and expensive shoes, Liz took photos and measurements of Tony's handsome furniture and oil paintings. She recognized the Richard Diebenkorn and Elmer Bischoff, stunning figurative works by Bay Area artists her mother had discussed in her classes. Angela Marino was crazy not to want any of these. As if reading her mind, Aasal approached her and explained that, after the divorce, Tony's daughter and son had sided with their mother, essentially disowning their father and his second wife.

"Janelle split ten years ago and little has changed," he said. "Tony corresponds with his son, and once in a blue moon he sees the grandkids. But Angela never calls." He stared down at his broad, sandaled feet, momentarily lost in thought. "I'm divorced too. But I talk to my kids every week. Tony needs to find a way to make peace with his family before you ladies"—he jutted his chin toward the second story where Gabbi was working—"put on a funeral."

Did Liz detect a note of distain in Aasal's voice? No one disapproved of putting on a party, but maybe planning funerals would be the kiss of death for Touchstone Events.

She met Aasal's gaze and nodded, agreeing with the notion of a reconciliation. She couldn't bear the thought of Tony facing the end of his life with so little tenderness, Grade-A Jerk or not. Her thoughts turned to Dusty and the boys, and a gust of gratitude swept through her. As terrifying as death was, she believed she would never leave this world alone and unloved.

Gabbi and Liz left Tony's house around 5:00 p.m., agreeing to return the next day bright and early. They'd each worked seven hours, earning a tidy sum for Touchstone Events. Even better, Tony had given them a generous retainer, assuring them his house projects would take weeks to complete.

At home, Dusty's truck was parked exactly where she'd seen it this morning, and Liz felt the buzz of a productive day seep away. Inside on the kitchen counter, she found a platter with four uncooked beef patties under cellophane, and a salad bowl full of greens. At least Dusty had a plan for dinner.

Eager to get off her feet, she sat down at the table to sort the mail and heard the door to Ben's room swing open down the hall. He strolled into the kitchen followed by a sporty girl wearing yoga pants and a baseball cap flipped backwards. Her smudged mascara, swollen lips, and wrinkled top clearly telegraphed what they'd been up to in the bedroom. These were not the circumstances under which she'd imagined meeting Maddy Chan. The girl straightened her cotton jersey self-consciously, and Liz wondered what the pretty teen made of her, a middle-aged woman in jeans and sneakers who hadn't applied makeup or brushed her hair in eight unforgiving hours.

"Hey, Mom," Ben said. The girl stepped forward and gave her a little wave.

"Hi, Mrs. Becker!"

"You must be Maddy. So nice to meet you." Liz didn't get up to shake her hand. She was playing it cool since Ben obviously didn't care about proper introductions.

"I'm going to take her home," Ben said, pulling out his keys.

"Where's Jamie?" she asked.

"In his room playing video games with the other nerds. Duh."

Liz stiffened, taken aback by Ben's rude remark—particularly irksome in front of his new friend. Before she could think of a parent-appropriate comeback, he and the girl disappeared out the back door and slid into the Prius. Irritated, she marched into the family room where Dusty was on the couch staring vacantly into his laptop.

"So, I thought we had a policy about no girlfriends behind closed doors."

Dusty pawed at his eyes, reluctant to engage. "In my defense, we've never had to enforce that rule before." He looked up at her for sympathy. "I was caught off guard."

"How long were they in there?"

"Not too long. Half hour?"

Liz frowned. That was ample time for things to go too far. Maddy was only a sophomore, and Liz hoped that Ben wasn't *pressuring* her in any way. Or maybe it was the other way around.

"Tell me, honey, what would you have done?" Dusty said.

Standing with folded arms, she wondered, would she have knocked on Ben's door and demanded he open it? Such an awkward thing, triggering who-knows-what kind of nastiness. She recalled the time her mother had banged on Ned's bedroom door after he—already criminally handsome at fifteen—sneaked a girl inside. An epic mother-son screaming match ensued as a mortified blonde wearing an inside-out shirt bolted from the room and raced away. Liz didn't have the stomach for any of that.

Dusty could sense that she was softening. He patted the sofa cushion next to him, urging her to sit down. When she complied, he leaned over and whispered in her ear. "Don't be angry. We were young and horny once too."

She rolled her eyes and chuckled as he reached under

to cup her ass, giving it a gentle squeeze just as Jamie entered the room. They separated quickly, and Liz peered at their other son, their moon boy, pale and shadowed from so much time in his shuttered room gazing into a screen. It occurred to her that it would be a relief to catch him with a girl in his bedroom, a friend in the flesh. Most of his pals were fellow online gamers, invisible to her.

"When's dinner?" Jamie asked.

"Dad will fire up the grill in a few minutes."

He nodded and retreated to his room while she and Dusty settled back against the couch. She touched his knee and asked him how his day went.

"I worked from home today. Just had paperwork, so I knocked it out here."

She paused, taking a few measured breaths. "What's the status on that remodel in Palo Alto?"

"Ty Leighton got the job," he said, dropping his gaze to the floor. "His numbers were lower than mine." He shifted his weight and turned to face her. "Honestly, I thought nobody could beat my bid. I can't see how Ty will make a dime on that project. It's like he's doing it at cost."

"Something else will come along," she said.

When Dusty headed outdoors to grill the burgers, Liz returned to the pile of mail in the kitchen. Sifting through it, she noticed a letter from the mortgage company that carried the loan for their second home. As she slid her finger under the backflap of the envelope, she tried not to worry. But the note was precisely what she feared. The teaser interest rate that had seemed like such a bargain in 2006—when Dusty was certain they could flip the house, pay off the loan, and put cash in the bank—was changing. The rate was jumping up, nearly doubling their payments, while the value of their home was sinking. She and Dusty were caught on the wrong end of the seesaw.

Chapter 6

*B*efore returning to Tony's house, Liz stopped by the high school to drop off two dozen chocolate crinkles for the bake sale supporting Ben's baseball team. After the awkward introduction to Maddy, she hadn't felt inclined to save him any. If he wanted one of her cookies, a reliable hot seller, he'd have to damn well pay for it himself.

When she pulled up to the house, Gabbi's old ("vintage," she liked to say) Mercedes station wagon was already parked at the curb. She hustled up the steps and slipped through the front door that was left ajar. In the library, she found Gabbi and Tony discussing his memorial service, which struck her as odd. What was the hurry? There was so much to do around the house, and Tony didn't appear on the verge of keeling over. On the contrary, he seemed extremely animated talking to Gabbi about his "After Party."

"I know my golf buddies will be there," he said. "So, I definitely want a full bar. Wine, yes, but also bourbon, gin, and vodka. And meat!" He pounded his desk for emphasis. "Pastrami sandwiches, hamburger sliders, that kind of thing. Absolutely no sushi," he added, making a face of disdain. He paused to acknowledge Liz. "Aasal is brewing a pot of coffee. Help yourself to a cup in the kitchen."

The earthy aroma of French roast led her to Aasal, dressed as before in an island shirt and drawstring pants. He appeared agitated as he tossed the coffee grounds into the garbage and pulled a carton of cream from the refrigerator.

"Are they still talking about his service?" he asked in his low, sonorous voice. Liz nodded. On the countertop, he assembled the mugs on the red tray and poured the coffee without another word. Then, he handed her the tray. "I won't listen to another word of that." Liz glimpsed a deep sadness in Aasal's black-brown eyes and felt a sudden warmth for him.

"I know. It seems so...premature. For now, we should be focused on his move. By the way—where's he going?"

"Last year, he bought an apartment in a retirement community just down the hill. They offer assisted living. Tony is certain he won't like it, but he knows he can't stay here. Too many stairs and split levels. Every night when I go home, I worry he'll fall and not be able to get up. Even so, he's still got life in him." He sighed and turned to the sink to put away the breakfast dishes.

As Liz carried the tray down the hall, coffee slipped over the rims of the mugs like waves over a break wall. How was she less graceful than a 300-pound man? From the threshold to the library, she spotted Gabbi with her pen poised above her notepad.

"And will there be a burial service? Or is cremation preferred?" Liz faltered and the tray nearly fell from her hands. The walls of the hallway seemed to bend away from her, and she moved her feet apart to regain her balance. Burial or cremation? How could Gabbi be so callous, so cavalier? She might have been asking their client if he preferred chicken or beef, real sugar or artificial sweetener. She leaned against the doorframe, reluctant to take another step.

"Oh, heavens, I'm an old real estate guy," Tony said. "A land man. I want a big plot with a roomy box and a hefty headstone." He leaned back in his leather chair and gazed briefly out the window where a mow-n-blow team was cutting the tender grass of spring. "Ashes in an urn? That doesn't work for me. It'd be like spending eternity in a damn condo."

"So true," Gabbi said, nodding sympathetically, as if the fact that she and Zoey had moved to a small, two-bedroom condominium following her divorce had slipped her mind.

Hoping the issue was settled, Liz entered the room, distributed the coffee, and sat down next to her partner. Tony reached for his mug and took a few swallows before clearing his throat. "I'd like to tell you a little about my life," he said, turning to face them square on. Liz and Gabbi smiled in unison, like two kindergarteners eager for story time. "It will help you write my obituary."

"Of course," Gabbi said.

Oh, hell, Liz thought. The man was obsessed with his own death. Perhaps the same could be said for her, but they were cosmic opposites. She fought daily to ward off thoughts of that dark country from which "no traveler returns." Just this morning, she'd bolted awake after a frightening dream where she'd been separated from Dusty and the boys in a strange wilderness, clawing at branches and finding no path back. Her sense of being lost and utterly alone had felt like a kind of death. When she awoke to find her warm, sleepy husband beside her, she had shuddered with relief. Tony, by contrast, seemed to enjoy being in the gravitational pull toward the great beyond.

As she spooned sugar into her coffee, Liz vowed to simply do as the old man asked. While she believed their time would be better spent helping him downsize, he was the customer. It was, as they say, his funeral.

She gestured to Gabbi for her pen and pad, and her partner quickly relinquished them. Gabbi was gifted in all things visual, but writing was not one of her strong suits. Over the next hour, Tony unspooled the threads of his life. His father, born in Genoa, arrived in San Francisco in 1919 and found a job working as a cook in North Beach. By the time Tony was born in 1924, he'd opened his own Italian restaurant, and it flourished for many years. But during the war, food shortages threatened their family business.

"At that time, I was on a naval ship in the South Pacific. I wrote my parents and told them to buy property on the Peninsula—dirt cheap in the '40s—so they could raise livestock and vegetables to supply their kitchen in the city." He tapped his chest and smiled. "Good thing they took my advice. After my father had a stroke, I sold the farm to help support my parents and disabled brother. That, young ladies, was the 'aha moment.' Buying and selling land in what became Silicon Valley was vastly more profitable than serving pasta."

He ran his bent, arthritic fingers through his thinning white hair, giving Liz a breather. She'd been diligently taking notes but sensed that the bulk of Tony's oral history wasn't meant for a newspaper column. It was meant for someone who would live beyond him and remember something of Tony Marino's life. She and Gabbi exchanged a knowing glance. They were stand-ins for his estranged children.

They heard a knock on the door and looked up to see Aasal. "Time for your cardiology appointment, Tony." The old man nodded and reached for his wallet on the corner of his desk.

"Gotta go see Doctor Doom," he muttered. "You gals can stay here and pack up. Sound good?"

"Sure," Liz said. "Plenty here to keep us busy."

"How quaint," Gabbi said, holding up a *Playboy* magazine featuring a Pamela Anderson lookalike with bee-stung lips and boobs bursting out of a gold brassiere. Gabbi and Liz were boxing up linens in a small bedroom closet and came across a stack of random publications.

"These days, most guys watch porn online, but our Tony prefers his girls in print."

Liz leaned over and squinted at the date on the magazine: August 2005. Only three years old. She shook her head, trying to square the well-dressed octogenarian with the type of man who pored over dirty pictures. Gabbi merely laughed. "Men!"

Liz wondered, would Dusty still be fantasizing about sex at eighty? A cloud of guilt scuttled across her thoughts. Last night, he'd reached out to her after she'd switched off the lights, rubbing her shoulders and spooning her so that she could feel his intentions. She'd moved away from him under the too-warm comforter, uttering, "It's nearly midnight. Another time would be better."

"That's what you always say," he'd complained. "It's never a better time."

He had a point. Sex rarely appealed to her these days. Occasional hot flashes made her inclined to avoid nightgowns, and the skimpy T-shirts she was wearing to bed at night to keep cool were sending the wrong signal to her amorous husband.

Six years ago, when Dusty turned forty, she'd given him a book her girlfriends had been gossiping about for weeks. Called *101 Nights of GRRREAT Sex*, the paperback guide offered descriptions of "sex-perimental" adventures hidden behind glued sheets of paper. Some suggestions were "For *his* eyes only." Others, "For *her* eyes," the rule being that partners took turns initiating romance and keeping the details a secret. As Liz carefully, nervously, ripped the perforated edges away, she discovered ideas she could try (and others she would not).

While she and Gabbi loaded Tony's old magazines into bags for recycling, Liz's thoughts drifted back to one memorable night. Suggestion #59 had been to recreate a teenaged boy's high school fantasy, and she'd followed it to a T. The evening entailed a long drive to a wooded lovers' lane...a few sips of sweet rosé...and old-fashioned, tried-and-true sex in a reclined car seat. There'd been a full moon visible through the windshield, and Liz had feared someone would see them—or murder them, Zodiac style. But they'd been all alone that night. When she'd lowered the zipper over Dusty's bulging fly, he had moaned with relief when he popped free and they'd both giggled. It had taken only minutes to satisfy him, and he'd been cheerful for days afterwards.

For her, Dusty had selected just the right interludes with candles, fragrant oils, and a velvet eye mask. Best of all was the sexy CD he'd made with songs like "Smooth Operator" by Sade and Clapton's "You Look Wonderful Tonight." Looking back, she had to admit, the pre-planned nights of intimacy had been good for them both. Maybe she could dig up that old book and put some heat back into their bedroom. Unlike Tony Marino, her husband only had eyes for her—he deserved a little TLC. Why not surprise him tonight and rock his world on a mundane Tuesday when he least expected it?

When they were finished for the day, Gabbi offered to take all the clothes, shoes, and linens to St Vincent de Paul. As they drove away in opposite directions, Liz decided to make a quick stop by the office to check her computer for any client correspondence. Maybe, she prayed, someone would need help planning a summer party.

Chapter 7

*A*lone at the office, Liz found a voicemail from a long-time client. Last week, Liz had phoned her hoping to ink in her family's annual Fourth of July party, an event Touchstone had managed for five consecutive years. But Mrs. Dalton—a woman who adored her flag-motif sweaters, "Independence Day Martinis," and sparklers for the kids who always swarmed the ice cream buffet—had sounded uncertain. Today she left an apologetic message. "I'm sorry, Liz. We're skipping the party this year. The optics of entertaining during a recession just aren't very good."

Liz sighed, frustrated that the local gentry was keeping their money on the sidelines. Throwing a party may appear frivolous, but it would help sustain small businesses like Touchstone. Her spirits rebounded when she opened an email from her neighbor, Julie Mohr, who was getting married and needed help with the plans. Because it was a second marriage, the ceremony and reception would be "casual and intimate." Liz knew this was code for *small budget*, but she was grateful—almost giddy—to find that Touchstone was still in the business of joy. She replied with enthusiastic congratulations and suggested several times to meet.

When she turned to the small bundle of snail mail, she discovered a check from Karl Perkins among the bills. What a dear man, finding time to pay them so quickly after his wife's memorial. He included a handwritten note on the bereavement cards they'd ordered for him, a lovely touch. She decided to deposit the money immediately and then treat herself to a pedicure, letting the day's talk of burials and obituaries lift away with a good, warm foot soak. By the time she got home, she'd be relaxed and ready for a little romance with Dusty.

She parked in front of the bank, and as she pulled the handle of the heavy glass door at Wells Fargo, a woman on the other side of the pane was pushing. Though she was wearing a baseball cap and oversized dark sunglasses, Liz instantly recognized her as Rachel Matsen, Mikey's mother. She flushed, uncertain what to say to this grieving woman. Last month, Mikey had overdosed on some undisclosed narcotic in a park near the public library. Liz heard about it from a friend while standing in the check-out line at Walgreens. The boy died a week before his seventeenth birthday.

In middle school, Ben and Mikey had played AYSO soccer together, and she and Rachel often chit-chatted on the sidelines while putting out snacks and Gatorade at half-time. But once the boys entered high school, Mikey drifted away from sports, falling into drugs and dealing. Liz had been relieved that neither Ben nor Jamie ran in the same circles as Mikey Matsen.

As Rachel emerged into the sunlight, Liz stepped aside to make room for her, still searching for the right words.

"Rachel," she began, reaching out to briefly touch her arm. "We were heartbroken to hear about Mikey. If there's anything I can do for your family—maybe drop off some dinner?"

Rachel pushed up her glasses to rest on her cap and leveled her gaze at Liz. "We're fine," she said. "We don't need help from anyone."

Liz rocked back, stung and baffled by the anger in her voice. She had expected sadness, but not—resentment? She tried again. "I'm sorry our boys grew apart."

"Well, not entirely," Rachel said. "We found Mikey's accounts."

Something in her face made Liz flinch.

"So, we know the kids who kept him in business. Your son, Ben? The *star* baseball player? He was a customer. Quite a pothead, your boy." She shoved her glasses back over her eyes and walked stiffly around the corner and out of sight.

Standing on the warm sidewalk outside the bank, Liz was frozen. Equal parts worry and fury overwhelmed her. *What else do I not know about my own son?* The pedicure would have to wait. Liz hurried to her car and headed straight for the high school baseball field.

Pulling into the school parking lot just after 5:00 p.m., Liz knew practice was over and that Ben would be making his way to his car. She wanted to confront him alone, to hear what possible defense he might have. It galled her to think he would pull this crap—couldn't he see how stressful it was just to keep a damn roof over their heads?

Through her dirty windshield, she watched her sandy-haired son materialize from the boys' locker room. After swinging his canvas baseball bag over his shoulder, he fist-bumped two teammates and then strolled out in her direction, looking as if he hadn't a care in the world. She felt a pressure on her heart, an unexpected warmth for her boy that she tried to shake off. When she finally caught

Ben's eye, he looked surprised but offered a friendly wave and hustled to her driver's side window.

"Get in," Liz said.

"But my car's right there!" He pointed to the Prius parked in the shade of an enormous maple.

"We're not going anywhere. I have to talk to you about something."

Ben looked mystified but neither guilty nor alarmed. *He must think I'm utterly clueless*, Liz thought, feeling the warmth dissipate. When he climbed into the van's passenger seat and raised his eyebrows in question, she paused, uncertain where to begin.

"I saw Mrs. Matsen at the bank today."

"Oh," Ben said, shaking his head and looking genuinely distressed. "That totally sucks about Mikey." He settled back against the headrest. "He was weird, but cool, you know? A really funny dude."

She turned to address him more directly. "So, I understand you connected with him recently." Now apprehension dawned on Ben's face. He glanced down, fiddling with the lid of his baseball cap.

"Not really, I mean, I saw him in the halls after class and stuff."

Liz was in no mood to hear Ben shuffle around the truth. "Mrs. Matsen told me that she found your name in Mikey's drug records. She said that *Ben Becker* had been a regular customer."

"Mom, chill. Don't go all STP on me."

STP was short for *Straight to Panic*. Liz hated the expression, something the boys had dreamed up to describe her tendency to "overreact."

"I'm not panicking; I'm extremely concerned."

"It was just a little pot."

Liz closed her eyes and drew a deep breath. "A little pot? And what would Coach Ramirez say about that? *A little pot* is enough to get you kicked off the baseball team. And without baseball, your college prospects get even smaller."

"Don't you think I know that?" he snapped. His cheeks and neck flared red. "And thanks for reminding me that I'm a fucking dumbass."

This was Ben's ninja move in every argument they had lately, commandeering her righteous anger and turning it against her. Why couldn't he just say, "I'm sorry, I messed up. It won't happen again"?

"Look, I know you won't believe this," he said. "But the weed wasn't for me. It was for a...friend."

Liz stared into his eyes, trying to decipher what was behind them. Was he telling the truth? Ben was so passionate about baseball; it was plausible that he wouldn't risk his position as starting shortstop for the chance to get stoned. Not that he was an angel. She'd found empty beer cans stashed behind the garage. And when she'd rolled the vacuum cleaner under his bed, she'd clunked against a bottle of Fireball Cinnamon Whiskey. But she hadn't come across any drug paraphernalia, and she'd never smelled that skunky odor of pot in his room.

"It's still illegal, Ben. Who would you risk that for? Was it...Maddy?"

"No, no way," he said, and Liz sensed that she'd touched a nerve. He reached for the van's door handle and yanked it open. Then, he grabbed his duffel and stepped outside the car.

"Mom, I'm done talking about this. You're way off base. Me buying a little pot is the last thing you should worry about." He shut the door with deliberate restraint and walked away.

Liz turned on the engine and started home in a funk. If Ben buying weed—from a young dealer who was now dead—was the last thing she should worry about, what, in God's name, was the first?

When she found Dusty stretched out on the sofa watching a ball game and stuffing his mouth with tortilla chips, she had to fight an impulse to explode. So much for her vow, just hours ago, to initiate some *GRRREAT Sex!* It was starting to feel like *Groundhog Day*. Here they were again needing to discuss Ben. And here she was, one more time, wondering when Dusty would find work and get off the flippin' couch.

Though it was faint, she could hear the screeching guitar solos of vintage Metallica coming from under Jamie's door—he wouldn't hear a word they said. She planted her purse on the coffee table and sat down to face her unshaven husband, noting that Brad Pitt rocked the stubble thing considerably better than he did. Before she could speak, Dusty pulled himself up to a sitting position and held up his palm.

"Ben just called me. I know about the pot."

She took in his crumpled T-shirt and relaxed brow. His calm eyes. Clearly, he was not as upset as she was.

"And it doesn't bother you? That he was buying drugs from a dealer at school?"

"Of course, it bothers me. But kids like Mikey have been peddling pot on that campus since you roamed those halls thirty years ago. And even good boys like Ben have been buying it. Nothing's changed."

"Correct. And marijuana can still get you busted and expelled from school. Your college dreams can still go up in smoke. Literally," she added. "And what if Rachel Matsen decides to hand over Mikey's drug records to the police?"

A roar from the baseball fans on TV made his eyes slide to the screen. She wanted to smack him. "Dusty, are you kidding me? Pay attention."

His head swiveled back in her direction. "Honey, what Ben did was wrong and we should definitely punish him. But you can't micromanage his every move. Boys in high school are going to drink. And smoke. And try really, really hard to get laid. It's just how they roll." The ghost of a smile appeared on his lips.

"Jamie doesn't do that stuff," she sniffed.

"Maybe we should be worried about *that*. Maybe he's not having enough fun." Dusty appeared truly concerned, and Liz felt a stitch in her gut. But she shook her head, refusing to believe Dusty knew better than she did.

"Don't be ridiculous. It's a comfort to know that he's safe and sound in his room. Not running around looking for trouble."

The front door opened, and Ben tip-toed through the foyer down the hall to his bedroom. As if they couldn't see him. Or hear him. Liz started to get up, but Dusty reached for her arm.

"Let me handle this. You've worked all day."

She started to object but then settled against the pillows. Truth was, she felt physically exhausted from hauling boxes of old linens down concrete steps to Gabbi's car. Mentally worn out after confronting Rachel at the bank and Ben at school. And maybe Dusty needed this small exercise in authority.

"Fine with me," she said.

"I suggest we ground him for a month."

"Yes, that sounds about right. But..."

"But what?"

"Maybe we should let him go to the junior prom. It wouldn't be fair to Maddy if we kept him home. I'm sure she spent a small fortune on her dress."

Dusty's eyebrows lifted in surprise. "And I thought I was the softy."

While Dusty had his come-to-Jesus talk with Ben, Liz got dinner underway. As she browned a skillet of ground beef for spaghetti, her thoughts returned to Rachel Matsen. Despite their upsetting exchange, Liz harbored no ill will towards the woman who had suffered the loss of a child. And if that wasn't hellish enough, Rachel had to endure the town gossip—all the wretched, behind-the-back judgement about her son's death from an overdose.

Poor Mikey. She hadn't lain eyes on him in years and could only conjure him as the sweet middle schooler in baggy shorts he'd once been. He was one of those kids always happy to share his Skittles or bubble gum with anyone. She wondered where he was now, and her thoughts slipped into the deep, dark well of her fears. Was the boy buried miles away in a deserted, wind-swept cemetery—like her sister? Or was he perched on a shelf in his family's home, reduced to dust in a "damn condo"? Either way, an unbearable choice for a mother.

Hot grease from the skillet popped and fizzled, bringing her focus back to the too-warm kitchen and her own sons. She pushed open the window above the sink, taking in the bracing night air. The twins were nearly grown, but still so unprepared to fend for themselves in the world beyond their front door. To think that Ben was messing with pot—at the peak of baseball season. And that sensitive, serious Jamie had so few friends. She felt she had failed them in ways she couldn't quite grasp.

Liz added linguine to a pot of boiling water and watched the ribbons of pasta bend and bob under the surface. She told herself to buck up. Though it had been a stressful, knocked-off-balance kind of day, she and Dusty would soon be sitting down to share a warm meal with their boys. There was genuine comfort in that.

Chapter 8

$\mathcal{A}$t **Tony's request,** Liz had prepared a first draft of his obituary, but there were missing dates and lingering questions. Did he want to mention both former wives, or was his second wife, Janelle, persona non grata? What about hobbies? Non-profit work? She emailed him her write-up and requested that he fill in the blanks. For three days, she had no reply. And then on Thursday, she received an attachment that looked less like an obituary and more like a tome on the life and times of Anthony Paul Marino.

She printed out and read five pages of single-spaced text, finding, to her disbelief, achievements dating back to his middle school years. When Gabbi wandered into her office looking for stamps, Liz handed her the top page. Gabbi glanced over it and clamped her hand over her mouth.

"Is this for real? He won top honors in his *Boy Scout troop*?"

"Keep going," Liz said, extending the additional pages. Gabbi took them and retreated to find her glasses.

On page two, Liz had found a succinct description of Tony's service in the Navy. But what followed was a long section describing his excellence in intramural basketball at Stanford. Liz, too, had played intramural basketball in college. The team was comprised of all the kids like her who had absolutely no shot at playing at the varsity level. Were intramural sports—and the Boy Scouts—truly obit-worthy?

Page three was devoted to Tony's real estate career and his position as a "philanthropic community leader." But he appeared to support only charity golf tournaments, "pay to play" events that allowed donors like himself to tee off alongside retired stars of the NFL. These donations didn't qualify him as a community leader. Not when Silicon Valley CEOs and venture capitalists were funding new wings at the Children's Hospital, complete with family recreation areas and whimsical outdoor sculptures.

In his final paragraph, Tony gave a glowing report of his children who "embraced his legacy of achievement, and who gave generously of their time, talent, and treasure." It was both lofty and vague, and it depressed Liz to realize how little he really knew them.

Gabbi returned, waving the pages overhead, and dropped into the chair next to Liz.

"¡Dios Mio!" she said. "Do you have any idea how much this would cost to run in *The Merc*? Or *The Chron*? Literally thousands of dollars."

"I know. But what worries me more is that Tony will be a laughingstock. I can already hear people snickering about his pitiful Scout badges."

"True. But he'll be dead. So, technically, he won't have hurt feelings."

"Gab—it's not funny. We can't let him do this. I admit he's no prince, but he's growing on me." Liz stood up and walked around her desk to face her partner. "It's our job as his"—and here she raised her fingers to make air quotes—"'death-planning consultants' to give him sound advice. I mean, when a bride is trying to choose between a wedding dress that looks sexy verging on slutty, and a wedding dress that looks a tad prissy, we recommend the prissy one. Because we know her grandmother—and future children—will find that dress more appropriate."

"Tony ain't no bride."

"But he needs our professional guidance. Besides, it will reflect poorly on us if we let him run this crazy thing."

"So, what do you propose?"

"I'll start by calling the local papers to get an estimate for placing an obituary with a gazillion words. Hopefully, the price will knock some sense into him."

Armed with prices from several newspapers, Liz drove to Portola Valley to meet with Tony. Earlier, she'd spoken with an editor at a community paper where she'd worked years ago as a reporter covering the local school beat. He'd politely refused to devote so much space to the obituary of a non-dignitary, adding, "We're happy to run something half as long, and, believe me, it will still cost a pretty penny." Delivering this kind of message to Tony required a face-to-face meeting.

The shutters were still closed when Aasal escorted her into Tony's office, and she was alarmed to find the old gent still in his robe as he sat behind his desk.

"I've got a cold," he grunted. He appeared sallow and dispirited, and Liz was hesitant to make matters worse.

"I'm sorry, Tony. I'll make this fast. I have the prices for what it would cost to run your obituary." She sat down and scanned her notes feeling awkward. Shouldn't this kind of thing be addressed after death by his adult children? Though she hadn't met them, she had a growing dislike for his self-righteous brood.

"Let's be frank; I can afford whatever it costs," he said, straightening himself to sit more erect. "But I'm confident that the papers will run my story free of charge.

They do that for individuals who have a certain *stature* in the community."

"Yes, Tony, that was true in the past. But with more people getting their news online, and advertisers moving away from print—especially in this down cycle—the papers have to charge for nearly every obit. It's part of their bread and butter so to speak. And with a submission of this length..."

Tony's head hung low, grazing his folded hands on the desk. After a long moment, he looked up.

"I know it's long. Stupidly long. But I want my children and grandkids to know something about my life. To have a record." His voice cracked, and tears glittered in his pink-rimmed, rheumy eyes. "Surely, they will read my obituary, don't you think?"

"Absolutely," Liz said, with more certainty than she felt.

He took a sip of his tea and leaned back in his chair. "And I want to send a message to Carol here, to let her know where she stands with me when it's all said and done." He picked up his draft of the obit and read aloud: "Following their wedding on October 16th, 1955, Tony and Carol settled on the Peninsula and raised a family. They enjoyed sailing, playing tennis, and visiting Italy with their two wonderful children. These were the happiest years of Tony's life." He took off his glasses and peered at Liz with a measure of satisfaction.

Liz nodded. "I'm sure Carol will appreciate those uplifting words. As well as the fact that you don't mention the divorce." What made her insert that little dagger? Her mother's disapproval of the man had crept into her voice.

The color rose in Tony's unshaven face. "I didn't include my divorce from Carol or my marriage to the other one. But there are no falsehoods in this obituary, merely omissions. I think it's fair that I have the last word on how my story is told."

"Of course," she said, feeling castigated and reminding herself that he was currently their only active client. "For planning purposes, let's agree to run the full obit in the papers' online format, and a shorter version in print. And we can put whatever you like in the program for your memorial service, including photos."

Lord, she was sounding like Gabbi now, talking about end-of-life details as if death was an event like any other, something to organize and embellish. But the capriciousness of death defied planning, and its cold indifference appalled her. Everyone was born thinking he or she was someone special, secretly destined for great things—and, quite possibly, immortal. But death was the faceless blow across the back of the head that confirmed you were not special after all. Your little sister was not special. Not even real estate tycoon Anthony Marino was extraordinary in any way.

Tony drained his cup of tea and sighed. "Honestly, I don't know if any of my relatives will attend my funeral. It's been years since the kids came to visit. I doubt they'll make the trip to California once I'm gone."

Liz scooted her chair closer to him. "I'm just thinking out loud here, but maybe you could make your children's inheritance contingent upon them attending your service." Admittedly, it was a crass thing to suggest. But why should his family be rewarded after years of neglecting him?

"Why didn't I think of that?" he said, brightening. "You're a smart gal, Liz." He looked at her intently, as if for the first time.

She smiled, relieved their little tête-à-tête was wrapping up on a positive note.

"As long as you're here, why don't you help me box up these books in the office? Aasal was going to lead the charge, but I'll send him to the pharmacy." There were cardboard boxes and rolls of tape already assembled in the corner, and a mid-sized ladder.

Liz slipped off her shoes and cotton blazer before getting to work. In bare feet, she scaled the ladder to reach a row of old novels dating back to the 1950s and '60s. She grabbed six books and noted her parents owned many of the same titles: *The Spy Who Came in from the Cold* by John le Carré; *The Godfather* by Mario Puzo; *Couples* by John Updike. On her second ascent up the ladder, she pulled *Dr. Spock's Baby & Child Care* from the shelf. Tony chuckled.

"I think we can toss that one away," he said. "Trends in parenting have completely changed—and not necessarily for the better. At least not for the men."

She glanced down at the old man and noticed he was in no hurry to help pack books from the lower shelves. He seemed very content to remain stationed behind his desk observing her work. It occurred to Liz that her backside was in full view. Dear God, was he staring at her ass?

"I'm glad I lived in the era I did," he said, folding back the cuffs of his robe. "Nobody ever asked me to change a diaper or warm a bottle." He paused to blow his nose. "The one thing I regret is that I missed the Sexual Revolution. It came after I was married. Maybe if I'd gotten that funny business out of my system as a young man, I would have been a better husband."

Liz felt her stomach clench, and she stifled a groan. Gabbi had warned her about this very thing while they'd discussed Touchstone's new target market over lunch.

"Old people have no filter," she'd said. "They've got loose lips. Like we do after a couple glasses of wine."

It was true. And to be fair, it wasn't just old men thinking about nookie. Years ago, when Liz was in high school, her recently widowed grandmother had traveled from Wisconsin to California to find solace by their kidney-shaped pool. As Liz sat next to her in the warm sunshine, her grandmother had gazed into the treetops and asked, "Lizzie, do you think folks in heaven have sex?"

At first, she believed she had misheard her Nana, the former Sunday school teacher who'd been dressed in a flowered polyester blouse, dark skirt, and sensible pumps. For as long as Liz could remember, her grandparents had slept side-by-side in twin beds and partook in separate morning rituals in different bathrooms. She had never seen them kiss or even hold hands. But now—after her husband was six feet under—her grandmother was wondering about making love in the afterlife?

"Well, do you honey?" The note of hopefulness in her voice was unmistakable.

At sixteen, Liz was still a virgin, having never gone all, *all* the way with Peter, her boyfriend. She was still figuring out how sex worked on earth; heaven was another matter entirely. As a student enrolled in human biology, she had to ask herself: In the absence of flesh—that is, without warm lips, knowing hands, and perky private parts—could spirits enjoy coupling above the clouds? She had turned to her grandmother and shrugged.

"Maybe, Nana. I guess anything is possible."

Later, Liz had noticed two Danielle Steel paperbacks in her grandmother's open suitcase. The romance novels were likely filling the mind of her white-haired Nana with lusty notions. As a teenager, she didn't know what to think about that. At forty-five, she still didn't know.

Stepping up to a higher rung, Liz focused on a new row of books, leaving Tony's comment unanswered. The thought of discussing the Sexual Revolution with an elderly man dressed in a loosely tied robe left her tongue-tied and squeamish.

After clearing a third shelf, Liz excused herself to get a glass of water from the kitchen. When she returned to the office, she found Aasal there armed with a variety of cold medicines and insisting that Tony take a nap. As the gentle caretaker led Tony down the hall, Liz repositioned the ladder under a set of ancient encyclopedias, relieved to work without an audience.

After leaving Tony' house, Liz sped off to Oak Creek High. There, in the bleachers overlooking the baseball diamond, she and her mother sat shoulder-to-shoulder watching Ben and his teammates take their positions on the field. Below them, Dusty and her father lingered near the dugout, chatting with an assistant coach and laughing at something the young man said. She had nearly an hour to watch the game. Jamie was meeting with his college counselor about merit scholarships and would need a lift home to prep for AP exams.

It was a mild day in the first week of May, and Liz enjoyed the late-afternoon sun on her face. Ben looked in their direction and raised his glove high above his head in greeting. He was like his father, quick to let go of hard feelings. Though he maintained he hadn't touched the pot he purchased weeks ago, he remained mum on who it was for and was resigned to serving out the terms of his punishment. He'd already missed a number of outings with his pack, including a pizza party in the Morgans' poorly chaperoned basement. But Liz was allowing Ben to study with Maddy after dinner in the family room (his bedroom was strictly off limits), and this concession had enabled them to broker a peace.

On occasion, Maddy stopped by with her eleven-year-old sister, Haley, in tow. Haley was a petite gymnast spinning with life, and she reminded Liz of her sister who'd adored tumbling classes and wearing bright leotards and tights. Last week, Haley had sprung up on Ben's back and ordered him to canter through the kitchen. "Faster, Benny, now down the hall!" Liz and Maddy shared a laugh as the hulking shortstop obeyed his tiny rider's every command. Despite their botched introduction, Liz looked forward to Maddy's visits, relishing another female presence—or two—in the house.

As the baseball game got underway, her mother applied sunscreen to her arms and passed the tube to Liz, who followed suit.

"How'd the Open House go on Sunday—any new offers?" Joanie asked.

"Only one, another low ball. We'd be crazy to take it. If we don't sell the house this summer, we'll put it on the rental market until the economy picks up."

"A sound idea," her mother said, patting her thigh. "And what about Dusty? Any construction jobs on the horizon? Or is he still camping out in front of the TV?"

Liz's shoulders sagged. She shouldn't have mentioned the couch potato thing to her mom. She had needed to vent and couldn't complain to Gabbi, whose ex-husband had been good for nothing as a provider. From time to time, Liz wondered what it would've been like to grow older with a sister. Would Maggie have become a trusted confidante? Someone with whom she could unburden herself about the ups and downs of husbands and sons— and mothers?

She turned toward Joanie, careful to keep her voice low. "Dusty is bidding on jobs; they're just not coming our way. Not yet," she clarified. "For now, we're trying to make ends meet on my income. It's stressful."

"I bet," she said, adjusting the brim of her straw hat to block the sun. "I read somewhere that even though women have come a long way, one thing never changes."

"What's that?"

"At the end of the day, every cave girl wants her cave man to drag home a woolly mastodon."

Liz laughed. "So true, Mom."

Her mother started to cough and reached for a tissue in her purse. "Darn allergies," she muttered. She was quiet for a minute and then turned to face Liz.

"Don't worry too much, Lizzie. Things will turn around. Trust me, your dad and I have lived through worse." She didn't elucidate in any way, but Liz had a feeling she wasn't talking about the economy. Joanie's references to the past were like that, always in code.

Below, a chorus of "HEY batter-batter, HEY batter-batter" filled the air. Liz glanced down at home plate where a towering boy swung at a fast ball and sent it rocketing out toward left field. Ben leapt into the air, catching the ball and firing it to second base where his teammate tagged out the runner. A double play—two outs! The students and parents in the bleachers cheered wildly, and her mother stood up, whooping and hollering with the best of them. Below, Liz saw her father throw his fist toward the sky.

Liz flushed with pride before silently chiding herself for caring about how the boys performed in front of her parents. Back when she was in school, they never attended her basketball games or Ned's tennis matches. Often, she stopped by the courts to watch her brother play, and he returned the favor once or twice. But it wasn't the same as having your mom and dad courtside. After they moved to Menlo Park, her father had buried himself in the auto parts business. As for Joanie, it seemed she couldn't bring herself to join fellow parents in the stands to root for their kids, not after leaving a little one behind in a plot of earth thirty miles south of town. So now, when Liz watched her mother jump to her feet and crow over her grandson's stunning catch, she had the unexpected satisfaction of getting a do-over.

When Ben's team was ahead by four runs, Liz left to pick up Jamie outside the college counselor's office.

Her parents had slipped out too. Something in the flowering trees near the field was aggravating her mother's throat, and she'd developed a persistent cough during the game. But they all parted ways in high spirits, and when Liz pulled up to the curb to find Jamie waiting, she felt a sense of well-being in the world.

As always, Jamie was wearing earphones under his cotton hoodie and his head bobbed ever so slightly to a beat she could never hear. When he clambered into the passenger seat, she asked him to turn off his music. Reluctantly, he complied.

"How was your meeting? What did Mrs. Strub say about potential scholarships?"

Jamie said nothing at first, staring out the windshield as she accelerated into the school's exit lane. "She thinks I have a shot at a few scholarships. Small colleges in the Midwest and East." He shrugged. "I've never heard of them, but they might be cool."

Liz stared at him blankly before turning her attention back to the traffic.

"Mom, seriously, what did you expect? It's not like I'm captain of the football team. Or Student Body President. Good grades aren't enough."

"I haven't said a word!"

"You don't have to."

She stepped on the gas to make a green light. When she glanced back at Jamie, he'd already replaced his headphones. She silently agreed to table the discussion, but she wasn't ready for him to ship off to a distant campus because she and Dusty couldn't pay the tuition for a school he'd prefer closer to home. At a stop light, she adjusted the rear-view mirror and caught sight of the tension in her eyes. Maybe worrying about future college tuition was crazy when bills that were due weeks ago lay heaped on her desk at home.

Tony Marino had provided a steady if modest income stream, but Touchstone needed more clients in the pipeline. Gabbi hadn't minced words when they talked last night. They needed to double down on end-of-life events and services. The question was, how?

Last week, Gabbi had phoned Tony and asked in her most charming voice if he might be able to recommend their services to any of his friends. He told her he'd be happy to, but, so far, he hadn't come up with a single name.

"He doesn't want to share us," Gabbi said. She sat on a stool in a storage closet near Tony's office, calling to mind Little Miss Muffet on her tuffet, while she fed years of old financial records into a shredder. It was one of several new to-do's he'd dreamed up to keep them busy.

"I don't mind being a kept woman," Liz joked.

"More like *unkempt* woman."

Liz was preparing to voyage into Tony's attic, the final frontier of the pre-move purge. She was dressed in her oldest sweats and sneakers and had fitted a shower cap over her bangs and ponytail. The thought of spiders and cobwebs clinging to her hair had been a no-go factor until Gabbi plucked the plastic bonnet from a guest bathroom down the hall.

"Wish me luck," Liz said. With flashlight in hand, she set off for the pull-down ladder that led to the attic. Job number one was to assess what was up there and then enlist Aasal to help her carry things down. Tony was certain there was nothing worth saving. "What you need up there are heavy-duty trash bags," he'd remarked before settling down with the newspaper on his sunny redwood deck.

Stepping into the musty space where the floorboards were covered in dust and smelled faintly of expired rodents, Liz swung around the beam of light. It landed on what looked like cast-off props from an old movie set: a faded leather trunk with brass latches, two rocking chairs decommissioned by holes in their cane seats, and an antique doll house with toppled over furniture, as if a tiny tornado had spun through it.

At the back of the room, she came upon a crate of old yearbooks with scribbled notes from classmates who were likely long forgotten or gone. Tucked between the books was a silver-framed photo, and Liz pulled it free. When she focused her light on it, a warm sensation flooded her chest. There, in a faded color print, was Tony and his preteen daughter sitting side-by-side on a piano bench. They appeared so happy and compatible, and Liz could almost hear the notes of their duet. She rubbed dust from the glass and looked more closely. Tony may have given his name to his son, but little Angela got everything else: his expressive brown eyes and dramatic brows, his full lips and narrow chin. It was inconceivable that this father and daughter were essentially strangers now.

Liz put the photo aside and kept moving. Inside a velvet-lined box, she found beautiful ornaments that had once sparkled on the Marino family Christmas tree. As she held a cool, silver bulb in the palm of her hand, melancholy slipped over her like a second skin. When she was a girl, she had loved these kinds of family keepsakes. But that was before the house fire devoured all that was precious in her world.

Her thoughts reeled back to that summer night in 1973, and she felt dizzy in the dim light, allowing herself to settle on the filthy floor. She'd been two blocks over at a slumber party, her brother away at camp. The details of that cruel blaze were never discussed, but Liz understood that a fire had broken out in their kitchen and swept down the hall to the bedrooms. Her mother phoned for help as her father raced through the billowing smoke for Maggie. Somehow, the local firemen managed to save large sections of that brick and clapboard home but not her little sister—the skipping, singing, stubborn child everyone couldn't help but adore. Liz had loved her fiercely, and she had long regretted the spat between them just before Maggie died.

She glanced around at the forgotten relics in Tony's attic and closed her eyes. A deadly fire and a painful divorce had awful commonalities. They both destroyed the bridge to the life that came before, a place in time that may have been imperfect, but was whole and beautiful in ways it would never be again.

Maybe Tony was right. Best not to keep any of this. She got to her feet and inhaled deeply to steady her balance. Then she trained her flashlight on the exit and backed down the ladder.

Driving home from work, Liz's phone rang from the bottom of her purse and she fished it out. California prohibited drivers from chatting on the phone while behind the wheel, but Liz was compulsive about taking calls. What if a client needed something—or the boys had some kind of emergency?

"Hey, Mom," she said, putting the phone on speaker mode.

"Hi there. How are things going on the Marino job?"

"We're making progress."

"And Tony is behaving himself?"

If Liz had sensed that Tony harbored certain impulses, that worry had receded over subsequent visits to his home. At eighty-three, he wasn't the Italian Stallion her mother had implied.

"Oh, yes, he's perfectly harmless."

Ahead of her, commuter traffic was merging into her lane and a truck swerved and nearly hit her. She cursed before remembering her mother was still on speaker.

"Sweetie, I don't want to keep you—I can hear that you're driving," her mother said. "I just wanted you to know I had my annual physical today."

Every year, Joanie called after her check-up to boast about her low blood pressure, her uncommonly good cholesterol levels, her strong heart. But following every glowing report, her mother reliably paused and added, "There's only one area of concern." Last year, it was a small lump in her left breast (it proved to be a benign cyst). The year before, it was worrisome post-menopausal bleeding (the result of her hormone replacement therapy). And in 2005, a disconcerting spell of vertigo was traced to a virus in her inner ear. What now?

"I've had that chronic cough, so the doctor took a chest X-ray. There appear to be a few small nodules in my lungs."

Typically, such news would send her Straight To Panic, but Liz pushed away her fear. She'd seen this movie before.

"What did the doctor say about the spots?"

"He thinks it's probably a passing infection."

"I'm sure he's right, Mom. Please don't worry."

"I won't. But to be on the safe side, he scheduled a few more tests. I'll follow up when I return from Sally's birthday party at the lake. By the way, are you sure you can't come?"

Her father's younger sister, Aunt Sally, was turning seventy, and the family was gathering at the cabin on Lake Winnebago to celebrate. Liz would miss seeing her cousins but didn't want to leave the boys during these final weeks of their junior year. Besides, the flights to Wisconsin were pricey.

"Count me in next time," she said, trying to sound upbeat. "Have fun." She shoved her phone back in her purse and felt a flush of irritation. Her mother just had to give her a little scare right before leaving town on holiday.

Chapter 9

After returning from an early morning run, Liz found an email from Donna Kohn, a friend from college who was now chair of the English Department at the boys' high school. Donna wanted to meet for coffee, and Liz wondered if her agenda was school-related or simply a desire to catch up.

They met at Starbucks in the late afternoon and chit-chatted in line about mutual acquaintances from Davis. When their drinks were ready, they sat down at a quiet table and Donna described a new school initiative that was being deployed through the English Department. As a former reporter on the school beat, Liz enjoyed hearing about innovative programs and settled back into her chair.

Donna explained that since the Columbine High massacre in 1999—and in light of the recent spate of teen suicides in Palo Alto—school administrators had tried to find ways to identify at-risk students. Who is being bullied by peers? Abused at home? Suffering from depression? The idea recently hatched at Oak Creek High was to require students to write journal entries every Friday in English class and to submit them to teachers who vowed to keep their secrets safe. Unless, of course, there appeared to be trouble.

"The girls have taken to *The Diary Project* like ducks to water," Donna said. "They're more than willing to write about their parents' wretched divorce. Or their unrequited love for the captain of the water polo team. The guys? Not so much."

"What a surprise," Liz said with a knowing smile.

When Donna paused and stirred a packet of sweetener into her coffee, Liz sensed a shift coming in the conversation.

"Actually, your Jamie is one of the few boys who has embraced the journal assignments."

"Really? He hasn't mentioned it." Alarm bells were sounding in her head, but Liz tried to appear calm.

"According to his teacher, Jamie has expressed feeling down." She released the word gently, and her hazel eyes were soft with concern. "Recently, he wrote that he's simply 'going through the motions' in class. That he has nothing to look forward to...."

"But he loves school," Liz said in disbelief. "He's getting virtually all A's!"

"It's easy to confuse high performance with happiness."

Liz slumped back in her chair. She was accustomed to getting mixed reports about Ben at school. But Jamie? He'd always been an introverted child, but she'd believed that under the quiet exterior, he was relatively content. "What else did his teacher say?"

"Apparently, Jamie got his brother into some kind of trouble," Donna said. "He feels terrible about that."

Liz blinked, not understanding.

"Lizzie, our teachers report only truly disturbing findings to the administration—that is, kids who may be getting hurt or who are harming others or themselves. Jamie doesn't appear to fall into any of these categories." Her assurance kindled little comfort. "I hear about these minor cases when teachers stop by my office to discuss them unofficially. Since you're a friend, I thought I'd let you know."

Halfway home, a dark hunch began to take shape in Liz's mind. Throughout his weeks of being grounded, Ben insisted that he'd purchased the weed for someone else. And now she knew that Jamie regretted getting his brother into trouble. When Rachel Matsen called Ben Becker a pothead, had she named the wrong twin?

Liz arrived home to a silent house and found a note from Dusty saying that he and Jamie were watching Ben play baseball. It was a high-stakes game against their school's archrival, and she'd meant to be in the bleachers too. But it had completely slipped her mind during her meeting with Donna.

She opened the door to Jamie's room and stepped inside, inhaling sharply through her nose. Did it smell vaguely of pot, or was it her imagination? She flipped on the lights and raised the shades, preparing for a thorough investigation. Riffling through his sock, underwear, and T-shirt drawers, she found only worn items that needed replacing. She moved to his closet, shoving aside the hanging clothes, and spotted two shoe boxes that looked like promising hiding places. Empty. When she dropped to her hands and knees and began searching under the bed, she heard footsteps and glanced up to find Jamie staring at her, clearly agitated. She noticed his unwashed dark hair and sunken eyes, the angry red acne along his jawline.

"What are you doing in my room?"

Liz climbed to her feet and pushed back her sleeves. "I'm looking for drugs." Though her heart was racing, she hoped she sounded in charge and unapologetic.

Jamie folded his arms across his chest. "Did Ben say something?"

"No."

"It's just pot, Mom. No big deal."

"That's exactly what your brother said. But it's been a big deal for him, hasn't it? He's kept your secret at considerable personal cost. Frankly, I'm floored that you let him take the fall for you."

A wave of shame moved across Jamie's features, and his face darkened. He pulled out the chair at his desk and collapsed into it.

"I know. I feel like crap about that. I was going to tell you and Dad this weekend. Anyway, the pot's long gone. After what happened to Mikey, Ben stopped getting it for me."

"Why are you smoking?"

"Everyone smokes."

"But not you, Jamie. This isn't like you."

He tilted back his head and stared at the ceiling. "It's not that I feel bad, exactly. It's that I don't feel much of anything." His bottom lip trembled momentarily. He picked up a pen from his desk and nervously clicked the end, pushing the ballpoint tip in and out of its plastic casing. "Every morning, the alarm goes off and the day feels just like the one before. And when I get home from school, it takes forever to do my homework. I keep rereading the same page over and over. Ben thought that smoking weed might help. Like, getting high would lift my crushing boredom."

Liz was momentarily speechless while her thoughts tumbled through the possibilities of what "crushing boredom" might mean. Growing up, she'd endured the loneliness of grief and the breathless panic of anxiety. But she couldn't remember a single day when she was overcome by the tedium of life.

"Did the pot help you?"

"It did at first. I was sleeping better, I guess." He shrugged. "But smoking alone sucks. Ben won't get high during baseball season. And my friends at school don't party. They're obsessed with getting into Stanford or Berkeley."

"So, Jamie, when you say you're bored, do you mean you feel...depressed?"

His eyes dropped to his feet. "I'm fine."

Liz went to him, wrapping her arms around his bony shoulders and leaning into his ear.

"I'm going to find someone you can talk to—a professional," she said. Part of her wanted to tell him that she'd suffered from bouts of anxiety too, but she didn't know where to begin. Her instinct had been to keep the bleak years of her childhood from casting shadows over the downy heads of her boys. They knew only the slimmest of details concerning the death of her sister and the aftermath. Now wasn't the time to unpack all that, so she made him a simple promise. "We'll figure this out together, okay?"

Jamie nodded wordlessly, and she saw both reluctance and relief in his weary eyes.

After the boys had closed their doors for the night, Liz told Dusty about Jamie's journal entries and how he'd been treating his depression with pot. As he adjusted his pillows and settled into bed next to her, he listened sympathetically and said little, somehow holding back the words *I told you so.*

"Jamie just needs to get out more. To spend more time with buddies," he said.

Dusty was probably right, but it wasn't a plan they could act on. Jamie was nearly seventeen. It's not like she could arrange playdates for him.

"I think Jamie should see a therapist."

Dusty rolled on his side to face her, his eyebrows knit in concern. "It's almost summer. The pressure of school will be off and he can relax. Why don't we wait and see. Therapists charge a mint, don't they? At least they used to."

Ah, a reference to her own brief stint with counseling years back.

"Yes, of course," she said. "Very expensive." Dusty's unemployment was a current of tension meandering beneath the surface of every conversation. "But with no classes, Jamie could actually get worse. More isolated—harder to get out of his room."

"Okay, okay," he said, disinclined to argue. "Maybe you're right. Let's look into getting some help."

She nodded, grateful to have him on board but weighted with the knowledge it would be up to her to find someone to counsel their son. And to pay for that someone.

As Dusty drifted off to sleep, Liz tried to console herself with the notion that Jamie's depression was the kind she'd read about in school bulletins. What had the staff counselor called it? The junior doldrums? She prayed he didn't have any kind of obsessive thoughts or strange ideations. Like she did. The compulsive thoughts about death and dying. Could that sort of thing be passed on? As Liz burrowed down under the sheets, she reminded herself that she hadn't been *born* with this peculiar anxiety.

Before Maggie died, she'd been an active, ten-year-old girl who'd embraced her classwork and free time with equal passion. Writing book reports and learning long division were as pleasurably consuming as whiling away the hours watching *Bewitched* with her siblings or biking to 7-Eleven to get Slurpees. But after the fire, the inner workings of her mind began to shift.

At first, she assumed that her fear of death was normal, especially given her family's sudden loss. It struck her that every living creature possessed this fear—even a spider, with a brain the size of a poppy seed. She recalled that shortly after Maggie's funeral, a squat brown spider had crawled out from under her bed, and she'd grabbed a sneaker and swung it above her, preparing to smash it. When the shadow from her shoe fell across the bug, it raced to the left, then zig-zagged right. Liz froze. She marveled that the creature understood its life was in jeopardy and she felt its tiny terror in her own heart. In the moment that she hesitated in killing it, the spider skittered back under her bed. She'd regretted that it might return in the night to creepy crawl on her body, but she'd been relieved to know it would live another day. That she wouldn't be the agent of its demise.

Suddenly, death was everywhere Liz turned. When Ned switched on an old Tarzan movie, she watched, horrified, as a man got sucked down into a pit of gritty quicksand. "He's the bad guy!" Ned had said, scowling at the way she covered her eyes. True, the villain had it coming. But the way he hollered for his life before being swallowed up haunted her for days. She kept wondering: Did Maggie call for help, too, when she awoke to find her room filling with smoke? Liz would never know. She'd been at that sleepover party for Mary Murney. And of course, she couldn't ask her parents. Though her father had given her and Ned a tearful summary of that hellish night, once they buried Maggie, her parents virtually never spoke of it again.

Worse than the movies was *National Geographic*, where deaths were real rather than make believe. While studying geography in sixth grade, her teacher had read aloud an article about ancient Mayans who sacrificed young girls to curry favor with the gods. Something about virgins being thrown alive into deep-water caves to please the god of rain. Liz had been appalled that the children's parents hadn't protected them. Was she secretly appalled her parents hadn't saved Maggie? She couldn't go there. Even now.

What followed were years of fearing that death would come for her too—a fatal car accident on the freeway, or a rare and terminal disease. When she and her friends partied on the beach during high school, she half expected a rogue wave to drag her out to sea. *Why should she be spared?*

She confided in no one about her anxieties, and no one seemed to notice. She was good at faking it, crowding out the menacing thoughts and focusing on the job at hand. It wasn't until the twins were born that she'd finally dropped her guard. She'd become overwrought with false intuitions that Ben or Jamie—or both—would follow in her sister's doomed footsteps. One night, after she'd been up a dozen times to check and recheck that the stove was off, the doors were latched, and that neither baby had succumbed to Sudden Infant Death Syndrome, Dusty had confronted her. Delirious from lack of sleep, she could mount no defense and had simply told him everything about her spiraling fears. He'd cradled her in his strong, thirty-year-old arms and hushed her, vowing to find the help she needed and promising to keep them all safe. Afterwards, she'd met with a therapist for several months and, in time, the little white pills turned down the worrying voices in her head. Just enough.

In the morning, Liz made a few discreet calls to trusted friends inquiring about a psychologist who treated adolescents. Gabbi referred her to Noah Greenberg, who'd treated Zoey during a difficult transition as she struggled with her parents' split and her identity as a queer teenager. Zoey's happy adjustment to college life gave Liz hope that Dr. Noah was a skilled clinician. She called his office and a cancellation made it possible for her to see him that afternoon.

Liz found his appearance reassuring. In jeans and a smoky-blue cardigan and with graying hair, Dr. Noah had the presence of a tenured professor. He offered her a seat on a comfy couch and then settled into a chair opposite her. Over the course of their meeting, they discussed Jamie's school performance, hobbies, and recent use of pot.

"His use of marijuana doesn't sound too serious," he said. "Unless there's a family history of substance abuse and addiction?"

Liz paused before answering. She and Dusty rarely overindulged. But what about her parents? There was no denying that her mother had abused alcohol. Yet, before the house fire, she and Arnie had been merely social drinkers—a cocktail or two before dinner or out with friends. And now, Joanie had her drinking under control again. "No," she said.

Dr. Noah made some notes. He seemed more concerned about Jamie's video game habits than the pot.

"We're seeing a rising incidence of mood disorders in boys who spend long hours in front of their screens," he said. "There's a chicken-and-egg question here. Does the excessive gaming cause depression? Or are depressed kids attracted to the escape that, say, *Grand Theft Auto* provides? Either way, it's detrimental to their health. Because if you're glued to a joystick, you aren't getting the exercise and sunlight that heighten our moods. Worse, you're becoming socially isolated."

Liz flashed on the closed shades in Jamie's bedroom, the cloak of darkness he seemed to prefer lately. "What can we do?"

"I'll have to see Jamie myself before I can make recommendations."

Liz had a final question, one that had churned in her thoughts all night. "Could Jamie's depression be inherited? I have certain…anxieties." She found herself choking on her words, blinking back tears as she considered that Jamie's unhappiness could be her fault. Maybe she hadn't shielded the boys from her old wounds as well as she'd believed. Dr. Noah handed her a Kleenex and asked her to explain. Briefly, she touched on the loss of a sister in childhood and the recent panic attack at the funeral.

"Depression and anxiety are known to run in families, but your condition and Jamie's appear to be quite different," he observed. "His issues don't appear to be the result of any kind of trauma." He opened his hands like a book and searched her face, ready to delve further into her story. But Liz, having neither the time nor the money to plunge down that rabbit hole, said nothing. Dr. Noah nodded and closed his hands; message received. "Whether or not there's a genetic link is really irrelevant," he said, getting to his feet. "We must address your son's symptoms and help him feel better."

Before she left, Liz gave her credit card to Dr. Noah's assistant. When the Visa was declined, she groped through her purse for a checkbook. She paid for the first session and made a hasty exit from the building, trying not to think about the unbudgeted expense.

Chapter 10

That morning, as the boys were leaving, Liz had reminded Jamie that she'd pick him up after school for his appointment with Dr. Noah. Jamie had glared at her, yanking his index finger to his lips to shush her. He was embarrassed, not wanting his brother to know he was seeing a therapist. But yesterday, Liz had found a private moment with Ben and had already told him. Stretched out on his bed flipping through *Sports Illustrated*, he'd been relieved to hear that Jamie was getting help.

"I guess the weed didn't really work for him."

"No," Liz said. "And it was reckless of you to buy it. But at least your heart was in the right place."

"About that," he said, tossing the magazine aside and getting to his feet. "Do you think you can unground me?"

"I'm afraid not." She started towards the door and then stopped and turned back. "Ben, I know I should have been the one to see that Jamie was struggling. But why didn't you tell me?"

"I figured you and Dad have enough to worry about. I mean, Dad's not working much, and the new house isn't selling. And when Jo-Jo told me that you have to plan parties for dead people now?" The corners of his mouth turned down, and his nose scrunched up, as if a disagreeable odor had passed into the room.

Liz sighed and looked away. She hadn't told the boys about her new business venture, hoping it would be only an interim thing. "It's true," she said, straightening to meet his eyes. "We're going through a rough patch. That's why I need you to quit messing around. You've got to step up."

"Okay," he said. He circled his muscled arms around her shoulders and gave her a gentle hug. "I'll try harder not to be a knucklehead."

Liz smiled and leaned into him, savoring the warmth of his unexpected embrace.

Café Borrone was jam-packed as Liz stood in line waiting for Gabbi to arrive. She ordered two lattes and found a small table near the window overlooking the fountain outside. At the café's entrance, she spotted Gabbi dressed in white jeans and a black ruffled blouse, her favorite leather tote slung over her shoulder. Gabbi acknowledged her with a brief wave but neglected to remove her sunglasses as she weaved toward her through the morning crowd. Liz suspected her partner was navigating under the dull throb of a hangover.

Dropping into her chair, Gabbi gripped her latte and took a long, grateful swallow before sweeping up her napkin to wipe away the foam from her lip.

"God, I needed that," she said, lowering her sunglasses to reveal dry, bleary eyes. "Had a date last night and the red wine didn't agree with me. Nor did the man, for that matter."

Liz chuckled. "Another online match?"

Gabbi nodded. "Should have just stayed home and watched *Breaking Bad*." She dug into her tote, pulled out a file and handed it to Liz. "These are the final details for Tony's memorial service. He wants it to be *Invita-*

tion Only. Yesterday, we reviewed the guest list, menu items, and music options. He's a long-time supporter of the Stanford a cappella group, Mendicants, and he'd like them to perform 'Life Could Be a Dream.' I suggested he also consider a video with photos of his family and highlights of his career. He loved the idea." She took another swig of coffee and smiled. "He told me, 'You only die once' and that he wants to go out with a bang. Can you work up an estimate?"

"Yes, of course. But then what?"

Gabbi shrugged. "I know, it's bizarre. To plan an event that has no date. I guess we put the file away and wait for him to...buy the farm?"

Liz rolled her eyes. "'Fess up. You like the old guy too."

"I do. And let's be honest: Tony has totally saved our butts. But someday soon, we're going to show up on his doorstep and he'll have *nada* for us."

"True. The obit's done, and now the service is planned. Aasal said that once we ship the art and rugs to his son in Seattle, Tony will be ready to move into his assisted living unit. The closets are virtually empty now."

"Speaking of empty closets, I have a little confession to make," Gabbi said. "You know Tony's suits? The gorgeous Italian ones?"

"Yeah."

"Well, I didn't take them all to St. Vincent de Paul. I gave *a few* to St. Vince's. The rest Zoey and I sold on eBay. The designer leather shoes too."

Liz set down her drink and leaned toward Gabbi. "But those weren't Tony's instructions," she said, her voice rising above the chatter of underemployed consultants and yoga moms nearby. "He was very clear."

Gabbi laid her hand across her heart. "I promise, he'll never know. When they gave me the donation receipt, it was a piece of cake to alter it. It looks like they got all of Tony's items."

"That's not right, Gabbi." She felt a fleeting concern regarding Touchstone finances. Would Gabbi be tempted to alter those too? No, she'd never stoop to that, even if she knew how. Which she didn't.

Gabbi opened her bag again, pulling out a thick envelope and waving it in front of Liz's eyes before handing it over. "Tell me if this feels right."

Liz slid her nail under the flap, finding a neat stack of hundred-dollar bills. She counted eight of them.

"I know how much Noah Greenberg charges," Gabbi said quietly. "That should cover Jamie's therapy, at least for now."

"I can't accept...all of this," Liz mumbled, shifting off the moral high ground where her feet were usually planted.

"Sure, you can. I kept eight hundred for myself and gave two hundred to Zoey. That girl of mine photographed the clothes, posted the descriptions, and handled all the eBay transactions."

Liz tucked the money into her purse, feeling sullied but lifted up too. Could she justify taking the money, for Jamie's sake? She wasn't sure. She only knew that he needed help.

"Okay, Gabbi, but next time, give me a heads up before you do something like this."

"And make you an accessory to the crime? Um, no. Better to keep you in the dark."

Liz gazed at her silently. Perhaps it was better not to know when she was bending the rules.

"So, new business idea," Gabbi said, changing the subject. "Zoey told me last night that the California Supreme Court is likely to make same-sex marriage legal next month. If and when that happens, we'll drive up to City Hall and pass out our business cards. Sound good?"

Liz nodded, quickly warming to the idea of more wedding events. She'd seen cake toppers featuring two plastic grooms, two plastic brides. "Gay weddings could be a great new market for us."

"Also—in terms of our current business—my cousin is a nurse in the ER at Kaiser. I was thinking she could tip us off when things don't go well in the operating room."

Liz groaned. "Why don't we just start tailing ambulances?"

"I'm totally down for that."

"I was kidding."

"I know," Gabbi said, smirking good naturedly.

Liz checked her watch and got to her feet. "Tony has a few odds and ends for me today. I better get going."

"Okay. Give our golden gander a squeeze for me." She dipped into her tote one last time. "And give him this."

It was the St. Vincent's donation receipt. The way Gabbi had doctored the number of items and value on the print-out looked totally amateurish. Liz glanced around the crowded café feeling caught in the act. She would have to redo it, making herself an accessory to the crime after all.

✳ ✳ ✳

Liz let herself into Tony's house with the key that Aasal had left for her under a pot of red geraniums. When she stepped into the old man's office, she saw him slam down his black handset, fuming. Her hands instantly felt clammy. Did he know about the ill-gotten cash from eBay? She clamped her elbow against her purse, making certain it wouldn't fall open to reveal the bulging envelope.

"Reporting for duty," she said, trying to sound lighthearted.

"That was my son," he sputtered. "He wants me to put my house on the market immediately. I didn't become a successful developer by trying to unload properties during a goddamn recession. Only a fool would sell now."

Fools like Dusty and me, Liz thought.

"Since he'll be inheriting the proceeds from the sale, you'd think he'd want to wait until the economy picks up. Makes me think he's in financial trouble."

Weeks ago, Aasal had mentioned that Tony Jr. worked in marketing for Microsoft. Just this morning, Liz had read that the company was planning layoffs and salary freezes. So, maybe he did need the money now. Maybe he, too, was falling behind in mortgage payments. But that's not what she voiced to her client.

"Tony, I'm sure he wants to get you settled into your new apartment, so you won't have to manage this big place." She lifted her hands towards the high ceilings and then pointed outside. "Just think. You won't have to worry about broken sprinkler heads, clogged drains, or a leak in the roof. It will all be taken care of for you."

"Exactly. I'll have nothing to manage. And absolutely nothing to do. That's what I call hell's waiting room."

He was making it impossible to cheer him up, but she took another stab. "Well, maybe when you move into your new complex"—she studiously avoided the term *assisted-living community*—"you'll meet someone special."

"Now you're sounding like Aasal. Me, with a new love interest? With this old ticker?" He jabbed at this chest. "Ridiculous."

Liz gave up and focused on the business at hand. "So, what can I do for you today?"

Tony struggled to his feet and pushed a stack of magazines toward her. "I'd like you to phone these publications and cancel my subscriptions. I'd do it myself, but I can't stand the automated commands. I always push the wrong buttons and get put on hold. Or disconnected."

She peered down at the titles: *Golf Digest, Boating World, The Wine Spectator*. No sign of *Playboy*. "Are you sure? You don't enjoy reading these anymore?"

"Well, I can't golf anymore. I sold my boat and gave up sailing eons ago. And, really, I don't need anyone to tell me what Cabernet to drink."

She started to fret. Cleaning out closets felt liberating. But cancelling the magazines that covered Tony's life-long passions was depressing. Before the recession, she and Gabbi had planned events for clients with so much life in front of them. Engagement parties, bar mitzvahs, Christmas galas. In hindsight, she recognized that she'd taken all that joy and swirling excitement for granted.

"Please don't cancel *Forbes* or *Business Week*, Liz. I want to keep up with the stock market."

Good, she thought. He's still invested in this life.

"After you finish with the magazines, I was wondering if you could run an errand with me."

An hour later, Liz found herself behind the wheel of Tony's vintage Alfa Romeo with the top down. She hadn't driven a stick shift since she was in college, tootling around in an old VW bug her father had fixed up with new parts from his store. After a few false starts, she eased the red Spider out of the garage and accelerated down the hill toward Palo Alto. Beside her sat Tony, sporting a checkered wool cap and blazer (thank God, Gabbi hadn't sold everything) and clutching two ancient albums full of "priceless stamps." Apparently, Tony's younger brother, Leo, had been a devout philatelist before his death last year.

Over the exhilarating roar of the car's engine, Tony filled her in. When he and his brother were kids, teachers believed Leo was mentally handicapped and they placed him in Special Ed classes. But he was quite smart—autistic perhaps—and a sweet, good man.

"My brother believed without a shadow of doubt that this collection would have strong returns. Except he never cashed it in—couldn't bear to part with a single stamp." Tony hugged the books tighter to his chest. "Leo never married, so he left them to me." He glanced at Liz with a gleeful smile. "Wouldn't it be a hoot if we had a small fortune here? Leo would be so proud."

Liz returned his grin while taming hair that whipped around her face. What a pleasure to see the curmudgeon focus on something other than his death planning. Perhaps this kind of outing would be the first of many. A new start for whatever time he had left.

They parked in front of a faded storefront on Cambridge Avenue and ambled inside, discovering rows and rows of brightly colored stamps and gleaming coins behind glass cases. An older gentleman in baggy trousers and suspenders was bent over an array of stamps, peering through a magnifying glass. With a pair of tweezers, he gingerly removed one for closer examination. *Right out of central casting,* Liz thought.

Tony cleared his throat and waved impatiently in the man's direction. Without looking up, the store's proprietor called out, "Be with you in a minute. Take a seat."

While they waited, Liz leafed through Tony's albums, marveling at the unexpected beauty in their pages. A lovely violet-colored stamp featuring a well-coifed Eleanor Roosevelt caught her eye first. Next to it was a series of orange stamps depicting pioneers in dusty covered wagons. Her favorite postage art was a golden spaceship rocketing through a midnight blue galaxy toward earth. The caption read: *U.S. Man in Space: Project Mercury 4¢.* Liz had never purchased a lottery ticket before; the odds of winning were absurdly low. But these exquisite stamps? They had "winner" written all over them.

At last, the old collector shuffled over to review Tony's goods. He laid out the albums on his desk and peered at them through his magnifier, flipping through the pages with a speed that confounded Liz. Was the quality so obvious he didn't need to take a deeper look? Or was it something else?

"No rush," Tony said. "We've got time." He glanced at Liz uneasily.

The collector leaned back and closed the books. "What," he asked, "is your intention for these stamps?"

"We want to sell them!" Tony said. "What do you think they're worth?"

The balding man removed his glasses and rubbed his eyes. "You have a nice and varied collection here," he began. "The stamps are in excellent condition. But you must understand one thing. None of these are particularly *rare*. And if they aren't rare, they're not as valuable as you may have hoped."

"I'm certain Leo wasn't wrong about these...."

Liz pointed to the *Project Mercury* stamp. "What about this one?" She had a sudden suspicion that this man, harmless as he appeared, was out to scam Tony.

"The U.S. government printed millions of those—they aren't very hard to find. It's probably worth about a dollar. Maybe less."

Liz recoiled in her chair, not wanting to believe a word. The store owner turned to Tony.

"Artists enjoy using these richly designed stamps in their collages and crafts. You might consider donating them."

She was afraid to look at Tony's face, to witness the disappointment. Reluctantly, she shifted to meet his eyes.

"Time to go, Liz," he said quietly. His shoulders sagged, and his arms appeared woefully thin as he reached for the albums.

Back in the car, Tony asked her to join him for a bite to eat and she quickly agreed. They drove to his country club, past trees in full leaf and foothills in transition from spring green to the warm wheat of summer. Soon, the meticulously maintained gardens of the Alta Vista Golf Club appeared, and Liz downshifted the car and nosed it through the wrought-iron gates. She'd been here before, not as a guest but as a wedding planner. She and Gabbi had staged a reception here for a lovely young executive from Oracle and her handsome groom.

An American flag fluttered at half mast, signaling the recent death of a member. A piercing sensation shot through Liz as she realized that the same flag would fly for Tony someday, likely in the not-too-distant future. It was on these very grounds that he intended to have his memorial service. Out of the corner of her eye, she could see that he was staring at the flag too, and she fought an urge to turn the car around and speed away.

While sipping lemonade and eating lunch under a wisteria-covered trellis, Tony gazed out at the rolling golf course where he no longer played. Other than ordering a turkey sandwich, he hadn't uttered a word.

"What a bummer about the stamps," she said, uncertain whether to address the subject but feeling she could no longer ignore it.

"It was foolish of me to get my hopes up." He set down his drink and removed his cap. "I had so wanted to justify the years Leo spent putting those books together."

Liz knew the question of legacy had been dogging him. "But he enjoyed himself, didn't he?" she asked.

He glanced down at his half-eaten sandwich, momentarily falling silent again.

"I suppose you're right, dear. Collecting and trading those stamps gave my brother a lifetime of satisfaction." He looked at Liz. "They really are quite beautiful, aren't they?"

"Stunning," Liz agreed.

"I'd never noticed before today." He leaned back in his chair and squinted at the sky. "As I recall, Leo passed his final days quite happily. Which is more than most of us can say."

Liz felt a spasm of guilt. It wasn't in her job description to keep Tony happy, but she pledged to do better anyway. As she poked at the remains of her salad, she wondered how she would pass her final days. Would she cancel her magazines and give away her keepsakes? Would she, as the poet Mary Oliver once asked, find herself sighing and frightened before entering that *cottage of darkness*?

The waitress arrived to clear their dishes, and when she asked if they wanted anything else, Tony suggested a little dessert.

"Perhaps some chocolate gelato will lift our spirits."

"I feel better already," Liz said.

She smiled, grateful that Tony had managed to end their outing on a sweet note. After polishing off her ice cream, she reached for her purse and spied the swollen envelope. In two hours, she would take Jamie to meet Dr. Noah and be able to pay him in cash for additional appointments. She was grateful to Tony for that as well, though she would never tell him.

Chapter 11

As Liz was finishing breakfast and watching the *Today* show, her mother called from the lake house in Wisconsin with a favor. Her little lung infection had not cleared up, and Arnie had injured his knee. Their plane was landing in San Francisco around 6:00 p.m., and she wondered if Liz could pick them up outside baggage claim. "The prospect of standing in a long line for a taxi is unbearable," her mother said, coughing incessantly into the phone. Liz promised to be there and to pick up a few groceries for their dinner.

At the office, she met with Gabbi to explore a new business strategy. Since Tony had yet to refer any friends to Touchstone, Gabbi suggested they contact local retirement communities to cultivate prospects who were still "alive and kicking" about the benefits of end-of-life planning. Liz agreed—anything beat waiting around for someone else to die. Together, they hammered out a presentation for retirees that included traditional events and "emerging services."

Their pitch opened with offers to produce family reunions and special birthday and anniversary parties, and then segued into end-of-life services. Now, in addition to memorial planning, obit writing, and liberating couples from burdensome belongings—"gilded crap" as Gabbi liked to say off the record—Touchstone was offering tours of final resting spots. The thought of milling around graveyards made Liz's flesh creep, but Gabbi insisted she wouldn't mind conducting the cemetery circuits. "I'll just think of them as walks in the park," she quipped.

As grim as this service sounded, it wasn't a terrible idea. In California, Liz didn't know a single soul who had planned ahead for a final resting spot, including her parents. Back in the Midwest, all her aunts and uncles had little fiefdoms pre-purchased in the most desirable cemetery real estate. Maybe the advance purchase of a plot or niche would catch on and this touring service would grow in demand. She wondered, had Tony selected a memorial park? Perhaps Gabbi knew. She, for one, couldn't ask.

Liz left work around 4:00 p.m. and hurried through the sliding glass doors of Safeway. There wasn't time to make a meal for her parents, but the store now offered roasted chickens and "homemade" soups in self-serve kettles. The offerings were hardly gourmet, but they were warm and hearty and certainly a grade above airplane fare. Before heading for the hot food section, she pushed her cart toward the produce department, intent on buying her mother some fresh-squeezed orange juice. A little vitamin C was in order.

It occurred to Liz that it had been ages since she'd shopped for her parents. In the years after Maggie died, when her mother was depressed and self-soothing with cheap vodka, the job of meal planning and food acquisition had eventually fallen on her. Aunt Sally had stepped in at the beginning, and her father had foraged for food at pizza parlors and Chinese take-outs. But after studying nutrition in her sixth-grade science class, Liz began writing out grocery lists for her dad in neat cursive handwriting. Fruits, vegetables, and whole wheat sandwich bread became staples. By the time Liz entered high school, her mother had recovered considerably, but the die was cast. A year before she could legally drive, Liz—propped up on a pillow to properly see over the dashboard—piloted the old station wagon to a market one town over to buy the family's food.

She hadn't enjoyed meal planning back then. At times, she had seethed with resentment that her mother couldn't pull together a pan of meatloaf, let alone bake a birthday cake from scratch the way other moms did. But, today, she didn't mind providing her parents with a little sustenance. Scurrying behind her thoughts was the worry about those tiny spots on the X-ray.

As she entered the produce area, she glanced over at the crates of bright summer fruits and a man there caught her attention. Something about the way his hair curled around his forehead and ears looked familiar. She watched him select a basket of strawberries. He peered at it from every angle, checking for bruises or mold on the fruit. *Fastidious as ever*, she thought fondly. It was Peter Levine, the guy she'd dated between her sixteenth birthday and the Thanksgiving holiday of their freshman year in college. After two years together, they'd reluctantly participated in the time-honored tradition of "The Turkey Drop," breaking up so they could return to their new college communities as free agents.

He'd put on a bit of weight since she saw him at their twentieth high-school reunion. Not in a bad way—he looked arguably more attractive with a stronger build. And his hair was still as dark and thick as she'd remembered it. When they began dating, she'd overheard her grandmother describe him as "a nice Jewish boy" in that way people talked back then. In fact, he *was* nice, and super smart. And, an unbidden voice in her head added, a really good kisser.

She ducked down the frozen food aisle, deciding not to approach him. It wasn't just that her clothes felt frumpy and that her lipstick was long gone. It was this: What was there to say? Their paths diverged after their breakup, never really to cross again. He'd gone to Dartmouth and married a classmate from Boston where they eventually settled. Liz had returned to the Peninsula and married Dusty, a young man she met at a barbecue hosted by a mutual friend. Dusty had played football at her rival high school and had graduated from the Construction Management program at Cal Poly. Big, blond, and charismatic, he'd quickly swept away any lingering feelings for Peter Levine.

She hustled to the ready-to-eat food display and found the roasted chicken and some decent looking tomato basil soup. As she loaded them into her cart, she heard a voice behind her.

"Liz? Lizzie Boyle?" At the sound of her maiden name, she spun around and looked at Peter with wide eyes and a slightly lowered jaw, hoping to appear utterly surprised.

"Peter! My gosh, what brings you to Menlo Park? Visiting your folks?"

"Yes," he said with a warm smile and sparkly green eyes that called to mind Paul Rudd, an actor her boys adored. He abandoned his cart and walked towards her, clean-cut in his crimson polo shirt, khaki shorts, and spanking new running shoes. She stood stock-still as he reached for her hand and kissed her chastely on the cheek, the scent of Old Spice lifting from his skin, same as ever.

"Time hasn't touched you, Liz. You're still the fit point guard from high school. What's your secret?"

"Oh," she sputtered, "you're too kind. Chasing after teenaged boys, I guess."

"Ah, yes. Twins, right? I've got girls, two years apart. One's at Exeter now, and the other is heading to college in the fall. We'll be empty nesters." His voice trailed off, a note of sadness surrounding his daughters' departures that struck her as sweet. At least he didn't have to fret about their tuition payments. She'd heard through the grapevine that Peter had done extremely well as an investor in the healthcare industry. While the recession was surely unpleasant for everyone, Peter appeared unscathed. Her heart slumped as she considered that the same could not be said for her and Dusty.

"And your parents?" she asked. "How are they?" She sensed this might be a loaded question. Historically, Peter and his father didn't get along. Years ago, Peter had confided in her about his dad's quick temper and dark moods, describing him as "half-Jewish, half-Polish, all asshole."

"Well, Dad has Parkinson's," he said. "It's pretty advanced. Last month, he took a bad fall so we're transitioning him into a wheelchair. My mom's been a trouper, but I need to help out more until we find a better place for him."

"I'm sorry."

"Don't be. The disease has actually made him humble. Nicer to my mother. But enough about them. How are your folks? Is Joanie still painting?"

Peter's face lit up the instant he spoke her mother's name. When Liz was in high school, her mother had insisted that Liz's friends call her by her first name. The informality made the kids feel grown up, and made Joanie feel like one of them. In today's terms, she might have been called a Cool Mom, even—ugh—a MILF. She and Peter had enjoyed a warm friendship, often chatting in her art studio near the garage while Liz finished homework or ran an errand. Just before he left for college—

at a time when he and Liz were vowing to stay together forever—her mother gave him an oil painting. The picture captured Liz's face in profile, her hair in a girlish high ponytail and a faint smile on her lips. It was the only portrait of her that she'd known her mother to create, and she was tempted to ask Peter if he'd held on to it. How she would love to see it again. But such a question would appear presumptuous.

"Oh, yes, Mom still paints from time to time," she said. "Mostly landscapes these days rather than portraits."

"Oh, that's too bad," he said. "Her portraits were so... lovely." He held her gaze for a long moment and then he reddened, glancing at his feet.

Liz looked away too, feeling the compliment warm her skin but also noting the past tense: *were* so lovely. As if the painting was no longer in his possession.

Over the store's PA system, she heard a request for more roasted chickens, and Liz became aware of the time. "My parents are landing at SFO, and I've promised to pick them up."

"I'll let you go," Peter said, reaching into his pocket to remove his wallet. He fished out a business card and handed it to Liz, grazing her arm before stepping away. "Give my best to your folks and have Ned give me a call sometime. I'd love to catch up."

"Will do." She waved goodbye as they pushed their carts in opposite directions. She'd almost forgotten. Peter and her brother, Ned, had played doubles together on the high school tennis team. One afternoon, she'd been lingering by the courts watching Ned play, and after they'd won, Peter introduced himself to her. That had been nearly thirty years ago. Another lifetime. And yet, there was a familiarity between them that was both comforting and disorienting.

When Liz pulled up to the curb outside baggage claim, she spotted her dad limping toward her and dragging two duffle bags on wheels. Her mother trailed behind him, and when she caught Liz's eye, her face brightened with relief. After helping her parents into the van, Liz made a beeline for home. They both looked utterly worn out.

"Good thing your follow-up with the doctor is tomorrow," Liz said. "Maybe he can give you something for that cough."

"Oh, I was going to postpone the appointment until next week. I need some sleep—in my own bed! Those mattresses at the lake house are positively *Jurassic*."

Liz glanced into the rearview mirror at her father in the backseat. He held her gaze, an unflinching intensity in his eyes.

"I'll drive you to the clinic, sweetheart," he said. "Maybe your doc can give me a referral for my bum knee."

"Sounds like a plan. Two birds with one stone and all that," Liz said.

"Well, if you two are going to insist...I have been feeling rather puny. Maybe I can start a course of antibiotics." She coughed into her fist and then sat back against the van's headrest and closed her eyes.

After dropping off her parents and their ready-to-eat meal, Liz headed home, suddenly wondering what she would serve her own family. Somehow, she'd forgotten to buy the pork chops and fresh vegetables she'd planned on for dinner. If running into an old beau wasn't enough to fluster a girl, her mother's cough had thoroughly rattled her nerves. Leftovers would have to do tonight.

Chapter 12

Friday afternoon had been an unexpectedly emotional one. After Liz had finished up the last of Tony's house projects, she gently removed the cane from his hand and gave him a hug, thanking him profusely. When she stepped back from their embrace, she noted that his dark eyes had misted over and his lower lip protruded like a child's.

"Don't be a stranger," he said.

A sudden swelling in her throat made it difficult to reply. Touchstone would miss the steady business provided by Tony Marino, but she would miss the old gent even more.

"I'll be baaack," she said, leaning on the old line from *Terminator*. She promised to swing by for Aasal's famous French roast and offered to help Tony move when the time came—*no charge*. Halfway home, sitting in Friday traffic, Liz was struck by the thought that Tony would likely not need Aasal once he moved into assisted living. Staff nurses would take care of his every whim and necessity. Being part of the Tony Marino support squad had given her genuine satisfaction and purpose, but the team was soon to disband.

She'd felt blue as she pushed her key into the front door, but Dusty met her on the other side and welcomed her home with a warm kiss. He'd just landed a small carpentry job helping a young couple build out a nursery. "It's a short-term gig," he'd admitted, but it lifted her spirits and managed to open a little breathing room between them. And though their spec house still hadn't sold, there was another open house on Sunday, and Dusty was certain the warm weather would bring people out.

Now the sun was setting, and Liz lingered over her dinner. Ben and Maddy were attending prom, and she had asked her parents to join them for supper so Jamie wouldn't feel so alone. He'd greeted them in his frayed *Pizza My Heart* sweatshirt, and she vowed that next year he'd be sporting a tux at prom too. And if Jamie needed a little extra support tonight, the same could be said of her father. Joanie had undergone more chest scans, but results wouldn't be back until next week. While her mother seemed unruffled, Arnie had confided in Liz that he was worried.

Yet, all things considered, it had been a pleasant evening, with lively discussions of popular books and movies, and the Giants' prospects for making the playoffs (slim-to-none). Over dessert, Jamie had opened his laptop and showed his grandmother designs from his class in digital arts, strange and wonderful depictions of distant galaxies and alien life forms. "Brilliant," she'd gushed, touching the screen. "But I can't hang these illustrations on my refrigerator!" Jamie had laughed for the first time in weeks. His kindergarten sketches of fire-spewing dragons were still on display under magnets in Joanie's kitchen. He promised to print out his artwork and deliver copies immediately.

After Jamie retreated to his room, Dusty poured her parents and her a second glass of Two-Buck Chuck and returned to the kitchen to get a head start on the dishes. She took a long sip and savored that letting go feeling of Friday night. A noise outside drew her attention to the window, and she was surprised to see Ben and Maddy pulling into the driveway. She checked her watch: 8:30 p.m. By now, the two of them should have been at the Sequoia Hotel ballroom, slow dancing and mugging for pictures in the rented photo booth.

Dressed in his pleated tux shirt and black pants—but no jacket—Ben leapt out of the car and trotted around to the passenger side door. Opening it slowly, he reached in and carefully pulled Maddy to her feet. She teeter-tottered in her high heels, wobbly as a Barbie doll not designed to stand, and then slumped her head against his chest. Liz could see that the front of her turquoise gown was stained and her wrist corsage was in tatters. The girl was indisputably drunk.

"Uh-oh," her mother said. "Looks like trouble in paradise."

Ben had paid a pretty penny for their prom tickets, and it was his first night out after weeks of being grounded. But he didn't appear angry; he looked deeply concerned as he guided his date toward the back door with a tenderness that Liz had never seen in him before.

She started toward them, but Jamie intercepted her as he hurried into the kitchen.

"Mom, I've got this. Maddy has, like, food poisoning? She needs to get to the bathroom. I'll help bring her in." Ben must have tipped him off, sending an SOS from his cell phone.

"If she's truly ill, shouldn't Ben take her home?" In her opinion, an intoxicated teenager should be under the care of her own mother.

"She'll go home later." He swung open the screen door and scrambled out to help his brother.

Arnie pushed back from the dinner table and got to his feet. "We should get going. You've got your hands full here."

Her mother nodded, threading her arms through the sleeves of her sweater and collecting her purse. She gave Liz a quick kiss on the cheek. "Don't be too hard on them," she said quietly. "I know it's hard for you to accept, but everyone makes mistakes. Especially the young."

Liz stiffened, alert to the criticism in her mother's advice, but she had no time to consider it. As Dusty ushered her parents out the front door, the boys bustled Maddy through the kitchen and into the bathroom. Moments later, Jamie returned, charged with delivering a request. He swept his dark bangs from his forehead and cleared his throat.

"We'll take care of this, okay? If there's something we need, we'll ask."

"Fine by me," Dusty said before Liz could answer, his hands planted on his hips. "We'll go watch a movie in our room. But tell Ben we want to talk with him the minute he gets Maddy squared away." Jamie nodded and was gone.

Liz followed Dusty into their bedroom, leaving the door ajar so she could monitor what was going on. Stretched out in bed fully clothed, they could hear water running and a series of toilet flushes, followed by soft music emanating from Ben's room.

"Where did they get the alcohol?" she wondered aloud. "I can't imagine the Fitzes served it at the pre-party."

"Not a chance. The kids probably paid some desperado outside 7-Eleven."

"At least Ben didn't drink and drive. He's sober, don't you think?"

"Yes. But, Maddy—she's a flyweight like you. It probably didn't take much to make her head swim."

"We really should call her parents. What if she has alcohol poisoning and needs to go to the ER?"

Dusty held up his palm, his favorite "slow down" gesture that never failed to get her engine running faster.

"I'm sure Maddy will be fine. Let's see if the kids can regroup." He turned on the TV, selecting an old *James Bond* movie, and they divided their attention between preposterous car chases and developments down the hall. After about thirty minutes, Ben pushed open their door.

"Hey," he said.

"How's Maddy?" Dusty asked, pausing the program.

"She got sick but feels better now. I'm letting her rest before taking her home."

"So, you're not attending any of prom?" Liz noticed that he'd changed into jeans.

"Nah. It's okay. Better that we're here. Three of Maddy's teammates—who also had too much champagne—got into trouble. If you show up drunk at prom, the chaperones don't just turn you away. They narc you out to the Vice Principal. Which means you'll get suspended from school and your coach will bench you. Like, forever."

"Where did the champagne come from?" Liz asked.

"The girls did their hair and make-up together at Dani Silva's house. Dani's older sister is twenty-one."

"Thanks for being honest," Dusty said. "For the record, we didn't buy the food poisoning bit for a second."

The shrill ring of the landline interrupted them, and Dusty crossed the room to pick it up. After speaking in a quiet, reassuring tone, he settled the phone back in its cradle.

"That was Maddy's mom. She's upset. Maddy had promised to text her from the party and she hasn't heard a word."

"What did you tell her?" Ben asked, pacing nervously at the foot of their bed.

"I told her not to worry. That the kids are fine. Which is true."

"Partially true," Liz said. "Ben, you should call her back immediately and tell her what really happened."

"Can't do that." He squeezed the bridge of his nose, as if a headache was blooming behind his eyes. "Maddy's dad is cool, but her mom's kind of a psycho. She expects

Maddy and her little sister, Haley, to be effing perfect. If they mess up, there's hell to pay."

Liz settled back against the pillows and gazed into Ben's face. Did he feel the same way about Dusty and her? That his dad was cool, but that she freaked out? All week, her thoughts had circled back to Dr. Noah's remark that her anxiety condition was likely the result of trauma. And it had occurred to her that if a ten-year-old girl returns from a slumber party to find her house half burned down and her sister dead, a tendency to over-react might be understandable. Normal, even. But all these years later, was she inflicting her angst on her boys? Was she as uptight as Maddy's mother?

"Maybe you're judging Mrs. Chan too harshly," she said.

Ben shook his head. As he explained it, the former rodeo queen was now an executive at a PR firm in San Francisco specializing in luxury hotels and high-end retailers. "She's really good at promoting stuff and looking good. That's what she cares about."

Liz was reluctant to side against another mother. But it jibed with what she'd observed at school. Though never available to volunteer at fundraisers, the impeccably dressed woman could be found front and center at soccer games and gymnastics meets where her girls were high scorers and popular teammates. She seemed to positively shimmer in their reflected glory. For Tammy Chan, it would simply not do to have your daughter gulping champagne, missing prom, and throwing up in her date's toilet.

Still, was it right to deceive the woman? And maybe Maddy shouldn't get off scot-free. Hadn't they grounded Ben for the pot thing? She locked eyes with Dusty who said nothing, waiting for her to make the call. Her mother's barbed comment—*It's hard for you to accept, but everyone makes mistakes*—echoed in her ear.

"Okay," Liz said. "Mum's the word this time around. But if we see this kind of thing again, phone calls will be made. For now, please have Maddy text her mother."

"Will do," Ben said, retreating down the hall to awaken his groggy sleeping beauty.

After the movie concluded predictably, with the spy's seduction of the latest Bond Girl, Liz padded to the kitchen in slippered feet for a cup of tea. As she passed into the family room, she spotted the twins playing a video game. On doctor's orders, they had been limiting Jamie's gaming, but on weekends they made exceptions. Maddy sat wedged between them, dwarfed in Ben's XL sweatshirt pulled over her gown. She was pale as an eggshell but perked up a little, offering Liz a self-conscious smile.

"Good to see you feeling better, honey," Liz said. "I'm making some chamomile tea. Would you like some?"

"That sounds nice."

Locked in cyber battle, the boys were oblivious to their exchange. After one final explosion, Jamie declared victory and leapt to his feet in triumph. The nerd had vanquished the jock. For Liz, it was an unexpected moment of grace to see Jamie enjoying himself on a night that had promised to be a lonely one for him.

After handing Maddy a mug of steaming tea, Liz returned to her bedroom where she found Dusty opening the covers for her, intent on a little seduction of his own. She laughed softly and obliged him, dimming the lights and shedding her clothes. Sometime later, she awoke to hear Ben unlocking the front door after dropping off Maddy at home. It was a shame he had missed his first prom, but at least the kids had averted disaster. Lately, that's all Liz could find herself hoping for.

Waking later than usual on Sunday, Liz pulled the faded floral comforter over her head to block the sun spilling in through the windows. Today, their realtor would be holding an open house at their spec home, but she and Dusty had no role in that. Except to pray that someone would come along and take the half-million-dollar burden off their backs. The higher interest rates on the house were now in effect, and if they couldn't keep up with the payments, there would be late fees. Not to mention a hit to their credit score. Though Dusty didn't like to talk about it, they both understood the worst-case scenario. Twenty months ago, they'd secured the loan for the spec house with equity in this, their family home, and they could end up losing both.

She closed her eyes and massaged her temples. At least the boys were in brighter spirits. Ben was no longer grounded and had dropped Maddy off "post-prom" with no complications. And yesterday, she'd found Jamie wearing sunglasses and reading a book on a lounge chair in their backyard. Rubbing his bare, ashen arms, he'd quipped that he was "soaking up Vitamin D" from the sun. It appeared Dr. Noah was catalyzing some healthy behaviors, and she reassured herself (again) that Tony's elegant suits were supporting a worthy cause.

Another item in the plus column—the boys had put their SATs behind them a week ago. On that morning of the college entrance exam, she'd tiptoed past their bedrooms to make scrambled eggs and blueberry muffins, comfort food for their weary brains and nervous stomachs. So much depended on those infernal test scores. Strong results for Jamie would mean better scholarship opportunities. Decent scores for Ben would bolster his prospects for playing baseball at the college level. God knows, she and Dusty couldn't make gifts to colleges to tip the scales. Nor did they know influential people on the boards of trustees. It was up to the boys to pave their own path forward. So, when they'd returned home visibly relieved to have the ordeal behind them, she'd fought the urge to ask them how it went. They would know soon enough.

She heard Dusty approaching from down the hall and pushed back the comforter.

"Want to walk downtown for a bite to eat?" he asked. He was already wearing his jacket and a baseball cap. Liz nodded, pining for caffeine. They'd established a moratorium on dinners out, but breakfast was an indulgence they occasionally enjoyed.

After a leisurely stroll, they ducked into their favorite diner moments before the sprawling corner church dismissed its hungry congregation. Finding the last open booth, they settled in, relishing their small piece of luck. Behind them, someone yelled, "Coach!" and Dusty twisted around to see three boys he'd trained in the Pop Warner football league. They'd been in middle school then, but now they sported the hallmarks of puberty—wispy moustaches, broad shoulders, and cocky grins. Dusty ambled over to their table and fist bumped each boy before sliding into their booth for a quick catch up. Liz studied her menu, pleased that her husband was getting a little love from his former players. Months of meager employment had dimmed his mojo, and it was good to see him laughing and trading sports trivia with the kids.

After polishing off the diner's signature dish of huevos rancheros, they returned to Main Street and noticed that the farmers market was in full swing. As they passed by the stalls of spring vegetables, fresh-cut flowers, and local honey, Liz spotted friends and neighbors filling up their cloth bags and stopped to chat. An hour passed before they headed home, cradling fresh berries and broccoli they'd found at reasonable prices. How she cherished this town of hers, where she and Dusty could find familiar faces and warm exchanges around every bend. If they lost their home, where on earth would they go?

Around dinner time, their realtor, Chuck Moonie, called Dusty with an update regarding the open house. They talked for several minutes and when Dusty hung up, he gave her a look of guarded optimism.

"A young hotshot from Facebook came through today. Apparently, he was looking for a larger lot size, but his wife likes the kitchen and great room—the open floor plan. And the location. She's excited that their kids could bike to school."

Liz clapped her hands together. She reminded herself that they'd lowered the price again and stood to make next to nothing, even if they received asking amount. But at this point, breaking even would be fine. A win. "Will they make an offer?"

"Chuck thinks so, but they have a few more houses to see. We should know something next week."

Liz wondered if this was a sign that the economy was picking up. Today she'd sensed an air of consumer confidence in the bustling diner and at the crowded farmers market. She stepped into Dusty's arms, and he gave her a hopeful squeeze.

Chapter 13

Liz heard the low, grinding gears of the garbage collection truck coming down the street and cursed. She'd forgotten to roll the bins to the curb, so she tightened the belt around her bathrobe and dashed out to the garage to get them. A neighbor bending down for his morning paper gave her a quizzical look as she stood flagging down the truck in her fleece robe and bare feet.

It wasn't like her to forget such things. But today was the day her mother's doctor had predicted that the additional lung test results would be complete. She considered calling her parents to check in but didn't want to appear overly concerned. Best to wait to hear from them.

At the office, she found Gabbi and Zoey working on the backyard nuptials for Julie Mohr, Liz's down-the-street neighbor who'd requested help with her "casual and intimate" wedding. Gabbi had worked a true miracle with the minuscule budget. The theme for Saturday's event was a Tuscany-inspired supper, featuring grilled meats and veggies, Chianti, and a tiramisu wedding cake. To control costs, Gabbi was making the centerpieces herself and had just finished a trial arrangement: bright yellow sunflowers and purple thistles in vintage watering cans. As for music, she'd tracked down a jazz ensemble comprised of four Stanford grad students looking to make a little money now that school was out.

Zoey was on summer break too. After she'd broken her leg in April, the bone had healed nicely, and her mother had wasted no time before putting her to work. "We've completely transformed Julie's backyard," Gabbi boasted, donning work gloves to handle the flowers. "Zoey strung twinkly lights over her patio to create the feeling of an outdoor café. What this girl can do with a ladder and a few extension cords is amazing." Gabbi slung her arm around Zoey's shoulders, and the nineteen-year-old girl rolled her eyes good naturedly.

"It's true, I'm freakin' amazing!" she mocked. Zoey had her mother's good looks, yet she was wiry and more toned, with short hair and an unstudied style. She didn't wear an ounce of makeup, but her heavily-lashed brown eyes and radiant smile turned the heads of young men and women alike.

"Thanks for your help," Liz said, hugging Zoey before the girl ducked out for coffee.

At her desk, Liz glanced through her inbox before returning to Gabbi's office. "I've got estimates from the vendors," she said, "and the deposit from Julie." She didn't mention that there would be little profit on this job, despite the fact that Gabbi and Zoey had put their hearts into it. The best they could hope for was the subtle cultivation of new clients at the reception, or a referral or two from Julie. That's how they landed most of their business anyway. It was, after all, an introduction from Karl Perkins that connected them to Tony.

"You don't have to work the wedding," Gabbi said. "We have it covered." She took off her gloves and reached into her pocket, pulling out a card. "I'll make sure to pass these out."

Liz glanced down to see a new version of their Touch-stone business card. Under "weddings, corporate events, and private parties" she spotted "memorial services and celebrations of life."

"Did you notice? Zoey added the memorial stuff to our website too. She found some tasteful graphics online so it looks good—nothing morbid."

Liz stared at Gabbi, at a loss for words. Her partner had made another executive decision without consulting her. First, the suits on eBay, and now this. Yes, there had been a discussion of "doubling down" on death events, but no agreement as to changes in their brand and marketing. She realized now, she hadn't been ready to go fully public with their new sector. The look of disdain on Ben's face when discussing "parties for dead people" flashed through her mind.

"Everything okay?" Gabbi asked.

"This looks fine," Liz allowed. "But anything involving our messaging—and expenses—I want to approve."

"Of course," Gabbi said, straightening and pushing back her shoulders. "It's just that you've got a lot going on these days. With trying to sell that house and helping Jamie. And didn't you say Joanie has health concerns? I didn't want to bug you."

"We're managing quite well at home," Liz said. "From now on, keep me in the loop." When Gabbi appeared surprised—and annoyed—she added, "Please."

Liz returned to her desk and began processing payables and receivables while Gabbi left to run errands. She was relieved to have the space to herself and regretted the chilly exchange between them. Undoubtedly, Gabbi had meant well, but sometimes she needed reminding that Touchstone was a *partnership*.

When her paperwork was done, she texted Dusty, asking if he'd heard anything from the realtor about the potential buyer. "No word," he replied. She sighed. No word from her parents either.

She scooped up the outgoing mail and walked briskly to the post office, trying to work off some nervous energy. When she returned, she found a voicemail from her dad asking her to stop by at her earliest convenience. They had the results from Joanie's additional tests.

Liz entered her parents' den and found only her father there, pitched forward in his favorite armchair. On the coffee table, she noticed a scotch on the rocks, half gone. It was 3:00 p.m. and the sunlight was streaming through gaps in the wood blinds. Arnie never drank before dinner.

"Where's Mom?"

"She's in bed, resting. The doctor gave her a sedative." A faint ringing sounded in Liz's ears, and she felt a sudden dryness in her throat.

"What did he say?"

"Sit down, Izzie."

Izzie, the old name from her childhood, coined by Ned when they were both toddlers and he couldn't pronounce the "L" sound. Always a nickname of endearment, today she detected something different. A warning. She found a seat on the couch nearest her dad and noticed that the whites in his gray-blue eyes were bloodshot, his lids swollen.

"The spots in her lungs aren't some passing infection. It's cancer."

Impossible, Liz thought. "My God, Dad, she hasn't smoked in years. Is the doctor sure?"

"I'm afraid the CT scan was very clear."

"Well, they can remove it, right? With surgery?" Liz cast about in her memory, trying to recall a distant cousin who had lived a decade or so with a single lung following a similar diagnosis.

"I don't think so. It's on both sides." He rubbed the front of his checkered shirt in a slow, circular motion.

118

"Then what's the plan? Where do we go from here?" She stared into his blotchy, lined face searching for answers. Her peripheral vision was getting fuzzy, and she tried to tamp down the panic storming her brain, inhaling sharply and blinking away the blur.

"Your mom is getting more tests this week—a biopsy and an MRI. When Doctor Kumar gets the results back, he'll devise a treatment program. He's the oncologist. We haven't met him yet, but we've spoken on the phone. He assured us that we have good options for attacking this thing. Radiation, chemo."

"Is Doctor Kumar a lung specialist? Maybe we should get a second opinion." She stood up and began pacing around the room.

"We will, of course. But we must deal with the facts and be strong for your mother. Put a good face on this, okay?" He leaned back in his chair, gripping the armrests. "This is such a shock, so out of the blue, and I'm worried that Joanie will...*relapse* in some way." He reached for his glass and took a deep drink. "We have to keep her spirits up, to give her a fighting chance."

"Have you told Ned yet?"

"No, I'll call him tomorrow. I wanted to tell you in person because you'll be part of Mom's care team."

Liz was instantly comforted by the sound of that. The notion of being on a team. Teams that pulled together and followed directions could win.

"I'm going to join your mom for a nap," he said, getting to his feet. He put his warm, weighty hands on her shoulders and pulled her into a hug. As his weary body sagged against hers, she felt the forging of an old, familiar pact: that the two of them would hold the family together. But this time around, he would need care too. At seventy-four, he wasn't the same man who, years ago, had lifted his family from the ashes and carried them into a new life.

With the twins attending a music performance at school, and Dusty at a Giants game, Liz came home to a silence marred only by the distant buzz of a lawnmower. It was the kind of quiet she usually relished, giving her a chance to unwind before the hustle-bustle of getting dinner on the table. But this evening she would have preferred a raucous full house and an endless list of chores—anything to keep her thoughts from looping back to her mother's diagnosis.

Though she had promised herself not to go online, Liz settled in front of her computer and googled lung cancer, metastatic. With just a few clicks, she learned it was the leading cause of cancer death in America, killing more people each year than breast, prostate, colon, liver, and melanoma cancers combined. Any warm feelings she had conjured about being on a winning team began to dissipate. If her mother's disease was truly widespread—stage IV—it was essentially a death sentence.

Her heart began to pound, and she felt lightheaded. Pushing away from her computer, she staggered into her bedroom, sinking to her hands and knees on the carpeted floor. She crawled into her closet, and there in the sound-proof darkness, under the hems of party dresses she seldom wore, she howled like a lost child. The thought of losing her mother flooded her with a bottomless terror. But an inner voice called from the dark and asked, *Why, why are you so scared? You've managed without her before.*

In the first months after the fire, Liz had tried to cajole her mother into playing boardgames or roller skating in the cul-de-sac, activities she'd always delighted in with Maggie and her. But her mother waved her away, complaining of headaches and fatigue. "Maybe tomorrow," she'd mumble, reaching for a drink. And if a parent phoned to ask if Mrs. Boyle was available to help chaperone a school field trip to the zoo, her father made excuses about his wife's delicate health.

One evening, as Liz searched out her father for help on math problems, she overheard her parents talking in the den. In a weepy voice, her mother said something about having lost the will to go on. "What about Ned and Lizzie?" her father pleaded. "What about me?"

After that night, Liz adjusted her expectations, making few demands on her mother. When she pedaled home from school each day to find her passed out on the sofa in front of *The Merv Griffin Show*, she felt only a sweep of relief. It was enough that her mama had not slipped out the door to leave another sucking hole in the family, shrinking their number to three. And each morning, when she awakened Liz with apologetic kisses and stale breath, she whispered that she, Izzie, was an angel, her perfect little helper. As fragile as she was, her mother had been Liz's champion.

Eventually, after a few years of counseling and a renewed passion for painting, her mother returned to a close facsimile of her former self. Though Liz was secretly peering over her shoulder—making certain the candles were snuffed out, the iron was unplugged, the oven was off—it was a pleasure to have her mother serve roast beef and scalloped potatoes for her family again. Ned, long adept at making himself scarce, was also buoyed by his mother's recovery and drifted back home with greater regularity. In a reversal of the natural order of things, fourteen-year-old Liz had felt proud of her forty-year-old mother who had regained her footing.

But as Liz entered high school, a power struggle emerged between them. When her mother directed her to do chores that Liz had long been doing without prompting, irritation flared in her like a fever. One evening, after a full day of classes and a grueling basketball practice, the tension came to a head.

"Hey, Mom. I'm going to take a quick shower. Be right back."

"Before you go, please wash your hands and empty the dishwasher so it's ready for loading after supper."

"You mean the way I always do? Like, *every single day*?"

"Don't use that tone of voice with me."

"Well, don't treat me like an infant. I haven't been a child since I was ten years old."

Her mother set down her oven mitt and stared at her, looking stricken. "What's that supposed to mean?"

"Nothing," Liz muttered and quickly got to work pulling coffee mugs from the KitchenAid and pushing them into the cabinet. But the damage was done; Joanie had heard the blame in her daughter's voice, the accusation of being a virtually absent mother. She retreated to her bedroom and locked the door, refusing to come out. When her father came home, Liz confessed to her "crime" and he—who'd never had cause to discipline her—marched her down the hall to apologize through the closed door. At first, there was no answer. Had her mother busted out a hidden bottle of vodka? Fallen asleep? Or had she finally flown the coop to soar beyond her sorrows?

At last, her mother cracked open the door, asking her husband to send in Liz for a private conversation. There, on the edge of the bed, they faced each other. To Liz's surprise, her mother had brushed her auburn hair, applied make-up, and changed into a pretty blouse. She didn't appear angry; she looked as if she was applying for a job.

"I'm sorry about what I said," Liz began. Her mother raised her hand to silence her.

"No, Izzie. I had it coming. You're right, you haven't had the privilege of being simply a child for a very long time. But I'm better now, and I want to be a good mother to you and Ned."

Liz nodded, unsure what being "a good mother" entailed anymore. More uncertain of what it was to be a child. But she vowed to give her mother a chance. She did her best to play along, allowing Joanie to select outfits for her school dances. Or to write permission slips to the teacher when Liz suffered from menstrual cramps and wanted to stay home. In time, their mother-daughter relationship grew roots in a common ground. They had their garden-variety arguments about homework and curfews. And there were still things unsaid, details about the fire that remained shrouded in secrecy. But Liz had her mom back.

And now, all these years later, she was determined to keep it that way.

Chapter 14

*L*iz and her parents crowded into a small consultation room at the hospital dressed in what they might have worn for a night out at an upscale restaurant: skirts and blouses for her mother and her, pressed slacks and a crisp button-down for Arnie. Though they hadn't discussed it, Liz understood that the first goal was to make a good impression on Dr. Kumar, the young oncologist recommended to them. It was vital to appear unified and respectable, a family deserving of his best efforts. Aside from her distracting cough, Joanie looked healthy and considerably younger than her seventy-two years. Her eyes sparkled and she smiled bravely at the dark-haired doctor with thick, navy-framed glasses. Surely he could see that she was worth saving, couldn't he?

After brief introductions, the doctor turned quickly to explaining the results of the MRI and biopsy, careful to feed them information in digestible chunks. There were "lesions in both lungs" and "suspicious spots along the spine." He kept it impersonal, never saying to her mother, "You have tumors in *your* lungs, cancer in *your* bones." The clinical nature of the report made it no easier to hear, and Liz had to remind herself to keep breathing. Finally, after feeding them so much terrible news, the doctor offered them a small serving of hope.

"The good news is there's no cancer in the brain." He dropped his pen into the pocket of his white coat, signaling the wrap-up of their meeting. "It's difficult for chemo to pass through the blood-brain barrier, but it can be effective in the body. Some patients have an excellent response."

An excellent response. She glanced at her parents where they sat side-by-side in tiny, armless chairs, and they nodded at the doctor, a look of solemn determination on their faces. No one asked what the prognosis was, how many months or years her mother might have ahead. They were aiming to leave the cramped, airless room on the high note of a potential excellent response. Chemotherapy would start after all of Joanie's lab work was done. As soon as next week.

"Try to get some rest before treatment," he advised. He gave her mother a prescription for a bronchodilator to help subdue her cough. Then they made their way through the crowded hospital parking lot and climbed into her father's sedan, relieved to have a game plan.

After her father dropped her off at home, Liz scrambled into her own car and headed to the pharmacy to pick up the prescriptions to ease her mother's cough. From there she drove to the shopping center to find a gift. The doctor had warned that fatigue was a common side effect of chemo, and Liz wanted to treat her mother to something that would make lingering in bed more pleasant.

She recalled with a rush of affection how Joanie had pampered her following the birth of the twins, who'd arrived after twenty-four hours of labor and an emergency C-section. As soon as Dusty had settled her and the babies at home, her mother had appeared with soft pajamas and fancy moisturizers for her stretched belly and swollen breasts. "From one mom to another," she'd said. Liz had allowed herself to be mothered by Joanie, who had tidied up the house and prepared hearty meals in those first post-partum weeks. Back then, Liz believed that recovering from Cesarean surgery while nursing twins was some epic ordeal. By comparison, what her mother was facing in the months ahead would be brutal, with an uncertain outcome. But she wouldn't let herself think about that.

At a boutique specializing in lingerie and bed linens, she found a lovely periwinkle nightgown with lace trim and a matching robe. The price was beyond anything Liz would typically spend, but she didn't care. After pulling out a charge card she prayed had credit remaining, she asked for the items to be gift wrapped. Then she started back to her car. It was nearly dinnertime.

When she finally entered the kitchen with her shopping bag, she found Dusty setting the table. He hesitated over a placemat, trying to remember if the fork was positioned on the right side or left.

"Still no word from the realtor," he said, settling the fork on the right side.

Through the window to the back patio, Liz noticed a thin curtain of smoke rising from the grill where dinner was underway. She should have been pleased that Dusty was reliably pitching in, but instead she felt frustrated. After all, he was the one who'd been so confident about remodeling a house and making a killing on it. She'd cautioned against it, calling it a gamble. And now? Here he was, a dish towel slung over his shoulder and no real plan for making things right. She wanted her caveman back. She wanted the woolly mastodon.

"They go on the left," she said.

"Huh?"

"The forks. They go on the left side."

"Oh." Slowly, he circled the table, correcting his mistake. "How'd it go with the doctor today?"

Liz dropped her bag and sank into a chair, a weariness overtaking her. "The cancer has metastasized, but it's not in her brain. We start chemo next week."

"Poor Joanie. How's she holding up? And what about your dad?"

"They have their game faces on. It's hard to know what they're saying behind closed doors."

"It's that whole Midwestern thing, right? Chin up." He rubbed his own chin absentmindedly as he went to the refrigerator and pulled out barbeque sauce for the ribs. "This disease may be hardest on Arnie." He gazed at her over his shoulder. "I'd hate to be in his shoes."

She looked away, unable to reciprocate his tender sentiments. After he passed through the porch door to tend the grill, she gathered her things and went to call the boys for dinner.

Hours later, Liz surfaced from a deep, blank sleep and found herself stretched out on the couch where she'd been watching TV. Moonlight sifted through the shutters, and the perfect stillness in the house telegraphed that everyone else was tucked away in bed. She vaguely remembered hearing her phone ring some time earlier, and she reached for her cell on the coffee table. There was a voicemail from her brother: "Lizzie, call me about Mom. We need to discuss this cancer thing. Is it as bad as it sounds? Or is Dad overreacting?"

She bristled at the suggestion. As far back as she could remember, her father's response to bad news had always been measured, reasonable. Had he *overreacted* when, after the fire, he'd found them a new home in a different town where they could try to start over? Had he *overre-*

acted when he finally told their mother that if she didn't get help for her grief and drinking, he'd take Ned and her and move out? And was it *overreacting* to stop supporting Ned when, out of the blue, he dropped out of college to play on a rinky-dink tennis circuit?

She peered at her watch and saw that it was nearly midnight—too late to return her brother's call. After a moment's hesitation, she deleted his voicemail and then crept though the darkness to her closet where she changed into a nightshirt and crawled into bed. Next to her, Dusty snored steadily but she felt wide awake, courtesy of her evening nap. Her thoughts returned to the hospital meeting where the patient-care coordinator had told them that fighting metastasized cancer was a family affair; the frontline caretakers would need reinforcements. But could she and her dad count on Ned for anything?

Although her brother was two years older and half a foot taller, Liz had never truly looked up to him. Born with an embarrassment of riches—a quick brain, a grin that made otherwise smart girls say stupid things, and the hand-eye coordination of a professional jock—Ned had squandered his gifts in a manner that was unfathomable to Liz. In high school, he had the long, dirty-blond hair and blazing two-handed backhand that reminded coaches of Bjorn Borg, the Swedish phenom. But by his senior year, he'd slipped down the tennis team ladder and was relegated to doubles matches—often partnering with Peter Levine—due to so many skipped practices and missed games. He'd bailed on classes too, taking off for the beach with fellow underachievers to skimboard along the foggy coastline, or to get stoned in local parks. Now, all these years later, Ned was an assistant tennis pro at a stuffy country club in San Diego. He was forty-seven and he'd never married, never had children.

Minutes ticked by, and Liz was still wrestling with her pillow at 2:00 a.m. In her medicine cabinet, she found an expired sedative and washed it down with a handful of tap water, praying it was still effective. When her cell rang again, she awoke to find the sun up and Dusty's side of the bed empty. She grabbed her phone and sat up against the headboard.

"Hello?"

"Why didn't you call me back?" Ned asked.

"I was just dialing your number...."

"So, is the cancer—"

"Yes, it's extremely serious. Late stage."

Ned said nothing at first, taking it in. "All right, I'll fly up next week. Okay if I stay with you? I don't think now's a good time for Mom and Dad to have company."

Perfect, Liz thought. *Then I'll have three adolescents under my roof.* "Well, it's just that the boys start final exams on Monday."

"I'll keep a low profile. I figure if your hubby isn't working much, the two of us could hang out. You know how much I love Mr. Dusty Pants."

A laugh snorted out through Liz's nose. From the beginning, Ned and Dusty had enjoyed a warm bromance. The two of them could jaw about Bay Area sports teams, new-model trucks, and the finer points of charcoal versus gas grills until the friggin' cows came home. Even though she'd told Dusty how often her brother had left her in the lurch after Maggie died, he was able to compartmentalize the backstory and enjoy Ned's company.

"Okay," she said. "You're welcome to the sofa bed in my office."

She hung up and heard a soft rap on the door as Jamie stepped in shouldering his backpack and finishing a toasted waffle.

"Hey, Mom. Ben and I are leaving for school. You okay? It's late."

"Just a little headache," she lied. She and Dusty had agreed not to tell the boys about their grandmother's illness until after exams.

Jamie studied her face, and she sensed he wasn't buying it. He moved closer to the bed and gently patted her feet where they were tucked under the comforter. "Feel better," he said.

She smiled and waved goodbye as he hurried out to the driveway to join Ben. It was likely only a matter of time before she deputized her tender son to be on his grandmother's care team.

Chapter 15

A week later, Liz was barreling down the 101 to pick up Ned at the San Jose airport. She was making good time, something that never failed to give her a small but vital sense that she was in control of her day.

Her mother had started chemotherapy two days before, in an old building on the Stanford Hospital campus where an acrid smell of cleansers and chemicals hung in the air. Liz and her dad had both attended the first treatment, making nice with the nurses who helped Joanie onto a scale to weigh her, settled her into a comfy recliner chair, and tapped her arm to find a good vein. Though Liz had come with an assortment of reading materials for her mother—everything from *Art News* to *People* Magazine—she'd had little time to read. Nestled as close as possible to his wife, Arnie had chatted incessantly to her. And if he took a break to use the bathroom or to get something to drink, a monitor streaming CNN droned on overhead.

After being tethered to an IV for hours, Joanie had told them that she felt neither nauseous nor overwhelmed. "Just a bit worn out." Though it was a warm June day, she'd requested soup for dinner; Liz had already prepared a hearty chicken stew. Back home, after eating more than anyone had expected, Joanie went to bed and slept without a stir while Liz kept her father company watching the History Channel. Driving home that night, she'd felt some of the tension lift from her shoulders and neck. So far, so good.

Yesterday had been nearly identical to the first day of treatment except that Joanie was either more relaxed, or more fatigued, and kept dozing off. Each time she closed her eyes, Liz jumped up to call Gabbi to see if anything was percolating at work. But it was quiet at the office, and though Julie Mohr's wedding had been an enchanting affair by all accounts, no referrals had surfaced. Liz was now pinning her hopes on responses from their presentation at the retirement community in Palo Alto. It had been well received—the fashionably attired older couples had been cordial and asked many questions. No new clients had yet emerged from the pitch, but folks probably weren't in a hurry to plan their final exit.

When she spotted signs for the airport, Liz prepped herself to be open minded, to entertain the possibility that Ned might be a capable contributor to their mother's care. Outside the terminal, she waited just a minute before he breezed out of the sliding glass doors gripping a small carry-on duffle. Tall and fit, dressed in stylish frayed jeans and a white polo shirt that contrasted sharply with his deeply-tanned face, he grinned and waved when he caught her eye. She smiled back, wary of his charms but feeling the undertow of his charisma even before he reached her driver side window and leaned in to peck her on the cheek.

"Hey, little sis."

"Welcome back to NorCal, bro."

"New car?"

"Very funny." Liz had been driving the same blue minivan for ten years, since the twins were in first grade. Ned, who'd picked up their father's passion for tinkering with old cars, always had a fashionable set of wheels. With no mortgage to pay—he was a serial renter—it was easy to splurge on what his father referred to as hot-rods.

"Where to?" he asked, climbing into the passenger seat and tossing his duffle in the back.

"Let's go to the clinic and see Mom. I bet Dad could use a little break."

"Okay if we stop by Starbucks first? I'd kill for a chai latte."

Liz nodded. "And do you want to pick up some flowers for Mom?" She seriously doubted there was any kind of gift for her in his carry-on.

"Brilliant. Yes, let's do that."

Before merging back into traffic, Liz glanced at her brother, taking him in from head to toe. Around his neck, attached to neon green Croakies, were his signature Ray-Bans. And on his bronzed feet were Hawaiian print flip-flops. As he swatted down the visor to check his look in the tiny mirror, it occurred to Liz that his attire hadn't changed one iota since he'd moved to San Diego when he was twenty. His sandy hair was shot through with gray, and the lines on his face gave testimony to the long, hot days he'd spent hitting tennis balls to suburban moms and their kids. But everything about his presence suggested he was still a young man. And that Peter Pan thing was apparently working for him. When they'd talked at Christmas, he was dating a thirty-something Pilates instructor.

Liz found a Starbucks near the hospital, as well as a florist in the same complex. After getting their hot drinks—addiction to caffeine being one of the few things they had in common—they headed to the flower shop. Liz pointed to a dozen yellow roses with a touch of pink on the petal tips, and Ned nodded in approval. "Very cheerful." Trying to channel Gabbi, she asked the florist to place the flowers in a simple vase and to add some greens and baby's breath—and maybe a pretty bow? When the arrangement was complete and Ned had paid, he scooped it up and they headed to the hospital.

Leading the way into the treatment room, Liz saw that her mother, dressed comfortably in a blue chambray shirt and leggings, was wide awake. She gazed over Liz's shoulder, and when her eyes fell on Ned, her face lit up with girlish delight. Her brother stepped around her and loped to their mother's side, dodging the infusion apparatus and planting a dramatic kiss on her lips. On the wheeled side table, he pushed away the magazines and Styrofoam cups of water and carefully set down the vase of long-stem roses. "For you!" he said with a flourish.

"My gosh, Ned. They're absolutely gorgeous! You remembered how much I adore the color yellow." She reached out for his forearm and gave it an affectionate squeeze. Liz watched wordlessly, nearly certain Ned wouldn't give her a lick of credit for suggesting the gift.

"I'm so glad you like them. And for the record, *you* look gorgeous. You must be tolerating this stuff pretty well." He flipped his thumb toward the IV bag.

"Well, it's only day three," their mother replied. "Too soon to tell." She swept her hand over her auburn waves, meticulously dyed to match the color from her youth. "I really hope I don't lose my hair."

"That's what wigs are for, Mom. Worst-case scenario? You'd be a killer blonde."

Liz wanted to pinch him for his cavalier attitude. The worst-case scenario wasn't just hair loss. But a young nurse passing by with a tray of meds heard his comment and laughed, and Ned reciprocated with a wink.

"Where's Dad?" she asked.

"He'll be right back—he went to get a sandwich." She looked at Ned and then back at her. "Honey, between Dad and your brother, I'm well-covered here. Don't feel you have to stay. I know the twins are in finals, and you probably have work to do."

She did, in fact, have to drive Jamie to an appointment with the therapist after his exams. Night after night, he'd been studying into the wee hours, and she was concerned that the stress would stall—or reverse—his progress. Still, she couldn't shake the feeling that she was being dismissed.

She turned to her brother. "Okay, then, I guess I'll go. Just have Dad drop you off at my house. Your bag's in the car. Need anything?"

"A spare key?"

"Don't worry about that. Dusty will be home." He was always home.

✳ ✳ ✳

As she swung her van into the school parking lot, she considered that Dusty could have taken Jamie to his therapist. But Jamie wanted to keep his counseling on the down-low, only willing to discuss it with her. Liz understood his instinct to keep quiet about his spiraling thoughts and debilitating lethargy. It was such a relief to get him the help he needed. Maybe with early intervention, he wouldn't end up like her—having panic attacks and groping for Xanax in musty church bathrooms.

She looked for Jamie's nondescript hoodie in a sea of cut-offs and T-shirts and spotted him slamming the door of his locker and twisting the dial padlock with a flick of irritation. As he made his way toward her and reached for the door, she vowed to keep things light.

"Hey there. Two exams down, only one to go, right?"

"Yeah, but the chem test. What a drag." He clipped his shoulder belt into place and tilted back his seat so he could stretch out. "I ran out of time and left a few questions blank. No chance I got an A."

"Chem is hard for everyone." She opened the console between their seats and pulled out some granola bars and a small bottle of Gatorade. Jamie looked unimpressed.

"Don't worry. We'll have a nice dinner tonight. Your Uncle Ned will be joining us."

"Ned's here?" he asked, sitting up. "Cool."

Nearly a decade ago, Ned gave Jamie his first video game. Was it *Pokémon*—or *Super Mario Brothers*? Liz could never keep the titles straight, but Ned had a middle-schooler's zeal for games. Last Christmas, he and Jamie had disappeared for hours playing *Halo*. Dr. Noah had placed restrictions on that kind of endless gaming, and she reminded herself to tell Ned about the new house rules.

"Why's he in town?"

"Oh, just to visit Jo-Jo and Grandpa. He'll help with some repairs around the house. Grandpa shouldn't be climbing up ladders anymore."

Liz was still managing to keep her mother's treatments hidden from the boys. Jamie, in particular, would find her diagnosis upsetting. While Ben and her father gravitated towards one another around sports, Jamie had happily orbited his grandmother, collaborating on jigsaw puzzles and art projects. From the start, they'd enjoyed an effortless companionship, one that she and Joanie had never known.

She pulled up to Dr. Noah Greenberg's office, blessedly located on a quiet alley where Jamie was unlikely to run into anyone he knew. After quickly scanning the area, he slipped out, leaving his backpack behind but grabbing his iPod and earbuds. "I'll walk home," he said. "See you at dinner."

She nodded goodbye, grateful there was no need to circle back. It would give her more time at the office to check in with Gabbi.

It was getting towards dinnertime, and Liz remembered she had four men to feed. As she made quick edits to a letter thanking their landlord for accepting late office rent—again—Gabbi went to the women's room to primp before a date. When she returned, she looked decidedly racy in a low-cut leopard print top and fitted black skirt.

"Meow!" Liz said, clawing at the air.

"Too much? I don't want to give my date a heart attack. I think he qualifies for senior discounts at the steak house." Gabbi glanced at her phone, looking mischievous. "Maybe I should just cancel dinner and join you and Neddy-Bear for a bite to eat."

"Ah, *no*," Liz said.

She hadn't forgotten the New Year's Eve party she and Dusty had hosted right before she and Gabbi joined forces at Touchstone Events. Ned had been visiting over the holidays, and when he was reintroduced to Gabbi (they'd met briefly back in high school) she was wearing a dazzling red sequin dress and tipping back champagne. Her marriage was already on the rocks—David's gambling addiction and debts had put divorce squarely on the table—and shenanigans quickly ensued. At the stroke of midnight, she and Ned started to smooch and then slinked off to a back bedroom. When Liz discovered their indiscretion, she was stunned they'd been so reckless. And now that she and Gabbi were in business together, she didn't want the drama of mixing Peter Pan with Cat Woman.

"You're no fun," Gabbi said.

Liz heard the genuine disappointment in her voice and considered changing her mind to include Gabbi. But her partner flipped off the lights and rushed out the door.

On the way home, Liz stopped by the boys' favorite Japanese restaurant and picked up enough teriyaki chicken and rice to feed a small army. Rolling into her driveway minutes later, she spotted Dusty and Ned out front. They were passing a basketball back and forth under a rim that had clearly been adjusted below regulation height. She laughed softly to herself. No harm in that. It was still sunny and warm, a perfect evening for shooting hoops. And it was good to see Dusty zigzagging around the makeshift court.

In all their years of marriage, Dusty had benefitted from plenty of exercise on construction sites. Though he was the head contractor, he never hesitated to assist his subs by swinging a hammer if they were shorthanded, or by unloading their trucks. She'd watched him carry in finished cabinets, stone slabs for counter tops, heavy mirrors for bathrooms. And after a long day building or remodeling a home, he'd often hit the gym. But months ago, Dusty had let his fitness membership expire in another cost-cutting measure. Afterwards, he'd vowed to start a program of early morning runs and weightlifting in the garage, but his cross-trainers were still in a box, his dumbbells untouched. Lately, he'd grown soft around the middle.

As she started for the front door, the men stopped playing and ambled toward her. She handed Dusty the aluminum tray of teriyaki chicken and asked him to put it in the warming oven. "I'll take a quick shower and then we can eat. Boys home?"

"Yep. They're both hitting the books."

"It's truly gratifying to see how much they take after their uncle," Ned said with a straight face. Liz smirked and headed inside to freshen up.

Feeling re-energized in a clean cotton tee and white jeans, Liz padded barefoot into the kitchen to check on dinner. When she cracked open the oven door, she was annoyed to find that a sizable portion of the meal was missing. She glanced through the window to the back patio where Dusty and Ned were bent over small plates of teriyaki chicken and enjoying a beer. Really? They couldn't have waited fifteen minutes to eat as a family?

Marching outside, she faced the men, a flush of anger rising in her cheeks.

"Lizzie, honey, we helped ourselves to a little appetizer," Dusty said before she could utter a word. "I'm sorry, but after all that B-ball, we were starving."

"*Starving*," Ned echoed with a giggle.

She leaned in more closely and noticed that her brother's eyes were red and at half-mast. She looked back at Dusty. Ditto. They weren't just hungry—they had the damn munchies.

"Ned, can I see you inside for a minute?" she said.

Her brother turned toward Dusty, giving him the mournful expression of a basset hound, and reluctantly got to his feet.

"Hon," Dusty began. But she'd already spun around and was making her way indoors. She led Ned to her office and closed the door with a firm click.

"Remember one thing, and one thing only," she said, raising her index finger. "You're here to help Mom. And Dad. This is not a vacation. And certainly not the time or place to get stoned."

Ned rolled his eyes. He was a single man unaccustomed to being scolded by anyone, let alone his younger sister. "I smoke a little weed to relax and take the edge off my back pain. Don't get so wound up. Jesus, Liz, you're absolutely no—"

"Fun? So I've been told." She was suddenly fighting tears, so tired of always being the grown-up in the room. "Ned, things are going to get much worse with Mom

before they get better. If they get better. We're in the effin'
Disneyland stage right now. Have you read the email I sent
you? About the chemo side effects?"

"No." His hands were resting on his hips, and he was
staring at his spotless Stan Smith tennis shoes. "Not yet."

She wanted him to look up and meet her eyes. "This
time around, I need you to do your part."

His head jerked back and he glared at her. "What's
that supposed to mean?"

"I mean after the fire, Ned. After Maggie died. Do I
have to spell it out? You kept disappearing." She struggled
to keep her voice from breaking. "You left me to pick up
the pieces. I was just a kid."

"That's ancient history," he said. "I was just a kid too.
And by the way? No one asked you to be Florence-Fuck-
ing-Nightingale."

His words grabbed at her throat. She wanted to
scream at him. Liar! But as she cast back through her
memory, she froze. Technically speaking, it was possible
that no one had actually requested that she step in and
run the show. But on the mornings when their mother
had flipped back her bed covers only to hunt down a cigarette or pour a drink, nobody had to ask.

"Okay, Ned. Maybe no one officially requested my
help back then. But right here, right now, I'm officially
asking for yours."

The shuffle of feet outside the door startled them
both, and Jamie stuck his head in the room. "Mom—okay
if Ben and I have some of that chicken? It smells amazing."

"Of course," Liz said, feigning cheerfulness. "Help
yourself. Be right out."

"And dude—I brought dessert!" Ned said. He unzipped
his suitcase and dug out a copy of *Grand Theft Auto*. Liz bit
her lip, silently cursing herself for neglecting to tell him
about the new gaming restrictions.

"Aw, that's killer," Jamie said. He glanced at Liz. "I know, I know. One more final tomorrow. We won't play long." She nodded, grateful not to be the heavy, and Jamie shut the door.

When she turned back to Ned, the anger in his glassy green eyes had cooled. "Don't worry about Mom and Dad," he said. "I'm all in." He sat down on the sleeper couch and kicked off his shoes, making himself at home.

Chapter 16

*T*wo weeks had passed since her mother started chemo, and her parents had established a tentative new normal. While Joanie delighted in Ned's visit and lavish attention—he was ever ready to pour her a cup of tea, fetch the mail, or wrap a shawl around her shoulders—Arnie insisted on shuttling his wife to treatment without the help of his children. So Ned returned to San Diego and his life of teaching topspin forehands and pursuing fit young women in beach attire.

For Liz, a new normal was getting underway too. Now that junior year was blessedly over, the twins were relishing the first days of summer. Ben had landed a job as an assistant coach at a baseball camp, and Jamie was helping underserved kids improve their computer skills. In short, each boy was getting paid to do what came naturally. In this atmosphere of relative calm, Liz had finally told them that their grandmother was being treated for cancer. She was matter-of-fact in her delivery, explaining the diagnosis as they noshed on Hawaiian-style pizza. And though Liz may have neglected to mention certain characteristics of the disease (metastatic, late stage), she didn't feel as if she had deceived her boys in any way. Jamie had asked if Jo-Jo was experiencing any nausea or hair loss "like they do in the movies," but Liz assured him his grandmother was doing quite well and was on her way to an *excellent response* to chemotherapy.

With the home front in a stable holding pattern, Liz headed to work and sank into her chair, ready to review her backlog of emails. As she waited for her ancient computer to load, she gazed out her window and noticed two more *For Lease* signs hanging in vacated stores across the street. So much for the "consumer confidence" she'd felt just last month. It was hard not to feel discouraged, especially since the couple from Facebook who'd shown genuine interest in Dusty's remodel had never circled back.

Her cell phone rang, and she found an incoming call from Tony. How glad she was to see his number; they hadn't spoken in many days. It was nearing the time that he would move into his assisted living complex—the place he grimly referred to as "Hotel Sayonara."

"Hello, Liz. Do you have a minute? I have a favor to ask."

His breathing sounded labored, and she hoped his oxygen apparatus was within reach. Aasal had been encouraging him to use it for his shortness of breath and trouble sleeping.

"Fire away. Happy to help."

"First of all, I'd like to thank you and Gabbi again for everything you've done for me. It's been a relief to get so many matters put to bed."

"It's been our pleasure, Tony. Thank *you*."

"My attorney and I have been discussing the notion of having my relatives' inheritance contingent upon them attending my memorial service. I've decided against it. Instead, I've written letters to my children and grandkids, and to Carol. To tell them how I feel. To make amends, I guess."

"Oh, that's nice. Much better," Liz said. "And I'm sure, when the time comes, they'll all be here in California to..." She groped for the right words. "Pay their respects."

"I hope so. It should be quite a gathering, and I'm sorry I won't be around to see it. But it's some consolation to know that my family will remember me as a lion, not a lamb. Not this shrunken, old ghost of a man."

"Oh, Tony. Don't be so tough on yourself."

There was a pause in the conversation, and Liz wondered if the call had dropped. Service in the hills was spotty at times, but then he continued.

"So, here's the favor I need. I've put some instructions on my desk regarding my final wishes. I'd like you to come by tomorrow to pick them up."

"Sure thing. What time works for you?" She glanced at her calendar, open as the summer sky. "Does late morning work? Ten-ish?"

"Whatever works for you is fine. The key is still under the pot at the front door. Just let yourself in. Nobody will be here."

"But, Tony, I'm happy to work around your schedule. I'd love to see you."

"That's not possible, dear. I'll be gone by then."

"Are you heading out of town?" Liz was surprised. In the months that she and Gabbi had worked for him, Tony had shown no interest in travel. Even a cruise on an ocean liner seemed beyond him now.

"I'm afraid you don't understand what I'm trying to say."

Gone echoed in her ear, and Liz felt a cold dread rise in her stomach. "Where's Aasal?"

"I've insisted he go on vacation. Caring for me has taken a toll on the poor man." He paused again, raking in his breath. "Now, when you get here, you'll see that I've reserved the bar and outdoor patio at the club and paid in advance for a service next month. You and Gabbi know who to invite and what to serve. I'm sorry to make you a party to this, Liz, but I know I can count on you."

"Tony, just hang on. Please." An image of the black pistol buried in his old war trunk flashed through her mind, and she shot up to her feet. "I can leave right now and be on your doorstep in minutes. Then, I'll take you up to Seattle myself. So we can visit your family. This is not what anyone wants."

"It's what I want, Liz."

"Please don't do this to yourself. Don't do this to me." She ached to tell him that her beautiful mother had a terrible disease, and that she was scared and couldn't take one more shitty thing. "Please," she said again. "You're my friend, Tony."

When she heard a click indicating the call was over, she punched in 9-1-1 and ordered an ambulance to Tony's address.

"Hurry!" she shouted. "He's got a gun in the house and wants to kill himself." Ignoring the dispatcher's instructions to stay on the line, Liz hung up and hurled herself down the steps to the garage, leaping into the van. Speeding towards Portola Valley, her heart hammering painfully in her chest, she called Gabbi. When there was no reply, she remembered that Gabbi was in Santa Clara with Zoey, trying to find housing for fall term. "Fuck!" she howled. She phoned Dusty next, and in a torrent of words, she told him what might be happening this very instant.

"Don't go in the house," he warned. "If the man's got a gun and he's suicidal, who knows where the bullets will land. I'm on my way."

Slowed by a peloton of neon-shirted cyclists—why weren't those *assholes* at work—Liz felt as if she might spontaneously combust. When she finally came barreling up Lupin Lane and pulled over, she discovered that she'd beat the emergency personnel to the house. Two steps towards Tony's front door, she came to a halt. Was she really going inside to find, what, a corpse? Gray matter on the ceiling and walls? A rubbery sensation in her knees and a foggy light headedness descended upon her, symptoms she knew all too well. She grasped the steel railing that bordered the steps and turned around, bent on retreat. But what if there was still time to change fate—to stay Tony's hand? Somehow managing to get up the stairs, she found the key under the red geraniums and pushed open the heavy door.

"Tony?" she called. "It's Liz. I'm here."

No reply. She crept into his office and circled his desk, alert for the slumped body she loathed to find and feeling as if she were in some awful TV crime show. There was no sign of Tony, but when she glanced at his desktop, she noticed the binder labeled *In the Event of Death*. Inside, she found a copy of his will and a list of contacts identifying his estate advisors. When she spotted her own name and number, she stepped back, her arms falling numbly at her sides.

She and Gabbi had brought Tony to this day. They had planned his memorial. Drafted his obituary. Prepared his house for sale. Above her, the looming, empty bookshelves seemed to stare at her in judgement. The only thing they hadn't done was pull the trigger.

Through an open window, Liz could hear sirens growing closer. She moved quickly through the other first-floor rooms, searching in vain. And then she had an epiphany. Hurrying to the living room, past the grand piano, she tugged open the thick, sliding glass door that led to Tony's expansive outdoor deck. There, her eyes fell upon the old man lying prostrate on a plastic chaise lounge, a faded beach towel covering his legs and torso.

Though she saw no blood, she sensed that she had arrived too late.

At their first meeting, Tony had described himself as a real estate developer, "a land man." In his final moments, he had been surveying his property, a mix of lean redwoods and stocky oaks, and a garden past its prime but beckoning all the same. Liz took a fortifying breath and willed herself forward, inching toward the body. For a strange, vertiginous moment, she thought of her own mother, approaching the lifeless form of her precious Maggie. The voices of EMTs were somewhere behind her—she had left the front door ajar for their quick access. But she wanted to reach Tony first. To ask forgiveness, to say goodbye. One step. Two steps. Breathe.

At the sound of her footfalls, the old man's head turned in her direction, and Liz stumbled to her knees with relief.

As the young medics guided his gurney down the steep driveway, Tony, tucked under bone-colored linens and belted into place, stared vacantly at the sky. When they reached the street where Liz was waiting, he gestured for her to come close. The moment their eyes met, she took his cold, limp hand into hers.

"I couldn't do it, Liz. Maybe I'm simply a coward." His voice was scarcely audible. "Please don't tell anyone about this. Let people think it was another heart attack." Neighbors were already gathering on their front lawns or gazing furtively out their windows at the hive of emergency vehicles and personnel.

"I'll keep your secret on one condition," she said, bending down on still shaky knees to graze his forehead with a kiss. "That you never try this again."

He nodded, and then his eyes fluttered shut as the men rolled him away and loaded him into the ambulance.

Liz reached for her phone, intending to break her promise to Tony immediately. She needed to track down Aasal and ask him to return home. Someone needed to watch Tony around the clock—and get rid of that gun. She'd found it half hidden under the beach towel and stashed it in the pool house.

Before phoning Aasal, she called Dusty who was only a few blocks away and told him that Tony was alive and unharmed. Only then did she feel her heartbeat and breath settle into a normal rhythm. But as she stood in the middle of the cul-de-sac watching the taillights of police cars disappear from view, her equilibrium was undermined by a deepening sense of guilt. She left a message on Gabbi's voicemail requesting an urgent meeting, and then walked over to consult with Tony's nosy neighbors.

Last night, after Dusty and the boys had turned in, Liz had wandered back to the kitchen and poured herself a third glass of wine. Two hadn't been enough to blot out the image of Tony being carted away to a hospital, or to stop her from fretting about his current condition. To think that he was utterly alone, with no family members to huddle with doctors and answer questions about his medical history—or psychological profile.

Now it was morning, and she felt dull headed and dehydrated. The restorative magic of a hot shower would have to wait: Dusty, who was hustling to make a meeting with a former client about a few home repairs, had already laid claim to the bathroom. She pulled on her sweats and plodded down the hallway, knocking on the boys' doors to make sure they were getting ready for school.

At her desk in the guest bedroom, reclaimed the instant Ned returned to San Diego, she settled in with a mug of tea and checked her voicemail. The first was from blessed Aasal, en route to the Bay Area. He'd been in contact with Tony Jr. who, in turn, had communicated with the hospital staff. The doctors had assured him that his father was medically stable and would be discharged following a psych evaluation. What's more, father and son had spoken directly, reaching some sort of understanding. As Aasal explained in his message, "Tony Jr. offered to come to the hospital, but old Tony insisted there was no need. Instead, I'll take him to Seattle for a visit. If Tony is fully recovered, we'll fly up next week."

Liz closed her eyes and exhaled, feeling the pressure in her head start to lift. She took a few sips of chamomile tea and played her second voicemail. It was Gabbi, suggesting they meet at Borrone's around noon to discuss "the Tony situation."

Seated outside hours later, Liz gazed down at the pigeons pecking at bits of scones and croissants. "I can't believe we didn't connect the dots, Gabbi. To think he nearly..." She wagged her head. "Seriously, we aided and abetted a near tragedy."

Gabbi took a sip of iced coffee and held her tongue.

"We may be experts in weddings and parties, but when it comes to this death business, we're amateurs," Liz said. "We simply don't know what we don't know."

"Of course, there's a learning curve," Gabbi said, setting down her glass. "And I feel terrible about Tony. You know that, right? But, Liz, we can't control our clients' actions after we provide services. Think about it. If, after we've produced an epic wedding, the bride and groom decide to get divorced, that's not on us."

"Apples and oranges, Gab."

"Let's just agree we'll know better next time. We'll recognize the warning signs."

"What 'next time'?" Liz asked. "This new venture is going absolutely nowhere."

"You're wrong. We're on to something," Gabbi said, a flicker of excitement lighting her eyes. "That presentation we did at the retirement community? It's bearing fruit. I've been in dialog with two couples. And in the mail today, I found a signed proposal and a hefty deposit."

In spite of herself, Liz felt a spurt of satisfaction that she and Gabbi could still close deals—even in this dark business, even during a recession. At the same time, she had a creeping conviction that what happened with Tony was merely the first of many unforeseen calamities in wait for them. Still, as she poked the ice cubes at the bottom of her soda cup with a straw, she considered what a "hefty deposit" might mean.

She glanced up at Gabbi and nodded, feeling like a hypocrite.

Chapter 17

On Saturday, as Liz jogged in the hills above Stanford campus, past grazing cows and the giant radio antenna known as The Dish, her thoughts drifted to Tony. Aasal had returned from his aborted vacation to help him get discharged from the hospital and settled at home. Days later, he accompanied his elderly employer to Seattle for a long-overdue reunion. By Aasal's account, Tony Jr. and his family had welcomed them warmly. Was it because Aasal had shared the secret of the attempted suicide that they felt compelled to reconcile? Or was it the knowledge that their inheritance was ever closer that they embraced the old man?

It hardly mattered, really. Yesterday, Tony returned to California in palpably better spirits. Over the phone, he shared with Liz that his daughter, Angela, remained estranged from him, but his former wife, Carol, had agreed to meet for coffee. "We managed to mend a few old fences," he said, his voice warm and full. "If only I'd said 'I'm sorry' years ago." Even better, he'd made genuine progress with his son and connected with his grandkids, learning the small but vital details about the sports they played and what they might study in college. Though Liz still felt complicit in Tony's plot to end his life, his improved outlook gave her a measure of comfort. Which wasn't to say she had no reservations about meeting new clients from the senior living community. She couldn't shake the notion that she and Gabbi were novices in a business with unpredictable stakes.

Trotting down the paved trail to the parking lot, Liz felt buoyed by the endorphins that made every run worth the initial aches and stiffness of her first mile. Minutes later, she breezed into Trader Joe's to pick up a bouquet of mixed flowers, chocolate chip cookies, and sparkling waters before driving to the house she and Dusty were still trying to sell. Their realtor, Chuck, was ushering another couple through the remodel, and Liz aimed to make the kitchen as welcoming as possible.

This time, it was a young engineer from a new electric car company called Tesla and his wife, a teacher. Tesla was preparing to open a dazzling new showroom in Menlo Park, a hopeful counterpoint to the shuttered businesses in town. Reports varied on whether the high-tech Roadsters would catch on outside the culture of early adopters in California. Would there ever be a convenient, widespread network of charging stations? But every man she knew, including Dusty and Ned, was itching to schedule a test drive. The buzz around Tesla shored up her faith that this young couple had the capacity to own their own home.

As she angled into the driveway, she found Dusty just leaving. Their lawnmower was stowed in the bed of his truck as well as some clippers and a rake. She noted that the grass and hedges appeared trimmed and healthy, and she smiled, flashing him a thumbs up. He winked at her and rolled down his window.

"Looks good, doesn't it? Hell, I'd buy this house."

She laughed, catching the updraft of his optimism. "I've got flowers and treats. And I'll turn on a little soft music." He slid his fist toward her, and she bumped her knuckles against his. Then he flipped over his palm and gave her hand a warm squeeze.

"I have a lucky feeling today," he said.

Liz gazed into his caramel eyes, finding both hopefulness and a flicker of desperation. The sale of this house would do more than improve their financial standing. It would ease the tension between them that had begun to feel like a wall of thick insulation, making it harder to hear and see one another. Touch one another.

"Me too," she said. "I feel lucky."

He squeezed her hand a second time before checking his watch. "Chuck will be here in twenty minutes. At eleven."

"I'll be quick."

Inside, she found a vase for the flowers and a pretty tray for the cookies. Before they'd put the house on the market, she and Dusty had staged the home in a spare but inviting style. Several trips to Ikea and Target had enabled them to find modern, affordable basics. Pieces from their own attic helped too. When Dusty assembled one of the twin's cribs in the small third bedroom and moved in her comfy rocking chair, the message was clear: *Behold, your ideal starter home!*

The house had been locked up for two weeks, so Liz pushed open a few windows and the screen door leading to the garden. Feedback from Chuck indicated that the backyard was something of a stumbling block. While it was large enough for a play structure and outdoor dining set, it was too small for a pool of any size. Well, not everyone could afford an "Atherton Acre," she reasoned. She stepped out on the patio and admired the Climbing Iceberg white roses she'd planted along the redwood fence, and the blooming rhododendron in the corner of the lot. If they were ever going to sell this place, a sunny day in June was the time.

Back inside, Liz set out the refreshments and flipped on the lights. Taking one last look around at the tasteful finishes, gleaming new appliances, and warm paint colors, she was struck by what a beautiful job Dusty had done. If it weren't for the stalled economy, a young family would likely have already moved in.

At home, Liz was eager to peel off her sweats and shower. Before undressing, she dropped to the carpeted floor in the family room, moving through several yoga positions to loosen her tight muscles. It was nearly noon, and the boys were still asleep. She couldn't fathom why they wasted so much of their summer weekends in darkened rooms, but they'd earned the time off. As Dusty explained, they were "recreational sleepers."

Last night, Ben had arrived home very late. Though the engine of his hybrid car was soundless and he could have made a stealthy entrance, he elected to whip up a fruit smoothie at 1:00 a.m. Liz had awakened to the high-speed whirr of their old blender. Annoyed as she was, at least she had proof of life. As her fellow mothers always said, nothing good happens after midnight.

Ben and Maddy had been out on their "half-year-anniversary" date. When Ben had mentioned their plans to mark this quasi-milestone and asked for a restaurant recommendation, she couldn't decide if it was sweet or absurd. Millennials never missed a chance to celebrate themselves. Even now, her sons, who would turn seventeen next month, expected an array of gifts and hoopla on their birthday. At forty-five, Liz could count the number of birthday parties she'd had on one hand. Of course, after the fire, her mother had little enthusiasm for balloons and pin-the-tail-on-the-donkey. Ned's birthdays, too, had come and gone with little fanfare.

As she flowed into a final downward dog, her untethered hair cascading toward the floor, she considered that a year ago she and Dusty had reached a truly legitimate anniversary: twenty years of marriage. The recession had yet to reach the Bay Area, and they'd both been swamped with work, agreeing to wait until things slowed down before properly celebrating the occasion. Ultimately, things slowed down too much, and they could no longer indulge themselves. Now she wished they'd booked a romantic getaway, or that Dusty had surprised her with a special ring or sparkling bracelet to mark the day. She moved to the couch and sighed. Maybe the kids were right to enjoy a half-year anniversary. Circumstances could change in an instant, and the opportunity would be lost.

Ready for a shower, she started down the hall as Ben emerged from his room looking positively Neanderthal. His hair spiked in every direction, his lips appeared parched, and his eyes were puffy. No doubt he had partied last night—but he seemed upset too. Perhaps there'd been some drama with Maddy. Was this a hangover with a side of heartache?

"Maddy just called." He raked his fingers through his hair and swallowed hard. "Haley—her little sister—was at Neptune's Water Park this morning with a bunch of friends. She was on a ride, and they think her seat harness was broken. When the boat took a sharp turn on the track, she fell out and hit the pavement."

Liz's hand flew to her mouth, stunned to think that the darling gymnast was injured. "Is she all right?"

He shook his head. "It was a long way down. She's at the hospital." He fumbled in the front pocket of his jeans and extracted his car keys. "I'm heading there now."

Jamie's door swung open and he stepped into the hall gripping his phone. His jaw hung open and he locked eyes with his brother, saying nothing. Dreadful news traveled fast. Even Jamie knew.

Hours dragged by as they waited on word from Ben. Liz tried to keep herself busy in the kitchen, scouring the oven and tossing out expired muffin mixes from the pantry. In a kind of parallel play, Dusty worked in the yard repairing sections of the back fence. At first, Jamie pitched in, pulling out the table saw from the garage and nailing a few new boards into place. But, eventually, he drifted inside and into his room, likely taking up his joystick.

Near dinner time, her mother called to discuss the Sunday matinee she and Liz had planned to attend tomorrow. Her father disapproved of his wife going to a theater where fellow viewers might have coughs and colds. What about her compromised immune system? But Joanie had her heart set on seeing *Slumdog Millionaire*.

"I heard there's a marvelous dance segment," she said.

"I'm sorry, Mom. I can't go." Liz was reluctant to share news of the accident, but her parents had met Maddy several times and had shown a genuine interest in their grandson's first love. Liz told her what she knew, little as it was.

"My God, I hope that poor child pulls through," Joanie said. "For everyone's sake, but especially for the mother."

"Yes, for everyone's sake," Liz said. "Maddy and Haley are so close," she added.

A beat passed between them. "No one suffers like the mother."

Liz suppressed an urge to hang up. Now was not the time to engage in a misery competition; an eleven-year-old's life hung in the balance. But it vexed her to think that, after all these years, her mother still didn't acknowledge the pain that she, Liz, had also endured.

"We can reschedule, Mom, once Haley is out of the woods. I'll call you tomorrow with an update."

Moments later, she received a text from Ben: *She's still in surgery. I won't be home for dinner.*

For six days, Haley Chan lay in a coma at the Children's Hospital, lingering between this world and the other. Ben took a leave of absence from his coaching job so that he could remain at Maddy's side. Each morning before he drove away to the patient waiting room on the third floor, Liz slipped bag lunches full of roast chicken sandwiches, summer fruit, and freshly baked cookies into his backpack. If nothing else, she could provide a little sustenance for Ben and the Chan family.

Around town, everyone knew of the shocking accident, and the tight-knit community was holding its collective breath. Unable to concentrate at the office, Liz found some relief digging in the garden at their remodel on Pine Street, pulling weeds and deadheading roses. The Tesla engineer and his wife had expressed a keen interest in buying their house and were reportedly meeting with mortgage brokers and writing up an offer. Liz and Dusty were relieved, but they wouldn't discuss their good news until Haley had turned the corner.

At home where Ben was largely absent, Jamie appeared restless, and he confessed to having difficulty sleeping again. In the evenings after work, he was sliding back into the video game vortex, ignoring Liz's requests to unplug. When she phoned Dr. Noah for advice, filling him in on their connection to Haley Chan, his recommendation surprised her. "This is a frightening time for your family," he said. "Maybe Jamie is managing his feelings of being powerless and anxious about death by vanquishing enemies in a virtual universe. Let him be for now. Talk to him when you can, but give him a little space." If dominating digital demons could relieve Jamie's anxiety in any way, Liz was onboard. She figured it was better than self-medicating with pot.

Late on Saturday, a week after the catastrophic fall at the water park, Liz and Dusty were watching TV when they received the text from Ben they'd all been dreading. *They're taking Haley off life support.* Liz moaned and pitched forward, feeling faint and fighting tears, while Dusty got to his feet and began to pace. He tried reaching Ben, but his calls went straight to voicemail. Eventually, she and Dusty drifted to bed where they slept fitfully until daybreak.

At 6:00 a.m. on Sunday, Liz sat at the kitchen table gripping her second cup of coffee. She peered out the window to see the delivery man winging folded newspapers from his battered station wagon. The *Mercury News* landed on her doorstep with a thunk, and she moved sluggishly to retrieve it. As Ben explained in a call after midnight, the doctors had tried everything to save Haley, including removing part of her skull to help relieve the swelling of her brain. But the little gymnast never regained consciousness. Ben and Maddy had been napping in the hospital's family center when Kyle Chan appeared, stunned and unshaven, to tell them his baby was gone. Tammy had refused to leave the girl's bedside.

Liz cracked the door and bent down for the paper, noticing the date: June 22, 2008, a day that would cast a pall over the Chan family for years to come. For Liz's family, the indelible page in the calendar was July 20th, 1973. That morning after the fire, when her father had picked her up from the slumber party, he, too, had been stunned and unshaven. He, too, had lost his baby. But he didn't tell Liz at first. He drove her to a motel where she would find Ned—fetched from camp by their uncle—but neither her sister nor her mother. She remembered her dad gripping her hand and smelling of smoke.

Liz heard a shuffling sound in the kitchen and came in to find Ben. He pulled out a chair at the table and sank into it, groaning with exhaustion. When he turned his face to meet her gaze, she couldn't locate her boy. She saw a man now, christened by sorrow.

"She was such a great kid," he said quietly. "Never could sit still. Always doing handsprings and backflips in the yard. And climbing on my back like a monkey."

Liz understood that Ben wasn't simply close to Maddy; he had insider status with her whole family. Over the past six months, he'd been Maddy's boyfriend, but Haley's older brother as well. And her parents had allowed him to witness the most intimate, final hours of their daughter's life.

"What can I do for the Chans?" she asked. "Can I bring them more meals?"

Ben rubbed the soft stubble starting along his jaw line. "Yeah, that would be good, Mom. And maybe you could help them with Haley's—what do you call it—arrangements? That's what you do now, right?"

Images of Maggie's small, pink coffin darted through her mind. *Not again,* she thought. Not another fresh-faced little girl bound for the earth. Planning services for old people was one thing. This was too hard; she couldn't do it. Getting to her feet, she cinched the belt around her bathrobe tighter and made her way to the microwave to reheat her coffee. She was buying time, searching for the words to form her excuse.

"It would mean a lot to me if you helped them out," Ben said.

Returning to her seat at the table, Liz reached out to squeeze his shoulder. "I'll give it some thought," she said. Knowing, and dreading, that she would do what he asked.

Chapter 18

*I*n the second week of July, Liz and Gabbi drove together to the home of Tammy and Kyle Chan to discuss their daughter's Celebration of Life. Strictly speaking, the arrangements had already been taken care of. The child's funeral and burial had taken place the Sunday before. It had been a small, mostly family affair at a Presbyterian church in Burlingame, just up the freeway. Liz had been deeply grateful that the pastor and a local mortuary had managed all the details for that terribly difficult day. But she'd been anxious about Ben and Maddy.

Just before Ben had left for the service, dressed in a dark, somber suit from the back of Dusty's closet, she pleaded with him not to go to the cemetery. "Take it from me. You don't want to see that little girl lowered into the ground—and that goes double for Maddy." She alluded so rarely to her sister's death that Ben had listened intently and nodded in agreement. Hours later, both Ben and Maddy had opted out of the graveside service. They'd returned home and slipped into his bedroom, closing the door. From down the hall, Liz could hear the click of the bolt being set and then the muffled sounds of the poor girl weeping. She'd let them be. It was not the day to enforce house rules, and she sensed that Maddy would find refuge with Ben behind that closed door many more times in the weeks ahead.

Gabbi pulled up to the Chans' mailbox and turned off the engine. On the doorstep of the two-story house with gray shingles and white wood trim, they spotted Tammy shaking the hand of a distinguished-looking man in a well-cut suit. He tipped his head to her before turning to leave.

"I wonder if that's their attorney," Gabbi said. Liz was wondering the same thing. Everyone in town seemed to know that the Chans had hired a powerful law firm to help them sue Neptune's Water Park for the wrongful death of their daughter. "You can't blame them for wanting to wage holy hell against Neptune's. I mean, you send your kid off for a little fun in the water and she winds up dead? Because of faulty equipment? Heads should roll for that."

"Agreed," Liz said, pushing open her door and stepping onto the quiet street. But she feared for the peace—the very survival—of Maddy's family. They needed time to mourn the child, to grow accustomed to the absence of her precious, singular voice in the house. To learn to look past the empty chair, the darkened bedroom. A lawsuit in the public eye would give them no such time. Even now, the local papers were feeding on the tragic accident with an appetite that appalled her.

Walking next to Gabbi toward the front door, Liz felt nervous about meeting another grieving mother. She recalled her awkward exchange outside the bank with Rachel Matsen after her son had overdosed in April. But Tammy Larkin Chan, neat and professional in a navy dress accessorized with pearls, appeared dry-eyed and ready to get down to business.

"Thank you for being so prompt," she said, brushing back a strand of soft brown hair and ushering them into her foyer. A sickly-sweet fragrance engulfed them, and

Liz glanced through an opening to the kitchen where flower arrangements covered every countertop and table. Unopened condolence cards hung from several of the potted orchids and lilies, and it struck Liz that the Chans must have a staggering network of friends and colleagues.

While Tammy poured coffee into china cups, the women exchanged what would have been pleasantries under different circumstances. Tammy thanked Liz for the dinners she'd sent over and remarked on what a fine young man Ben was. "Haley had quite a crush on him," she said, her voice catching momentarily. "She'd always dreamed of having a brother." Liz assured her the feelings were mutual, that Ben had taken a real shine to Maddy's little sister.

In the dining room, wrapped in elegant pinstriped wallpaper, they took their seats around a polished oval table. Moments later, Kyle Chan joined them with an air of reluctance. In contrast to his wife, the trim, black-haired man wore jeans and a long-sleeved T-shirt, loafers without socks. The circles under his eyes and the sallow cast of his skin suggested insomnia. When he shook Liz's hand, he seemed to gaze right through her, searching for someone else in the room he would never find. His expression was unsettling yet familiar to her. Thirty-five years ago, she'd seen it in the face of her mother.

Tammy's manicured hands lay on a thin stack of papers, and Liz understood that their client had a clear view of what she wanted. She passed out her agenda notes and looked up, removing her reading glasses.

"Haley was such a special girl," she began. "I know every parent feels that way about their kids. But she wasn't just a good student and gifted gymnast, she was a *performer*." Gabbi and Liz nodded in unison. They'd read the girl's obituary—presumably Tammy had written and distributed it to the press—describing her medal-winning competitions at the local and state levels. And Liz had seen a video clip on the evening news featuring one of Haley's dazzling routines. She'd marveled at the child's graceful leaps and perfect flips. It seemed impossible, unbearable, that so much exuberant talent had been snuffed out on the hot pavement of an amusement park.

"Our girl loved to dance and sing too," continued Tammy. "So, Kyle and I thought it would be appropriate to hold her memorial at the new Burkhart Performing Arts Center." She turned toward her husband, waiting for him to chime in, but he stared at his coffee mug, saying nothing. "The stage and multimedia capabilities will allow us to have music, video, and a range of speakers. And, with a 400-seat capacity, everyone will be welcome to come."

"For God's sake, Tammy, we aren't putting on a show," Kyle said, sitting up in his high-backed chair and grimacing. Liz raised and lowered her chin ever so slightly in a gesture of solidarity.

"I didn't say it was a show," Tammy snapped. "It's a fitting tribute to our baby—whom we'll never see again—because of those idiots, those *murderers* at Neptune's." She grabbed at a box of tissues and furiously dabbed her long-lashed blue eyes.

"Your family has been through so much," Gabbi broke in gently. "You can trust us to create a beautiful celebration of your daughter's life that will strike just the right balance. Nothing too showy," she added, nodding at Kyle.

Typically, Gabbi reserved her honey voice and kitten gloves for distressed brides or nervous party hosts. But Liz could see that her calming, confident manner was a godsend in emotionally wrought situations like this one.

"Why don't you tell us a bit more about your vision for the tribute. And then we'll come back next week with a proposal," she added.

"That sounds fine," Kyle said as he pulled himself to his feet, the antique chair creaking and sighing as it gave him up. "I'll let Tammy take it from here."

After he left the room, Tammy visibly relaxed. "He's not himself," she said. "Kyle drove Haley to most of her meets and was her unofficial coach in many ways. They were so tight. And now, with a lawsuit getting underway... well, he just isn't sleeping. Or eating."

"I can't imagine how devastating this must be," Gabbi said, glancing sideways at Liz.

Liz didn't have to imagine. Should she share her story of losing a sister—and, for many years, a mother? No, she didn't want to make this meeting about her. What she wanted was to jot down the details for the poor child's service and get the hell out of there. She couldn't bear thinking about Haley's ghastly accident and memorial much longer.

"Why don't we discuss the particulars," Liz said. "Looks like you have a strong start here in your notes."

Tammy had set the date for Saturday afternoon, August 16th, 4:00 p.m. It was a week before classes resumed in the local schools, so Haley's friends and other community members would likely be in town and free to attend. Thankfully, the performing arts center was available.

"I'm reaching out to those who meant the most to Haley about giving eulogies. Her coach will speak, and so will one of her favorite teachers," Tammy said. "By mid-August, I'm hoping Maddy will be ready to go on stage too." Liz trained her eyes on her notebook. She didn't like the idea of pressuring Maddy to eulogize her sister. The girl was feeling fragile and depressed. Pre-season soccer workouts had begun, and Maddy confided in her that she was having trouble keeping up. Liz worried that Tammy would push her too hard, especially now that she had only-child status.

Tammy moved through more agenda items. "Between speakers, we'd like to present a reel of Haley's competition highlights put to music. And what do you think about having her teammates perform a routine of floor exercises—in her honor?"

"That sounds marvelous," Gabbi cooed. "It would add such an upbeat element to the program." Under the table, Gabbi stepped on Liz's foot, prodding her to act more engaged. But it seemed to Liz that they were hurrying down the path toward producing the very show Kyle had feared. Under no circumstances would she let a child's memorial service become a three-ring circus.

"So, you can handle all the AV production, as well as the food and beverage?" Tammy asked. "And the programs? The printing?"

"Of course," Gabbi said. "Soup to nuts."

Tammy gazed out the divided windows of the French doors to the rose garden beyond. "I've worked in public relations for twenty years. Designed and run countless events—hotel openings, product launches, presentations for the press. But I can't do this without help." She reached for another Kleenex and wiped her cheek where a few tears had appeared, streaking her powdered blush. "I really need you both to do the heavy lifting." The woman looked utterly spent, and it dawned on Liz that the attorney had probably been here for hours before their arrival.

"Tammy, we're here for you," Liz said. "Whatever you need, just let us know." She reached across the table and touched Tammy's arm, then gathered her notes and stood up. It was time to go. "We'll check out the website for the performing arts center and get the layout. As I recall, there's an outdoor courtyard that would be a lovely spot for a reception following the service."

Tammy looked up at Liz and nodded. "Yes, I was thinking the same thing."

Gabbi joined Liz and the two of them said goodbye, assuring Tammy they could find their way out.

As she drove Liz home, Gabbi was unusually quiet. Typically, following a meeting with a client to discuss an event, they brainstormed all the way back to the office—mulling over design themes, entertainment options, sit-down dinner versus buffet. But today, Gabbi turned on the radio and appeared lost in thought.

Pulling in behind Dusty's truck in the driveway, she faced Liz but kept the engine running. "It hadn't occurred to me that this would happen."

"That what would happen?"

"That we'd have to plan memorials for children."

"It was always a real possibility for me," Liz said.

"I get that now. Jesus, I can't believe your mom and dad survived this hell. And you and Ned too."

"Somehow, we muddled through," Liz said.

"Once this service is over, we'll try to book more weddings. When the economy picks up."

"*If* the economy picks up," Liz said, heaving herself out of the car.

Chapter 19

*L*iz was aggressively ignoring the to-do list for Haley Chan's memorial that lay on her desk. Yesterday, she and Gabbi met to discuss the timeline for speakers and performances, music playlists, and party rentals for the reception. The event was squarely in Touchstone's wheelhouse, and for her partner it seemed to have become just another job. How she envied Gabbi's ability to compartmentalize things. In stark contrast, Haley's death resuscitated painful memories for Liz. And once she started rolling down a dark path, Liz could spiral after simply watching the morning news.

Earlier, at breakfast, she'd seen a segment about a British journalist who'd been killed—beheaded—by a terrorist in the Middle East. The image of the disheveled, doomed war correspondent kneeling in the desert while a masked figure prepared to saw his neck with a knife had made her head swim. Hours later, she couldn't stop summoning the horror of that murder.

Liz understood that most people could watch that segment on NBC and enjoy a poached egg on buttered toast a moment later. Not her. Morbid thoughts had stalked her since she learned that firemen had lifted Maggie's small, lifeless body from a closet where she'd hidden from the flames. That day, while her mother lay sedated in a local hospital, her father had assured her and Ned in a voice hoarse with grief that "the fire never touched your sister. She put her blankie over her head and drifted off to sleep." It had been comforting to know that Maggie hadn't been burned in any way. But then Liz began to fret that her six-year-old sister had been all alone in that closet, terrified and gasping for air. Did she cry for their mother? For *her?* These were questions that still slithered their way back to her.

Determined to chart a new course for her thoughts, Liz got up to refresh her coffee and reviewed a preliminary budget for the memorial with Gabbi. The ping of an arriving email drew her attention back to her computer screen. Members of her high school class were planning a belated twenty-fifth reunion at the end of the year. She scanned the names on the planning committee and noted that Peter Levine, her old beau, was among them. To spark interest and attendance, the committee had started a Facebook page where alumni could share photos, RSVP to events, and track down long-lost classmates. There was a push for everyone to join Facebook, but Liz was reluctant to initiate an account. Wasn't that online social stuff meant for the kids? More to the point, there was something creepy about creating a profile that revealed aspects of your family and work that virtually anyone could see.

"Just do it," Gabbi said, peering over her shoulder. "You can include a description about Touchstone Events. It's essentially free advertising. I did it ages ago."

Liz wondered what in her life would be worth viewing. As far as a description of their business was concerned, she was inclined to leave out the death-related events. No need to give her classmates something to gossip about. *Did you hear that Liz Boyle Becker and Gabbi Rossi are, what, undertakers now?*

"Okay, I'll do it," she sighed. "But I'll have to wait until I dig up a decent picture of myself."

"Lame excuse," Gabbi said. She disappeared for a moment and returned with her digital camera. Liz hadn't seen it since the Perkinses' funeral where she dropped it and nearly cracked the lens. "Why don't you go brush your hair and put on some lipstick? I'll take your pic and then help you upload it to your page. No charge," she added with a wink.

Liz hauled her purse to the bathroom where the florescent light made her skin tone look positively corpse-like. Here it was midsummer, and she still hadn't found the time to get even a hint of a tan, a single freckle. Groping in her bag, she found a comb and a tiny tube of lip gloss, but no blush. She pinched her cheeks to bring some color into them, something she'd seen her mother do long ago while standing before a mirror in a restaurant bathroom.

"Okay, ready for my glamour shot," she muttered. Gabbi flicked open the blinds, letting in some warm July light, and positioned her near a potted ficus tree. Then, she raised her camera and pointed it at Liz, who unfastened the top buttons of her linen blouse, hoping to appear less like a schoolmarm. Gabbi nodded approvingly.

"Smize!" she instructed: *smile with your eyes.* Liz tried to oblige, flaring her eyes as wide as possible to animate her smile. "No, please, stop doing that," Gabbi said, lowering her camera. "You look like a serial killer. Just relax and think of something that makes you happy."

Now Liz was frowning; her mind had gone blank. She searched for an image that would light her up from within and came up with nothing. Of course, her family brought her happiness. And her home. But how long could she and Dusty hold on to it? The Tesla engineer still hadn't presented an offer on the remodel. Then, out of the blue, a scene appeared in the reel of her memory, and she savored it momentarily before turning toward her partner.

"Got it," Gabbi said, putting away the camera. "And whatever's going through your mind? I'll take two."

Minutes later, Liz's Facebook page was done. When she saw the profile photo that Gabbi had uploaded, she blushed. The memory that had put a dreamy smile on her lips was of a lingering kiss in the public library just blocks from where she now sat. No doubt, thoughts of the class reunion had stirred up the stolen embrace. During her junior year of high school, she and Peter Levine had discovered that though they were in different U.S. History classes, they'd both requested to write their World War II term paper on the Marshall Plan. Weeks earlier, Ned had introduced them after a tennis match, and she'd felt a spark of mutual attraction. But their paths hadn't crossed again until they bumped into one another outside the school cafeteria.

"So, you're the one who's checked out all the books I need," he'd teased. "Any chance you could share at the town library tonight? I'll smuggle in some snacks."

When Liz arrived at the bustling public library, Peter had already staked out a table in the back and spread around a few books to lay claim to it. At first, he was all business, speaking in hushed tones about the plan to help rebuild Europe and impede the spread of Communism. But after an hour of scribbling notes, he led her to a back room full of dusty reference tomes where he pulled a box of Raisinets from his pocket and then a package of Red Vines. Somehow he'd known her favorites.

Seated side-by-side on musty industrial carpeting, they'd talked for hours. Peter had his sights on going away to college, as far as the East Coast. For Liz, a California school was probably in the cards, accustomed as she was to keeping an eye on things at home. When they found themselves down to the last Red Vine, Peter swiped it up and held it before her. She leaned in to bite the twist of candy, but he whisked it away and boldly introduced his mouth to hers. As she'd tasted the sweet flavor on his lips, he'd reached around her waist to pull her closer and she had felt both lost and found in him.

Screeching tires and the blast of an angry horn outside her window jolted Liz from her daydreaming. She shook her head to free herself of those ancient, foolish memories and gazed back at her computer screen. As she moved the cursor to quit her Facebook page, she was amazed to find her first friend request, sent from Tammy Chan.

She accepted the request and navigated to Tammy's home page where she encountered dozens of photos of Haley at every age, every stage. In one, the child in a blue tutu couldn't have been more than six, Maggie's age for the rest of eternity. An old grief coursed through Liz as she considered the terrible luck that struck them both down.

While every picture of Haley was heartbreaking, Tammy's photo commentary made Liz twitch in her chair. Above a close-up of Haley with a gold medal around her neck and her arms raised in the V of victory, she'd typed: *Our little champion, taken too soon but forever our pride and joy.* And next to an image of the gymnast captured in mid-air above a balance beam, *How we miss our soaring baby girl. When she left us, she took the sun with her. Today, I couldn't get out of bed.* Beneath the various posts, scores of friends had left messages of condolences and others had, bizarrely, "liked" her entries. Liz was dumbfounded by the entire exchange and motioned for Gabbi to take a look.

"Tammy shouldn't be posting all this stuff online," she said while Gabbi leaned in to survey the pictures. "It's too personal."

"We can't judge her. Imagine if it were you."

"I am imagining it's me. The last thing I would do is make a spectacle out of my child's death."

Gabbi straightened and removed her reading glasses. "'Spectacle' is your word. She might say 'sharing her grief.'"

"Someone should tell her to stop."

"That's definitely not our place. Besides, Tammy Chan is our client, remember? And the customer is always right."

Though never a quiet sleeper, Dusty had caught a summer cold and his congestion had morphed his snore into a roar. After an hour of trying to tune him out, Liz dragged a blanket and pillow to the couch in the family room. The silence there did nothing to summon sleep, and she found herself thinking about Tammy Chan and Facebook. Maybe the woman was actually onto something. Maybe unpacking your grief before a community of watchful eyes helped you move forward. *A trouble shared is a trouble halved.*

It seemed to Liz now that when they'd buried little Maggie, laid out in her favorite *Scooby-Doo* pajamas, they'd buried so much more. They buried the freedom to talk about her, to openly miss her. In the Puritan tradition of pushing pain into the past, they'd buried their feelings of anger and guilt, and love. Trying to keep that impish, curly-haired child below the surface of their lives had driven her mother to the liquor cabinet, and Ned to the boisterous homes of neighbors and friends. It had turned her father—once a man who loved nothing better than trotting through the back door to greet his family at suppertime—into a workaholic. And what had burying Maggie so entirely done to her, exactly? She wasn't sure, but Liz had sometimes wondered: If she had been the one to perish in the fire, would her family have tried to un-remember her?

She recalled the first anniversary of her sister's death in July of 1974. In a break from their custom of iron-clad silence concerning Maggie, her parents had decided to visit her gravesite. They agreed that she and Ned could remain alone at home; after all, he had just turned thirteen, and she was eleven. Ned had shot her a sidelong glance, flashing a thumbs-up, and her knees had nearly buckled in relief. She dreaded the idea of going to the cemetery, of spotting the small, rounded headstone that bore witness to the terrible brevity of her sister's life: *Margaret Ann Boyle, 1967–1973.*

As her mother stepped toward the front door holding a bouquet of flowers and a stuffed bear with the tags still on, she turned to her and said, "Don't worry, honey. We'll be back in a jiff." Her voice sounded normal, almost cheerful, but the dark crescents under her glassy eyes and the odor of cigarettes on her breath made Liz's stomach clench. Her mother had supposedly quit smoking a year ago—right after the fire—but in recent weeks she seemed to be always hunting for matches.

After their parents' Oldsmobile wagon had disappeared from view, Ned jumped to his feet and dashed outside to the tree fort where they'd stashed their candy from Chip Taylor's twelfth birthday bash. Liz chased after him, afraid he'd scarf down her share. The party favor bags were like the second coming of Halloween, stuffed with chocolate bars, Bazooka bubble gum, and jawbreakers. In the boys' bags, Mrs. Taylor had also included a small cap gun. Liz marveled at the loot; their mother would never allow so many teeth-rotters, let alone a toy that produced the sound of a gunshot.

Sitting cross-legged on the plywood floor littered with dead leaves and the crispy carcasses of assorted bugs, Liz sucked on a giant jawbreaker while Ned loaded his gun with a roll of red caps. When he was satisfied that it was ready, he pointed the gray gun with the plastic ivory handle directly at her forehead.

"Close your eyes," he said quietly. "This won't hurt a bit."

She gagged, spitting out the purple ball of candy into the palm of her hand, and screamed. "Put that down or I'll tell Mom!"

"Relax, Izzie. I'm just foolin'." He sighed in a way that made her feel small, like a dumb little cry baby. Then, squinting his left eye and looking down the length of his bare right arm, he aimed the gun outside the opening of the treehouse and pulled the trigger. Nothing happened. He yanked back the cheap, metal trigger again and again, to no avail. "What a piece of crap," he said, dropping it with disdain. But then an idea dawned on him, and he reached up to a shelf their father had built and found a sturdy, boy-sized hammer. He pulled the strip of caps from the gun and laid it flat on the floorboards before raising the hammer above his head.

"Watch this," he said, grinning. And when the blunt nose of the tool struck the small black dots of combustible powder, the treehouse shook, and the loud crack of the caps made Liz cover her ears in alarm. A smoky, burning smell filled the small interior space of the fort, and Ned's smile vanished, replaced by a grim line at odds with his freckled nose and summer-bleached hair.

"Our old house smelled like this—after the fire," he said. "Dad and I went in to get some stuff while you and Mom stayed at the motel." Liz met his troubled green eyes and nodded, grateful that he'd confided in her. But when she started to ask a question about that day, he shoved the hammer back on the shelf and slipped the broken cap gun into his back pocket. "I'm hungry," he said. "Let's make lunch." He retreated down the ladder and disappeared into the house without another word on the subject.

Sometime later, their parents returned from the cemetery, and when her mother came indoors, she neglected to remove her Jackie O sunglasses. Her father guided her down the hall to their bedroom and hurried back minutes later, rubbing his hands together in a display of excitement. "Turn on the TV," he said. "They're rebroadcasting the first landing of Neil Armstrong and Buzz Aldrin on the moon!" Liz had been too young to care about the moonshot five years earlier, but now she found her father's enthusiasm contagious.

She settled on the sofa next to him while Ned went to the kitchen for chips and dip. As she stared into their new TV with built-in speakers, video appeared from Apollo 11's historic four-day journey. Images of the vast, black galaxy and pinpoints of starlight had always given Liz a jittery feeling. Now the emptiness of space took on a terrible meaning. It struck her that on their voyage from Earth to the distant moon, the astronauts had never passed through heaven. NASA cameras had failed to beam back pictures of a great, gated kingdom in the sky. They had captured no silver-winged angels. No white-bearded God in flowing robes to gather children into his loving arms. What did this strange vacancy in the cosmos mean? Was her little sister's spirit wandering lost and alone among the cold stars?

Sitting stock still, tears momentarily spilled from her eyes. She turned to her father for answers, for comfort. But he was staring past the slow-mo images of Neil Armstrong moving about in a clownish white spacesuit. She followed his gaze out the window to the fresh-cut lawn of their new house, a yard where Maggie would never kick a ball or turn a cartwheel. She knew, then, that her father was only pretending to care about Apollo 11. And that, down the hall, her mother was weeping behind a locked door.

Chapter 20

*L*iz and Gabbi arrived at the venue for Haley Chan's memorial nearly three hours before the service was scheduled to begin. Gabbi beelined indoors, intent on finding the in-house AV guys to do a test run of the featured video, and to make sure the podium and mics were set up. For her part, Liz headed to the courtyard behind the performing arts center to check on prep for the reception. She was relieved to find staff from the rental company setting up tables and chairs, and a dozen market umbrellas to offer mourners relief from the late-afternoon sun. Everything was being placed precisely to her specifications. But when she spotted two men hauling in boxes of liquor and tubs for ice, she felt a spike of concern.

At a meeting with the Chans a week ago, Liz had expressed the opinion that it wasn't necessary to serve alcohol at an eleven-year-old's memorial.

"I'm afraid I have to respectfully disagree with my partner," Gabbi broke in. Rotating her attention from husband to wife like a plug-in fan blowing cool air, she explained that though they had meticulously planned the memorial to feature upbeat music, images, and eulogies, "tears will be shed, and hearts will ache over the senseless loss of your gifted little girl." She paused before adding, "It's my belief that at the reception following the service, your close friends and relatives might find a bit of comfort in a mixed drink or glass of wine." Tammy had nodded in full agreement, brushing away a sudden tear, and added a full bar to the list of "must haves" for the event. Kyle, as usual, said little, deferring to his wife.

Though Gabbi's reasoning hadn't been wrong, Liz suspected her real motive was to secure another way to beef up the bill. Every added element would put more money into Touchstone's meager coffers. But were Tammy and Kyle aware of the ballooning expenses? Liz had dropped off a preliminary budget nearly a month ago, but so much had changed. Recently, Tammy had become fixated on the notion of creating special leotards for Haley's teammates to wear during their tribute performance—leotards with Haley's face imprinted on the front. "When the music starts and the eight girls step on stage, Haley will be one of them," Tammy said in a voice thick with emotion. Liz quickly agreed, scribbling down specs and wondering who on earth could fabricate custom gymnastic outfits in ten working days. Miraculously, she'd found a vendor, but expediting the order had nearly doubled the cost. And then there was the climbing headcount.

Liz had been enjoying a quiet evening at home after fixing dinner for her parents. While paging through the local paper reviewing tips for drought-tolerant gardening, she'd happened upon a "come one, come all" invitation to Haley's memorial. She'd been absolutely stunned. It was one thing to post information regarding the service in an obit, but placing a half-page announcement in the town rag opened the door to countless more attendees. And why hadn't Tammy mentioned her intention to run it? After all, Touchstone was supposed to be in charge of all the details.

It was impossible to know if Haley's classmates and their families would spend one of the last days of summer attending a memorial (or if parents even approved of such an early introduction to death). But she and Gabbi had to assume that the venue would be filled to capacity. Providing food and beverage for up to four hundred people would cost a fortune. Liz had emailed the Chans with updates of the escalating expenditures and requested approvals with signature. But Tammy had neither signed nor initialed the revised estimates, merely replying that "everything looks fine." Though they had received a deposit from the Chans, Liz had distributed every penny to their subcontractors, promising that their client would pay in full when the service was over.

Moving toward an umbrella for cover, Liz sighed, feeling guilty for worrying about money at a time like this. But she and Gabbi were in no position to comp their services or underwrite hard costs. Zoey was returning to college next month, and Gabbi had a stream of incoming bills, while she and Dusty still had the two mortgages. The engineer from Tesla had finally made a solid offer on their home—how thrilled they'd been! But as they were finalizing terms, he learned that his wife, after years of fertility treatments, was pregnant with triplets. Understandably, the expecting mother wanted to be near family, so they returned to Sacramento. With summer drawing to a close, Liz's hope of selling the remodel during the high season was fading.

She glanced up to see Manny from The Flower Hour pulling a wagon loaded with floral arrangements. The color theme of the memorial was blue and gold, "the color of champions" as Tammy explained, and Manny had prepared dozens of vases brimming with periwinkle hydrangeas and yellow roses. Liz waved him over.

"Those look gorgeous. But is it too early to put them out in this hot sun?"

"Oh, no, they'll be fine. I've got them in some nice cool water."

A young woman on the wait staff was positioning crisp linens on the tables, and Manny set down a vase at the center of one.

"All this blue," he said. "It looks like the shower for a baby boy that I arranged flowers for last week."

"If only we were here for a baby shower," Liz said, pushing back a wave of fatigue. She helped him unload more vases and distributed them around the courtyard. When they were done, he handed her a cheerful bouquet of daisies and gave her a gentle hug.

"Thanks—as always—to you and Gabbi for the business. Hang in there."

After he left, Liz returned to the building's entrance and found Zoey parked out front, the hatchback of her Subaru gaping open. Inside were boxes of freshly printed programs. Her digital art classes at college were paying off nicely. She'd designed and produced Haley's eight-page program by working with Tammy on the content and importing photos from Facebook.

"Hi, Liz! Can you run these in? I need to go back to the office. I forgot the dang butterflies!" She unloaded the programs on the curb and then jumped in the car and sped away.

Good Lord, the butterflies. They'd been another point of contention with Gabbi. Tammy had wanted something "uplifting and dramatic," and Gabbi had pitched the idea of releasing live monarchs at the onset of the reception. "My angel would love that," Tammy said, crossing her hands over her heart.

But Liz absolutely hated this sort of thing. Live butterflies had to be FedExed the day before the event and stored at cool temperatures to keep them calm. Yet, in order for the insects to properly fly, they had to be warmed up prior to their release. The trick was to keep them from getting too cold or too hot. She remembered all too well the wedding in Napa where she'd left one hundred black and orange painted ladies in the back of her van. Although she'd cracked the windows to provide fresh air, the temperatures had soared and the interior grew too warm. At the allotted time for the bride and groom to set them free, she'd removed the lid of the container to find nearly all of the beautiful creatures dead. The bride had expressed only a fleeting disappointment—it was on to the couple's first dance. But Liz had been crushed by the sight of all those folded wings that would never open.

When she'd grumbled to Gabbi about having yet another logistic to manage, Gabbi hadn't been the least bit sympathetic.

"Stop being such a party pooper."

"It's not a party," Liz countered.

"Look," Gabbi said, setting down her latte. "Tammy Chan will never have the chance to throw her daughter a party for prom. Or graduation. Or for her wedding. Let her go big with this memorial. Whatever she wants, we're going to give it to her."

Liz had left it at that, sucking it up and ordering five dozen live butterflies and a pricey viewing-release cage. But she'd insisted that Zoey keep an eye on the delicate colony during the service, shifting them to the shade when necessary. If anything could make a child's memorial even more depressing, it would be a batch of dead monarchs.

She glanced at her watch, stunned, as always, by how time accelerated before events when there was still so much to do. She left the programs on the table near the front doors and hurried inside to see if the caterers were set up in the industrial kitchen. Gabbi intercepted her in the foyer.

"Food is here," she said, wiping her mouth with a paper napkin. "The grilled cheese sammies with Gouda are perfection."

According to her mother, Haley's favorite post-workout splurge had been to go to Johnny Rockets café, score a booth, and devour grilled cheese sandwiches, French fries, and a shake. In her honor, Gabbi had arranged for the caterer to prepare a gourmet version of the diner's menu. There was little doubt that a buffet featuring grilled cheese triangles, pommes frites, and mint-chip shakes served in tall shot glasses would be a crowd pleaser.

"Great," Liz said. "And the video's all set? Mics working?"

"Affirmative. We're in good shape."

Minutes later, the Chan family arrived. Tammy appeared ready for Prime Time, wearing an elegant ivory suit accessorized with a lapis-blue scarf and gold jewelry in keeping with the color scheme. Her hair was swept up in a neat bun and her make-up was immaculate. Kyle, too, was dressed for the occasion in a navy sport coat, yellow tie. Maddy trailed behind in a sleeveless, powder-blue dress and ballet flats, her dark hair tied back with ribbons. She looked both fragile and exquisite, and Liz, knowing how terrified the girl was of public speaking, felt a pinch in her heart.

Tammy gripped the program, rolled like a diploma, and pointed it toward Liz. "This looks good," she said in a flat voice. "Will the boys be here to pass them out?"

As if on cue, Ben, Jamie, and several of Ben's pals from the baseball team filed in through the front doors. They were all wearing khaki pants and blue collared shirts, as requested. Bringing up the rear was Dusty, dressed like the boys, only his stomach sagged over his belted pants and his hair was alarmingly long—shaggy, even. How had she not noticed before? How had *he* not noticed? He waved at her and smiled briefly, careful not to appear cheerful under the circumstances. She waved back, tuning out the critical voice in her head. Dusty was here for her, ready to pitch in.

Ben sidled up to Maddy and took her pale hand into his, giving it a quick squeeze, and Liz saw her shoulders lower and her face brighten. How tender they were with each other, how truly in love. Last week, when Liz had unlocked the Prius to put the new registration and insurance cards in the glove box, she'd found a stash of condoms. She felt neither anger nor concern, only relief that they were being careful. How differently she'd felt just a few months ago. In the wake of Haley's death, whatever comfort the kids were finding in each other's arms was okay by her. Tammy—or Kyle—may have felt differently, but it wasn't her place to tell them what she knew.

"Hey, honey," Dusty said, his hand on her back. "I noticed the Event Parking signs and orange cones stacked in a corner out front. Shouldn't those be out?"

"Yes!" she said, her palm flying to her forehead. "The staff was supposed to put them out hours ago."

"I'll track someone down and get them in place. Be right back."

Something was always falling through the cracks. She pulled out the schedule in her tote to check the timeline. There was no sign of the minister who had conducted Haley's private funeral weeks earlier. When the Chans had approached him to open this public service with a prayer and to act as Master of Ceremonies, he'd kindly agreed. Surely he hadn't forgotten?

She heard a side door squeak open and was pleased to see a fit, fortyish-looking man carrying a gym bag. Liz recognized him from his photo in the program as John Wu, Haley's storied coach, and she raised a hand in greeting. On his heels were eight of Haley's former teammates. She was anxious to see how the custom leotards turned out, but the gymnasts were all wearing sweats over their body suits. The nervous hive of pre-teen girls buzzed into the auditorium to check out the enormous blue tumbling mat already on stage. When they were out of sight, the coach approached her.

"John Wu," he said, extending his hand and acknowledging Tammy with a nod. "Quick question. The girls are slated to do their routine at the end of the program. I was wondering, could they perform earlier? They're pretty wound up and keeping them on hold for nearly an hour is going to be tough. As you can imagine, losing Haley has been brutal for the kids. For all of us."

Before Liz could answer, Tammy spoke up. "I've given the program tremendous thought, John. I think the girls' tribute performance at the end will be so moving, so powerful. Each of those athletes has performed under pressure before. They'll be just fine." She touched his elbow and looked resolutely into his eyes before moving away in her shiny heels.

"Sorry," Liz said.

"Me too." He hurried off to find his girls, and Liz shifted her concern back to the minister, wondering what Plan B would look like if he didn't show. Though Gabbi had been raised Catholic, it wasn't likely she could wing an opening prayer. But she could certainly introduce speakers and adlib where necessary. "My best lighting is the limelight," she often joked.

The early birds were starting to arrive. No matter what the event—wedding, holiday gala, funeral—these folks arrived well ahead of time to secure the best parking and optimal seating. Her own parents were famous early birds. They'd considered coming today to support Maddy, but four o'clock was Joanie's post-chemo nap time, and Liz had encouraged them to stay home. Her mother appeared increasingly tired these days.

Out front, the twins were welcoming guests and handing out programs, and she took a moment to watch them. Ben smiled warmly and shook many hands whereas Jamie's smile appeared fixed, even mechanical. Interacting with so many people was daunting for him, but he was holding his own, and she felt the flush of a mother's pride. Behind him, she caught sight of Kyle Chan embracing a gray-haired man wearing a white-banded collar and blazer. The minister, Robert Barnes, was here. It was back to Plan A.

The auditorium was nearing capacity. Tammy's Facebook posts and newspaper announcement had spread the word far and wide. Entire families were filling up row after row of plush-back seats. Liz recognized a few Silicon Valley big shots—possibly clients of Kyle who, until recently, had worked in the mortgage banking group at Wells Fargo. Whether he'd left of his own choosing or had been released in the face of declining mortgage business, she didn't know.

Below her, she spotted the familiar faces of local middle school teachers and various pals of Ben and Maddy. The kids were stealing glances over their shoulders, checking out who from their pack was here. For many, it was their first memorial, and as tragic as it was, the service was nevertheless a *happening*, and there was a strange charge in the air. She vaguely remembered a similar stir at her sister's funeral.

The door clanked shut at the back of the theater, and Liz looked up to see Max Kohn, editor-in-chief for the local paper, stride in and take a seat. What was he doing here? No matter—it was time for the program to get underway.

The Chans settled into the front row. Tammy and Kyle were flanked by the minister and Laurie Yob, the fifth-grade teacher who would say a few words about Haley as an outstanding student. Ben sat next to Maddy, who was silently rehearsing her lines, her lips moving feverishly. Other relatives greeted one another in somber, hushed tones.

Near an exit, Dusty and Jamie had staked out three seats. Liz would join them and keep an eye on the speakers while Gabbi focused on AV issues. Somewhere outside, Zoey was tending butterflies and overseeing the last of the reception setup.

Just after 4:00 p.m., Liz asked Minister Robert Barnes to take the stage. He appeared to be her father's age, and, like Arnie, he was still in reasonable shape. He climbed the stairs to the podium and deftly adjusted the microphone. Then, spreading his arms, he thanked everyone for coming to honor the short but exceptional life of Haley Chan. After a brief recitation—"It broke our hearts to lose you, but you did not go alone, a part of us went with you the day God called you home"—he asked Miss Yob to share her thoughts about Haley.

As the attractive young teacher traded places with the minister, Liz received an SOS text from Zoey: *Cocktail bar is short on ice. Need $$ to get more.* She grabbed her wallet and slipped outside to deliver the cash. After the girl drove away, Liz checked on the monarchs, tucked under a flowering dogwood. The linen cover was still draped over the cage, and she lifted a corner to take a peek. A few of the butterflies were stirring, languidly opening and closing their velvet orange and black wings. So far, so good.

When she crept back to her seat, the video was playing and the soundtrack was deafening. Images of Haley dressed in adorable Halloween costumes and opening gifts on Christmas day gave way to the highlights of her gymnastics career. To the pop tunes of Taylor Swift and Justin Timberlake, the audience watched Haley in full living color on a thirty-foot screen as she spun around the uneven bars, flipped off the balance beam, and stuck every landing. Though it was a memorial service, people clapped thunderously at the end and many wiped away tears. Tammy acknowledged the crowd's response, glancing back over her shoulder and waving like the rodeo queen she once was.

Next up on the program was Maddy. As the video screen disappeared into the rafters, she fiddled with the microphone and laid her notes on the podium, appearing small and alone on stage. Viewing her from an angle, Liz could see her knees shake uncontrollably. Her eulogy was entitled "The ten things I'll miss the most about my sister Haley." Liz had a death grip on her armrests as she watched Maddy stumble through her first words. She glanced at Jamie, who looked as if he might be sick, and then turned to Dusty. "Don't worry," he whispered. "She'll settle in."

"...Number six: on Thursday nights, we loved watching *Gilmore Girls* and took turns braiding each other's hair. Even when she was really little, Haley could weave my hair into a perfect French braid...Number four: making chocolate chip and banana pancakes on Sunday mornings when there were no meets or soccer games. Best mornings ever!...Number one: whenever we lost power during a storm, Haley would crawl into bed with me. I'll miss being able to hold her close and comfort her." Her eyes fluttered shut and her voice broke as she added, "Hales, I'll miss everything about being your big sister."

Liz heard a strange sobbing noise and was mortified to discover it was coming from her own throat. Jamie stared at her in alarm, and she swallowed the next moan that threatened to escape. How she'd missed her own sister after the fire stole her away. Even decades later, the pain could possess her entirely. Feeling clammy and exposed, Liz focused back on Maddy. The dear girl, still shaky in her delicate blue dress, turned her attention to the front row where her mother nodded in approval. Smiling with relief, Maddy said a quick thank you, collected her notes, and scooted off the stage.

It was time for the grand finale: the tribute routine performed by Haley's teammates. The minister announced each of the girl's names, and they gathered stage left as John Wu gave them final instructions. Theater lights illuminated the mat where the gymnasts would do their tumbling, and the music began.

As the girls stepped into the downlighting, Liz could see the image of Haley's face on the front of their leotards. The first four girls to perform were a bit younger, nine or ten years of age, and Haley's eyes, button nose, and bright smile were clearly visible across their taut, flat chests. They darted toward the blue mat, and one after another they executed a flawless routine of diving somersaults, round-offs, and pirouettes.

But when the older group, the eleven- and twelve-year-olds, lined up to face the mat, the tallest girl, Sonya, pulled uncomfortably at her leotard and glanced at her coach, whispering something out of earshot. He motioned her forward, and when the light fell across her body, Haley's face appeared wildly distorted—in a Picasso cubist kind of way—due to the girl's breasts pushing against the skin-tight material. Next to Sonya, an elf-like teammate pointed and giggled. As Sonya initiated the sequence, she charged the mat like a crazed bull, over rotated on a front handspring, and landed unceremoniously on her rump. Groans and gasps escaped from the audience and Liz held her breath. Humiliated, Sonya leapt to her feet and fled the stage as tears streamed down her crimson cheeks.

After an excruciating standstill and several skipped beats, the three remaining gymnasts completed the routine. But there were more awkward missteps and fumbled elements—the jitters appeared to be as contagious as the chicken pox. When the music mercifully ended, the girls formed a line across the stage, held hands and bowed, their young faces grim with disappointment. Guests in the auditorium applauded politely, including, Liz noticed, Kyle and Maddy. But Tammy, her hands motionless in her lap, looked on with undisguised disapproval. Liz turned away, tamping down a feeling of intense dislike for her client.

As the applause waned, women collected their purses, and kids glanced around aiming to make a hasty escape. It was a far cry from the enchanting, poignant ending for the service that the Chans had scripted. Liz felt helpless, having no clue how to turn things around. The minister was scheduled to give a closing remark, but Gabbi hurried to the stage and grabbed the microphone, pulling it close to her glossy, coral lips.

"Thank you all for coming," she called out in a cheery voice that was over amplified. "Please join us in the courtyard for a special, yummy supper. We're serving Haley's favorite foods, including mini milkshakes, grilled cheese sandwiches, and beef sliders. For you adults, please help yourself to a refreshing drink at the bar."

Instantly, murmurs of genuine interest filled the auditorium and crowds began to push toward the exits. It amazed Liz how fast people could switch from mourning to excitement where free food was concerned. She peered down at the front row and was surprised to find the Chans already gone.

Dusty and Jamie left to check on the buffet stations—Liz was worried about yellow jackets swarming the meat—and Gabbi appeared at her side. Together, they made their way to the lobby where a young man in a gray suit was frantically distributing pin-on buttons with Haley's photo. "1997–2008" was printed at the top, "Taken too soon" at the bottom. Liz glanced at Gabbi who merely shrugged. "We never ordered those," she said. Tammy had gone rogue once again.

As they streamed through the doors into the warm, five o'clock sunlight, Liz was surprised to see the majority of the guests still gathered out front rather than around back at the reception. They appeared to be staring into the parking lot. There, she spied Tammy talking to a statuesque blonde reporter while a cameraman circled them, shifting his lens for a better angle. Kyle stood behind his wife with an arm wrapped stiffly around Maddy's shoulder. Rolling up close to them was a white van emblazoned with a red and black logo: *Channel 2 Eyewitness News*. A satellite dish was mounted on the roof.

Wordlessly, Gabbi and Liz wove their way into the throng of onlookers until they were within hearing distance of their client.

"Over four hundred people came here today to pay their respects to my daughter," Tammy said, dramatically dabbing at her eyes. "The callous, reckless owners of Neptune Water Park should know that Haley Larkin Chan was no ordinary girl. She was a phenome!"

"What on earth?" Liz wondered aloud. But Gabbi said nothing, leaning in to catch every word.

The reporter sidestepped over to Kyle, and Liz hoped—expected—that he would decline to comment. "And how about you, Mr. Chan? Do you feel your daughter was a potential Olympian?"

"I d-d-do," he stuttered into her menacing black microphone. He tipped his head back and paused, seeming to search for the right words. "The terrible, *avoidable* accident has broken our hearts and dashed the Olympic dream held by our close community." Here, the bearded cameraman panned the crowd. For her part, Maddy stared intently at her feet, and Liz felt a surge of affection for her—mixed with outrage that her parents would subject her to the media.

"This is exactly the kind of circus we wanted to avoid at all costs," she said.

Gabbi shook her head. "This is brilliant," she whispered. "Don't you see?"

"See what?"

"This was the plan all along. To get a ginormous crowd to show up today and put pressure on Neptune. Their legal team can play hardball with a single family, but they don't stand a chance against an entire town." She gazed admiringly in Tammy's direction. "In the court of public opinion, they'll lose big, and the waterpark will be doomed unless they pay up. My guess is that the lawsuit gets settled pronto."

"So, let me understand this," Liz said, feeling the temperature rise under her skin. "Our memorial service for a darling little girl is really a public relations campaign? A fucking stunt?"

"Jesus, Liz. For once, can't you look at the bright side? Trust me, the Chans will be richly compensated for that horrible accident. Neptune will be forced to fix their shitty equipment. And us? You've been so worried about how the Chans will pay for all of this." She paused to swing her arm out toward the sea of guests, the mounds of food and drink at the buffet stations. "This will be pocket change. We have nothing to worry about."

Liz stared into the face of her partner and stepped back. She felt dirty, duped, part of a charade. She'd been right about this death business. Unforeseen calamities had been in store for them. But her anger was dissipating, replaced by a staggering sense of defeat. For they had not properly celebrated the life of Haley Chan. Had not properly said goodbye with tenderness and love. The child had been crushed under the weight of their production, becoming almost an afterthought.

She looked up to see more media trucks driving through the gate. "I can't do this," she said. And without another word, she slipped away to her van and drove home.

Chapter 21

*L*iz's alarm went off and she reached over to silence it, hoping it didn't wake Dusty. After she'd bailed out of the memorial, she'd called him in tears, and he and the boys offered to stay to the bitter end, breaking down tables and boxing up the leftover booze. Understandably, he'd been exhausted by the time he returned home. When she was certain that he remained in a deep sleep, she crept out of bed to get the Sunday paper.

After a fortifying mug of dark roast, she flipped to the section that featured news on the Peninsula. There, she spotted a large color photo of Tammy Chan releasing the monarch butterflies. Around her, the little gymnasts reached for them, their fingertips just below the cloud of orange and black wings, and Liz exhaled a breath of relief that they'd survived to fly away. Below the picture, the caption read: *Four hundred attend memorial for Haley Chan, killed at Neptune Water Park.* She had to admit, the butterflies made for a perfect photo op. They would be viewed as a sweet offering to the spirit of little Haley—and add fuel to the outrage swirling around her death.

She poured herself a bowl of cereal and sat down to read the article. The reporter reviewed the grim details of the fatal accident and speculated on the lawsuit, suggesting that the Chans stood to gain as much as $20 million—more than even Gabbi could have imagined. Liz didn't begrudge them the money. If it could, in any way, mitigate the anguish of losing their child, she hoped they collected every last cent from the amusement park. What she hated was the calculated way the Chans had used their daughter's memorial to manipulate public opinion and influence the future outcome in court.

As she turned the page to finish the article, she was startled to find a quote from Gabbi.

> *"At Touchstone Events, we were honored to create a memorial tribute that helped people see what an extraordinary girl we had in our midst," said Gabbi Rossi, owner. "Haley Chan was a brilliant star in the making."*

A small photo of Gabbi was included, the "taken too soon" pin just recognizable on her blouse. How quickly she'd aligned herself with Tammy, amplifying her message seamlessly. And while she was at it, she'd repositioned their event business, hadn't she? By working her way into the press, Gabbi had found a way to highlight their memorial planning. But as Liz told Dusty after he'd poured himself a well-deserved beer last night, she didn't think she could handle one more job in what Gabbi blithely referred to as the "Touchstone death sector."

She put down the paper and recalled with a strange nostalgia a particularly chaotic wedding reception they'd planned. As the band started its second set, the groom, emboldened by shots of tequila, had decided it was time to demonstrate his new dancing skills, a modern take on the jitterbug. Flushed and grinning, he'd presented his clammy hand to the mother-of-the-bride. Across the room, Liz and Gabbi had exchanged glances, knowing with perfect certainty this dance would not end well. Seconds later, the groom missed a catch, spinning his new mother-in-law into the horn section of the band. She'd landed on a tangle of power cords—miraculously unharmed—but the back of her Vera Wang dress split open. "Cringeworthy" didn't begin to describe it, and Gabbi had covered her mouth with a linen napkin to conceal her nervous laughter. What Liz understood now is that the stakes for "happy" events weren't very high. Nothing compared to the heart-clamping discomfort of watching young gymnasts bumble the tribute for a dead friend.

She got up and carried her dishes to the sink, feeling upset with Gabbi but also missing that sense of being on the same page, the same team. Yesterday she'd told her partner, "I can't do this," and Gabbi had said nothing. What was Gabbi thinking now?

Her phone rang, and she saw that her mother was calling. Before this work fiasco, Liz had promised to take her to the Cantor Arts Museum today to see a photography exhibit followed by lunch. After a two-week hiatus, Joanie was due back in the clinic for more chemotherapy, and Liz wanted to give her a pleasant outing. Although she was anxious to sort things out with Gabbi, that would have to wait until tomorrow.

It was a quiet, mid-August day, a shade cooler than it had been at the memorial. When Liz pulled up at her parents' home, Joanie spied her from the front window and came right out, wearing white Capri slacks and a pale turquoise sweater. Like Gabbi, her mother was always well turned out, selecting clothes a notch or two above whatever Liz threw on. It didn't bother her—at least, not anymore. Rather, it comforted her to know that Joanie was well enough to keep making an effort regarding her appearance. Today, her hair was pulled back under a pretty silk wrap she'd never seen before.

"Cute scarf," she said as her mother stepped into the van.

"Do you think so? It's not too old-ladyish?"

"Not at all."

"Good." She clipped the seat belt into place and turned to face her. "The chemo is hell on my hair. It's starting to fall out." She patted the side of her head and tucked under a few wispy strands. "Might be time for a wig."

"I'm sorry, Mom. I read about the side effects. But I didn't realize—"

"What was it your brother said—that I'd be a 'killer blonde'? Maybe I'll give that a whirl. Do a Marilyn Monroe thing."

Liz smiled, impressed that she was maintaining a sense of humor. But sirens were sounding in her head. Until recently, the cancer had been invisible, making it possible to almost believe it didn't exist. Now, the side effects were making the disease come alive. She studied her mother's face more closely. It wasn't just the hair loss. Her cheekbones were more pronounced, and the pink in her skin tones had turned slightly sallow.

"Thank you for making time for the exhibit," her mother said. "Some of Dorothea Lange's work will be there. Everyone knows her images from the Dust Bowl. But the photos of Japanese families from the '40s—in U.S. internment camps? They're even more powerful."

Liz nodded. "And if we have time, we can tour the permanent collection too." Her mother loved the bright Wayne Thiebaud paintings of lollipops and pastries, and the abstract landscapes by Richard Diebenkorn in that heavenly blue.

As they lingered in front of Lange's photos of the wartime internment camps, an image of a young girl caught Liz's eye. The girl was bundled up in a drab coat of coarse fabric and an ID tag hung around her collar. Despite being captured in bleak black and white, the child projected a fierce vibrancy that reminded Liz of Haley Chan. She wondered what had become of this girl after the war. Was her life cut short too, or did she live to fulfill her bold dreams?

After taking in the photographs and admiring the sculptures in the museum's gardens on Stanford campus, Liz and her mother settled into seats at the café. Joanie didn't have the energy to view the paintings upstairs, and Liz thought it best to relax and enjoy a healthy meal. They ordered soup and salads.

"Have you heard from the Chans regarding the service?" her mother asked. "Are they, well, happy isn't the right word. Satisfied?"

"They haven't reached out—at least not to me. After all, I abandoned ship just as the reception was getting underway." She'd already confided in Joanie about the media mayhem.

"I don't blame you for that," her mother said. "Tammy sounds rather awful." She paused to sip her Arnold Palmer. "That said, I do empathize with the woman. I understand her pain."

"Each of you lost your baby girl," Liz said, careful to keep her voice low.

"Yes, but strange as it sounds, in one way Tammy Chan is lucky."

Liz set down her fork and gazed into her mother's deep-set eyes. "In what way?"

"She has someone to blame for her child's death. Neptune's." Joanie stared into her lap where she twisted her paper napkin.

"I'm not sure what you mean."

"I blamed...*blame*...myself for what happened to your sister."

All her life, Liz had wondered about the silence, the secrets surrounding her sister's death. She'd had her dark inklings, yet she was wholly unprepared for any sort of wrenching enlightenment. She scanned the sunny, public café where diners were casually discussing art and nibbling on turkey sandwiches and felt suddenly exposed. Her instinct was to provide cover for her mother, herself—to stick to the narrative that had been established all those years ago.

"But Mom. The fire was caused by bad wiring. Faulty electrical stuff in the kitchen. Remember?"

Her mother nodded vaguely, picking at her salad, and then lifted her chin to speak again. But Liz caught the eye of a roving waiter with a full pitcher of iced tea and beckoned him to the table.

"Anything else I can get you?" he asked.

Liz glanced at her mother. "Dessert?"

"No, thank you," she said. "Just the check, please." She reached down for her wallet. "I'm a little tired, honey. Would you mind taking me home?"

Stationed behind her desk on Monday morning, Liz had arrived at work extra early, flipping on the lights, brewing a pot of coffee, and turning on some mellow music. She'd even brought a bouquet of dahlias, placing them on the coffee table in the common area. After a fitful night's sleep, she'd determined that now was as good a time as any to have a candid discussion with Gabbi about their business. Getting to the office before Gabbi gave her a territorial advantage, yet she also wanted to set the stage for an amicable exchange. After all, she and Gabbi had been partners for six years now, friends for thirty.

As she waited for Gabbi, she logged into her computer to check her email. The online edition of the local newspaper appeared in her inbox with the subject line: *Gymnast's memorial attracts national attention.* Clicking on the link, she discovered a story written by Max Kohn, the editor she'd seen in the auditorium. She scanned the content, certain that she'd find criticism of the event—perhaps even a reference to the botched gymnastics routine. But it was a "just the facts, ma'am," account, describing the number of people in attendance, the line-up of speakers, and the arrival of the news crew outside. One photo featured a reporter from NBC; another showed Maddy at the podium clutching a tissue. Liz sighed, admonishing herself for being so paranoid.

But as she was about to close out the page, she noticed the comments section below the story where readers were allowed to post responses—anonymously—to the article. She found a growing number of remarks:

> *How that little girl died was tragic, and how she was laid to rest was bad too. What a zoo. Between the hordes attending the service and the media trucks, traffic on El Camino was at a dead stop.*

The post was signed by "Long-time Resident." Liz was floored that anyone would complain about the traffic. How insensitive! But the zoo remark? She really couldn't take issue with that. Though she was afraid to read what was next, she pressed on.

> *I attended the memorial and thought it was beautiful. When Maddy Chan spoke about her little sister, I cried.*

Me too, Liz thought, comforted by the review from "Still Weepy in MP." When a third post popped up, she leaned into her screen, promising herself she would read just one more.

Totally agree with Long-time Resident. The service was over the top. Did Spielberg direct the Haley Chan all-star video? What a production. BTW, who runs Touchstone Events? I bet they made bank on that memorial. Cha-ching!

Liz tilted back in her chair, gasping for air like a fish at the bottom of an old rowboat. It was mortifying to be called out in such a public way. And she was angry—furious—that Touchstone was being accused of taking advantage of a family in mourning. Yes, Gabbi may have pushed for booze and agreed to every bell and whistle proposed by Tammy Chan, but they had reduced their mark-ups and underbilled for hours served. In fact, she wasn't charging a nickel for working the memorial. She viewed it as support for Maddy.

When she heard the familiar click-click-click of Gabbi's heels on the stairs, she looked up.

"Something wrong?" Gabbi asked, walking toward her and studying her face.

Liz pointed to her screen and waited while Gabbi browsed the various posts.

"No big deal," she said, brushing back her hair with a gesture of indifference. Gabbi had a way of weaponizing cheerfulness. "Bunch of old trolls with too much time on their hands. Let's just agree that any press is good press, okay?"

Liz shook her head. "Not for me." She closed the window of her email and folded her arms on her desk. "I don't like people making disparaging remarks about our business. Our integrity. For God's sake, Gabriela. We grew up in this town."

"The thing is, Liz, I can't afford to be thin-skinned. I grew up on the *other* side of this town, remember?" She pulled up a chair and shirked off her tote. "It's not like I have a husband—or parents around the corner—who can back me up. It's just me trying to take care of myself and Zoey. Death events can pay our bills and then some. Did you see the story in the *Merc*? I've already got two leads from that."

I've got two leads? What happened to "we"? And Liz resented the implication that she was living on easy street. But it was true that Gabbi's financial resources were scant compared to hers. After her parents split up, her mother moved to a tiny apartment in Pacifica and barely made ends meet on her fixed income.

"Did the inquiries come through our website?" Liz asked.

"Yes."

"Good. That means the potential clients saw our whole range of event services."

"In theory, that's true. But the two women who reached out to me weren't interested in our other services. One has a husband who recently died of Alzheimer's. The other has a brother who is terminally ill. Both need help planning memorials."

"What fun," Liz said, rubbing her temples where a headache was taking root.

"At least they're not kids."

Liz had imagined this sit-down with Gabbi going differently. A little heart-to-heart where they brainstormed about new directions for their partnership. But Gabbi was set on the death market. Talk of anything else seemed fruitless.

"Listen, Liz. If you can't get behind this new line of business, just tell me."

"Are we completely abandoning our old lines of work? What about your idea to focus on gay weddings? Now that gay marriage is legal in California—"

"When the economy picks up, the wedding market will come back. But let's face it. There's a ton of competition—a wedding planner in every zip code around here. No one is targeting memorial events. We could own that market."

Gabbi had obviously given this a great deal of thought. But the notion of going "all in" on the death business, even after the economy recovered, was untenable. Between the grief and fury of the Tammy Chans in the world, and the loneliness of the Tony Marinos, there was too much darkness in the work. Too much sadness and fear.

"If I have to, I'll go it alone," Gabbi said. She paused before adding, "Or find another partner. What are you thinking—are you in? Or out?"

Liz planted her hands on her desk and pushed herself up to a standing position. "What the hell, Gabbi. You're giving me an ultimatum?"

"I guess I am."

With as much self-control as she could muster, Liz shut down her computer. "I'll think about this, but I won't be rushed. You'll hear from me when I'm damn well ready." She collected her purse and sweater and walked swiftly past Gabbi and out the door.

Chapter 22

arked in the underground garage below her office, Liz sat in the front seat gripping her steering wheel. Her legs were shaky, and she didn't trust herself to drive. What's more, she didn't know where to go. The boys were at school registering for fall classes, but Dusty was undoubtedly at home. Until recently, she would have beelined toward him to explain her side of the Gabbi-Liz drama. But today, she knew that her unemployed husband would counsel her to reconcile with Gabbi and take whatever business came in the door. For an instant, she hated him for putting her in this predicament. Under no circumstance would she crawl back to the office on Gabbi's terms.

Her cell phone buzzed and it was her father, calling to report that her mother had taken a fall in their bedroom.

"She's not hurt, thank God. She fell on the carpet. But she's a little shaken."

"It's probably another side effect of the chemo," Liz said, switching gears and trying to sound calm. She'd reviewed the literature again last night. "Neuropathy is pretty common in the feet."

"That's what I'm thinking too. To be on the safe side, the doctor wants her to get a brain scan. We'll do that first and then head over to the infusion center."

"A brain scan? Do you want me to go with you?"

"Well, yes, but don't you have work?"

"It's fine, Dad. Gabbi can hold down the fort."

At the hospital, she sat in the changing room with her mother who stepped out of her clothes and into the thin flannel gown provided for patients. Liz couldn't help but notice that Joanie hadn't simply lost weight—she'd also lost muscle tone. Her skin appeared loose and wrinkled, sagging around her arms and legs in a way it never had before. Wasn't it just weeks ago that they had exercised Cheddar in the neighborhood? The old retriever had lagged behind on the leash, struggling to keep up with her mother's brisk pace. Now she worried that Cheddar would knock Joanie off her feet. Even though she had warned Ned about the debilitating side effects of chemo, she hadn't been prepared for this rapid decline.

After pulling on the yellow, hospital-issue socks with rubber grippers, Joanie sat down and yawned. She'd taken a sedative to make the forty-five-minute scan in the MRI tube more tolerable. "I can't decide what's worse," she said. "The racket that machine makes, or the feeling of being trapped."

Liz reached over and squeezed her hand. "Just close your eyes and try to take a little nap. Dad and I will be right here." She glanced at her mother's purse, wondering if there were more sedatives inside. The thought of her mother lying in that tomb-like scanner gave her the willies, and she craved to take the edge off. Seconds later, a nurse arrived to lock away the purse and other belongings.

While her mother was down the hall behind closed doors, her father shuffled around the waiting room, nervously slurping from the drinking fountain. Liz drifted through old *People* magazines, unable to focus even on celebrity gossip.

An hour later, her mother emerged, dressed and ready to leave. Assuming it would take a few days for test results, Arnie began to herd her toward the exit, curling his hand around her elbow to steady her step. An aid sitting behind the appointment window called out "Joan Boyle," and Liz hurried over to consult with her. Apparently, Dr. Kumar had an opening in his schedule and wanted to see them right away.

When he walked into their examining room, the doctor took the time to look each of them in the eyes and to shake their hands. Liz found his behavior unsettling. The exaggerated eye contact and human touch struck her as something he'd learned in a patient management playbook. He glanced at some notes and then asked her mother to describe her general health and the circumstances of her fall. When she finished, Arnie added, "The chemo is hitting her pretty hard."

The doctor cleared his throat before responding. "I'm not sure the fall is related to treatment. There's a chance it's related to the cancer." He removed a sheet from his folder and pointed to several indecipherable grainy images. "There appear to be a few small lesions in the brain."

Joanie covered her face with her hands, and Arnie slipped his arm around her. He looked at Liz, his mouth opening and closing without a word.

"So the disease is spreading," Liz said. She hardly recognized the matter-of-fact tone in her voice. Perhaps this was some form of shock.

"I'm afraid so."

"Clearly, my mother isn't having an 'excellent response' to this treatment. What's the new plan?"

The doctor blinked twice, registering the bite in her question. "Radiation is an option. We can target the tumors with a great deal of precision, but there are risks.

It's not uncommon for patients to experience headaches and fatigue, or nausea." He glanced at his notes and then met Liz's stare. "A larger concern is cognitive issues. Speech and memory problems."

"No one is zapping my brain," Joanie said. She was terrified of memory loss. Her own father had died after years of senility, and she'd often said: "Better dead than an empty head."

"Are there alternatives to radiation?" Liz asked.

Dr. Kumar nodded. "We have other chemotherapies to consider. I'll consult with my colleagues and develop a recommendation."

"Does that mean we suspend current treatment?"

"Yes. For now, rest up. I'll be in touch in the next day or so."

Liz and her parents filed out to the parking lot saying little. Three months earlier, they'd been buoyed by the prospect of Joanie's cancer being arrested and reduced by the first wave of chemotherapy. Liz, for one, hadn't let herself think about the opposite of an excellent response.

When they reached her father's sedan, Arnie helped his wife into the passenger seat. Normally, she would have declined his assistance, insisting she wasn't a darn invalid, but today she nearly collapsed into his arms. When she'd settled into her seat, he gently closed the door and turned to Liz.

"We can't give up hope."

"No, of course not."

"Doctor Kumar will figure out another treatment strategy."

"And if he doesn't, we'll find someone who will."

"Well, let's not change horses midstream. Let's stay the course for now." He hugged her goodbye and slipped sunglasses over his weary eyes. "Thank you for being here, honey. Now, go back to work. I'm sure Gabbi is wondering where you are."

If Gabbi was wondering where she was, she didn't say so, or text. Which was fine with Liz. What she desperately wanted was to go home, rest her head on a cool pillow, and fall into a dreamless sleep.

When she arrived home, she found a note from Dusty. He and the boys had gone to Staples to get back-to-school supplies. "Meet us at Baskin Robbins at 3:00 p.m." It had been their annual ritual since the boys were little: buy the required three-ring binders, pencils, and calculators and then go to BR for a double-scoop cone, a treat to cheer up the boys as they mournfully counted down the last days of summer. When it dawned on Liz that this would be the last time they shared this tradition—the boys would be off to college in a year—the stoicism that had kept her upright at the hospital fell away. Sinking into the worn cushions of her couch, she allowed herself a little cry. She was losing on every front: with Gabbi; with her mother's disease; with the cursed remodel that wasn't selling. Before long, she would lose Ben and Jamie to a life apart from her and Dusty.

When she awakened sometime later, Liz felt disoriented and chilled and went to her closet to find a cotton zip-up. After pulling it on, she noticed a business card in the front pocket.

Peter Levine, Partner
MedTek Capital
Funding innovations that save lives
plevine@medtek.com

She'd forgotten that Peter had passed his card to her at the grocery store several months earlier—and it had slipped her mind he was a healthcare investor. Wide awake now, she wondered if he knew anything about innovations in cancer care. Before she could talk herself out of it, she sat down at her computer and dashed off an email to him, summarizing her mother's diagnosis and treatment, and the discovery of tumors in her brain. She included her contact information and hoped she wasn't being too forward, but time was of the essence. After she clicked *send*, she glanced at her watch. If she hurried, she could join her family for their sweet tradition one last time.

When she arrived at the ice cream parlor, Dusty and the boys had already been served and were sitting elbow-to-elbow at a small table, focused intently on their melting cones. She waved to them, vowing not to mention the dreadful hospital visit nor the fight with Gabbi, and got into line behind a young mother and her small children. The woman appeared harried, counting dollars in her wallet and trying to get the kids to commit to a flavor. "How about cookie dough? Or rainbow sherbet?" Liz felt a pang of envy, her days of having children milling around her waist long over. How would she and Dusty fill their days once the boys were gone? She'd entertained a vague notion of connecting more deeply with her mother, puttering around the garden together. But now?

"You better hurry," Dusty said, appearing next to her. "We're already down to one scoop." He reached past her, tugging a handful of napkins from the metal dispenser, and shuffled back to Ben and Jamie. When it was her turn to order, Liz requested coffee chip, grateful to have even a few minutes with her boys before heading back home.

After they returned from town and the twins had retreated to their rooms, she took Dusty aside and told him about the MRI scan and the progression of her mother's disease. His shoulders slumped and he briefly closed his eyes.

"Damn," he said. "Not the brain." Liz recounted the possible next steps regarding treatment, and he was instantly drawn to radiation. "I think we should go with the nuclear option," he said. "Bring out the big guns and blast those cancer cells to hell." She felt a surge of affection for him. Naturally, her husband the contractor would choose the most powerful tool. But her mother wasn't on board for that, at least not yet.

They agreed to tell the twins over dinner, though Liz hated to worry them, especially on one of the last evenings of summer. On the other hand, the boys were headed into a rigorous senior fall schedule with college applications getting underway immediately. Perhaps it was better to process the bad news now.

In the measured voice she had adopted with Dr. Kumar, she told the boys about their grandmother. When she was done, Jamie pushed away his plate.

"Poor Jo-Jo. That totally sucks." His eyes reflected the ache in his heart, the fear. "Can I go see her tomorrow?"

Liz nodded. "I think so. We'll call Grandpa about a good time to visit."

"Such a bummer the meds aren't working," Ben said, twirling spaghetti around his fork. "But it could be worse."

Liz cocked her head. "How so?"

"It's not like Jo-Jo is a kid. She's not eleven."

"Benjamin," Dusty said.

"I mean, this isn't the same as what Maddy's family is going through."

Stung, Liz shoved away from the table and got to her feet. "You're right, Ben. Jo-Jo is seventy-two. Not worth saving."

"That's not what I said."

"We're talking about your grandmother. My *mom*." She heard the anguish creep into her voice and fought to maintain her composure. "And by the way? I've already lived through exactly what Maddy's family is experiencing. I've already lost someone I loved. Which is why I'm going to do everything in my power to help Jo-Jo beat this disease. So, Ben, if you can't be in this fight with me, at least keep your mouth shut."

Ben poked at his chicken breast and said nothing, apparently embracing the new policy.

She turned to Dusty. "I'm going to take a walk to clear my head."

"I'll come with you."

"No. Thanks. I need some time alone." She grabbed the jacket from the back of her chair and walked out into the cool evening air.

She'd expected Ben to be compassionate and supportive. After all, she'd done everything he'd requested for the Chans and then some: cooked and delivered them meals; planned and executed the memorial; offered a sympathetic ear when Maddy needed one. On top of that, she'd learned to look the other way when he and Maddy disappeared into his bedroom and locked the door. She had a mind to revoke what she had come to think of as his "comforting privileges." He needed to learn a lesson about empathy, about living on a goddamn two-way street.

She set off at a good pace, trying to inhale the tranquility of the trees that were collecting the last of the setting sun and casting benign shadows around her feet. It felt good to be moving, to set free some of the anxieties that had made her legs feel heavy and stiff.

When her phone vibrated, she assumed it was Dusty—or maybe Ned. Had her parents called him in San Diego to bring him up to speed? But it was an unknown number with a 617 area code.

"Hello?" she said.

"Liz, it's Peter. Levine. Is this a good time to talk?"

"Oh my gosh, Peter. Thanks for calling. I know it's late out there in...Boston?"

"No worries. My wife and kids are at the Cape until Labor Day, and I just got home from the office. I've been catching up on paperwork, and I saw your email. I'm so sorry to hear about Joanie. I have some ideas."

As Liz meandered through the quiet streets and cul-de-sacs of her neighborhood pressing her phone against her ear, Peter shared his views on clinical trials, targeted drug therapies, and the importance of second opinions. How strange it was to talk at length with him after all these years. His voice was lower, fuller than it had been when they were young. But his inflections were the same, and his kind words and expertise soothed her.

Eventually, Peter turned the conversation to the personal. "How's your dad holding up?"

"He'll be better once a new plan comes together."

"Does he still drink scotch? It's medicinal at times like this."

She laughed softly into the darkness. "He's probably on his second dose by now."

"Good. And you? How are you doing?"

A knot swelled in her throat. "Oh, I'm fine," she said. To her own ear, she sounded unconvincing, and she wondered if Peter could hear the wobble. "And how about you? All good?"

"I'm okay too."

A pause in the conversation opened up, and Liz was tempted to step into the gap. To tell him everything. She recalled the night when, after three months of dating, she'd told Peter about the fire, about leaving her sister behind and moving here to Menlo Park. They'd been soaking in his parents' backyard hot tub and nursing a few cans of Coors in their bathing suits when the story spilled out of her. Peter had listened intently, never looking away or appearing uncomfortable. When she finished, he gathered her into his arms and kissed her wet hair. He'd been only sixteen, but he already had a man's heart, a man's understanding.

She looked up from the dark pavement to find that her feet had brought her home. The light near the kitchen window revealed Ben's face above the sink where he was likely finishing up the dishes from dinner. The moment to say more had passed.

"Peter, thanks so much for your call. I'll follow up on your suggestions tomorrow."

"Happy to help. I'll get you the names of those other oncologists. Until then, take care of yourself Lizzie, okay? And give my best to your folks."

She put away her phone and felt a flicker of hope catch fire inside her. At least she had new leads to pursue regarding her mother's treatment. But the flame wavered when she considered what to do about Gabbi. Their office was like a second home to her. When would it feel right to return? She hadn't pulled together a plan for a way forward. Maybe Gabbi would make the first move.

Chapter 23

On Friday, Liz opened her mailbox and found an envelope from Touchstone Events. She rushed inside to open it, wondering if this was the reconciliation letter she'd been hoping for. Instead, she found a check made out to her, and when she saw Gabbi's signature at the bottom, she felt as if she'd been slapped. It had always been her job to cut the checks, to manage all the bookkeeping functions. Was Gabbi assuming her work—conducting the business without her?

Three nights ago, just as they set aside their books and switched off their bedside lamps, Liz had told Dusty about her and Gabbi's falling out, about the ultimatum. As she knew he would, he had taken her side. And, just as predictably, he'd encouraged her to "put up with the funeral stuff" until the end of the year.

"Then what?" she'd asked. "When the calendar page turns to 2009, we're not going to magically have new jobs."

"True. But we'll have more time to figure things out. For starters, I think we should take the Pine Street house off the market and rent it. Chuck said that with the job market so unstable, folks are nervous about buying. For now, he believes we can get enough rent each month to cover the mortgage payment. Or most of it."

"And what about *this* house?" she said, throwing her hands at the ceiling. "To pay our bills, I've been drawing from savings for eight months in a row. The account is nearly depleted. And our credit cards are maxed out."

Dusty pulled the sheet up and tucked it under his chin. "One of my subs, Miguel, just got hired to work on a substantial renovation in Woodside. He thinks he can get me a spot on the crew. Honestly, I won't mind pounding nails for a while."

Liz hated the way they were going backwards in their lives, sideways in their careers. But there appeared to be no alternatives. "Okay," she said. "You follow up with Miguel and tell Chuck that renting the spec house is a go."

"And you'll call Gabbi?"

"Yes," she said.

But she hadn't phoned Gabbi. It was noon on Friday and making that call to mend fences would be harder than ever. What if Gabbi preferred that she not return? What if she'd somehow forgotten that, before Liz Becker came on board, her business had been a mess? Liz had been dumbfounded by the number of unpaid bills, half-baked proposals, and uncollected receivables that had hamstrung her friend's little enterprise. In fact, it had taken her months to right the ship that eventually became Touchstone Event Planning. But was she replaceable? Maybe, she thought miserably, Gabbi had already found someone who was happy to line their pockets by working in the dismal trade.

She tried to pull her thoughts together and rehearse what she would say. But her attention ricocheted around the kitchen. Sitting down at the table, she rifled through the rest of the mail, absently sorting it into piles for recycling, reading later, paying now. Back-to-school sales were featured on every catalog, and her mind turned to the boys who had started their senior year.

When they drove away this morning, she noticed that they didn't turn left out of the driveway toward Oak Creek High. They turned right, toward the Chans' home. She felt comforted knowing that Ben and Jamie were taking Maddy to school and escorting her through the halls. No doubt, everyone on campus was still talking about Haley's accident—and perhaps the over-the-top memorial. After her own sister had died, Liz and Ned moved to a new school district, but word of a death in the family preceded them. Teachers and students alike were extra kind and solicitous, yet it had made Liz uncomfortable to have a weird kind of celebrity status. She prayed that Maddy, considerably older than she had been, would weather the attention better.

As she stacked the catalogs destined for recycling, her phone rang, and when she saw Gabbi's name on the display, she hesitated. She felt like a pathetic teenager who spots the number of her boyfriend and fears the incoming message: "Let's just be friends."

"Hello?"

"Hey, Liz. I ran into your dad at the drugstore this morning—he told me about Joanie. God, I'm so sorry."

Liz exhaled slowly. This sounded like the Gabbi Rossi she knew and trusted. Not a business partner ready to give her the axe.

"I thought you said her treatment was going pretty well?"

"That's what we were told," Liz said. "Her doctor had no clue the cancer had spread."

"Poor thing. How does she feel?"

"She's tired. She says the chemo makes her feel puny. But she's not in any real pain. Not yet."

"Thank goodness for that." She paused and cleared her throat. "Listen, I know your parents are going to need a lot of help going forward, and that will probably fall on you. Have you thought about what you want to do, workwise?"

"I was just about to call you—"

"Because I was thinking that maybe you could do the bookkeeping and proposal stuff from home. Part-time. And to keep things simple, you could just bill me hourly."

And there it was, the gentle swing of the cleaver.

"No," Liz said. "What we have is a partnership. I'm not interested in working *for* you." Her heart was racing and she felt breathless but pushed on. "And to be clear, I'm not just a bookkeeper. I manage all our vendors and bring in as much business as you do. Tammy Chan hired Touchstone because of me."

"I've got no argument with that. But I thought you hated this memorial business. I was trying to give you a graceful way out. A way to make a little money before you find other work. What the hell was I supposed to think, Liz? I haven't heard from you in days."

"I do hate it," Liz said. "But I need it. The economy is still tanking. There is no 'other work.' And Gabbi, you still need *me*. So, I'll see you at the office next week." Before Gabbi could even say goodbye, Liz hung up. She stared at the phone for another minute, and then she endorsed the check that Gabbi had mailed her, picked up her purse, and headed for the bank. A timely deposit would keep checks from bouncing.

The line to use the outside ATMs was long, so Liz ducked indoors to join a short queue. She took out the check and glanced again at the memo line: *Partial payment/ Chan service.* She was relieved that the Chans weren't waiting for the Neptune settlement to begin disbursing payments. Had they sent enough to pay the caterer and Manny? The printer? She would find out soon enough. Though it'd been less than a week since she'd stormed out of the office, it seemed like an eternity.

As she scanned the tellers looking for an empty window, she became aware of someone staring over her shoulder. She turned around to find Rachel Matsen examining her check and deposit slip. A ghostly feeling of déjà vu swept through her as she stuffed them in her purse.

"My neighbor told me you made a killing on that funeral," Rachel said. She was no longer wearing the baseball cap and dark glasses to disguise her grief, but the heaviness of her son's death was still recognizable on her flesh, in the way she clutched her own hands.

"Your neighbor has been misinformed," Liz stammered. Those trolls who'd posted online—*cha-ching!*—had evidently hit their mark. "For the record, we tailored that memorial to meet our clients' wishes. Every detail reflected the way they wanted to honor their child."

Liz shifted back to face the tellers, praying someone would wave her forward. For months, she'd been grateful that Rachel had never turned over Mikey's drug accounts to the police. That Ben hadn't been called in by the authorities. But now she was pissed at this woman who was directing her bitterness at her.

"You know, we didn't have a service for Mikey," Rachel said quietly behind her. Liz heard the note of confession. "Given what happened, we kept it in the family. Maybe we should have handled it differently."

Liz rotated slowly in Rachel's direction. She met her dark eyes and noticed a nervous twitch. "Losing a child, it's so awful," she said. "Maybe there's really no right way or wrong way to grieve." Her own words surprised her. Did she truly believe that?

"Next!" called the teller with a harried look on her face. "Next!"

Liz reached out to touch Rachel's shoulder and then hurried to the open window.

As promised, Peter emailed Liz a short list of highly regarded thoracic oncologists to provide her mother with a second opinion. Each of them was within an hour's drive of Menlo Park, but the doctor who caught Liz's attention was someone named Dr. Emma Jacobs. Liz followed the link to her medical bio, which included a photo, and she liked what she saw. It wasn't just that she was a Harvard-trained physician who conducted clinical trials focused on lung cancer. Emma Jacobs was clearly older than Dr. Kumar, and something about the gray touches in her unruly hair and the warmth in her smile gave Liz solace.

She replied to Peter's email, thanking him profusely and telling him that she would call Dr. Jacobs immediately. Just before sending, she paused, pondering the appropriate sign-off. *Sincerely?* Too corporate. *Fondly?* No, that was sending the wrong message. She settled on *warmly* and sent it off.

When Liz contacted Dr. Jacobs' office, the receptionist seemed to have been expecting her call and told her an appointment had opened up. Next step was to convince her parents to release Joanie's medical files to the new doctor for review.

"Happy to send the records," her father said over the phone. "Yesterday, when we talked with Doctor Kumar about new treatment plans for your mom, he seemed indecisive. So I broached the idea of getting a second opinion."

"Was he offended?" Liz asked.

"Not at all. He encouraged us to consult another doctor."

Well, Liz thought. *Maybe he's eager to unload patients who fail to have an excellent response.*

"By the way," her father said. "Where did you get the referral for this new cancer doc?"

"A friend from high school in the medical field," she said. "I don't think you'd remember him." Liz felt it best not to mention the old boyfriend thing to her parents—or Dusty. It might raise questions and complicate matters unnecessarily. Peter lived in Massachusetts, for heaven's sake. She had no expectations of seeing him.

Despite a withering wait at the hospital—the doctor was running nearly an hour behind—when Liz and her parents met Dr. Emma Jacobs in Room 3A, their spirits rebounded. She shook their hands with a friendly firmness that had none of their previous doctor's practiced, by-the-book formality. After asking everyone to take a seat, Dr. Emma pulled her chair close to them so that their knees were only inches apart.

"I've reviewed Mrs. Boyle's scans and treatment history, and Doctor Kumar's notes," she said. "I don't have to tell you this cancer is very aggressive."

"Yes, we understand," Liz said.

"My approach is to be frank—to tell it as I see it. Okay with you all?" Her parents exchanged looks and nodded in unison. Dr. Jacobs shifted her attention, locking eyes with Joanie. "Mrs. Boyle, in my opinion, it's not likely we can cure your cancer." She paused, letting the information settle, before continuing. "But, if you qualify for our clinical trial, perhaps we can contain it. A realistic goal would be to manage the cancer as a chronic disease."

"How do we know if I qualify for the trial?" Joanie asked. She lifted her chin in a way that made her appear proud, unafraid, but Liz could hear the tiny tremor in her voice.

"We'll do another biopsy and more analysis of your tumor type. The fact that you're in generally good health helps qualify you too." Joanie straightened in her seat and pushed back her shoulders, looking as vigorous as possible.

After scheduling a biopsy and additional lab work, Liz and her parents left the clinic with a new mantra: *Manageable chronic disease.* Hard to believe that these were the words that now made Liz's heart sing, the words on which her family would heap all of their hopes.

When Liz returned to the office after more than a week's absence, she was surprised to find Gabbi there ahead of her. Perhaps it was her turn to stake out her territory. She was deeply engaged in a phone conversation, so Liz simply nodded at her and settled behind her desk. A few minutes later, Gabbi hung up the phone and approached her, stopping a few feet away and holding a notepad to her chest. Liz tried not to appear as nervous as she felt.

"Welcome back," Gabbi said.

Her tone wasn't exactly warm, but it wasn't sarcastic or hostile either. Liz exhaled slowly. "Thanks," she said.

"I need you to start—and finish—a proposal today. You up for it?"

Gabbi still *needed* her after all. Liz liked the sound of that. And though she didn't appreciate the demand for such fast turnaround, it struck her that death events weren't like weddings or parties, planned with the luxury of time. There was an urgency to get a body laid to rest, and a desire to get the whole sad affair over with, wasn't there?

"I think so. What are the details?"

"I just talked with a woman who wants to celebrate her father's life in a creative way," Gabbi said. "He was a decorated navy pilot and flew jets for Pan Am and United. She wants a flight theme of some sort. So, I said, why not do a 'destination memorial' and host it at the Norton Aviation Museum in San Francisco—the one with all the vintage planes suspended from the ceiling. She loved the idea."

Everyone had heard of a destination wedding. But a destination memorial? New to Liz. New to most people, no doubt. She had to admit, Gabbi possessed the entrepreneurial spirit that might save them. For now at least, she had to get on board. Be a part of this unlikely startup.

"So," Liz said, "I guess our pitch to new clients is: 'This Is Not Your Father's Funeral.'"

"Oh my God, are you making a joke?" Gabbi asked. She smiled and stepped closer, leaning on Liz's desk.

"I'm trying, Gab. I'm really trying."

"Well, good. Nice to see a glimmer of your old sense of humor."

Gabbi reviewed the specs for the memorial, and then Liz called the museum to talk with their events manager about seating capacity, catering options, and costs. Within hours, she had a preliminary proposal ready for Gabbi to present to the client.

"This looks good," she said. "And I think this event will actually be fun to produce. I mean, the dude was old, Liz. According to his daughter, he had a wonderful life. Flew all over the world, retired on a golf course, and then died in his sleep. Good life, good death. Nothing sad about that."

"A good death?" It was a concept Liz had never considered. "Okay, Gabriela. I'll take that under advisement."

After Gabbi left for her presentation, Liz called her father, anxious to hear whether her mother had qualified for the clinical trial. The trial was the only thing standing between her mother and a terrible certainty.

"We just heard," he said. "We're in! Honestly, we feel like we've won the lottery."

"Thank God," Liz said, blinking away a sudden tear.

"When does the trial start?"

"Soon. Right after Labor Day. We thought we'd drive down to Carmel tomorrow and spend a few days walking the beach. Your mother wants a change of scenery before entering this next phase of treatment."

"You should definitely go, Dad. Take her shopping. Spoil her rotten."

"Roger that."

She hung up and leaned back in her chair, propping her sandaled feet on the desk and taking a moment to savor the news. It struck her as uncommonly good luck to have found an opening on the schedule of Dr. Jacobs, a woman who, by all reports, was in tremendous demand. And then to have her mother qualify for the clinical trial too. It was as if an invisible hand was opening doors for them. And she wondered if that hand might belong to Peter Levine. On a whim, she texted him to report the good news. His reply was nearly instantaneous: *Thrilled about your mom! Driving to the Cape to join the girls. Cell reception crappy at cottage, but will check back soon. Cheers.*

Cheers. A perfect sign-off. Confident and friendly without being the least bit romantic. Which was good. And yet, she found herself parsing his words for hidden messages. He was driving to the Cape to join "the girls." Did that include his wife? Why did she care?

She closed her Excel spreadsheets and opened Facebook. Peter Levine was evidently not on the social network, but Meryl Bradford Levine of Boston was. She clicked on her page and discovered a blonde-haired woman whom her Midwestern relatives might describe as "pleasantly plump," a term never heard in California.

Below Meryl's photos were assorted pictures of Peter, their two daughters, and their home on the Cape. The ocean-side retreat was breathtaking—hardly a cottage, more like something torn from the pages of a Martha

Stewart magazine. The white clapboard home with dormer windows and handsome, hunter green shutters was perched on a bluff overlooking the Atlantic. Enormous pink hydrangea shrubs surrounded the porch, and a windswept boardwalk led to the beach.

No wonder Peter returned to the Bay Area so seldom. He'd left behind a difficult father and unhappy mother and created his own version of paradise three thousand miles away. She swung her feet back to the floor and peered more closely at a picture of him sailing. Alone in a small catamaran on a cloudless day, he looked so content, so...free. Had she ever felt that way? It occurred to her that since she was a child, she'd felt weighted down by the imperative to avert another disaster. Another cruel death. For her, there'd never been a boat where she could climb in, pull up anchor, and sail away.

She leaned away and closed Facebook. Viewing Peter's picture-perfect life was dampening the euphoria she'd felt just minutes ago when she'd learned about the clinical trial. How childish to feel envy when simple gratitude was what she owed him. Because of Peter, her mother was back in the fight.

She glanced at her calendar and was reminded that she had to be at Ben and Jamie's high school in thirty minutes. The head of the college counseling office was addressing the parents of seniors about application strategies and financial aid.

Before leaving for school, she placed a quick call to Ned at the tennis club down south, filling him in on the new treatment path.

"I know," he said. "I've talked with Dad." Liz could hear the groan and punch of a ball machine working in the background. "It's going to be easier for Mom now. No more chemo crap."

"Huh?"

"In the trial, she'll take the meds orally—in pill form rather than intravenously. Which means they won't have to spend hours at the clinic."

Liz felt irritation prickle on her skin like a rash. Her father hadn't mentioned any of this. What, he was giving Ned more details than her, when Ned had done so little to help manage their mother's care?

"Hey, I gotta go," Ned said. "The ladies are lining up courtside for their short-game lesson."

"Okay."

"And Lizzie?"

"Yeah?"

"Thanks for all you're doing—all you've done—for Mom."

As far back as she could remember, she'd never heard those words from her brother's lips. Not when they were young and she'd packed Ned's paper-bag lunches as well as her own, washed and put away their laundry. Even mowed the lawn when he skipped out to join buddies in another neighborhood. As she stood there holding her phone, she felt something shift behind her sternum and she experienced a strange but pleasant lightheadedness.

"Sure thing," she said. "I'll keep you posted."

Chapter 24

*I*n her neck of the woods, the past few weeks had been relatively good ones for Liz.

"We've got another live one," Gabbi said on Friday, and Liz glanced up from her spreadsheet and grinned. Thanks to another presentation at a local retirement community, senior citizens were contacting them about end-of-life planning. It was a market both she and Gabbi could embrace. For many of these energetic clients—avid golfers, competitive bridge players, world travelers— death was real only in theory, the way it was for young people. Selecting a final resting spot wasn't categorically different from buying a life insurance policy. It was easy to believe you would never take ownership, just as you couldn't fathom your heirs ever collecting payment from Liberty Mutual.

And for her mother, the threat of death had receded behind a distant door. After several weeks of taking oral tablets from the clinical trial, Joanie was experiencing some annoying acne and dry eyes, and her appetite was off. But it was generally life as usual where she filled her birdfeeders with seed and did a little oil painting in her studio. Her father took profound comfort in her routine. Yesterday, he'd told Liz, "Now, it's the ordinary things that send me over the moon." Liz had emailed Peter to thank him again. He'd assured her it was his pleasure and privilege to help the Boyle family and had signed off with an XO. It was good to know that someone she'd loved long ago was still looking out for her parents.

If Liz's world was turning a little less wobbly on its axis, the same could not be said elsewhere. As Ben and Jamie raided the pantry for snacks before heading to school, the Monday morning news reported chaos on Wall Street and Main Street. The Dow Jones was dropping precariously, and both domestic and global financial institutions were releasing grim reports. While she and Dusty had nothing to lose in the stock market, their past—and future—clients certainly did.

Liz tried not to dwell on these disturbing reports as she nosed her van onto streets crowded with kids pedaling like demons to make it to class before the first bell. She hadn't seen Tony in weeks, but she was headed to Portola Valley to spend a few hours with him. It was not a business call. Ever since she had sat across from him at his kitchen table and apologized for being so blind to his pain, their professional relationship had ended. How gracious he'd been, how forgiving, insisting that she was not to blame for the harrowing episode with the gun.

"Liz, you're the only reason I'm still alive," he'd said. "The last thing you told me before I picked up that pistol was that I was your friend. When I felt the truth of that, I decided to stick around. It's been so long since anyone called me that." A lifetime ago, she'd been wary of him, dismissing him as a dirty old man. Now she thought of Tony Marino as a dear uncle of sorts.

Though he'd missed the ideal window for selling his home, Tony had decided it was time to put his house on the market, and Liz prayed he'd have better luck than she and Dusty had. It wasn't pressure from Tony Jr. that had changed his mind, but that Aasal needed more time off and Tony couldn't muster the energy to groom a new caretaker. As he'd told Liz on the phone, it was "time to face reality" and move into his assisted living quarters.

She found the front door of Tony's house unlocked and let herself in. As always, the smell of French Roast beckoned her to the kitchen where she found Aasal putting away groceries. A pleasant feeling of rejoining the team slipped over her.

"Such great news about Sam," she said in greeting. Sam, short for Samson, was Aasal's middle child, an exceptional local football player who'd been recruited to play for the University of Oregon. Among his fans in the high school bleachers, Sam was famous for his thick mane of dreadlocks and his leadership of the gritty, growling Haka dance before kick-off. Dusty and the twins had witnessed his skills as the star wide receiver of their rival school, but she'd only recently learned he was Aasal's son.

"Pretty cool, huh?" He poured her a cup of coffee and stirred in some cream before handing it to her. "I'm headed up to Eugene on Friday to catch his first home game." He was dressed head to toe in green and yellow, the colors of the Oregon Ducks, and Liz grinned at the proud papa. Oregon was on Ben's list of target schools, but their baseball program hadn't shown much interest in him. At best, Ben could walk on, though playing at the club level—with no financial assistance—was more likely. But that was a worry for another day, and she headed down the hall to Tony's office.

When she knocked on the wood frame of his door, he looked up and a warm smile brightened his face.

"You look vaguely familiar," he said.

"I know—it's been too long." She pulled out a chair and sat down.

"How's the family? Your mother doing okay?"

Liz had confided in Tony about her mother's illness. He'd been concerned and sympathetic, remembering Joanie Boyle as a long-ago friend of his former wife. "Thanks for asking," she said. "Mom is still pretty active, all things considered."

"Glad to hear it." He paused before adding, "You know, today I see a family resemblance between you and Joan. Except she was a redhead, as I recall."

"Now she's a blonde." Recently, her mother had taken to wearing a wig to cover up her thinning hair as Ned had suggested. But she hadn't captured the Marilyn Monroe look they had collectively imagined. Rather than soft and curvaceous, Joanie appeared more like a skinny Carol Channing, her face overshadowed by the volume of pre-styled hair.

"So, when do the movers arrive?" she asked.

"Next month. Middle of October."

Liz glanced around the room. "Looks like the house is all set to go on the market."

"It is. But before we get my nosy neighbors tramping through, I'd like to ship the valuables to my son. The Persian rugs, the large paintings. I think I'll send my mother's sterling silver too."

"Won't the rugs help show the place?"

Tony grunted. "I don't think they'll matter much. According to the realtors I've consulted, I'll only get lot value for my home. They didn't come right out and say it, but they figure it's a teardown."

"That's crazy," Liz said. But it was likely the truth. Her parents' ranch house, built in the '50s, was probably the same. That's how it was in California. Everyone wanted new.

The boxy telephone set next to Tony began to ring. He leaned over to view the LED display and froze. "Oh my God," he whispered, gripping the edge of his desk.

Liz stood up and peered at the phone. She read MARINO, ANGELA followed by a phone number with a 212 area code.

"It's my daughter," he said in disbelief. The phone rang again and again. Liz couldn't stand it. On the fifth ring, she grabbed the handset and pushed it into Tony's trembling fingers.

"Hello? Hello?" The old man looked terrified, not knowing what would come from the mouth of this lost daughter, this ghost of a girl. Or *woman*, as Liz reminded herself. Angela was likely older than she was, at least fifty by now.

Liz picked up her coffee and scooted from the room to give Tony some privacy. As she walked back to the kitchen for a refill, she glanced out a window and saw Aasal dragging the recycling bins into the storage shed. Whatever was transpiring between Tony and Angela, he would want to know.

She sat down at the small kitchen table and glanced at the newspaper. Five minutes passed, then ten, fifteen. Finally, she heard Tony call her name and she hustled back to his office.

"I have the most wonderful news," he said. His hands were clasped together in thanks.

"What is it?"

"Lehman Brothers filed for bankruptcy. They're going under! Angela has lost almost everything."

Liz stared at him, afraid that he'd suffered some kind of stroke that was affecting his cognitive abilities. But he wasn't slurring his words; his mouth wasn't crooked.

"How is that good news?" she asked gently.

"She needs my help." A sob broke from his throat, and his eyes and nose began to run. But he was smiling too. "Liz, you're not going to believe it. Angela wants to come home."

Tony shuffled to the bathroom to blow his nose and collect himself. When he returned to his desk, Aasal appeared and took the seat next to her. Together, they listened while Tony recapped his conversation with Angela, the first meaningful communication they'd had in nearly two decades.

"At first, she was crying and I couldn't make out what she was saying. But then she calmed down and gave me the blow-by-blow." Angela, a partner at Lehman Brothers, had nearly all her net worth tied up in the investment bank, and it was unlikely she'd get much—if anything— back. "The firm was so overleveraged," Tony said, shaking his head. He was quick to add that Angela had nothing to do with the doomed, real-estate hedge-fund business. "She worked on the fixed-income trading floor," he said, as if that absolved her of all wrongdoing.

Liz nodded, not really understanding the nuances of his explanation, but getting the gist of it. "How devastating for her."

"Yes, to say the least," Tony said, pushing back his sleeves and taking a few hasty swallows of coffee. "She's utterly exhausted and wants to return to California. And here's the kicker." He leaned forward, modulating his voice to a dramatic whisper. "She's coming alone. She and her husband are 'taking a sabbatical.' Which suits me just fine—I never really cared for the man. In fact, I hold him largely responsible for her long absence. He's a native New Yorker and has basically held her hostage there."

Aasal cast her a sidelong glance, and she held it momentarily. Tony was tweaking history here, seeming to forget his infidelity and subsequent divorce that had hardened Angela's heart against him so long ago. But neither of them interrupted the old man to split hairs. He looked happier and more vigorous than Liz had believed possible. It must have been terribly difficult for Angela to ask for help like this, to be so vulnerable. And yet, her unfortunate turn of luck was drawing the family together, just as Tony's attempted suicide had.

"Angela arrives on Sunday for an indefinite stay. Aasal, let's put her in the master upstairs. She'll love the deep tub in the bathroom. And the view of the foothills!" Tony stood up and began walking excitedly back and forth behind his desk. Gone was his shortness of breath, the hitch in his step. He stopped abruptly and looked at Liz as if he'd completely forgotten why she was there. She prompted his memory.

"About the move to your new apartment. Do you still want me to get those items shipped?"

"Heavens no. For now, the move is on hold. I'm not going anywhere. On the days that Aasal is in Oregon watching Sammy play football, Angela and I will keep an eye on each other right here." He sat down and rubbed his hands together, warming to the new plan that was falling into place with the speed of a miracle. Liz wondered if Angela had any idea that eldercare would be part of her homestay package, but she didn't let on about her concerns.

"Tony, I'm so happy for you," she said.

"Thank you, dear. The global markets are crashing and my stocks are in the toilet, but I feel like the luckiest guy in the world."

She stood up, preparing to leave.

"Oh, don't go," Tony said. "I haven't taken my daughter out to dinner in ages, and it just occurred to me that you gave away all my nice clothes. Any chance we could get some of those back from St. Vincent's?"

Liz averted her gaze, feeling the heat rise in her cheeks. "Um, I'm not sure. Gabbi dropped that stuff off months ago."

"I'm just kidding. I want new clothes! You know how well-dressed New Yorkers are. Let's go shopping. You can help me buy a few outfits to impress my girl."

"Sounds fun," Liz said, laughing.

In the elegant white Jaguar, Aasal drove their little trio to Nordstrom where they selected some new trousers for Tony as well as coordinating sweaters and a pair of comfortable shoes. In addition to his own purchases, Tony bought Aasal a rain jacket for Oregon and a bottle of pricey perfume for Liz, despite their protests that it was totally unnecessary. When it was time to go home, Aasal helped Tony onto the escalator and over a few curbs, but otherwise Tony navigated largely under his own power.

Liz prayed her mother would show the same signs of improving health in the coming weeks. A scan that showed the tumors shrinking away would provide the elixir of sweet relief. With Angela's call from out of the blue today, anything felt possible.

Chapter 25

While the national media feasted on the Lehman Brothers cataclysmic closing, the local papers circled back to the Haley Chan story like scavengers to roadkill. As Gabbi had predicted, Neptune's Water Park had been forced to make a hasty settlement in the face of so much public outcry—sparked, in no small part, by the child's memorial service. Earlier in the day, when Liz picked up the Friday paper, the headline read:

As Ticket Sales Sink,
Water Park Settles with Chans for $17M

According to the article, payments would come from Neptune's as well as the mechanical raft manufacturer and the ride's maintenance provider.

Liz stirred a pot of chicken chili and wondered if the settlement would bring some kind of peace to Tammy and Kyle Chan. Ben had confided in her that Maddy's parents were bickering incessantly in recent weeks, and that Mr. Chan was bunking in the guestroom. None of that was surprising to Liz. After Maggie died, her parents' marriage barely survived. Grief had uncoupled them, and while they didn't openly argue, the silence between them was stifling. Liz had long suspected that only an old-fashioned commitment to their vows had enabled them to muddle through their sorrow to the distant shore of acceptance and renewed love.

Letting the chili simmer, she turned on the evening news and was startled by the image of Tammy Chan being interviewed in her front yard by the *Channel 2 Eyewitness News* team. As always, Tammy appeared camera ready, dressed in a crisp, black suit with fresh makeup and styled hair. Kyle was conspicuously absent. Perhaps this was one of the things the two had quibbled about—how to handle the press. The statuesque blonde reporter from the memorial service stood next to her, tipping the mic toward Tammy's angry, pursed lips.

"And remember, it was not an accident that killed my daughter. It was *negligence*," Tammy said, shaking her fist. "I vow to put part of our settlement toward improving amusement park safety. And to holding people account-able! For starters, the Neptune's director of operations should be charged with involuntary manslaughter."

A shadow skated across the kitchen window, and she saw Ben and Maddy pull up. They scrambled out of the car and hurried inside.

"The reporters are trying to track down Maddy," Ben said, ripping off his baseball cap and tossing it angrily on the kitchen counter. "Such assholes! We're going to lay low here."

Liz clicked off the TV just as Maddy appeared wearing her soccer sweats and lugging a backpack. She looked on the brink of tears, and Liz went to her and wrapped her in her arms. They weren't much different in height and weight, but Liz felt the strength of a grizzly coursing through her as she led the girl to the couch.

"Somehow, a reporter got my cell number," she said. "He asked me what it felt like to be a millionaire."

Liz closed her eyes and shook her head in disbelief.

"It's not like we're having some kind of party now," she said. "Hales is still gone." The grinding sound of a blender interrupted her as Ben whipped up a fruit shake for them and assembled a plate of cookies. Maddy stared morosely into Liz's eyes. "We haven't gotten the money yet, but my parents are already fighting about how to spend it. Dad wants to move away and build a house in the mountains. Everything here reminds him of Haley. He hates driving by the gym...knowing she's not inside."

"You're not going anywhere," Ben said, handing her a shake and settling next to her on the sofa. He kissed her lightly on the ear, and she beamed at him. Liz found herself wondering, would they be together this time next year, when Ben was away at college? She and Peter had not survived the separation, but she'd been grateful for that first love that helped her put many painful memories behind her. Ben's love would do that for Maddy too. She was certain that, years from now, Maddy would remember Ben Becker with enduring tenderness.

After finishing their snack, the kids migrated into Ben's bedroom. Liz noted that they left the door ajar. In addition to his homework, Ben had college essays to write and applications to fill out. Maddy had actually been helping him with all that; she was an excellent student. And keeping busy was good for her—a healthy break from all the tension at home. As she had many times before, Liz would set an extra place for Maddy at dinner tonight. She had assured Liz that her parents didn't mind, and Liz believed her. No one wanted to attend a family dinner minus one.

She returned to the stove to check on the chili just as Jamie came through the front door. "Bye, Grandpa," he yelled. "Thanks for the ride." Through the window, she watched Arnie wave before pulling away from the curb.

Lately, Jamie was spending more time at his grandparents' house where he and Jo-Jo brainstormed storylines and designs for potential video games. Liz and her father were delighted that Jamie was keeping his grandmother engaged as she learned to manage her "chronic disease." In turn, her genuine interest in his game concepts seemed to energize him.

At the kitchen table, Jamie dug into his backpack and pulled out a folder. "Look at these sketches," he said. "Not too bad, huh?" He grinned and blushed, casting his eyes briefly to his feet. "I'm trying to decide which one of our characters to create digitally."

Liz sifted through the drawings depicting Jamie as a comic strip character. In one, he donned dark goggles and a menacing cape. The second featured him in high tech armor brandishing a weapon. In the third rendering, he wore a gold helmet and had a jetpack strapped to his shoulders.

"Wow," Liz said.

"Yeah, Jo-Jo wants me to work on my inner superhero." He laughed softly, and then his face grew more serious. "She said that life can be hard. That I need to be ready for hidden *roadside bombs*."

Liz nodded. Whether her mother was referring to house fires or cancer, she wasn't sure.

"I think I'll go with the jetpack," he said, helping himself to the leftover cookies and dregs in the blender. "Ben and Maddy here?"

"Yep, in Ben's room. He's working on his college essays. How're yours coming along?"

"Well," he began, wiping froth from his upper lip, "I thought I had a good draft for my main essay. But that got torpedoed at our senior assembly today."

"Why?"

"A visiting admissions officer from the Ivy League told us to stay clear of three subjects." Jamie held up his fingers. "Sports. Divorce. Grandparents. She said they'd seen every version of those essays. Nothing new to say. So, there goes my story about Jo-Jo."

"That's ridiculous," Liz said. Undoubtedly, Ben was crafting an essay about sports this very instant. No one in school admissions could understand Ben if they didn't know how much he loved the deep *thunk* of a baseball slamming into the heart of his leather glove. And as far as Jamie was concerned, his grandmother was the only soul on earth who really got him.

"You keep your essay about Jo-Jo," she said. "Don't let a jaded old counselor dictate what you say about yourself."

Truth be told, she wanted Jamie to write that story about her mother for selfish reasons too. It would be a tribute, a record, a page she could turn to somewhere down the road.

Chapter 26

Though Joanie had tolerated the new treatment quite well for many weeks, when Liz helped her on the scales that morning, she'd dropped another three pounds. And when Rafael, the physical therapist they'd hired, encouraged her to do strengthening exercises with medicine balls and elastic bands, she had begged off, complaining of fatigue.

Arnie tugged gently on Liz's sleeve and led her into his den. "We're failing her," he said. He briefly covered his face with his broad palms to hide the tears that threatened to spill from his eyes. "Maybe we should take her to a skilled nursing facility. Do you think they'd do a better job of feeding her? Making her stronger?"

"I don't know, Dad. Doctor Jacobs gets back on Monday. I'll call her first thing and see what she recommends." Liz didn't want to send her mother away for fear she might never come back. For her, the solution was to try harder to increase her mother's calorie intake and find new forms of exercise. But maybe the stress of managing her care was too much for her father.

"Dad, why don't you get out of the house for a bit. I know Cheddar would love a W-A-L-K." On cue, the old retriever began to bark and scurry around in small circles.

Her father nodded. "I could use a little fresh air."

After he left, she returned to the bedroom where she found her mother pulling on a sweater and pants. Joanie suggested they sit on the back patio and enjoy a cup of tea. Though summer had come and gone, it was still pleasantly warm in the sun where they settled into their porch chairs.

"Look, Lizzie. Aren't the leaves on the maple trees glorious this time of year? We had maples at our first house too." She squinted up into the treetops and smiled. "When you and Maggie were little, we used to collect the fallen leaves and trace them on construction paper with crayons. Do you remember?"

"I do," she said. *Maggie* was a name that now slipped freely from her mother's lips, seemingly without pain. On one hand, it was a pleasure to hear it, to share a memory of her ginger-haired younger sister. But it marked a change in her mother, and, under the circumstances, change was something Liz didn't trust.

"Maggie always colored her leaves purple—and you always tried to correct her. Because autumn colors are red, orange, and yellow. Not violet."

"That sounds like me," Liz admitted, laughing.

Her mother set down her mug and turned to face her more directly, a wistfulness in her eyes.

"We had some good times, didn't we? Way back then?"

"Of course, Mama. Of course, we did."

"I'm glad you think so. And I hope, honey, that you'll remember those good times. Long after I'm—"

"Don't say it."

Her mother sighed and settled back against the sun-faded cushions. "Okay. Not now. But soon, Lizzie. There are things I want you to know."

When her father and Cheddar returned home, Liz made a hasty exit. Arnie was showing signs of battle fatigue, and her mother appeared resigned to lose the fight. From her car, she phoned Dr. Jacobs' assistant and asked for a consult with the oncologist as soon as possible. When the young woman asked if there was some kind of medical emergency, Liz hesitated. "No," she said after a long silence. She refused to believe the situation was dire.

Back at the office, she searched her email, hoping to find a request from a client or vendor that needed attention—anything to keep her thoughts from racing into dark corners. She was grateful to find a number of items requiring her feedback, but just as she was digging in, an email appeared from Peter Levine. Subject line: *In town 'til Tuesday*. She opened the note and discovered that Peter had arrived today, Friday, to help his parents downsize. They were moving into a senior living residence, and his job was "to make forty years' worth of old furniture—and crappy memories—disappear." He wanted to know if Liz had time to catch up over a bite to eat. "Of course, bring your husband too, if that works."

Liz hadn't expected this, but she quickly warmed to the notion of seeing Peter and thanking him face-to-face for all his vital help. She texted him that she was free tonight, but her husband had another engagement. Dusty was managing a coaching seminar for the middle school football league he'd agreed to help run. Since his construction work was still intermittent, Liz had encouraged him to take the voluntary position. He loved everything about youth sports, and the meetings, practices, and games were getting him into a better frame of mind. She wondered if she should tell Dusty in advance about her meeting with Peter but didn't want to worry him in any way. After a quick meal, she'd be home long before he was.

"*Meet at the Dutch Goose?*" she texted. Seconds later, her phone buzzed and it was Peter.

"That joint is still open?" he asked, laughing. "Much as I'd love a greasy burger, I think I better go lighter. How about Leland's Tavern?"

"At the Hoover Hotel?"

"Yep, I'm staying here. Dad moved into my old bedroom after he got Parkinson's. Is 6:00 p.m. too early? I'm on East Coast time."

"Not too early at all. See you there." She put away her phone and tried to ignore the fact that her heart was racing.

Liz stepped out of her car wearing fitted black jeans with ankle boots and a lavender silk blouse. As she had told herself in front of the full-length mirror at home, she looked good but not "hot to trot," a term her mother once applied to the young divorcee who lived next door. She doubted that she would bump into anyone she knew—generally, only hotel guests frequented the restaurant—but if she did, she wanted to appear as innocent as her intentions for the evening. Namely, to thank Peter for helping her mother access a new doctor and clinical trial. And if they reminisced about their youth over a drink or two? No harm, no foul.

She found Peter already seated in a leather booth in the rear of the restaurant, reminding her of that discreet table in the back of the public library from their first date. He waved at her while holding a full glass of red wine.

"Elizabeth, over here."

A smile played across her lips. No one ever called her by her full name, which was precisely the reason Peter often did when they were a young couple. "Elizabeth" never failed to get her attention. She cast back to the last time she'd heard him say it. They were both eighteen and departing for colleges in different directions. "See you at Thanksgiving, Elizabeth," he'd whispered in her ear. "Don't forget me."

"Hello, Mr. Levine," she said as he stood to give her a brief hug. And he did look like a *Mister*. Dressed in jeans, buffed loafers, and a houndstooth blazer, he appeared mature and successful. A far cry from the skinny, tangle-haired boy she had once known. It occurred to her that if her father could see Peter now, he'd say, "Here is a man who makes money in his sleep."

"What can I get you to drink?"

"A glass of white would be great."

He gestured to a waiter and ordered her a glass of Chardonnay. When it came moments later, he turned to her and said, "Tell me about Joanie. How's she responding to the new treatment?"

She paused, not wanting to tell him that her mother appeared to be weakening. She was afraid of sounding ungrateful or discouraged. And, she realized with sudden clarity, she didn't want to talk about the illness. "Well, Pete, I'd say she's in a holding pattern."

"Perhaps that's all we can hope for," he said gently.

Nodding, she changed the subject, asking about his parents and the moving process. He told her it was a relief to have his parents transitioning to a facility with gradu-ated care, where his mother could live independently and his father had access to good nursing. "But enough about the old folks," he joked. "Tell me about your kids."

They traded stories of their children, sharing the delicate dance of describing their strengths and passions without bragging. Then, Liz asked about life in Boston and at the Cape. Visions of the stunning beach house still lingered in her mind's eye.

"Despite the endless winters, New England has its charms. But you have to understand. Meryl's family is full-on Boston Brahmin—they literally descended from the *Mayflower*." He shook his head and took a drink. "After twenty-five years in Massachusetts, I'm still considered new-ish in Meryl's community. And still Jewish," he added.

"Poor you," she said, and he threw back his head and laughed.

"I don't mean to complain. But I must say that California will always be home. Whenever I step off the plane, there's that West Coast spirit that reinvigorates me. People here look forward. They don't give a shit about your lineage."

"Do you get home very often?" She'd been under the impression that his visits were infrequent.

"I have business here and, of course, my parents. But I was always in and out." He whirled his index finger in a circle, like a revolving door. "My girls had so many activities to attend—theater productions, lacrosse games. You know the drill. But now they're essentially launched. These days, I have more time to haunt the old neighborhood...and see old friends." He smiled at her sentimentally and raised his glass, tipping it toward her, and she clinked her goblet against his.

"And what about Ned? Still a tennis coach?"

"Yeah, and still in San Diego." She wondered if *coach* was a stretch. A coach made a commitment not only to perfecting technique, but helping a player learn to win, to be resilient. Did her brother have any of these strengths? She honestly didn't know. A worry began to take hold as she realized she would need him to help coach their mother—and father—to be tougher in the face of a ruthless opponent.

The waiter reappeared and handed each of them a leather-bound menu. Famished, she scanned the array of appetizers and entrees, meticulously described in a gilt, cursive font. She had come here determined to pay for dinner, a small way to thank Peter for his kindness, but the prices on the menu nearly made her choke.

"By the way," he said, eying her over his tortoiseshell readers, "dinner's on me."

"No, Peter. My treat."

"I'm meeting with a healthcare startup on Monday. This is officially a business trip—I can expense the meals." She looked at him doubtfully. "Please," he said, reaching out to cover her hand. "Let's not worry about this." His warm touch was a comfort, and it occurred to her what a rarity it was these days to feel taken care of, pampered. She nodded, allowing herself to be wined and dined just this once.

Eventually, the conversation meandered back in time to their wonder years. Over a gourmet dinner of "autumnal salads" with figs and goat cheese, Chilean sea bass, and generous pours of wine, they laughed about their high school escapades. Nearly all were conducted under the cover of darkness: pitching rolls of toilet paper over the boughs of trees and admiring the white streamers that were hell to clean up; stealing rum from Arnie's liquor cabinet and mixing it with fizzy coke. And skinny dipping in Half Moon Bay on the first evening of summer, just days before her seventeenth birthday.

"Lord, the ocean was cold that night. My teeth chatter just thinking about it," Peter said.

"And do you remember? We only had one towel!"

"That was no accident," he chuckled. "Oldest trick in the book to keep a girl close."

Liz wagged her head in mock disdain. "Boys."

When the bill came, she peeked at her watch. It would be another hour or two before Dusty came home, and the boys would be out late watching *The Dark Knight* movie debut. Peter handed the waiter his charge card. Then, he leaned over the votive candles at the center of the table so that he was just inches away from her.

"This has been so special for me, Liz. I'm reluctant to let you go. How about a cup of tea upstairs?"

The dining room began to close in on her so that she could only see Peter's face. She stared into his eyes, a mix of earthy greens and browns, trying to interpret his invitation. Of course, she knew what Dusty would expect her to say at this juncture. And surely Meryl Levine would feel the same.

"Oh, that sounds nice, Pete. But I should get going."

"I promise I'll be good." His gave her the three-finger salute of a boy scout and then got to his feet. "Just a quick cup."

"All right, then. A quick cup," she said.

As they walked to the bank of elevators, Liz glanced nervously around the lobby. She was more than a little drunk and feeling paranoid. If anyone recognized her—and got the wrong impression—her life would be turned upside down. She stood a few feet away from Peter, trying to create the illusion they weren't together, and he kept his distance. Seconds later, when she heard someone call her name, she thought it was just her jumbled brain playing tricks.

"Mrs. Becker! Mrs. Becker!" Through the heavy doors of the hotel's entrance, a stocky young bellhop hustled in wearing a red vest and carrying two suitcases. Liz recognized the catcher from Ben's baseball team who'd recently graduated.

"Hi, Hutch. How's the new job going?" she asked. A clammy heat broke out at the back of her neck and under her arms.

"Oh, it's fine for now." He lowered the suitcases to the floor, taking a breather. "I'm still living at home and saving up for college. I guess you could call this a gap year." He looked past her, no doubt in search of Dusty.

"I'm...I'm meeting with a client," she said.

"Oh, well, if she needs help with her luggage, let me know!" He smiled and then hustled off with the suitcases. As he turned the corner toward the reception desk, Liz sent Peter a telepathic SOS and bolted for the ladies' room.

The bathroom, with amber lighting and flocked wallpaper, was blessedly empty. Taking a few deep, restorative breaths, she rinsed her hands in cool water, then lifted her hair and patted the back of her neck with a damp paper towel. Hutch had called her "Mrs. Becker," and it was imperative to remember that's precisely who she was. She needed to say good night to Peter and head home immediately. Squaring her shoulders, she walked briskly back to the lobby, rehearsing a polite but efficient farewell. But when she spotted Peter, he smiled at her with such disarming affection, her resolve melted away. When the elevator dinged and opened, he waved her in and she obliged.

They exited on the fourth floor. He swiped his key card to open the door, and she hesitated briefly before stepping across the threshold. Inside was a well-appointed room with a king-sized bed, wide-screen TV, and a table with a hot water carafe and an array of coffee and teas. Peter selected a music channel on the TV and switched on the hot water. So, the invitation for tea was legit.

When he handed her a mug of chamomile that was dangerously full, she brought it to her lips, hoping to reduce the volume with a few quick sips. Instead, the steaming herbal tea spilled down her silk blouse.

"Hot," she yelped, setting down the mug. Peter scrambled to the bathroom to grab a hand towel and then rushed back, madly dabbing the front of her top.

"I'm okay, I'm okay," she said, laughing softly. "Geez, all grown up but still a klutz."

"A beautiful klutz," he said, pressing the towel against her.

She smiled, feeling a warm blush sweep through her, and gave him a playful look. "You're not trying to cop a feel, are you?"

He tossed the towel on a chair and leveled his gaze at her. "Is that what you want?"

This time, his face was easy to read. There was a vulnerability, but also a look of hunger. She stood still, barely breathing. And when she didn't say "no," Peter took her hand and led her to the foot of the bed where they sat down and faced each other. Slowly, deftly, he slid one hand along her cheek and leaned in for a kiss, transporting her back in time. She was no longer a wife, a mother, or a daughter. She was Peter's girl, with the all-consuming desires of a teenager. His hand traveled down her side, grazing her breast and sending a shudder through her. When she reached out to caress his thigh, a moan escaped through his lips and vibrated in her throat.

With eyes half closed in a mutual dream, they maneuvered their way up the bed, and Peter pulled back the duvet. There was blind unbuttoning and unhooking, and they found themselves half naked, skin against bare skin. Peter's kisses were deep and knowing, and the very scent of him excited her—a spicy masculinity that she'd always found irresistible. Yet, even as she was lost in his arms, flashes of Dusty tormented her. Liz knew it was unforgiveable, but she pushed the images away. She wanted Peter to take her completely, to release her from the fears that had gripped her for months. Sensing her permission, he rolled on top of her and kissed her with growing urgency. But just as she settled under him, Peter hesitated. Did he need more encouragement? She pressed her hips against him to convey her willingness. Instead of responding in kind, he lifted himself away, falling on his back and groaning against the pillows.

"I'm sorry," he said, staring at the ceiling and catching his breath. "I thought you'd stop us. You always stopped us back then. You held the line."

Liz closed her eyes and sighed. "I was a virgin," she said. "I think we can safely say that condition has changed."

A brief silence passed between them before he began again. "My wife, your husband. They deserve better than this."

Liz said nothing, feeling deflated and ashamed. And pissed that he had somehow taken possession of the high road. Hadn't it been *his* idea to come upstairs? No matter; it was time to go. She discreetly fetched her clothes from various places on the bed and slipped into the bathroom, shutting the door. After dressing quickly, she glanced in the mirror and discovered that the girl she felt herself to be just minutes ago had changed back into a woman in her forties. There were the familiar lines around her blue-gray eyes, the traces of silver in her dark hair. She rummaged through her purse and pulled out a comb and some lipstick, then checked to see that her buttons were aligned and everything was properly tucked in. When she opened the door, she found that Peter was fully dressed too.

"I feel like such an ass—I didn't mean for it to go this way," he said. He reached for her hand, and it struck Liz that he, too, looked middle-aged. Earlier, she hadn't noticed the gray at his temples and the heaviness starting under his chin. She let him briefly touch her fingers and then withdrew her hand.

"It's dark. Let me walk you to your car," he offered.

"Oh, no. The parking lot is very well lit. I'm fine, really." The last thing she wanted was for the two of them to risk another encounter with Hutch the bellhop. She turned toward the door and then remembered the reason she'd come to the hotel in the first place.

"Thank you again for all you've done for my mom, my family," she said, feeling the dread of her mother's disease recolonize inside her. "And thank you for dinner." With nothing left to say, she darted out the door and down four flights of stairs to a rear exit from the building.

When she arrived home, neither Dusty's truck nor the boys' car was in the driveway. Hating herself and feeling undeservingly lucky that she wouldn't have to explain where she'd been, she let herself into the pitch-dark house. Then, she undressed for the second time that night and stepped into the shower, washing away any trace of Peter Levine. After toweling off, she pulled on her nightgown and took a sleeping pill, hoping it would combat the hangover already clouding her head. Shivering under the covers, stripped of any lingering romantic notions, she felt as haunted as ever. And she wondered, did he feel foolish as well? For believing that Lizzy Boyle, his old flame in California, could offer an escape from his too-perfect, Boston Brahmin life?

Her thoughts turned to her husband. No one could say that Dusty Becker suffered from a too-perfect life. His father had died before they met, and his mother had remarried and moved to North Carolina, a woman who showed little interest in her only son and grandchildren. And Dusty's construction business was always at the mercy of swings in the economy. Yet, despite these unpleasant realities, she and the twins had always been enough to make Dusty a contented man. Before dozing off, she texted him a message of good night. Then she switched off the lamp and vowed to love him better.

Chapter 27

At her father's request, Ned flew up to the Bay Area to attend a family consultation with Dr. Emma Jacobs. This time, her brother didn't stay with Liz. After arriving that morning on an open-ended ticket, he moved into his former bedroom at their parents' house.

"We need reinforcements," her dad said to her wearily on the phone.

Earlier in the week, Joanie had undergone more CT scans, and Dr. Emma had called to say the results were back and they needed to discuss them. Her dad heard the urgency in the doctor's voice and understood the news was likely not good. But no M.D. had to tell them that Joanie was in trouble. At night, she picked at the dinners Liz prepared and left her glass of wine untouched. What's more, she'd skipped another of her beloved book club meetings and—the largest tell of all—no longer took a seat before her easel and paints. Yesterday, she had trouble walking and confessed to having no idea what day of the week it was. Arnie had called Ned, feeling overwhelmed. Liz shared her father's fatigue and wondered what her brother could bring to the table.

At the hospital, she led the way into the consultation room, and Ned trailed their parents. Gone were his tennis shorts and flip-flops, and the Ray-Ban sunglasses that had long created the illusion of youth. Today, he was dressed in slacks and scuffed wingtips, and an ill-fitting button down with sleeves rolled to his elbows. He'd turned forty-eight, pushing fifty now, and Liz saw him through new lenses. He appeared like a sun god fallen to earth. His handsome face was deeply tanned, but there were creases and crow's feet, and the silver in his thinning blond hair glinted in the fluorescent lights. Perhaps their mother's illness was taking a toll on him too.

They took their seats around the table just as the doctor appeared in the doorway. Though there was a seriousness in her eyes that alarmed Liz, Dr. Emma greeted them warmly, and Ned stood to shake her hand.

"This is our son," Joanie said, a dreaminess in her voice that was at odds with their visit. "Our oldest." It still irked Liz that Ned had claim to being the oldest, a title that carried weight and implied maturity. The birth order in their family had never made sense. For the six years of Maggie's life, Liz had been the middle child. But after her sister died, she became the youngest. Yet never the baby, never the child who was coddled and indulged. Liz had been the responsible one and Ned the eternal boy. She stole a glance at him as he settled in his seat. Did his changed attire, wingtips and all, indicate he was finally stepping up?

Dr. Emma joined them at the table and picked up a notepad and pen. Then she slipped on her glasses and focused on Joanie.

"How are you feeling today? Can you describe your symptoms?"

"I'm a bit tired, and..." She wobbled back and forth in her chair to demonstrate how she felt. "Shaky on my feet. My thinking is a little froggy."

"*Foggy*," Arnie clarified gently.

Dr. Emma nodded. "These symptoms are consistent with what I'm seeing on the CT scans. I'm afraid the targeted drug therapy isn't working as well as we'd hoped. The drugs are arresting the tumors in your body, but the cancer cells are spreading in the brain, causing a build-up of cerebrospinal fluid." She stood up and touched a detailed poster illustrating a cutaway of the human head. "The excess fluid here affects balance and cognitive functioning."

Dusty had been right. They should have brought out the big guns at the get-go. Nuked the little tumors straight to hell. She wished he was here, but he had to take work when he could get it. And after the fiasco with Peter, she didn't feel as if she could ask her husband any favors. Not that he knew anything about that night. By some inexplicable grace, he hadn't noticed her skittish behavior, hadn't detected the cheat in her eyes.

"Is radiation still an option for Mom?" she asked.

"No, whole brain radiation would be devastating. But there is another option: we could implant a shunt to drain the fluid. I'd also recommend raising the dose of the targeted drug therapy to see if that improves efficacy."

Her mother turned to face her father, appearing confused and unable to decipher what the doctor was saying.

"So, brain surgery," Arnie said.

"Only if that's what Joanie and your family want to pursue," Dr. Emma said. She sat back in her chair and removed her glasses. "A perfectly acceptable alternative is to stop treatment and enter palliative care. Hospice can—"

"No," Liz said. She looked at her parents and then Ned. "We want to keep fighting, right?" Nods all around.

"Please understand that the shunt will offer only short-term benefits. As many as nine months, but possibly fewer."

"We'll take whatever we can get," Liz said. In that instant, nine months stretched out before her like a lifetime. Her mother would live to enjoy another Christmas, to see the twins graduate in June. And maybe, while they bought more time, a new drug would become available, allowing them to cheat death yet.

A week later, a team of healthcare workers rolled her mother, sitting upright in a wheelchair and projecting a hopeful smile, out of a van and into her home. With no wig or makeup, she appeared vastly diminished but determined to impress her family. The back of her head had been shaved where the shunt was inserted, and Frankenstein-like stitches zigzagged down her scalp in a way that made Liz wince. Yet the drain had delivered immediate benefits. In the foyer, her mother stood up and walked tentatively toward Liz to give her a hug.

"The fog has lifted," she said triumphantly.

Game on, Liz thought. She looked at her mother with the pride and thrill she'd felt when Ben took his first steps, and then Jamie.

Ned and Arnie emerged from the guest bedroom where Joanie would be staying temporarily in a hospital bed until she regained her strength. They showed her around, pointing out their handiwork where they had installed grab bars in the shower and plugged in a new TV. Her father had also added books and magazines to the bedside table, as well as a baby monitor. "So that I can hear your every wish," he said. And if she needed assistance moving about the house, the closet contained a walker and cane.

"What's that?" Joanie pointed to a recumbent stationary bike pushed into a corner.

"That's for you, Mom," Liz said. "Dusty got it at a garage sale down the street."

Her husband's thoughtfulness momentarily gutted her as she flashed on Peter—who still hadn't so much as emailed her since their misguided tumble in bed. Not that there was anything to say. But Liz wondered, was he tip-toeing around his wife, terrified she might be able to see the crack in his integrity? The shadow across his heart?

"Oh, that was nice of Dusty," Joanie said.

"You can sit down and pedal when you watch the news. To build up your muscles." Liz reached down to grab her own thighs in demonstration. Her mother was pale and waif-like; it was time to remedy that before she grew even weaker.

Joanie eyed the equipment with a look of ambivalence.

"Do you want to give it a try?"

"Liz, are you kidding?" Ned asked. "She just got home." He slid his arm protectively around their mother's shoulders. "Give it a rest."

"I'm not asking her to bike the Tour de France. Just to check it out." As she suspected, her brother didn't have the guts of a true coach. Didn't he understand? Going easy on their mother wouldn't save her.

"Why don't I give it a spin after lunch?" Joanie suggested.

"Great idea," Arnie said. "Let's eat. I picked up some hot soup and turkey sandwiches."

"Fine," Liz said, feeling chagrined that her parents had to broker a peace between their grown children. She wondered how long Ned would stay on this tour of duty. However long it was, job number one was to get on the same team.

She glanced at her watch and remembered her meeting with Gabbi and their new client later today. As Ned accompanied their parents to the kitchen, she felt a spurt of relief—she was free to go.

"What do you think about 'Death Concierge'?" Gabbi asked, sweeping her hand in an arc above her head, as if imagining her name in lights on a marquis. "I'm thinking of putting that on my business card."

Was she joking? Liz couldn't tell. "Go for it," she said. "But I think I'll pass. Happy to use the old cards." It never ceased to amaze her that Gabbi contemplated death only in terms of a new market with promising revenue streams and branding opportunities.

The doorbell rang, and Gabbi's head turned in surprise. "You expecting someone? The O'Learys are coming in to discuss the memorial at the aviation museum. But that's not for another hour."

"No," Liz said. "Hope they're not early." She was still finalizing the costs of the specialty cocktails and buffet dinner.

Seconds later, a young man with a messenger bag trotted up the stairs. "Package for Elizabeth Boyle," he said—and Liz knew instantly who it was from. She carried the thin, rectangular box to her office and placed it on her desk. *Fragile, handle with care* was written by hand across the front, and she recognized Peter's careful script. After gently removing the packing tape and bubble wrap, she pulled a framed canvas from the box and was momentarily overwhelmed.

"My God, it's you," Gabbi said.

Liz raised her head to meet Gabbi's dark, wondering eyes. She hadn't been aware that she'd followed her in.

"Well, it used to be me," she allowed. It was the oil painting her mother had given Peter before he'd left for college. In a few places, the paint had cracked over time, but the color was as vivid as she remembered. The artwork featured her seventeen-year-old self on the brink of womanhood. Her hair was in a girlish ponytail, and the portrait captured her in partial profile, giving her a dramatic appearance that accentuated her long, dark eye lashes and tentative half smile. Her mother had always admired Vermeer's *Girl with a Pearl Earring*, and some of the rich blues and yellows in the painting recalled that famous image.

"Where on earth did this come from?" Gabbi asked.

"Oh, an old flame from high school," she said, swatting the air as if the whole thing was a nuisance. But that wasn't how she truly felt. Each day that brought no word from Peter had deepened her humiliation and given rise to swells of guilt. At the very least, this package was an acknowledgment of sorts. He hadn't simply extinguished her from his thoughts.

"And...?" Gabbi asked, leaning in for more details. But Liz had no intention of spilling her secret to Gabbi or anyone else. She offered only the partial story of Peter's parents moving to a senior living community and the need to get rid of old junk.

"You and I both know this isn't junk," Gabbi said.

"No, you're right. My mother painted it." She felt a flush of pride warm her face.

"I thought so. It's stunning. And to think your old beau kept it for so many years. If that's not unrequited love, I don't know what is."

"Don't be ridiculous. I'm sure it's been collecting dust in the garage."

"If you say so," Gabbi said, drifting back to her desk on the other side of the office. Free to look more carefully through the cardboard box, Liz found a small card.

Dear Liz,

On my visits home over the years, I've enjoyed reacquainting myself with this lovely girl. But now that the old house has sold, it's time to return her. Please thank your mother for the special painting. Something tells me she'll enjoy seeing it again. She (and *you*) are in my thoughts.

Peter

Liz exhaled, more than willing to accept this closing of the unexpected chapter with Peter. Not that the note absolved her in any way, but she did feel somewhat restored—and grateful, in the end, that Peter had limited their indiscretion. She replaced the painting in the bubble wrap and tucked it back into the box, unsure what to do with it. Hanging it at home would trigger unwelcome questions about how it came into her possession. Showing it to her mother would do the same. For now, she'd stow it in the back of her van.

With that decided, she returned to her computer and finished the estimates for the O'Leary memorial. The event was still a few weeks away, but it promised to be a grand gathering. As Liz reviewed the numbers, she realized she and Gabbi would net about the same profit as a mid-sized wedding. And that was a piece of welcome news.

Chapter 28

*L*iz should have been grateful for her brother's help, but Ned's presence was a constant aggravation, an itchy wool sweater on a too-warm winter day. She'd been trying to get their mother to eat more, but each time she carried in a tray of carefully prepared food, Joanie raised her palm in the international gesture for HALT. Yet today, after Ned breezed in from a weekend away—he'd been invited to play in a swanky tennis tournament in the Wine Country—her mother developed a sudden appetite. A renewed desire to be compliant. When he brought in a bowl of tomato basil soup and lifted a full spoon to her gaunt face, her jaw dropped open like a Christmas nutcracker.

"Thank you," her mother said, swallowing with some difficulty. "It's yummy."

Liz busied herself at the foot of the bed, layering an extra blanket across Joanie's legs. She averted her eyes from Ned, dodging the look of satisfaction on his perennially sunny face, and slipped out of the room.

After their mother had finished her soup and cheerfully consented to a cookie and cup of tea, Ned ambled into the kitchen and scooped up his car keys.

"I'm headed to Starbucks for a chai latte. Want anything?"

"Not for me," Liz said, drying her hands on a dish towel. She wondered how long he'd be MIA. An hour? All afternoon? "But if you could swing by the pharmacy, Mom needs more lotion and eye drops." The pills from the clinical trial were still causing skin and eye irritations.

When Ned was gone, Liz returned to her mother's room, bent on getting her up. Slumped into her pillows next to the morning paper, she looked disinclined to move an inch.

"Please, Mom. You don't want bed sores, do you?" Liz asked.

Joanie shook her head, remaining mute as Liz lifted the nightie over her raised arms and helped her into some faded, velour sweats. They didn't bother with a bra or makeup; her mother rarely left the house anymore except to see Dr. Jacobs. Last week, Joanie's visit to the hospital for more scans had been an ordeal, making her cross and on the verge of tears.

Liz rolled the walker to the bedside, and Joanie heaved herself up to a standing position, squeezing the hand grips and grunting with exertion.

"Good job," Liz chirped, the ubiquitous compliment she used now, just as she had when Ben and Jamie were tots, learning to master the potty and brush their teeth. She directed her mother down the hall and shadowed her closely, ready to catch her the instant she tilted off balance. Her spirits flagged as she noticed that Joanie had lost more weight. The way her sweats slipped below her hips and sagged called to mind rappers who stormed the stage wearing pants that slinked halfway down their asses. It was a look her mother despised.

Hunching forward, Joanie shuffled past Arnie's den where he waved from his cluttered desk. Liz smiled reflexively, tamping down a spike of frustration. Her father, like her brother, had proven incapable of pushing their favorite patient to regain her strength. Instead, he holed up in his office for hours at a time, ostensibly managing her medical paperwork.

They forged on. After making two snail-paced laps around the kitchen island, her mother stopped to rest, fingering a wisp of hair away from her eyes and panting softly. A black crow cawed outside the window, and she lifted her gaze to witness the last of the gold and crimson leaves of autumn brushing against the glass.

"Can we go back now?" Joanie asked.

"Not yet."

Her mother slouched briefly and then inhaled, pushing back her thin shoulders and picking up speed. Progress! But as she rounded the kitchen island a third time, rolling past the stovetop she hadn't used in weeks, Joanie clipped the edge of the counter and lost her footing.

"Mercy!" she cried, and Liz lunged for her, grasping her arm and repositioning her hands on the grips of the walker. The instant Joanie was stable again, she shot Liz a withering look.

"Okay," Liz said, rattled but still resolved. "Let's try something else." She motioned down the hall. "After you."

Once she had Joanie resettled on the edge of her bed, Liz returned the walker to the closet and picked up a small, two-pound dumbbell coated in bright pink neoprene. If nothing else, her mother liked the color. Liz kneeled before her, pressing the weight into Joanie's curled fingers, and instructed her to raise it above her head.

"Like this, Mom," she said, and thrust her fist into the air.

Joanie lifted the weight as far as her nose but paused when they heard the front door click open and footsteps drawing nearer. Ned had finished his errands in uncharacteristically good time.

But it wasn't Ned. Liz looked up to find her mother's oncologist, Dr. Emma, standing in the doorframe, her dad lingering just behind her. The doctor made house calls?

She didn't know whether to be touched by her kindness or alarmed by her presence.

"What are you doing?" Dr. Emma asked, crisscrossing her arms under her sturdy bosom. Her tone of voice caught Liz by surprise. The note of disapproval.

"I'm helping Mom build her strength." Obviously, she added silently.

The doctor removed the stethoscope draped around her neck and stuffed it into the pocket of her white coat, skipping the protocol of checking her mother's vitals.

"Liz, the scans from last week indicate the disease is very advanced. It's time we stop trying to make Joan stronger. From now on, we must focus on making her *comfortable*."

It took a moment for the doctor's meaning to register. When it did, Liz locked eyes with her father who nodded in agreement and knuckled away a tear. And just like that, it was official: they were giving up the fight to save her mother's life.

She glanced back at the doctor, who, in the span of seconds, had morphed into the Grim Reaper. Then slowly, fearful of how her mother was absorbing the sudden change in course, she turned toward her.

"Thank you, Doctor," Joanie said, relief blooming in her face. "I'm so very, very tired." She dropped the pink dumbbell to the carpet where it made a dull thud, and she crawled back into bed.

Hours later, as she folded laundry in the mudroom, Liz was still reeling. Team Joanie was throwing in the towel, embracing defeat. Her mother's death was now a certainty rather than a vague phantom hovering offshore on a kind of bleak Never Never Land. A heaviness settled in her chest, and she unzipped her sweater, finding it difficult to breathe. Liz was tormented not only by her fear, but from the accusation in Dr. Emma's voice. In her fervor to keep her mother alive, had she been too hard on her? It pained her to think that Ned's light touch may have been the better, kinder approach.

Matching up her father's dark socks, she tried to cut herself some slack. Maybe she'd been on the front lines too long. It'd been six long months since the oncologist confirmed that Joanie's persistent cough was not related to seasonal allergies but, rather, to metastatic cancer.

She heard the back door swing open and the hushed voices of Ned and their father. Invariably, they were discussing the doctor's visit, the new operating instructions for their mother's care. She stuffed a load of towels into the washer and then stacked the clean laundry into a basket before carrying it into the kitchen. There she found Ned fixing himself a snack. Beside him on the counter was a bag from the pharmacy and a dozen roses still wrapped in cellophane. The blossoms were the warm, sunny yellow color their mother adored.

"Hey," he said. "Mom's still asleep and Dad is taking Cheddar out to pee."

"Sounds good." She noted his clear eyes and relaxed brow, the untroubled way in which he munched on a potato chip. Maybe he hadn't been updated on their mother's grim status after all.

They moved into the family room and settled in front of the TV. Ned reached for the remote and switched on ESPN, never asking what she might like to watch. When he parked his enormous, loafered feet on the antique coffee table she'd polished that morning, Liz sighed. Ned acted as if he owned the damn place.

"Something buggin' you?" he asked.

"You mean other than the fact that Mom—"

"Liz." He gently tugged the loose ends of her pony-tail. "We've known from the beginning it was only a matter of time."

Liz shook her head. She'd never believed that.

"There's something else. C'mon, sis. Just spit it out."

Her instinct was to say no, she was perfectly fine. That's what she always said. But the truth was she sensed the ragged edges of her limits and was simply too tired to suck it up anymore.

"It drives me nuts," she said.

"What?"

"That I spend hours trying to get Mom to eat…to exercise…or to go into the garden for some fresh air. But nine times out of ten, she shoos me away. Then you arrive and, presto, she's Miss Congeniality. Like you're the second coming of frigging Jesus."

"Oh, that's just horseshit," he said, looking pleased. He surfed his fingers through his hair and then reached into his pocket, pulling out a fat joint from a tiny plastic bag.

"You can't be serious. Put that away." It dawned on her that Joanie's renewed appetite might be the result of so-called medicinal marijuana. "Don't tell me you're getting Mom to smoke that stuff."

"Not yet, but it's a damn good idea." He held the joint up to his nostrils and inhaled deeply before returning it to his jean pocket. How he loved to push her buttons. "So, what are you trying to say, Lizzie? That Mom likes me best?"

"Well—"

"I mean, we could just ask her, right?"

"Of course not," she said, panic creeping into her voice. She didn't want to know. But Ned got to his feet and started loping in the direction of their mother, a reckless smile on his face. Liz raced after him—castigating herself for being lured into his middle-school antics. For heaven's sake, she was a grown woman!

As they simultaneously entered her room throwing elbows, their mother stirred under the covers and opened her eyes. She seemed to register something electric in the air, a charge passing between her children. Ned crouched next to her bedside, close to her ear.

"Hi, Mom," he said, taking her pale hand into his broad palm and immediately putting Liz at a disadvantage. "Did you have a nice nap?"

Her mother nodded.

"Excellent," he said in his impossibly warm, seductive voice—the same voice he undoubtedly called upon to encourage comely young wives at the country club. Excellent volley. Excellent return of serve. Excellent form.

"Listen, Mom," he said. "We know you love both of us, of course. But we've been wondering—"

"I have not!" Liz said.

"Who is your *favorite* child? Just give us a little hint. Is it Lizzie—or me?"

A palpable silence engulfed the room, and Liz was vaguely aware that she'd stopped breathing. She was already dismissing her mother's answer, telling herself that the constellation of tiny tumors in Joanie's brain would undermine her judgement or distort her true feelings. For a long, tick-tocking moment, her mother's expression was cloudy, unreadable, and then an unexpected lightness broke across her face. She folded back the bedsheets and raised herself higher on her pillows.

"My favorite child's name," she said, "begins with the letter E."

Liz glanced at her brother who tossed back his head and laughed. She reddened—late to the game—and expelled a knowing breath: *Edward and Elizabeth.*

Rising from the carpet, Ned reached for Liz, gathering her into his arms. "Our mother, what a clever girl," he whispered into her ear. "I think we can safely say she's not dead yet."

And then Liz started to laugh too, laughing until her giddiness turned to tears.

After the favorite child stunt, Ned assured Liz that he and their father could manage the rest of the afternoon without her. Dinner would be simple: pizza from Amici's for them, leftover soup for their mom.

"Get out of here," he said, suddenly serious. "You look beat." She nodded and collected her things.

When she arrived home, the house was quiet. Dusty was in Cupertino for the day, helping a friend build an in-law unit off his garage. Lately, she felt only relief when his truck was gone, a sign that he had work to do, a hint that life might be inching back to normal. And when she was alone, she didn't feel the undertow of guilt grasping at her each time Dusty poured her a glass of wine or rubbed her shoulders. But in this moment, she wanted to fold herself into his arms and be consoled. Dr. Emma was removing her mother from the clinical trial. She wasn't going to get those nine months after all. Maybe not even nine weeks. A last Christmas together with the boys was questionable at best.

Another wave of tears threatened to engulf her, but dinner wasn't going to prepare itself. She tossed her sweater over a chair and got to work, sliding a seasoned pot roast and scrubbed potatoes into the oven minutes later. But as she was unloading the dishwasher, she knocked her shin into the metal corner of the lowered door and a bloody gash opened on her leg.

"Dammit," she cried. She grabbed a paper towel and pressed it against the wound, sinking to the hardwood floor and curling up in a fetal position. Despite the stabbing pain in her shin, it felt so extraordinarily good to be lying down. As the bright blood rushed across the white panels of paper towel, she felt overcome with sleepiness and closed her eyes.

"What are you doing?"

Again, this question. But this time it didn't sound accusatory. Rather, there was concern in the voice, alarm. Liz blinked open her eyes to see Jamie inches from her face, peering through his long, black bangs and reaching for her hand.

"Hey, buddy," she said. "I must've dozed off."

"You don't look so good, Mom." It was the second time she'd heard that too.

He helped her to her feet and threw away the stained paper towel. The bleeding had stopped, and the pain in her leg was merely a dull throb now. She sank into a chair at the kitchen table, and Jamie took a seat across from her.

"It was a long day," she said.

"At Jo-Jo's?"

She nodded.

"How is she? Any better?"

"No." She felt the corners of her mouth twitch downward. "Honey, your grandmother isn't going to get better. The truth is, she's getting weaker every day."

Jamie's expression went slack with disbelief.

"You mean she's going to...die?"

She paused, mulling over a realization that had taken root while she dozed off on the floor. "Yes. But I learned something today. I don't think Jo-Jo's afraid. I think she's getting ready."

Jamie's hand floated to his heart. "But I'm afraid, Mom. I'm so afraid."

Liz reached over and squeezed his arm.

"Me too, honey."

They heard the rumble of the automatic garage door opening and watched as Dusty entered the kitchen. He'd removed his work boots, but Liz could see flecks of sawdust in his hair and on the shoulders of his plaid flannel shirt.

"Pot roast?" he asked. "Smells great."

Liz and Jamie exchanged glances, agreeing to tuck away their fears for now. She got to her feet, remembering to check the oven, and Dusty intercepted her, pulling her into a hug.

"I talked to Ned," he said quietly. "I'm so sorry."

She sagged against him, grateful for his sturdy tenderness. When he released her, she managed to get dinner on with a semblance of normalcy. As a nod to her artistic mother, she set out pretty place mats and lit tall, ivory candles to create an atmosphere of tranquility. Minutes later, when Ben hustled through the door to join them at the table, the peacefulness was swept away. But as she glanced into his face, ruddy from the chilly evening air, Liz didn't mind his bull-in-the-china-shop energy. It was a soothing contrast to her mother's waning strength.

"Let's dig in," Dusty said, his fork raised in anticipation of the hearty meal lumped on his plate. The boys nodded, shoveling the warm roast into their mouths and ignoring their green salads.

"My counselor signed off on my college essay," Ben said between bites. "The rest of my app is done too."

"Congrats, Ben," she said. "Do you want me to proof it before you hit the 'submit' button?"

"That's okay, Mom." She heard the unequivocal "no" pass between them. "You take care of Jo-Jo, I'll take care of college stuff."

Jamie looked up from his plate, and Liz could see the temptation in his eyes to clue in his brother on the grim reality.

"I think Ben's right," Dusty said. He reached across the table and topped off her wine glass. "You've got your hands full. Let the boys take care of themselves." He turned to Jamie. "You're ready to send off your apps too, right?"

"Almost," he said, clearing his throat with a swallow of water. "But I need help with the financial aid applications. Like, I have no idea what your annual income is."

Dusty lowered his eyes, appearing tongue-tied, and Liz stepped in. "I can help you fill in those questions after dinner," she said. "Anyone want ice cream?"

After she and Jamie made progress on the paperwork and Ben and Dusty had washed the dishes, the four of them relaxed in front of the TV, watching back-to-back episodes of *CSI*. The warmth of her men beside her and the lingering buzz from the wine gave Liz an unexpected sense of calm.

But later that night, as she lay in bed listening to a steady rain tip-tap the gutters outside, sleep escaped her, and she felt weighted to the mattress by a blanket of dread. Death was coming for her mother, and she was powerless to change that. The image of her father smearing away a tear as he acknowledged that the mission was no longer to save his wife—but merely to limit her suffering—agonized her.

Before today, "till death do us part" had seemed like a quaint, romantic notion, a poetic line in an old-fashioned vow. But now she understood that it was a warning, that every deep marital love ends in a forced separation. In grief. That grief was circling her parents and closing in, just as it would someday circle her and Dusty. She'd been blind not to see it before. It had been so much easier to look away.

Chapter 29

$\mathcal{A}$unt Sally, her father's younger sister, had arrived from Wisconsin to offer her capable hands and durable good cheer. Joanie had always enjoyed her sister-in-law's company and perked up the instant Sally arrived in her cable-knit sweaters and sensible shoes, bearing gifts from the homeland. For Arnie, there was a collection of gourmet cheeses, mustards, and chutneys. And for Joanie, a pair of warm, flannel moccasins with the Green Bay Packers' logo. Perhaps the kindest gift of all was for Liz: a reprieve from cooking and nursing duties. The break couldn't have come at a better time. Although she was trying to adjust to the new program of simply keeping Joanie comfortable, Liz felt a lingering guilt for capitulating to her mother's disease. She desperately needed to step away from the sick room.

"Take this time to catch up at the office," her father advised, ever worried about her and Dusty's finances. In the paper that morning, the Labor Department reported that the economy had lost 240,000 jobs last month alone. He didn't want her to become a part of that statistic.

Liz spent the morning hours onboarding two new clients, developing proposals, and preparing bills. Gabbi's office was vacant as she was "in the field" touring final resting spots. Against all odds, their "end-of-life concierge services" appeared to be catching on.

Gabbi made a point of keeping her aging Mercedes in mint condition, tucking elderly couples into the back seat and squiring them to cemeteries up and down the Peninsula. After a recent tour, she remarked that "Old people are good company. They're not in a rush and they know what they want." Sam and Pamela Walker desired a plot near the coast with a view of the Pacific. (A view? From six feet under? Liz didn't ask.) Glen and Dottie Gruber, on the other hand, wished to be laid to rest under a stand of redwoods a few miles from their church. Gabbi encouraged their clients to "lock in today's prices" for the resting sites they desired. In these turbulent economic times, even cemeteries were offering discounts. Liz had been trying to negotiate a sales commission with the directors of the memorial parks, but nothing had been finalized. For now, she was billing clients on an hourly basis.

After finishing her proposal work, Liz reviewed Touchstone's online bank accounts. Income was covering their office overhead and allowing Gabbi and her to take decent salaries. Nothing like the previous go-go years, but still. And though she and Dusty hadn't found a buyer for the remodel, their realtor was negotiating with a couple eager to rent. The husband and wife had two young children, and they'd expressed an interest in owning the house downstream. In the moments when her thoughts weren't circling back to her mother, Liz allowed herself to feel hopeful.

As she browsed her email, she noticed a new message from Tony Marino. Subject line: *Lunch today?*

Dear Liz,

Aasal is in Eugene watching Sammy play ball, and Angela is in the city meeting with fellow refugees from Lehman's. I find myself hungry and alone. Any chance you're free for lunch? How about the café at Neiman's around 1:00 p.m.? Their warm popovers with honey butter sound darn good on a chilly day like today. Please call to confirm, or schedule for another time.

Tony

Two hours later, Liz pulled into the parking lot at Neiman Marcus feeling underdressed but unconcerned. She assumed there would be few people shopping in "Needless Mark-up" during what pundits were now calling a Depression. But once inside the tinted glass doors, she was startled to see a bevy of well-coifed women in the shoe department caressing high heels and leather boots, while others enjoyed make-overs at the cosmetic counter. And just past the escalators, Liz noticed a striking young woman standing before a mirror. She was pressing a velvet holiday gown against herself, admiring its effect from every angle.

Clearly, there were creatures in Silicon Valley who were recession-proof. Were they uber realtors who'd made a killing in the dotcom buying frenzy a decade ago? Software entrepreneurs who'd sold their app for a fortune? Or wives of venture capitalists who would never have to wait for this—or any—market to recover? Whoever they were, these women were hardly an endangered species. In nearly every department, they were milling about, and the sales staff appeared cheerful and attentive.

Feeling as if she were an uninvited guest at the party, Liz made her way up the escalator to the café. She finger-combed her dark hair and straightened her wool scarf, grateful at least that today she'd pulled on her black jeans rather than blue. Sitting front and center in the restaurant, Tony offered Liz a welcoming wave. The popovers had already arrived at the table draped in white linens, and he'd ordered two cups of English tea. What a joy it was to see him.

"How's it going with your new roomie?" she asked, grazing his cheek with a kiss.

"Angela? Oh, fine. I must say, it's been nice to have a woman's presence in the house again. It's the little things, you know? Like fresh flowers in the kitchen." He sat back against his chair and unbuttoned his cardigan, warming to his subject. "And I'd forgotten how well Angela plays the piano. The way her concertos float down the hall to my office reminds me of when she was a little girl, practicing for her recitals. By the way, I gave her that photo of us sitting together on the piano bench. She loves it." He smiled indulgently. "That said, she's not the cook her mother was. From what I gather, New Yorkers mostly order food for take-out or delivery."

"Oh, Tony," Liz said. "It's wonderful to hear that it's all working out." She could scarcely believe this happy old father was the same man who had contemplated taking his own life last June.

"Well, to be honest, it's not *all* working. There have been a few complications."

"Like what?"

"For starters, Angela and Tony Jr. are at each other's throats."

"I'm sorry," Liz said, feeling simultaneously concerned and comforted. At least she and Ned weren't the only middle-aged sibs to feud from time to time. "What's the beef?"

"My son is convinced that Angie is trying to worm her way into my good graces—just to get her hands on my house and assets."

Liz nodded as she helped herself to the basket of popovers. She understood how Tony Jr. might feel that way. After all, his father had abruptly cancelled his plans to sell his home and ship his valuables to Seattle. And he'd flung open his doors and his arms to his long-lost, prodigal daughter. *Was* Angela trying to horn in on Tony's estate after so many years of wanting nothing to do with him?

"That does sound complicated," she agreed. "What are you going to do?"

Tony dabbed the corner of his mouth with a napkin where a small glob of honey butter had collected. "My attorney suggested I simply split my estate in half. Fifty percent for Tony Jr., fifty percent for Angie. He said any other division would create 'malignant dynamics.'"

Liz nodded sympathetically. It occurred to her that the subject of her and Ned's inheritance had never come up—her parents were still in their early seventies. But now, she wondered, would those questions start to emerge? And would a fifty-fifty split be appropriate considering that she and Dusty had two kids, and Ned had never married?

"What looks good to you?" Tony asked. He was perusing the menu, and Liz was happy to drop the awkward subject of inheritance. When the waitress arrived to take their order, Liz and Tony decided on a selection of finger sandwiches and two bowls of minestrone soup.

"I've been remiss in not asking, dear. How's your mother?"

Liz took a deep breath and brought him up to speed, explaining that the treatment had failed and that they were resigned to letting the disease run its course.

"I hate feeling so helpless," she said. "There's literally nothing we can do to save her."

Tony settled his cup of tea into its saucer and gazed at her thoughtfully.

"Maybe there are ways to help your mother that have nothing to do with extending her life," he said. "For me? All I want is a little assurance from Tony and Angie that I wasn't all bad. That we had some beautiful years together. And that they know how much I've always loved them." He paused to wipe the lenses of his glasses. "I guess what I'm talking about is peace of mind. Perhaps you can find a way to give her that."

Liz felt a quickening in her blood. Tony was right. She didn't know how exactly, but there was still a way to take care of her mother. She would stay vigilant, ready to offer any service, sentiment, or touch that would help her mother take gentle leave of this world.

Chapter 30

For weeks, Liz's father had been listening to her mother's every breath, every call for assistance, every mutter from a dream. Next to her rented hospital bed in the guestroom, he'd placed a baby monitor, and he carried the speaker with him throughout the confines of their home.

In general, Joanie seemed fine with this round-the-clock eavesdropping. But today, when Liz bustled in with a tray of herbal tea and crackers, she rolled on her side and switched off the volume on the monitor.

"I want to discuss a few things with you," she said.

"And Dad can't hear?"

"No. He gets squeamish about certain subjects. Some men are funny that way. No stomach for how a baby is born into this world, no stomach for how a body leaves it."

Liz didn't like the sound of what was coming in this little talk. Her gut clenched, and she felt queasy. Apparently, she was mannish in this way.

"You might want to write some of this down," her mother added.

Liz nodded, setting down the tray and rummaging through her tote until she found a pad of paper and pen. She pulled up a chair and sat close to her mother so that she wouldn't have to raise her voice. Speaking was sometimes an effort for Joanie now.

"I'd like to be cremated," she said. "No need to take up any of our precious California soil."

"Got it," Liz managed, battling images of her still-exquisite mother being slid into a kiln. She didn't write these instructions down—as if she could possibly forget. Her thoughts turned to what Tony had quipped about cremation: "Ashes in an urn? That doesn't work for me. It'd be like spending eternity in a goddamn condo." But if Liz had learned anything in her career as an event planner, it was that everyone wanted something a little bit different. A custom solution. Even in death.

"About my obituary," her mother continued. "You remember the relevant dates, don't you? I was born in 1936. Met your dad at the University of Wisconsin. Married in '59." She paused, coughing into a Kleenex. "And in 1973, I lost my youngest child in a house fire."

Liz glanced up from her notes. "Are you sure you want to include that?"

"Of course. It's an essential part of my story." She reached out to Liz, her fingers, creased and freckled from years in the garden, lingering in the air between them. Liz took her mother's hand into her own and was surprised by the strength of her grip.

"There's a part of that story that you don't know, Lizzie. That I kept from you."

Liz pushed back in her chair, her spine rigid, and let her mother's hand slip away. "You don't have to tell me."

"But I want to. It's vital to me that you know the truth."

A strange memory surfaced in Liz's mind. In a college seminar on seventeenth-century British culture, she'd read a chapter about sin-eaters. They were destitute people who, in exchange for coin, agreed to consume a ritualistic meal that would transfer the sins of a dying person onto themselves. The soul of the dead would then be absolved, and the sin-eater would carry the burden of the transgressions forever more. Why did she recall this now? Her mother's secret might be something small, inconsequential. She laid down her pen and paper and braced herself. Whatever it was, Liz was willing to hear it, to take it on. Her thoughts wheeled briefly to the advice she'd received from Tony. Maybe this was the moment to provide peace of mind.

"Okay, Mom. I'm listening."

Her mother gazed up at the ceiling where a spider was making its way across the cracked plaster. She exhaled with a heaviness that frightened Liz, as if she might accidentally release her last breath, her very life force. But then her breathing grew more measured, and she turned to face her. "You grew up without a sister because of me," she said. "My carelessness caused the fire."

"Mom, no," Liz said, shaking her head. "It was the bad wiring in the kitchen. That's what Dad told me. Ned was there too. He heard the same thing."

"It was a lie he concocted to try and protect me. Arnie didn't want others to know that I was responsible for our daughter's death. He was afraid that our family and friends would never forgive me. That even our neighbors would turn against us." She sat up taller and drew her bedcover over her chest. "He was especially adamant that you and Ned never know."

Liz groped for words, for answers. "If not faulty wires, then what?"

Her mother's eyes fluttered shut momentarily. "That night in July, Arnie had gone out to play poker with a few friends. I was angry with him for leaving me alone on a Saturday night. You were at Mary Murney's house, and Ned was away at that mountain camp. Only Maggie was home. I'd planned on putting her to bed early and having a romantic dinner for two. But then the guys called and lured your dad off to play cards."

"Yes, I remember being at the Murneys' that night."

"I felt sorry for myself, so after tucking Maggie into bed, I had a few drinks and a smoke and watched some TV. Though I'd intended to wait up for Arnie, I got sleepy and went to bed." She paused and touched the base of her throat. "The thing is, Lizzie, I forgot to snuff out my cigarette in the den. I left it too close to a stack of newspapers."

Liz flashed on her first childhood home and could see her mother's blue-green ceramic ashtray brimming with lipstick-stained butts, a cocktail glass nearby. She bent over, peering at her mother more closely.

"Mom, how can you be so sure?"

"When the fire broke out, I knew instantly what I'd done. Back then, we had no smoke detectors so by the time I woke up, the flames had spread quickly. I remember thinking I had only one child at home, only one child to save. I heard Arnie come through the front door screaming for me. I called the fire station, and your dad ran down the hall through the smoke to Maggie's room. But she wasn't there."

Her mother tugged a tissue from the box and pressed it against her eyes.

Liz was stunned. What about her father's explanation all those years ago? That they'd found Maggie under her *favorite blankie* in her bedroom closet—untouched by the flames. Had it all been a lie? She stood up from her chair and walked briskly to the windows, pulling up the blinds and letting the slanted light of November filter into the room. She fought an impulse to dart into the damp, chilly garden and gulp the autumn air. Instead, she willed herself back to her mother's bedside.

"If Maggie wasn't in her room, where was she?"

Her mother's glistening eyes reflected a reluctance to reply. "I've said enough for now. I'm really quite tired."

"Mom."

She fell silent and seemed to gather her strength. "At first, we thought she'd escaped outside. Dad went to find her in the front yard, and I searched out back. But, Lizzie, the firemen found her in your room. We never knew why she'd fallen asleep in there."

Liz groaned, tipping her head into her hands. In the weeks and months following the fire, she had replayed the last encounter with her sister a thousand times, and now that tape streamed through her memory again. Before she'd left for the sleepover, Liz had run back to her bedroom for a swimsuit and caught Maggie there, listening to her favorite *Jackson 5* album. Perched on a chair next to the phonograph, she was singing along to "ABC" in her squawky, little girl voice. Maggie had already scratched one track, and Liz was certain she'd ruin another. "Get out!" she had shouted at her sister. "You're such a pest!" Now, she had an awful hunch. What if—when the coast was clear—Maggie had crept back to play that record? Or, waking up to flames, she'd forgotten that Liz was away and had dashed to her room for help?

"Where they found Maggie doesn't change the facts," Joanie said. She took a sip of tea and licked her parched lips, settling back against the pillows. "I was her mother—and I caused the fire. Too much drinking and smoking. If only I'd known that my dirty little habits would conspire to take my baby's life."

Liz leaned forward, gripping her knees. "Why didn't you just tell me, Mom?" Her voice caught as she tried to swallow the anguish billowing up in her throat. "It was a horrible accident. I would've understood."

"You were just ten years old, Ned only twelve. So very young. I was afraid that if you knew the truth, you'd never feel safe with me again."

Liz fell silent. The truth was, she hadn't felt safe with her mother after the fire. Ultimately, Joanie gave up smoking, but for many years the drinking grew worse.

Her father, worried sick that she'd crash the car with Liz and Ned in the back seat, had often hidden the keys to the Oldsmobile. Back then, Liz never went to bed at night without making sure that the appliances were turned off, and that embers from the fireplace had died down to a dead-cold gray. Her dad made a sweep of these fire starters too, but Liz had to always see for herself. Even today, she checked and rechecked these sorts of things and left windows cracked open for hasty exits. Whenever Dusty remarked on her OCD tendencies, she quipped, "Better safe than sorry."

"As you grew older, I wanted to tell you what really happened," her mother continued. "But was there ever a *right time* for that?" She shook her head. "And when the boys were born, you were such a good mother from the beginning. So conscientious. I was afraid that if you knew how reckless I'd been, you'd think I was a monster."

"Oh, Mom," Liz said, noting the exhaustion in her face. "I'd never think that. But, honestly, I don't know what to say."

"You don't have to say anything. I only hope you can forgive me. Before..."

"Hush now, Mom. You need to get some sleep, okay?" She stood up and reached for her purse, desperate to leave. Her mother nodded, watching her intently.

Liz slipped out of the room and darted past her father's office, choosing not to say goodbye or to discuss her next visit. He had kept the truth about Maggie from her all these years too. Her thoughts were spinning, and she needed time away from her parents. She wasn't ready to forgive either of them.

Out in the driveway, she climbed into Dusty's truck. The engine in her van had been making a clattering noise, and Dusty had offered to look under the hood. She shifted the truck into drive and rumbled away, unsure where to go. Before long, she found herself at a local park over-looking the duck pond. It was the place that had called to her when she was a girl with a shiny new driver's license. Here, in view of the old fountain that reigned over the murky water, she would ruminate on her young life, drink cheap beer with friends under a summer moon, or share secrets and caresses with Peter.

She switched off the engine and leaned back against the worn seat. Shaken as she was that her parents had deceived her, she was more distraught that her mother had suffered the guilt of Maggie's death for decades—and that she'd suffered virtually alone. Only her father had known the truth, and perhaps a fire inspector back in the day. The burden of that was staggering, and now Liz understood with stark clarity why her mother had anes-thetized herself with alcohol all those years...why she had lain listlessly on the couch staring at vacuous daytime television. If Joanie had shared the terrible truth with her family, might those lost years have been avoided? If they had each forgiven one another for the small and large parts they'd played in the tragedy—Joanie may have sparked the fire, but Arnie, Liz, and Ned had not been home to save Maggie from it—how would life have been different? Better?

Liz shifted in her seat. The "what ifs" only served to agitate her more. She gazed out the windshield, and though storm clouds were clustering overhead, she stepped out of the truck and picked her way to the muddy edge of the pond. There, she spotted a pair of geese rather than the common neighborhood ducks. When they gracefully launched into the water side by side, she was reminded that her parents, too, had mated for life. They had endured the slings and arrows in their marriage, and while her mother would not survive the cancer, her father would carry their love forward. As she watched the birds disappear behind the reeds, Liz felt a deep conviction that the pact to hide the truth about the fire had likely damaged them all. Yet, simultaneously, she experienced an undercurrent of gratitude that her parents had weathered the loss of Maggie together, giving her and Ned a fighting chance at happiness in this life.

A light sprinkle began to fall, dotting the surface of the water and awakening Liz to the realization that the afternoon was slipping away. Sorting through her mother's confession would have to wait. Tonight, she would discuss everything at length with Dusty and place a call to Ned. Back in the driver's seat, Liz headed to town as the cold rain beating against her windshield accelerated to a downpour.

When Liz opened the back door holding a bag of groceries, she spotted Dusty at the kitchen table staring at something in a bed of bubble wrap. For an instant, time froze, but then her heart began to pound and her face grew hot. *Please, not this,* she thought. *Not now.* Dusty was staring at Peter's painting of her. He'd found it in the back of the van.

He turned slowly in her direction, holding up the small notecard that Peter had enclosed with the canvas. His eyes narrowed and his face was dark with suspicion.

"Do you want to tell me why your old boyfriend is sending you gifts? Why *you* are in his thoughts?" There was a snarl in his voice she'd never heard before.

Explanations hinging on excuses and half-truths took shape in Liz's mind. But just as she was about to speak, to see if she could make any of them fly, she recognized what a pathetic hypocrite she was. Hours earlier, she hadn't been prepared to forgive her parents for lying— and yet she was on the precipice of doing that very thing. Instead of launching a phony defense, she set down the grocery bag and took a seat next to her husband.

Struggling to speak in a measured voice, she revealed how her mother had gained access to the clinical trial, that Peter Levine had "pulled some strings." Dusty listened silently, staring at her in a way that was unnerving. When she got to the part about dinner at the Hoover Hotel and being in Peter's room, she faltered, grasping to find the right words for something entirely wrong.

"For Christ's sake, Liz. Are you telling me you slept with that guy?"

She watched as his large, capable hands curled into angry fists. Dusty had always been so gentle with her, but they were in uncharted territory now.

"We didn't have sex."

"What exactly did you have?"

"I mean, we didn't go...all the way." She felt like a scared teenaged girl being interrogated by her father.

Dusty closed his eyes and grimaced. "Un-fucking-believable." He pushed away from the kitchen table and headed down the hall to their bedroom. Moments later, he returned with a packed overnight bag.

"Where are you going?" Liz asked, frightened and fighting tears.

"I'm going to Pine Street. I can't stay in this house with you another minute."

"What should I tell the boys when you don't come home tonight?"

For a fleeting second, Dusty's features softened, but then his face grew stern again. "That's not really my problem, is it?" He snapped his fingers in front of her face. "I need the keys. To my truck."

Liz hated the way he was talking to her, treating her. But she couldn't blame him. She fished in her purse and grabbed the keys, handing them over.

"I'm sorry," she said. "It will never happen again. I swear." She heard the whimper in her voice, the stupid cliché. Dusty ignored her, slamming the front door in a way that made the windows rattle, and screeched away in his pickup. How long would he stay at the remodel?

Her heart contracted as she remembered that last Saturday, they had finally signed a renter, that charming couple and their two preschoolers. She and Dusty had made plans to celebrate at the local steak house tomorrow night. The young family wouldn't take possession until the first of the year, and January was still six weeks away. Surely Dusty wouldn't be gone until then, would he?

When Ben and Jamie returned home from school, Liz told them that their father was at the other house, checking on a few things before the new renters moved in. She explained he might have to spend the night there to observe how the new heating system performed. In fact, Dusty had been planning on doing precisely that, and she was relieved to have a plausible story for his absence. When the boys nodded and settled into their rooms, she collapsed on the sofa. Instead of making dinner, she ordered pizza for delivery and poured herself a glass of wine, hoping to steady her nerves.

That night, although exhausted, Liz was unable to coax herself to sleep. Images of her little sister trapped by flames sparked from their mother's cigarette collided with flashbacks of Dusty's angry eyes and bitter words. In the middle of an endless night, she texted Dusty, telling him that if he could forgive her, she would love him better. She heard nothing in reply. When dawn seeped through her blinds, Liz longed to talk with someone she could trust. Gabbi would certainly provide a sympathetic ear, but that's not what her heart ached for. She wanted, needed, her mother.

After the boys left for school, Liz put Peter's rewrapped painting in the van and drove to her parents' home, noting that Dusty had fixed the engine. She felt a fresh pang of remorse as she considered how truly devoted he was to her, and prayed he would respond to her messages soon.

With the package tucked under her arm, she entered her mother's kitchen where her father and Ned informed her that Joanie had slept relatively well during the night and had just polished off a piece of buttered toast. She nodded and moved quickly to the guest bedroom. When she pushed·through the cracked door, Joanie searched her face, and Liz offered her a reassuring smile.

"You came back," she said.

"Of course, Mama." Liz settled in the chair next to the bed uncertain where to begin.

"Have you thought about what I said?" her mother asked.

Liz nodded. "I'm sorry you carried the weight of that terrible truth alone. The story you told Ned and me back then—about faulty wiring causing the fire—I understand it was meant to protect us."

"Are you saying that you can forgive me?"

"Yes. But more than that, Mom, I want you to know that I've made dreadful mistakes too. We aren't so different."

"Really? Your brother would be surprised to hear that." Her face brightened, and she brushed away the wispy gray bangs that had fallen over her eyes. "Behind your back, he calls you 'Little Miss A++.'" A thin smile formed on her mother's lips, and Liz felt the heaviness in the room begin to lift. But she was compelled to set the record straight—she was not the eternal Girl Scout they all imagined.

"Mom, I want to show you something." Liz picked up the painting, and when she removed the brown paper wrapping and held it up, her mother covered her mouth with her hand, astonishment glittering in her eyes.

"Oh, Lizzie. That's so beautiful—if I do say so myself. Come closer." She reached for her reading glasses on the bedside table and peered closely at her artwork, admiring the brushstrokes, the rich pigments. "What a pretty girl you were. How on earth did you get this back? Did that old boyfriend...Peter was it?"

"Yes, you remember." She gently took the painting from her mother and then told her the story of how Peter Levine had tapped his network to get her into Dr. Emma Jacobs' practice, and into the clinical trial.

"What a kind young man," she said. "I always liked him."

Liz pressed on with her story, describing the dinner with Peter at the Hoover Hotel. "My only intention was to thank him for his help. His generosity," she said. "But..."

"But, what?" her mother asked.

In more detail than she had shared with Dusty, Liz confessed that after a dangerous mix of too much wine and tender recollections of their courtship, she'd found herself on the fourth floor with Peter.

"I let myself believe we were just going to have a cup of tea. But then one thing led to another." When she finished speaking, she felt the shame of what she'd done burn through her all over again.

Her mother turned away, saying nothing for what seemed like a long stretch, and Liz wondered if she'd made a grave miscalculation—that her admission had only served to push her mother farther away. *My God*, she thought, *is there anything more destructive than the truth?* Had it jeopardized her marriage *and* her relationship with her dying mother?

Finally, Joanie shifted in her pillows to face her. "I know my illness has been a strain on you," she said. "Physically and emotionally. Meeting up with an old beau at a hotel isn't like you, not one single bit. And I feel bad for Dusty—you know how much I love him. But I have to tell you, Lizzie. That story makes me feel better."

Liz sat up in her chair, expelling a breath of surprise.

"Is it perverse to be happy knowing my daughter isn't perfect?" Her smile turned wistful, and she gazed thoughtfully at Liz. "All those years that you covered for me when I could barely get out of bed. I was grateful—don't get me wrong. But I was resentful too. Because I was the adult, and yet I felt small next to you."

An exquisite ache swelled in Liz's chest. All those times when her mother had seemed indifferent to her—or critical—was it really self-doubt? An insecurity rather than an absence of love? "I'm so sorry I made you feel that way, Mom. It was never my intention. To be honest, I also felt resentment. But even when you were...not yourself, I adored you."

"You mean when I was a holy mess?" She allowed herself a little laugh and then patted the space next to her in bed. "Lie down next to me, darling."

Liz did what she was told, stretching out next to her mother in the narrow bed, careful not to hurt her. Joanie laced her fingers through Liz's hand and squeezed gently.

"Let's forgive ourselves for all the terrible things we never meant to do," her mother said.

"I'll try," she whispered. As diminished as her mother was, Liz felt the power of her love in a way that was entirely new to her, and she felt deeply comforted. When her mother drifted off to sleep, Liz conjured Maggie singing songs in her moonlit room and let the old pain and guilt of losing her fade away. But when her thoughts turned to Dusty, she knew she couldn't let go of what happened between her and Peter. Only Dusty could release her from that.

After Liz left her mother's bedside, she drove to a PTA meeting about the holiday canned food drive and then headed to the office. The celebration of life for Frank

O'Leary, the former pilot, was a week away, and there were still several items to put to bed. Liz needed to call Manny about the flower deliveries, and request that the caterer bring a third bartender. Gabbi had a sense that the O'Learys were going to be "enthusiastic imbibers."

Liz noticed that her partner had been in high spirits recently, coming to work dressed to the nines and disappearing for a variety of meetings. It was starting to feel like pre-Recession days. Of course, there was always the possibility that Gabbi had found a new beau on Match. com. Liz wouldn't know; it had been weeks since the two of them had found a scrap of time to catch up over lattes. She missed those chats with her old friend, and she wondered if there would ever be a time she could confide in Gabbi about the mess she'd made with Dusty.

Throughout the afternoon, Liz checked her phone for messages from him but found nothing. She worried that every pathway into his loyal, generous heart was closed to her. Tonight she would have to tell Ben and Jamie what was going on. But what *was* going on, exactly? Surely Dusty wasn't planning on leaving her. Or had he already left? She texted him again, reiterating that there'd been one indiscretion with Peter, there would never be another. She'd left a voicemail too. "I love you, Dusty. But if you can't forgive me, please come home for the boys."

Hours later, pulling into her driveway in a haze of misery, Liz nearly rear-ended Dusty's truck. She parked and her hands released from their death grip on the steering wheel, falling into her lap. It was possible he was home only to collect more clothes before leaving again, but at least Liz would have the chance to talk with him, to plead her case.

Inside, she nearly walked right past Dusty. He was sitting on the couch in the family room, where the lights were off and the TV was uncharacteristically silent. He pushed back the hood on his sweatshirt, and Liz could see the pain in his gold-brown eyes, but the fury had subsided. She took two steps toward him and stopped.

"Sit down," he said. He flipped his thumb toward the seat cushion next to him, and she quickly complied. "For now, I'll stay at home for the sake of the boys." He paused, letting the words settle over Liz. "In a matter of days or weeks, they're going to lose their grandmother, and it will be damn hard on them. The last thing they need is any of our crap."

"True," Liz said. She didn't elaborate, afraid she'd say the wrong thing. Instead she waited, hoping he'd piece together more words to bridge the chasm between them.

"And, of course, losing Joanie is going to be hell on you. On both of us," he added. "She's been kinder to me than my own mother." A huskiness in his voice betrayed his emotion, and Liz reached out to touch his hand, but he quickly withdrew it and got to his feet. "I'll sleep on the pullout tonight. We'll tell the boys my snoring is driving you crazy."

Liz nodded. It wasn't the reconciliation she'd hoped for, but it was a start.

Chapter 31

*L*iz sat at her kitchen table shuffling through photos of Ben and Jamie. Before the boys had sped off to school, they'd handed her large envelopes stuffed with color and black-and-white proofs. It touched her that they wanted her opinion on which images were the most flattering for their senior page in the yearbook. When she'd opened Ben's envelope, she found pink post-it notes already marking several of the portraits. "Maddy likes those best," he explained. "But I'm giving you veto power."

"Same for me," Jamie had chimed in. Maddy had taken a first cut at his photos too, a gesture that only added to Liz's affection for her. Maddy always found ways to connect with Jamie—chatting in his room about music or helping him pick out new sneakers at the mall. It was as if she were providing the training wheels for having his own girlfriend someday. Dr. Noah had been right about restricting Jamie's gaming and getting him out more, that it would improve his mental health, but Maddy's friendship was another cornerstone supporting his better spirits. And Liz sensed it was a mutually bene-fitting thing. After losing Haley, Maddy had found a sensi-tive brother figure in Jamie.

She glanced up and noticed that the kitchen counters were clear—the boys must have put their cereal bowls in the dishwasher and returned the cartons of milk to the fridge. Such tidiness was not the norm during the get-to-school tornado that blew through her kitchen each morning. Had Dusty advised the twins to be extra considerate of their mother given the circumstances? She clung to the possibility that his heart was softening towards her.

Shifting her attention back to the photos, it dawned on her that it had been months since she'd truly studied the faces of her sons. Lately, she'd only had eyes for her mother, sensing at a cellular level that the earthly pleasure of sharing this life with the woman who'd borne her was nearing an end. Now she felt a piercing tenderness for her boys and a stab of regret for essentially ignoring them. Holding up their pictures side by side, she could see that Ben's features had shifted and thickened into those of a man, while Jamie still had the delicate qualities of a boy. They had always changed and grown at different rates, but they would fly the coop at the same time. This time next year, they both would be gone.

And what about this time next month? Would her mother be out of her reach, out of her sight forever? A feeling of panic rose in her chest, and she felt compelled to go to her mother's side. And yet, she was unable to lift herself from the table. In the days since they had shared their secrets, Liz felt closer to her mother than ever before. Why then, when she found herself seated next to her now, did she struggle to find a single thing to say?

Her phone rang, and it was Ned. Though he'd returned briefly to San Diego to check in with his employer and sort through his mail, he was back in Menlo Park, bunking at their parents' home and taking the morning shifts with their mother.

"Hey, can you come over?" he said. "I need to run to the pharmacy. Dad woke up with a bad cold and can't get near Mom. He doesn't want to get her sick."

"Doesn't want what?"

"To get her sick-*er*," he clarified.

"I can swing by the drugstore. What does Dad need?"

"No, I'll go. I've got a few other errands to run." He sounded anxious to get out of the house. Maybe he was tongue-tied too.

On the drive over, Liz rehearsed things to say, settling on some local news about a historic movie theater getting a make-over. Her mother had once been a member of the town's beautification council, and Liz felt a bloom of hope that the topic might engage her.

When she slipped through her parents' back door, it struck her why she was at a loss for words: the future was off the table for discussion. In all the hours she and Joanie had spent walking Cheddar along tree-lined streets, sharing a pot of English tea on the back patio, or catching up on the phone once the kids were in bed, there had always been the topic of *what's next*. Who would host Thanksgiving this year? What time was Jamie's art presentation? Ben's next baseball game? Joanie liked nothing better than to ink in the slots of her TimeMaster calendar with activities and adventures. Now, they were beyond pretending that an endless stream of tomorrows stretched before them.

In her mother's sick room, she found Ned sitting guard in a chair reading the sports page. Stacked on the bedside table next to an array of pill bottles were two family photo albums from their childhood, the few that had survived the fire. Her brother had already learned to cast backwards, not forwards, with their mother.

"How long has she been asleep?" she whispered.

"I'm not sleeping," her mother said. She blinked open her eyes and raised her index finger in greeting.

"Well, I'll leave you to your girl talk," Ned said, and Liz instantly forgot what she had prepared to chat about. He stood up, tucking his shirt into his khakis and raking his fingers across his bangs before vanishing out the door. A whiff of cologne lingered in the air.

"He looks rather dapper for a trip to the drugstore," her mother observed. Liz agreed, wondering what her brother was up to. She cleared the nibbled toast from her mother's bedside and asked if she wanted anything else.

"Could you read to me?" she asked. "The books are so heavy now, and I keep losing my place. The sound of your voice would be a nice distraction."

Liz felt a surge of gratitude for her mother who had neatly solved the problem of conversation between them.

"Which book?" she asked.

"You pick."

In an antique armoire in the living room, Liz found all the novels her mother had read over countless seasons in her book club. But what caught her eye on the top shelf was an anthology of poetry. Short and melodic, poems might provide just the soothing words her mother needed. Joanie brightened as Liz returned to the room with the thick volume of verse and settled in the chair. Balanced in her lap, the book fell open to a page marked with an old grocery receipt. "Fern Hill" by Dylan Thomas.

"Oh, I love that," Joanie said. "It's an Irish poem, but it always reminds me of Grandpa's farm in Wisconsin."

It occurred to Liz that she'd never read to her mother before, and she felt a fleeting moment of performance anxiety before clearing her throat and plunging into the page. The poem's lyricism, its aching nostalgia for lost youth, made the words alternately flow from her lips and catch in her throat. A few stanzas in, her mother recited lines with eyes closed, her memory undaunted by the sea of tiny lesions in her brain. Over the course of an hour, Liz read dozens of poems, ending with "Stopping by the Woods on a Snowy Evening," by Frost. When she concluded with "'But I have promises to keep,/And miles to go before I sleep,'" her mother dozed off.

Liz's thoughts drifted back to the nights when she read favorite bedtime stories over and over to her boys, calming their minds after a stimulating day. Now she was reading familiar poems to her mother to settle her mind after a long life, one marked by blessings and tragedies and many years of the in-between.

While her mother slept, Liz wandered into her parents' kitchen and perused the pantry for a suitable snack for her father. She heated a container of chicken soup and served it to him in his bedroom. Propped up against his California King headboard, he was watching *Seinfeld* reruns with a vacant look on his face, swiping at his runny nose with a hanky. The side of the bed where her mother usually slept was untouched, the decorative pillows and lace coverlet placed just where she'd left them what, six weeks ago? Seven? Back then, Liz had dared to believe her parents' loving arms would find each other under the same sheets, in the same bed, in no time. She'd been a fool.

"How's my girl?" her father asked.

"She's asleep," Liz said.

"I was asking about you."

"Oh, I'm fine."

"Why don't you get out of here for a while. Langi's coming in thirty minutes, and she can take it from here."

Langi was Aasal's cousin, nearly as large as Tony's indispensable assistant and equally kind. A former hospice worker, she was now an independent contractor devoted to helping the terminally ill and their families. According to Aasal, "Langi" was the Tongan word for heaven, and she was just that: heaven sent. On Monday, she'd lifted Joanie from her bed, weak as a feverish child, and carried her to a chair in the shower. There, as Liz looked on, Langi had gently washed her mother's tender patches of hair and sponged her body clean. Joanie hadn't made a peep of protest, trusting the wisdom of Langi's warm, broad hands. Liz had felt deeply soothed, knowing she had capable back-up when Ned was absent and her father was too distraught to be of much help.

Back in her car, she headed to work. Frank O'Leary's memorial was on Saturday, and she had calls to make. The rains of November had begun falling in earnest, and as she neared her building, she saw people scurrying for cover under awnings and doorways. When she spotted Gabbi huddled with someone under her signature red umbrella, she slowed and honked. As Gabbi turned and tipped back her umbrella for a better view of the street, a man's face appeared and Liz locked eyes with her brother. He froze, then waved awkwardly before giving Gabbi a brief hug and bolting away.

Coward, she thought. That explains the dapper attire and constant need to run errands. Ned was wooing her partner. Come to think of it, that also explained Gabbi's alluring outfits and frequent meetings as of late. How long had this courtship been going on?

She steered her van into the underground parking area and got out. She was angry and yet couldn't put her finger on exactly why this Ned-Gabbi thing was so upsetting. She trusted that when she marched upstairs to face her friend, it would all become crystal clear.

As she mounted the last step, she spied Gabbi in the foyer, dressed in a clingy knit dress and black leather boots that her brother undoubtedly found attractive.

"I'm sorry I didn't tell you sooner," Gabbi said. "Don't be mad."

"Too late."

"Liz—"

"Listen, Gabbi, we both know this won't end well," she said, her argument coming together in a flash. "In a matter of weeks, Ned will return to San Diego for a girl half his age. Or—you'll leave him for some older VC on Match who can properly spoil you. Either way, I'll be stuck in the middle of the mess. Which, as you might imagine, is the very last thing I need right now."

"Wow, Liz. Why don't you give us a little more credit than that." She dropped her umbrella on the carpet where it made a dramatic thud and scattered droplets of water in a wide pattern. "Ned and I are just looking for a little companionship during a particularly shitty time."

Liz was momentarily speechless. She hadn't seen the misery-loves-company defense.

"Don't you think your mother's illness—her dying—affects Ned? And that it doesn't bring back all that pain about your sister? You know, Liz, you've got Dusty and the boys to go home to every night. He doesn't have anybody."

"Okay, I get that," Liz said, shrugging off her jacket and sinking into a chair. Gabbi followed suit so that only a few feet stretched between them. "Ned needs someone to confide in. But why does it have to be you?" Liz felt embarrassingly close to tears. "And why would you want to date him?"

Gabbi lowered her chin, staring at her manicured nails, before looking up to answer the question. "I'm lonely too. Zoey's off to college, and I spend hours working by myself—because you can't handle many aspects of this business. That's fine. I can live with that. But don't judge me for wanting to meet Ned over a cup of coffee or bottle of wine. He's a hundred times more attractive and more fun than the drips I meet online. And you know what else?"

"What," Liz murmured.

"I know Ned comes from a really good family."

Liz sighed. Hard to argue with that.

At her desk, she sat behind her monitor, pretending to work, and fumed that Gabbi and Ned had been deceiving her. But simmering beneath her anger was another emotion entirely: jealousy. Gabbi was her partner and friend, and she had absolutely no desire to share her with her brother.

Chapter 32

$\mathcal{A}$t 5:00 pm, the celebration of life for Frank O'Leary was just getting underway when Liz arrived with last-minute items, including a guest book and memory box for cards and photos. She was pleased to see the banner she'd ordered hanging in the foyer of the aviation museum: "Join Us for Frank's Farewell Flight."

Knowing how very ill Joanie was, Gabbi had suggested that Liz not attend the memorial and had tentatively booked an assistant to help her manage the event. But Liz didn't want anyone stepping into her role, and she needed a good excuse to get out of the house. Dusty's interactions with her remained cold and clipped, and Jamie had taken notice. ("What's up with Dad?") So, here she was, determined to help showcase Touchstone's new format: *Not Your Father's Funeral.*

When she entered the building, she felt little of the anguish and anxiety that had consumed her at Haley Chan's service. The grown children of Frank O'Leary, Clara and Liam, had cherished their father and believed that he'd lived to a ripe old age and was now "up above with our mother." As a result, they had helped to plan Frank's service with more gusto than grief. Their acceptance of their father's death had enabled Liz to work on the memorial with a measure of calm she hadn't imagined possible.

Once in the primary venue, she marveled again at the vintage aircraft suspended from the ceiling. An elegant, white bi-plane seemed to float above the dinner tables, and a Viet Nam-era helicopter hovered near the buffet station. Guests, who had arrived as requested in festive attire rather than mourning clothes, lined up at the bar featuring *Cocktails for Lift-Off*: the B-52, Paper Plane, and Skyy Diver. Liz had spent hours hunting down vintage recipes and new concoctions that were in theme. When she'd narrowed down the options and purchased the various liquors, she conducted a taste test with Ned after their parents had gone to sleep. "Maybe I should crash this funeral," he said as he savored the bourbon in a Paper Airplane. "It sounds like a damn good party." They'd enjoyed a small laugh together, so rare these days as they took shifts caring for their mother. And now Liz was coming to terms with the Ned-Gabbi romance.

To recreate the glamour of air travel in Frank O'Leary's heyday, Gabbi requested that the catering staff come in costume. She'd tracked down Pan Am stewardess uniforms for the female servers, and pilot outfits for the male waiters. As they passed hors d'oeuvres, the women looked striking in their royal-blue blazers and skirts and white gloves. And the men appeared spiffy in crisp, cuffed shirts and black-and-white flight caps. Liz was amazed to see so many of the attendees smiling and laughing. They were utterly charmed by the servers and the venue itself. Benny Goodman's big band music filled the elegant space, and Liz wondered if people would actually start to dance.

Halfway through dinner, Clara and Liam took turns reminiscing about their father on a small stage with a podium and mic. Clara recalled how, when they were young, her dad had set up their family in first class on a Boeing 747 flight to Hawaii. He'd allowed her and Liam into the cockpit and, afterwards, had spoiled them with

Shirley Temples and extra desserts, and an orchid lei for their mother. "When we were growing up, Dad was gone a lot," she admitted. "But he always found a way to make it up to us."

When Clara passed the mic to Liam, a tall man with intense gray-green eyes and a neatly trimmed goatee, he thanked everyone for coming and assured them his father was resting in peace. "Which isn't to say his passing hasn't been difficult," he said, a thickness collecting in his voice. He quoted W.H. Auden, expressing the notion that his father had been his "North, South, East and West," guiding him through a difficult divorce and challenges in his business. "He was our captain in every sense of the word," Liam said, laying his hand across his heart. "And he taught us well." He paused, looking skyward, and concluded, "We can take the controls from here, Dad. Thank you for showing us how to navigate through pockets of turbulence and come in for a safe landing."

There was a smattering of applause and nods of approval while Liam left the stage and joined his family at their table. Liz was momentarily stricken as she wondered, when the time came, would she find the right words to eulogize her complicated, beautiful mother? A text from Gabbi brought her back to the job at hand: *Dim the lights now.*

As the wait staff served champagne and dessert, Liz lowered the lights, and the museum's AV technician rolled a video that was shot the week before. On the large screen, a young pilot and Liam appeared ready for take-off in an open cockpit airplane with tandem seats. Liam held up a burlap bag containing his father's remains while the words "Frank's Farewell Flight" scrolled along the bottom. As the small aircraft lifted into the sky and headed for the Pacific where the popular old aviator would be scattered three miles from land, "Come Fly with Me" by Sinatra built to a crescendo. "To Frankie," someone yelled, holding up his glass of champagne. "The friendly skies of United will never be the same without him!"

Laughter rippled across the room and Liz found herself joining in. She glanced over her shoulder and spotted Gabbi handing her business card to an attractive, older woman in an exquisite suit. Gabbi waved her over.

"Liz, this is Dana Ferrari. She's an investor in the hospitality industry."

"Nice to meet you," Liz said.

"Congratulations on creating a marvelous tribute to Frankie," Dana said. "He was my neighbor for twenty years, and I'm certain he would have enjoyed every minute of this. Now, as I was telling Gabriela, I'm intrigued by what you two are doing in the end-of-life services space. It's ripe for disruption."

She spoke with confidence and authority. "It's time to replace the cookie-cutter funerals directed by men in black suits with customized events like this one. There's been a missing link in the events business, and you two women might be just the ones to exploit that."

"That's exactly what we've been thinking," Gabbi said.

"The market is largely untapped. You could expand this business regionally and see where it goes. With the right business strategy—and financial backing—the sky's the limit." She slipped Gabbi's business card into her purse and gave each of them one of hers. Turning to leave, she promised to call them in the new year when she felt certain the economy would start to recover. "Until then," she said and glided away.

Gabbi's dark eyes were dancing with excitement. "How brilliant is that? A potential investor!"

Liz smiled and crossed her fingers. "Our luck appears to be changing."

An hour later, they helped guests collect their coats and make their way to the exit. Clara and Liam approached them and handed both Gabbi and her a bouquet of crimson roses.

"Thank you," Liam said, "for making Dad's service one we'll always remember with pride," he said.

"And joy," Clara added. She hugged them warmly before she and Liam hurried off to say goodbye to family and friends.

"We're doing good work," Gabbi said. "Important work."

Liz nodded. There was no denying that they had helped Karl Perkins and the O'Learys through a difficult time and brought them a measure of peace—even joy. She and Gabbi had made mistakes with Tony and the Chans, but they would be smarter going forward. She closed her eyes and inhaled slowly, surprised to think this way. *Going forward* in the death business.

"Time for a little R&R," Gabbi said. "Before they take down the bar, let's get a Skyy Diver."

"I can't," Liz said. "Ned's been with my mom for hours. I should relieve him of duty." The drive home from San Francisco would be nearly an hour.

"Won't your mom be asleep by now? I bet Ned's on the couch watching a movie. C'mon. Just one drink."

"Okay. On the rocks, please. I'll be right back."

As Gabbi sidled up to the bar, Liz phoned her father to see how her mother was faring.

"Honey, don't worry about your mom. She's tucked in for the night, and Ned and I are watching an old shoot 'em up."

"Sounds good, Dad. I'll see you first thing tomorrow."

She hung up and joined Gabbi at the bar, settling on the stool next to her and relishing the feeling of being off her feet. "Mom's asleep and Ned is in front of the TV. You're quite the psychic."

"Lucky for us," Gabbi said. She handed Liz a cocktail and raised her glass. "To making a good living by creating beautiful endings."

"Cheers," Liz said, starting to actually believe that death events could give them a shot at the Silicon Valley dream. She stirred the ice in her drink and then looked up to meet her partner's eyes. "And Gabbi, thanks for keeping Touchstone together. I know I haven't been at my best."

"Well, these have been challenging times." She reached out and patted Liz's arm. "Especially for your family. But, Lizzie, I take you in good times and bad, for richer or poorer." She smiled good naturedly and clinked her glass against Liz's. "Let's just try to focus on the *richer* part, okay?"

"Okay," Liz promised.

Gabbi tossed back her drink, and when her cell phone rang from the bottom of her tote, she slipped away to take the call privately. Perhaps it was Ned suggesting a nightcap somewhere.

All the guests had left the building, and the museum personnel were hovering nearby, anxious to lock up and casting Liz thinly veiled looks of annoyance. Normally, she would have been just as eager as they were to call it a night. But the atmosphere at home was still chilly. Dusty made an effort to speak to her in a civil tone around the boys, but in private his voice was acerbic, his gestures impatient. She wondered if he'd already retreated behind the closed door of the guestroom. Her body felt heavy with a deep longing for all the nights he'd stayed up late to welcome her home after an endless fundraising party or wedding celebration.

When someone from the staff flickered the lights on and off, she sighed, surrendering her barstool. She gathered the crimson roses off the countertop and headed home to her cold, empty bed.

Chapter 33

*I*n a corner of her mother's room, Liz and her dad sat opposite each other at a small card table playing Gin Rummy. Her eyes traveled from her cards to the motionless form in the bed, and her ears were tuned to the sound of weary sighs and uneven breathing. Joanie no longer desired to watch the morning news, to listen to poetry, or to accept visits from the doctor or old friends. "No more intruders," she'd said three days before. Last night, when Dusty and the boys stopped by after dinner, she'd perked up for their small talk about senior year pranks and the homecoming football game. When Dusty bent over her bed and gently wrapped his arms around her, thanking her for loving him like a son, they had all wept, even Ben. But after Dusty and the twins filed out of her room, calling sweet dreams, she'd made Liz promise not to allow them back. "Let them remember the real me," she'd said. "Not this shadow."

And so she and Arnie fell upon new ways to kill time, new ways to wait for the thing they dared not discuss. Though Liz had finished writing her mother's obituary and received brief input regarding her memorial ("no church service"), she and her father pretended that the inevitable was still miles offshore.

She took a swig of coffee-gone-cold and laid down four jacks, emptying her hand and winning the round. When the doorbell rang seconds later, Arnie got to his feet. "Loser answers the door," he said with forced good cheer. As he lumbered off to the foyer, her mother opened her eyes and peered around the room with a disheartened expression.

"Oh, I'm still here," she said. "Dying is such hard work."

An ache pulsed through Liz's heart, and she sat rooted in her chair, at a loss for how to respond. After a moment passed, she asked if there was anything her mother wanted. A drink? A nibble?

"No," she said. "Something else." Liz brightened, ready to fly in the direction of whatever that something was. She stepped closer to the bed.

"What is it?"

"I need you to help me...move things along."

"What do you mean?" Liz asked.

"Honey, you know. What's that stuff you give me? For pain?"

"Morphine?"

"Yes, that. Give me enough to go to sleep." She inhaled a ragged breath through her dry lips and coughed before adding, "And *stay* asleep."

Liz leaned away from her, not quite believing what she'd heard. "But, Mom."

"Izzie. I can't ask your dad. He'd keep me going in any form. Even this." She moved her hand down her skeletal body, covered in a wool blanket. "And your brother?" She merely shook her head. "It must be you."

"Please don't. Don't ask me this." Tears gathered behind her eyes, and she felt gripped by a sudden, righteous anger. Did she have to say it out loud? She was unprepared to let her mother go. Terrified by the approach of her death. "I'm afraid," she said, despising the cowardice in her voice.

Her mother rotated her head on the pillow to face her more fully. Her skin was ashen and her hands lay still at her sides, but her eyes shone with a rare intensity.

"Yes, I see that. Of course. I was afraid too. But now?" Her gaze drifted momentarily over Liz's head as she searched for the right words. "Whether I fall asleep forever, or I wake up with Maggie in another world, I'll be okay. It's just nature, honey, taking its course."

The front door closed with a heavy click, and Liz could hear Arnie starting toward them. "Flower delivery for one Joan Annette Boyle," he called from down the hall. He entered the room carrying an elegant potted orchid finished with a lavender ribbon. "From the book club gals," he said. Cheddar was at his side, wagging his tail and appearing equally pleased with the presentation.

Her mother, the formerly passionate gardener, appraised the flowers without so much as a flicker of interest. She turned away from the delicate pink and white blossoms and pulled the blanket up to her chin before shutting her eyes. And that's when Liz knew. Joan Annette Boyle was ready to leave this life.

When the boys arrived home for dinner that night, the sky was dark and she could only make out their silhouettes as they reached for their backpacks and hip checked their car doors closed. Where had the long days of summer gone, when Dusty grilled chicken and burgers on the back patio warmed by generous daylight?

Before this grim autumn, the notion of time flying had rarely troubled Liz. In fact, as a girl, she'd been grateful for it. The way the years between her tenth birthday and her eighteenth had galloped by had been a blessing, allowing Maggie's death to recede into the hazy past. Even when she was a young mother, when the speed with which Ben and Jamie left behind *Good Night Moon* and *Power Rangers* had saddened Dusty, she faced the headwinds of time with steely serenity. Every year that they grew bigger, stronger, and more capable diminished the chances of them being snatched away by a tragic accident.

And then there was her event business, where she had reveled in taming time, the queen of logistics who got the ball rolling, got the show on the road. Now was the time for the bride, arm-in-arm with her father, to start down the aisle! For the birthday cake to be cut! For the orchestra to strike up "White Christmas" at the holiday gala. It was exhilarating how the hours raced by, catapulting the event toward its happy conclusion when she and Gabbi could pack up and go home. A job well done.

But now time was Liz's sworn enemy, devouring her mother's final days with its careless appetite. And yet Joanie perceived it completely differently. "I wish I knew when this would all be over," she'd said. She was tired of living, exhausted from dying, and she longed for release. Only the rapid passage of time could grant her wish. Or Liz. Liz could grant her wish.

Lying in bed that night, Liz felt lonely and afraid. She longed to talk things over with Dusty, but he remained committed to the sofa bed down the hall. She had texted him goodnight, and that she loved him, and he'd replied, "I know." But then she added something new—and true: *I need you, Dusty. I can't face what's coming without you.* There had been no response, and well past midnight Liz was still awake. Yesterday, she'd slipped a bottle of her mother's sedatives into her purse, and they beckoned her now. Morphine had replaced all her mother's drugs, so it hadn't felt like a theft. She moved silently to the bathroom and tapped the open bottle of pills against her palm. One blue tablet inched out and then two. As she was about to place them on her tongue, Dusty appeared in the doorway.

"Come 'ere," he said. "You can put those away." He led her back to bed where he joined her for the first time since her confession. At first, she couldn't relax, afraid he'd change his mind and leave.

"It's been so long since I've heard you say those words," he said after a stretch of silence.

"You mean, 'I love you'?"

"No," he said. "The part about needing me." He rolled over on his back and stared at the ceiling. "It's been killing me to think you needed your old boyfriend more than me. That he could help Joanie and your family in ways that I couldn't."

Liz shifted to face the ceiling too, her shoulder resting against his. She'd been blind to the possibility that Peter's influence over her mother's medical care was as painful for Dusty as her night in the hotel.

"I'm sorry," she said. "I guess I did believe that for a time. I've been so scared, and I've made stupid choices. Can you forgive me?" She glanced as his profile, barely visible in the darkness, knowing and loving every contour of his face. "I need to know if you're going to stay—not just for the boys, but for me too."

Liz felt Dusty take her hand under the covers and she held her breath.

"I'm here to stay," he said. "I'm here for you."

Despite her mother's explicit instructions regarding no more visitors, Dr. Emma Jacobs was scheduled to arrive for what was likely a final assessment. Five days had passed since Joanie had requested the dreadful favor, and her condition had quickly declined. She was no longer eating as food caused her to choke, and on the rare occasion that she opened her eyes, she accepted only sips of water. Liz had come to believe that her mission of mercy was no longer necessary. But just a few hours ago, as she entered the bedroom to adjust the thermostat and tick up the heat, her mother had shot her a pleading glance. Her lips pursed together momentarily, forming the word "please." Or was it just a trick of Liz's imagination?

When Dr. Emma arrived, dressed in her weekend jeans and a sweater, she checked her patient's vital signs and reviewed the chart that Arnie meticulously kept with the time, date, and amount of each medicine administered to his wife. But he, Ned, and Liz no longer wrestled off the caps of myriad bottles—there were no more chemo tablets, eye drops, or vitamins. Only the opiates to control her pain remained on the bedside table.

Liz had confided in no one about her mother's request to *move things along*. Her father would be dead set against it. Ned would likely be in favor but unwilling to help. And Dusty, in an effort to allay her deep-seated fears, might have offered to take care of it himself. But her mother had asked her, Liz, to do the deed. What she needed was to somehow summon the courage, and for Dr. Emma to confirm that her mother was near the end. It was vital to know that she was not escorting death through the front door. That it was already hovering in the room.

"Liz, at this point, there are *no limits* on how much morphine you can give your mother," the doctor said before leaving. She gave her a long, meaningful look and reached out to squeeze her shoulder. Then she handed Liz a hospice pamphlet entitled *Journey's End*. "If you have any questions, call me."

It was a quiet afternoon, a week before Thanksgiving. As she heard the doctor's car drive away, Liz stared out the window where a squirrel zig-zagged up the trunk of an old redwood and disappeared behind a cluster of branches. Arnie was watching a college football game in the den, and Ned and Gabbi were attending a matinee. The opportunity for carrying out her mission of mercy had presented itself. Liz approached the small tray next to her mother and lifted the pre-loaded, pre-measured plastic syringe of morphine. The syringes were identical to those she'd used to squirt liquid Tylenol into the mouths of her babies when they had a fever. *You can do this*, she said to herself. But her heart was thumping madly, and she felt terribly warm and lightheaded in her cotton turtleneck.

Not yet, she thought, setting the drug back into place. She pulled up a chair to the end of her mother's bed and folded back the covers to reveal her small, tender feet. Liz had been massaging her mother's feet for weeks, and Joanie had savored every minute of it. But now she appeared to be in a deep sleep, in full retreat from the world. Liz pumped lavender lotion into her own palms and reached for her. As she worked the cream into her mother's dry arches, Joanie's grimace softened and her eyebrows lifted almost imperceptibly. She was past language but aware of her daughter's presence, and Liz felt a mix of grief and gratitude that she could rub against her flesh, her molecules, her elemental self. One last time.

Spreading the cream over her mother's toes, Liz gently tugged each one. *This little piggy went to market.* How her mother had loved the summer farmers' market, where she had filled her straw basket with ripe tomatoes, sweet berries, and bouquets of dahlias and zinnias. *This little piggy stayed home.* Yes, together they were here at home. Not in some drafty hospital room where beeping sensors and the ever-changing guard of doctors and nurses would have unsettled them. Even in this dark hour, Liz felt the grace in that.

Her mother uttered a grunting sound and twisted in her sleep. She appeared agitated, as if working out a problem. Was it the puzzle of how to escape the body? The tethers of her family's love?

Liz returned to the bedside table and tried to steady herself. Her hands trembled as she picked up the syringe of morphine, but she pressed on, squirting it under her mother's tongue. Between doses, she stroked her hair and small clumps of it fell away in her hands. At first, Liz was frightened by the sight of auburn and gray strands strewn across her palms. But soon she understood that death would be a series of releases culminating in a final expelled breath. Within the hour, she noticed a bluish cast around her mother's lips and she began to fret. *Was it possible to die the wrong way?* Blinking back tears, she hurriedly paged through the hospice pamphlet and found a passage assuring her this strange coloring was a sign her mother was nearing the last of life. Liz picked up her phone and texted Ned, and then she leaned over the table and spoke urgently into the baby monitor.

"Come quick, Dad. I think it's time."

What Liz hadn't dreamed possible was that in the first hours following her mother's passing, she would feel a curious lightness in her spirit. As she went about the sober business of calling family and friends and the volunteer at the hospice center, who in turn phoned the mortuary, she experienced a benevolent floating quality. The dread of her mother's death had been a stone on her heart that had suddenly lifted away. Liz realized that the weight of that stone had been there not only in recent months; it had always resided inside her. Since the day the fire had swept Maggie from their arms and ravaged their home, she had been terrified of losing another beloved one. And now she had. And yet, somehow, she was surviving what she had long believed would be a personal apocalypse.

After two men from the funeral home transferred her mother's body to a gurney, covered her with an ordinary linen, and wheeled her away, Liz wondered if this day had been part of a plan. By asking Liz to facilitate her ending, had Joanie known they would both be liberated? That by some strange, pretzel logic, Liz's active participation in her death would actually free her from the fear of it? Yes, she thought. It was all by design. A parting gift from her wise, flawed, precious mother.

In what they would always refer to as Jo-Jo's kitchen, Liz prepared a scotch on the rocks for her father and poured Dusty and Ned each a beer. The three of them were sitting silently in the den watching a pre-season basketball game. *Thank God for televised sports*, she thought. It gave the men a chance to grieve together without having to utter a single word. Across town, the twins were at school preparing the gym for a Homecoming dance and did not know their grandmother had died. Liz would tell them in person.

For Jamie, the news would be crushing, and she had already consulted Dr. Noah about how to manage the aftermath. Noah had advised Liz that Jamie would be taking cues from her. If she could process the death in an open, healthy way, Jamie would find comfort in that. Liz had seriously doubted that she'd be capable of modeling a "healthy" response to the very thing she feared most, but now she felt a trickle of hope. Maybe she was up to the task. She found solace in knowing that soon it would be Thanksgiving. As wrenching as that tradition would be without their Jo-Jo, at least the boys had time away from classes to cope with the loss.

As she entered the den balancing the tray of drinks and nuts, her eyes rested on her father. He was in shock now, but in the weeks and months ahead, the grief and loneliness would be punishing. She noticed Cheddar dozing on his feet and felt a morsel of relief; her father still had another creature in the house that adored him. When she handed him his cocktail, he nearly dropped it, but Dusty was at the ready, sliding his palm under the glass to support it. "Thank you," she whispered and felt a rush of love for this man who was literally the steady hand in her life. For months, she'd forgotten that truth, obscured by the worry over their finances, the terror of her mother's death, the debacle with Peter. But now she could see again, breathe again. Somehow, they would get through all this turbulence and sadness. And with her business picking up and the remodel rented, maybe they could keep their house after all.

After passing out the drinks, Liz returned to the kitchen for a cup of tea. She heard the low hum of an engine and glanced outside to see a car she recognized pull up. It was Gabbi.

When Liz swung open the front door, Gabbi stepped into the foyer and slipped her arms around her. Only then did tears overcome her. As she rested against Gabbi's comforting shoulder, she went rigid as it dawned on her that her friend and partner had come for her brother.

"Ned's inside," she said.

"Don't be silly," Gabbi said softly. "I'm here for my BFF."

"Good thing," Liz said, dabbing her cheeks with the sleeves of her shirt. "Because there's a celebration of life to plan."

Gabbi released her embrace and took a step back. "Too soon?"

Liz shook her head. "Mom said 'no church service.' And it's the holiday season so most event spaces are probably booked."

"Don't worry. I'll come up with a plan."

"*We'll* come up with a plan," Liz corrected.

"I like the sound of that," Gabbi said.

Liz took her hand and led her to the den where Gabbi hugged Arnie and Dusty and gave Ned a brief but tender kiss. Outside the sliding glass door, the wind picked up, and Liz noticed that her mother's pink camellias were in bloom, swaying their lovely heads in the crisp autumn air. When she turned back to face Gabbi, her friend gestured toward the kitchen, and Liz nodded. There, the two of them pulled out chairs at the old wooden table, and they got to work.

Acknowledgments

Many writers, friends, and relatives supported my journey to become a novelist, but at the top of my gratitude list are two writing teachers from Stanford University: Ammi Keller and Malena Watrous. Years ago, when I was a mother with three kids under my roof, I enrolled in several fiction-writing classes with Ammi. In 2017, she encouraged me to apply to Stanford's novel writing program, and an exhilarating new chapter opened for me. Malena was indispensable once my story was underway, suggesting where to trim the fat and where to go deeper. In addition to being a gifted editor, Malena invariably makes me laugh. Thank you both.

Fellow writers Tracey Lange, Bob Murney, and Jessie Weaver have become trusted friends and we've swapped chapters over the course of several years. Their honest feedback and notes in the margins have made every page better.

To my dear friend Deb Fitz, always my first and most supportive reader: your encouragement to *keep writing* has simply made all the difference. And to Julie Brody: your sweet notes and gifts in my mailbox always cure what ails me. I'd also like to thank my friends (starting with ML Robinson) who I've walked beside for many years.

The stories we've traded about marriage, parenting, and losing loved ones inform this book. A special nod to Amy Reardon and Lisa Stuart for sharing their fears about death with me. (Aren't we all a wee bit terrified?)

I'm deeply grateful for readers of early drafts who offered thoughtful comments and support: Leah Fitz, Claire Gilhuly, Stephen Godchaux, Todd Harris and Amy Powers, Julie Helfrich, Lynne Jacobs, Maggie King, Beth Mondry, Jenna Signorelli, and Jacquie Walters. A big shout-out to my wonderful daughter, Dani Moragne, and to my loving (and patient) husband, John, who read many drafts of this novel. To my sons, Hutch and Tyler, thank you for always being on my team (even if women's commercial fiction really isn't your thing!).

To my agent, Beth Davey, I bow down. Your experience, network, and insights into the ever-changing publishing world have been my guiding light. Lucky me to have such a warm, witty, and wise friend in the trenches. (Thank you, Claire, for introducing us.)

And to the team at Post Hill Press: Debra Englander, Heather King, Dev Murphy, and Tiffani Shea—thank you for welcoming me into your fold and keeping me on schedule. I'm also honored to have Blackstone as my audiobook publisher.

To Cathy Danzeisen: it was a pleasure to brainstorm with you on book cover concepts—you nailed it. And to Annie Barnett, thank you for photographing me in the kindest light.

Before signing off, I'd like to thank my father, Jim Young, for moving us from the Midwest to the San Francisco Bay Area when I was a child. He embodies the best of midwestern values and the California ethos to dream big. His steady devotion to his beloved wife and growing family always kept the ground firm beneath our feet—even in earthquake country.

In the Event of Death:

Questions/Themes to Discuss in Book Club

1) Liz and Gabbi live and work in Silicon Valley, and yet they don't enjoy the lavish lifestyle of those who work in big tech—or who invest in it. Do you think this feeling of being an outsider gives rise to their entrepreneurial spirit?

2) Because of the early tragedy in Liz's life, she is reluctant to produce funeral and memorial events. But she is desperate to make money for her family. Have you ever worked in a job you disliked but did it anyway to pay your bills?

3) The death of Liz's younger sister, Maggie, results in a kind of undiagnosed PTSD for Liz. Death is a very scary concept for most children. Do you remember when you first realized that you and your loved ones are mortal?

4) Liz is something of a perfectionist who strives to control her children's behavior and ensure their safety. How did the circumstances of her childhood contribute to Liz's anxiety and need for control?

5) In chapter nine, Liz wonders if the trauma she experienced as a child has been passed on to her son, Jamie. What else might contribute to Jamie's depression? Academic pressure? Too much screen time? Feelings of being the "lesser" twin?

6) Secrets play a big role in this novel. Ben keeps his brother's depression and pot smoking a secret from their mother. Joanie keeps her role in her daughter's death hidden from her older children. Little secrets abound too. Gabbi sells Tony's suits on eBay and doesn't tell Liz. How do these secrets (and others) damage family dynamics and friendships? Do the confessions help—or harm—these relationships?

7) Liz appears to have traditional views of sex. At first, she was judgmental about Tony's affair and subsequent divorce, and she was worried about Ben and Maddy going "too far" in his room. Later, Liz finds herself in bed with her old boyfriend. Is this a double standard, or has she changed in some fundamental way?

8) When Liz meets Peter at the hotel for dinner, Peter's intentions are unclear. Do you think he planned to seduce Liz—to take advantage of her vulnerable psychological state? Or do you think he succumbed to old feelings before his conscience got the better of him?

9) Gabbi and Liz are partners who attended high school together, but they come from different economic backgrounds. As Gabbi reminds Liz, "I can't afford to be thin skinned. I grew up on the *other* side of this town." How does this difference impact their partnership and friendship?

10) Death is seen from many perspectives in this novel. Liz fears death. Tony tries to prepare for and control it. Gabbi wants to build a business around it. Liz's ailing mother longs to die, and Liz's father and brother don't like to discuss the end of life. Which character do you relate to the most?

11) Over the course of the book, relationships bloom in unexpected ways. Liz and Tony become confidantes. Jamie and Maddy become mutual support systems. And Gabbi and Ned become lovers. Does surviving hardships bring them together?

12) Liz and Dusty's marriage is tested on all fronts. Do you think their reconciliation at the end of the book is believable? Why or why not?

13) The setting for this novel is during the Great Recession of 2008. Since then, the world has endured a global pandemic and political upheaval. But what elements seem unchanged as they relate to parenting, the "sandwich generation," and financial insecurity?